# THE SECOND DARK AGES

## *An Unofficial Review of the Third World War*
## Daniel R Steiner

# CONTENTS

## INTRODUCTION

*I compiled and completed this report nearly five years after what has become known as the Third World War. I attempted to capture, to the best of my ability, the events of this devastating war, and to do so in a sequential manner. This report is the first in a series that I hope to make public. The primary objective is to describe the actual events of the war at a strategic level.*

*Most of the information came from interviews combined with observations and knowledge of the relationships and capabilities of the major nations involved. At one point in my life, understanding how events like this conflict might take place was my job, and I was good at it. Perhaps that is why I was informally asked to write this report, but I will never know because those who asked are gone.*

*I am sure the faculty of any of the United States War Colleges would grimace at this particular report as well as the validation processes I utilized. Footnotes, a Bibliography, and validated references were not part of my process. Not only did I feel those standard actions would be unachievable, but they are irrelevant. What I have attempted to capture in this series is what took place and why as well as the impact of such events. If someone wishes to question or challenge my depiction of what happened, they are free to do so. This report is not a government-authorized account of the conflict, but I'm confident that it captures the significant events and their consequences.*

*If any organized government is in the process of conducting a more detailed review, I am not aware of such a project. At this point in human history, I'm not sure any functional government can even compile such a report. The fact that some semblance of what was called the World Wide Web is operational is the only reason this publication maybe might be read by someone outside of my sphere of contacts. In reality, I don't know whether there is a right or wrong way to tell this story, but I have attempted to capture the history of this tragedy).*

The format for these reports is based upon a review of the critical areas listed below.

**The Series of Issues:** *Events set the stage for this conflict?* (First Report)

**The Road to War:** *A strategic-level review of what events took place.* (First Report)

**Post-Conflict Events:** *The status of the world by the end of the war? (Second Report)*
**Analogy:** *Status of the world, five years after the war. (Second Report)*

**Side Note:**
The level of data lost as a result of this war is amazing. And the amount of false information that impacted all parties before and after the conflict is frightening. The world truly did not comprehend the dependency linked to the World Wide Web, nor did it understand just how deeply daily life was dependent on being able to access this data. As to the topic of false information, the rapid rate at which the world lost confidence in nearly everything they were reading or, more importantly, seeing seems to have guaranteed that the war spun out of control. Finally, the speed at which this war took place had never been witnessed in the history of warfare. The events leading up to the war were ignored by a global society that was too busy to see the warning signs.

The Series of Issues
The following is a simplified list of events and circumstances that had a direct impact on the war. Each of these will be reviewed in greater detail later in this report. Although I struggled with the sequence of the issues listed below, after countless restructuring reviews, I concluded that I have the series of events incorrect order.

**The Wrong Leaders at the Right Time:**

Throughout history, dynamic individuals have shaped events that changed the world. Often, these figures acted unilaterally with other fellow leaders merely reacting to the actions that were put into motion. One man or one woman

5

altering the course of history was somewhat the norm. That was not the case in the Third World War. What took place this time could only be described as the Perfect Storm. This time, all the key nations in this conflict were represented by men who fit the description of "Dynamic" Each of them was driven. Each of them was resolute in his vision of where his country should have been and what obstacles were in his way. Uncompromising, paranoid, and some prone to kneejerk reactions, each of them played collectively into the spiral that ended in nearly uncontrollable warfare. One leader would hold the key to the crisis that changed the course of humanity. The Chinese leader represented a core group of individuals who truly believed the time had come for Asia to control the future of the world, and to the Chinese, the definition of "Asia" was China.

**Social Media and the Communication's Crisis:**

As far back as 2012, I and many others sounded the alarm bells about the impact that social media was beginning to have on the concept of governance. Even before 2012, the actions of the so-called Arab Spring had shown the world the power of spontaneous, ungoverned, raw communications. Students in Tunisia were talking directly to fellow students around the globe. Video clips on YouTube began to replace organized media coverage. Governments were reacting to the messages painted by social media with little or no lead-time for developing a logical, believable response. By 2014, the civil war in Syria and the world opinion of that war were no longer controlled by any government or any form of recognized news media. Social media fueled the conflict in Syria, and the world struggled to keep up with what was being shown "live" from any battlefield inside the war-torn country. It should have been an omen, and it was a prelude of things to come, but only on a much larger scale and with a far more disastrous impact. Un-vetted social media messages and video clips on platforms such as Twitter and YouTube almost instantly led to world opinion clouding the actions of the nations involved. At first, governments tried in vain to suppress the ability of the public in the area of the conflict to show the rest of the world what was happening. These suppressive actions were taken in Tunisia, Egypt, and Syria during the Arab Spring. In both cases, the governments proved ineffective and even counterproductive.

Simply put, suppression of social media was not only physically impossible, but it also damaged the credibility of the governments that tried to execute the destruction. It made a bad situation much worse. Attempted overthrow led to a loss of confidence and a complete collapse of trust. In the end, the attempt to suppress social media communications contributed significantly to the expedited failure of the government. Social media fueled the winds of war, and the efforts to contain it made the conflict even more destructive.

**The Horror:**

Just as some had predicted the impact of social media on modern-day governance, some had spoken of the lost reality of a truly global conflict. Most of the world no longer understood the concept of death on a massive scale. It had been over seventy years since the world had witnessed collective causality numbers in the tens of thousands and then millions. All of this took place in less than thirty days.

As modern militaries became equipped with weapons that would allow them to inflict damage on their enemies without producing massive casualties, primarily civilian casualties, the world became accustomed to conflicts where reports of ten deaths were dramatic. No nation was more susceptible to the unrealistic expectations of conflict casualties than the United States. Not only had the US's weapons advancement resulted in a society that was shocked by a dozen deaths, the medical capability had grown to the point that the odds of service members dying on the battlefield were lower than anyone could have imagined. Desert Storm, Iraqi Freedom, and all actions the US had been involved in since Viet Nam produced causality numbers that in no way depicted what would take place in a modern, global war. In the eyes of the US, civilian losses occurred in the form of small, but visual and emotional terrorist attacks. The deaths of September 11, 2001, were so shocking to the American people that the nation came to a virtual standstill for three days. The cascading reports of losses in this war not only shocked the population of civilized nations, but it also sent them into a nearly uncontrollable panic; the type of fear that was seen in science fiction movies for decades. Horror was the most accurate term used as the war unfolded. The Horror that seemed to get worse by the hour was fueled by social media accounts that no government could control. Instantaneous communications, at least in the first few days of the war, created a level of panic that stopped nations in their tracks. Death on a massive scale was acceptable to a select few countries in the early days of the war, but even those who were reluctant to unleash their full capabilities were forced into doing so with little or no explanation to their citizens. The speed of this war was unlike anything ever seen. The degree of violence was just as shocking.

**Religion:**

Wars were fought over religious issues for thousands of years. This war was no different. Was religion the primary cause of this conflict? No. Was religion a critical factor in this war's initial phase of conflict? Yes. Did the issues behind the conflicts in one particular religion provide the "spark" of war? Yes. The deep-seated rift between the Shia and the Sunni had been an emotional tool used by leaders on both sides, leaders who were more interested in power than in healing the wounds of their faith. Religion was the exposed nerve of the ordinary people, and a few key nations knew it. Getting the youth of a movement to die in the name of their religion was not unique to the Muslim faith, but convincing a country it must attack another country in the name of their religion, that was an obvious starting point for this war.

Power and religion. The two have had a long relationship that has too often ended in death, but the tools of warfare had allowed man to kill at a level far more significant than at any moment in history. Nuclear capabilities in the hands of a nation whose professed cause was the fulfillment of their religion could have had only one outcome on the world. The world was unwilling to invest in the future of the human race by making hard decisions on ownership of the ultimate tools of war. In the end, religion was not the primary cause of the beginning of this war, but it was the excuse needed to sacrifice millions of lives. Those who were willing to kill and die in the name of their religion were given the tools to drive the world into crisis, and that crisis would lead to an end-state one nation had planned on for a very long time. Religion was the tool to start a planned conflict.

### Technology Lost:

The events of this war were sequential, but the speed at which they took place and the magnitude of their impact overwhelmed the world's ability not only to respond but also even to comprehend what was taking place. The average person was unable to grasp the magnitude of the war, and they could not process what was taking place. Panic was the only logical, predictable action, and fear became a cascading, global event. The day-to-day technological lifestyle of most of the civilized world was so quickly disrupted; many people sat and watched the world come to a crashing halt. The fragility of the modern world had long been a topic of great debate, especially amongst the governmental sponsored "Think Tanks" as well as major universities. How many aspects of day-to-day life would be impacted after one day, two days, or a week of lost connectivity? In the end, answers to such questions were nothing more than educated guesses, and, not surprisingly, the "experts" were not even close. Technological fragility had one fatal flaw, and that flaw guaranteed the rapid collapse of society. Panic. When the people panicked, technological processes collapsed but not just because of physical or software issues. Societal structures fell apart because the humans responsible for their execution panicked. *At one point in my career, I was involved in a planning process that dealt with preparation for a pandemic event in the US and the rest of the world. After only a few, initial meetings with a state-level health department, it was clear that the ability to keep simple infrastructure processes functional once the public began to panic was never going to happen. The picture painted by the Centers for Disease Control and Prevention (CDC) was too much for most state-level planners to comprehend. The issue of who would continue to operate the local water treatment plants once the public was convinced a pandemic event was underway was just one of hundreds that came up at the planning table. The number of people who truly made things work was never really known. How would they be replaced if they suddenly didn't show up for work? That question was never answered to a level anyone would accept. Even after working on this project and a few others that dealt with public infrastructure, it shocked me how fast it all fell apart.*

Not only did day-to-day technology collapse at an unanticipated rate, but the ability to restart processes was lost as well. Mining operations, needed to produce the rare minerals required for manufacturing, could not be restarted. Inventories that were not lost in the war became depleted quickly. Coordinated transportation didn't exist. Not only was the ability to fabricate complex items lost, even the most simplistic necessities were no longer obtainable. Most of the modern world was utterly unprepared for a raw, simplistic life. When the US government attempted to capture the total number of lives lost in the US and the world, they had overlooked this issue. The number of those who had died from non-attack events was never indeed calculated.

Today, five years after the war, most of what was manufactured in the world is either gone or has been replaced by much more simple processes. The collapse of the pharmaceutical industry has led to nearly as many deaths as the war itself. Disease is now the number one killer in the world. Later in this report, I will go into greater detail about the impact that the technological losses have had and will continue to have, but it is safe to say that modern man has suffered the most significant setback in history. History shows that the Black Plague of Europe pushed the European nations into "The Dark Ages." This war propelled the world into a whole new level of darkness, and recovery is a topic few even mention.

## THE ROAD TO WAR

In a military mindset, the one I lived in, the concept of "how" something might take place or might have taken place was referred to as "The Road to War." It was typically a detailed review of what actions would be required or what steps may have been taken before a conflict getting underway. That is the process I understand. Wright, wrong, or indifferent that is the way I have structured this first report. Conflicts have always had a "Road to War." There are still traceable "reasons" why wars take place. The reality is that the human race never really became capable of learning from past mistakes and therefore made this war unavoidable.

In the end, this war was not unlike others in the past five thousand years. Was it "unavoidable"? It should have been. Was it "probable or predictable"? Yes. Was this war deliberate? Did someone or some nation or even some group of countries plot a world war? Yes. The Chinese concept of "reset," something I will cover in detail later in the report, was the catalyst of this conflict. The tragedy was that virtually no modern nation, other than China, believed a global war was possible, much less probable. A global market. That was the answer to preventing another World War. It now seems the "reset" theory was built around the belief that no nation would plot an event that would bring down not only its economy but those connected to it. No country other than China that is. This conflict was no different than many in the past. It was about power and leverage. It was about a nation's desire to shape the future in a way that ensured that nation's growth. This war was about greed. This war was predicated on the assumption that those who were given access to weapons they longed for would use them in a reckless drive for power. Iran, North Korea, and a few others gained the ability to destabilize the world, and it was that cascading destabilization that the Chinese had anticipated. In their minds, they would not be held responsible for a cataclysmic event, but they would be in a position to leverage the outcome. In short, it was the perfect storm. A storm unlike any in the history of the human race, a storm that was born of confidence, a storm that grew virtually without limits.

# CHAPTER ONE:
# THE MIDDLE EAST
# AND THE BEGINNING
# OF THE CRISIS:

*Iran's Miscalculation*

A
S is the case with all wars; this one had a point of origin. Before the start of the war, I posted a blog story about the US's attack in Syria in 2017. (*https://coldansviewpoint.blogspot.com*) I had been posting on this site since the Arab Spring began, as I was one of the many who believed that the events in the Middle East could lead to a biblical prediction coming true. My point was this: Reckless actions have ignited many conflicts over the past few thousand years. Operations that were poorly thought through. These were actions based on emotions and an unsound understanding of possible repercussions. Throughout the history of war, concepts such as Second- and Third-Order Effects or the Law of Unintended Consequences had seldom been given the level of importance they should have been. The events in Syria in 2017 were no different. The attack by the US on a Syrian airbase was reckless not just on the part of the US, but also on the part of the Russian government and the Iranian leadership, leadership that provoked the event. When the Russian government decided to make Iran responsible for the event that nearly brought two superpowers to war, it became clear that the Iranian dream of becoming the

next regional power was gone. The Tsar, as I called Putin at the time, had to make a decision, and cutting lose his Iranian puppet was far less damaging to Mother Russia than continuing down the road to war with the US. Both nations were desperately looking for an "off-ramp" from the event, and trading away Iran's plans was a smooth action for Putin. It's difficult to prove that this agreement, and it's possible the US never knew the Russians had decided that Iran would be collateral damage in a far more critical plan. In the end, the future of Mother Russia was the nightmare of the Persian dream. Iran would not control their future in the region, and that placed the Persians in a position they could not accept.

Out in the cold, that is where Iran suddenly found itself. Gone were the dreams of the old men in Tehran. Gone was the vision of the new Persian Empire. The picture painted was not only believable, but it was also correct. The Iranians had secretly convinced Assad that European Christians could not decide the future of Syria. Not again. Just as President Trump was ready to capitulate on the status of Assad in Syria, the Iranians realized why. Assad's time was coming to an end. That was the "deal" the Russians had struck with the US. Russia would bring the US to the table on the issue of NATO in Eastern Europe, and the US would get what they wanted, Assad out of power. It may have been a plan that would take time, but in the end, the Iranian program for Assad was going to be swept away. Worse yet, it seems the deal was struck, and the Iranians were not given a chance to vote. The region was changing, and peace was being negotiated without a voice from the Persians. The Russians would pay hollow homage, but those who tracked the region understood where the Iranians stood. The Iranian informed Assad of the Russian plot for his demise, along with a plan to make the US and Russia's compromise fall apart. The scheme would call for extreme measures by the Iranians, but the risk was far less than the known outcome of the Russian / US agreement. Iran would create a new dynamic in the region, and the prominence of the Persians guaranteed.

As for the Russian / US plan, it was simplistic and unified. Unified by the Arab League, the US, and the Gulf Cooperative Council, GCC, and all the while the Russians remained publicly opposed, as that was the stance that would make the whole process work. A charade on their part that just about everyone saw through.

Iranian backed forces were to leave Syrian soil by an unrevealed date. It was Lebanon in 2005 all over again, at least from the standpoint of the Persians. The superpowers would decide Syria's future, and Iran was to abandon their dreams immediately. When the Iranian leadership became aware of this concept, the result was dramatic. Tehran was a tinderbox. With the ever-present tension among the so-called "moderates" and the hardliners, this insult could have only been seen as a huge, perhaps devastating setback for the government in power. Iran's leadership was injured and injured severely. They had gambled to save their dreams for the region and lost. Wounded and without their historical protector, Russia, not only did Iran's leadership believe they were vulnerable, their true enemy was convinced. Saudi saw an opportunity, and a young prince's vision of victory was put into action. Iran's meddling in the future of the Middle East was ending, and the Saudis were more than willing to hasten the process.

A byproduct of this "deal" would also set into motion the pending crisis. The disengagement of Shia militias in Syria was a process that did not go according to plan. Yes, the Iranians had no leg to stand on as even Assad understood the price he would pay for insisting the Iranians remain in his country, but, as is often the case, departure proved to be almost as damaging as staying. There was no validated exit plan designed around the withdrawal of Iranian support in Syria. The only thing that was genuinely holding the Syrian military together was Iranian support and Russian airpower. The rumor of the Iranian departure exposed what everyone already knew. The Syrian military was incapable of defending its homeland. Russia's reaction to the Iranian displeasure did further harm to the Syrian government. Putin was not a man known for taking betrayal lightly. The Iranians were expected to follow the Russian lead, even if they disagreed where the Russians were taking them. When it became clear to Moscow that the Iranians were not cooperating with the process the Russians had agreed to, it was predictable what would happen next. Creating a peaceful Syria or even a peaceful region was never the Russian plan. Leaving Syria to disintegrate further was a price the Russians were willing to pay for the desired outcomes in Eastern Europe, but watching Syria fade away was almost more than the Iranians could stand.

In the end, Russia had what it had been working towards from the very first day it intervened in Syria. The US had brought the one topic to the table Putin longed desired. NATO. If the US agreed to stop the spread of NATO alliances into Eastern Europe, Putin would walk away from the Persians and let the Middle East travel a path determined by someone else. Some were even of the opinion that the region would finally stabilize. The Iranian threats to the region would be gone; at least, that was the theory. As most theories go, it didn't hold. Desperate to show that they could still influence the future of the Middle East, they could decide the fate of nations around them. Iran pushed Iraq into yet another crisis that would impact the Saudis more than most realized. Shia militias pulling out of Syria were tasked with creating a level of disruption not seen in Iraq since the Daesh nearly drove into Bagdad. The Shia militias and Iran's Islamic Revolutionary Guard Corps (IRGC) easily manipulated Iraq's slide into violence.

Within a month of the understood, undeclared plan between the Russians and the US, the Iranians had also turned up the heat in Yemen. It was the events in Yemen that began the spiral into war, not only for the region but also for the rest of the world. Deliberate planning by the Iranians mixed with the overreaction of the Saudi leadership led to an escalation in Yemen not seen to that point. Few believed that the events in Yemen would lead to a regional crisis, a crisis that only took three days to explode into something the nations of the Gulf had not witnessed since the 1973 war with Israel. Iran's desperate attempt to stay relevant in the region resulted in the area being the first casualty of what is now considered the Third World War. Again, the speed of events overwhelmed almost everyone who tried to control or even understand what took place with Iran. Iran wished to show its relevancy, but, in the end, all it achieved was its destruction. When the dust settled in just a few short days, it was apparent Iran had not only miscalculated the impact of its actions on the region, but it had set into motion the destabilization of the entire world. In reality, Iran had begun a process that the Chinese had anticipated for years.

*Saudi Arabia's Overreaction*

Iran's intent in Yemen had been known for several years before the deployment of Shia militant units, units that were openly supported by the IRGC. Iran understood the movement of weapons, and specialized units into Yemen would not go unnoticed. To Saudi Arabia, the concept of blaming Iran for the prolonged conflict in Yemen was nothing new. What was new was the sudden increase in support from Iran. Support that was clearly out in the open. The coincidence of this sudden increase of support in conjunction with the ordered withdrawal of Iranian-backed forces in Syria was there for everyone to see. The problem was, the decision to react to the Iranian actions were slow and mixed at best. The Russians were indifferent to the Iranian plans to increase support in Yemen. As far as they were concerned, transferring trouble in the region was not part of the deal they had quietly reached with the Americans. When the Saudis realized what was taking place, the protest fell on deaf ears. Agreements were made in the region, and once again those agreements were based upon old colonial powers and world superpowers, not the actual nations in the region.

When US intelligence was shared with Saudi on what was being moved into Yemen, the reaction should have been an indicator of just how quickly the event might escalate. It was clear that the ships off the coast of Yemen were delivering Iranian weapons. What was stunning was the delivery of well-armed and well-trained battle-hardened units, units that had seen three years of operations in Iraq and Syria. Groups that were clearly placed in Yemen to threaten the Saudi-led operations there. Saudi reaction to the US intelligence should have been another indication of just how desperate they were becoming. Saudi understood the US's ability to track these types of movements. It was also clear to them that the process had been taking place for days, and yet there had been no warning. In their minds, once again, the US and others were making decisions without the input of the nations in the area. Trust was a concept the Saudis had didn't accept. All the major Western networks covered news of this dramatic escalation of the crisis in Yemen. Speculation about what it would mean to the conflict was a hot topic until Saudi Arabia gave the world their answer. It would mean war, a war that would quickly spin out of control.

Two days after the verification of Iranian-supported units arriving in Yemen, the Saudis reacted. The attack on the Islamic Republic of Iran's naval ship supporting the offloading of combat units shocked everyone who was paying attention. The act was uncoordinated with the US or any other nation. The decision to attack seems to have been made by the Saudi government within hours of the US intelligence briefing. US intelligence intercepted the communications between Saudi military commanders, but the typical notification process was too cumbersome and prevented a US response before the act. Put, by the time US leadership understood what was about to take place, the attack was underway. The result was a stunned US administration and nothing less than pure panic among Western and regional news media organizations.

Social media coverage of the attack was on the Internet within fifteen minutes of the strike. Fishermen in the area took photos of the smoke plume and then attempted to help those who were in the water. Posted images and short video clips depicted the event for the first several hours, and nowhere were these images more potent than in Tehran. A retaliation by Iran was anticipated, but, again, the speed of the response was not expected. The Iranian vessel was attacked at 8 a.m. CST, and the second attack by Saudi Arabia took place within ten minutes of the initial attack. The Western media headlines of open conflict between Iran and Saudi and its GCC Allies were poorly developed, and the response of other vital nations was confusing and seemed uncoordinated. Canned words such as "we urge all parties to show restraint in this crisis" were utterly ineffective. People couldn't get timely information on the event from the standard media or government statements, so they went to what they knew, social media. Within two hours, Iranian, Saudi Arabia, and the US were in a conflict that seemed uncontrollable, and the world could not believe what it was witnessing.

The Iranian Navy's encounter with the US Navy off the coast of Yemen took place somewhere during the second attack event launched by Saudi Arabia. Within one hour of the event between the US and Iranian navies, an exchange was occurring in the Strait of Hurmuz. Restraint was being called for, but only from those who were not actively engaged in the conflict. After the first several hours of the event, it was clear that the primary objective of the US and its allies was to keep this event limited to a naval operation. That objective changed rapidly as the incident continued to unfold. It's still not clear whether Iranian missiles struck the oil refineries on the coast of Saudi first, or whether the Saudis attacked the naval bases of Iran. What was clear was that this phase of the crisis was no longer confined to the waterways of the region. Tanker traffic in the straits attempted to follow the known protocols for conflict in the region. In the early stages of the conflict, those measures seemed to be working. Civilian ships were not targeted for the first several hours. All tankers made full speed for the safety of open waters. When the first missile strikes took place in Saudi, the threat shifted quickly to the landside of the fight, and many of the ships in the area were able to continue to make full speed. That changed shortly after the initial strikes on Saudi refineries. The accuracy of some of the Iranian anti-ship weapons was underestimated, but worse than that, the location of Iranian boats that could attack both landside and seaside operations had been completely miscalculated. Covert boat capabilities, ships that were not recognized as Iranian weapons platforms, were able to inflict damage far beyond anything that had been anticipated. The regular Iranian naval vessels took an anticipated level of attack from both the US and the British task force in the Straits. But, the Iranian ability to counterattack soft targets, especially land-based facilities, was something the rest of the world had not anticipated. Iran's priority of effort surprised the US, and that required time to recalculate counter actions.

Saudi Arabia had set the conflict into motion, but Iranian leadership had begun the process that the Saudi government could not ignore. The decision to attack the Iranian operations off the coast of Yemen was one that propelled further events, and that was an issue the Saudi government may or may not have anticipated. It should also be noted that this phase of the conflict produced a reality many had not expected. Both the Iranians and the Saudis had weapons in their arsenals that could do damage far more significant than their leadership realized. Both sides inflicted damage on the other much faster and with a degree of severity both had not anticipated. This strategic misunderstanding led the Saudi government to believe that they could disable the first Iranian ship off the coast of Yemen and perhaps send a broader warning to the rest of the world. A warning on the tolerance level for Iranian "meddling" in Saudi affairs. Whether that was their intent is unclear, but there is speculation that the Saudi government never truly understood the potential consequences of their actions. By the end of the first day, those not directly involved in the conflict were demanding that the whole event stop immediately. More ominously, those in the area who believed that the event would continue to spiral out of control would not wait for their interest to be jeopardized. Preventive actions were decided upon by a few key nations, and that set into motion the escalation that pushed this crisis outside the Middle East.

## Israel's Fateful Actions

The fate of Syria was to be decided by the Russians and the US. The negotiated issues were informally briefed to Israel by the US and Russia. Israel's concerns over Syria were simplistic. Hezbollah and the Iranian-backed militias could not and would not be allowed to exist in what was southern Syria. Even more important, the power of Hezbollah in Lebanon was to be reduced drastically. With the loss of Iranian influence inside Syria, the ability for Tehran to control the events in Lebanon were becoming nothing more than a shattered dream. The Iranian plan to create a new level of crisis inside Iraq was less concerning for Israel, but the idea of active, Shia militias supporting a much-improved Hezbollah was a known nonstarter for the Israelis. The US intelligence capabilities for monitoring the actions of Iran's Shia militias as well as the IRGC were well known. But Israel was the leading expert on that topic, and as such, it was no surprise to them when the support shifted to Yemen. There was even speculation that Israel informed Saudi Arabia of those actions before the US. Within hours of the Iranian and Saudi conflict, the Israeli Defense Force (IDF) recommended a plan that had been developed several years before the current actions. This plan called for the destruction of all Hezbollah assets in Lebanon as well as in Syria. Israel believed that Iranian leadership was heading into a death spiral; otherwise, why would they openly send support into Yemen? Provoking Saudi would not be enough. To win the help of the Arab people and hopefully split the GCC nations' commitment, the accusation of a Saudi-Israeli secret partnership would have to be exposed. What was then underway in Saudi and Iran would lead to Iran lashing out with the most effective tool they had, Hezbollah. Israel would not wait for Iranian backed missiles to rain down on them. The IDF would enter the fight with Iran, not as the secret partner of Saudi but as the loyal ally of the US. A partner the US wanted desperately to leave out of the conflict, given that the US truly believed the event could be stabilized within a few days.

In the early morning hours of the second day, IDF raids into Lebanon destroyed the hope of a limited conflict. The Iranians had what they wanted, a battle cry of betrayal, a betrayal by the custodian of the two holy mosques. The picture they so desperately wanted the world to see, a unity of Israel and the GCC, was there. But the Iranians realized too late that this unity didn't matter. Even more importantly, it didn't matter to the Arab population in general. As they watched the crisis quickly encompass nations outside the region, the fear of what was taking place left no room for anger based on betrayal. The ability to communicate in the region, at least concerning public communication, was lost after the third day. What the people of Egypt thought compared to what the people of Jordan or Saudi thought never mattered.

Israel's actions in Lebanon were more than dramatic. The events of the first day were stunning enough, but the strikes on Hezbollah by the IDF came without warning and at a tempo that let everyone know the actions of the IDF, this time, were unlike any in the recent past. The ability of the Israel military to mobilize and fight at the same time was the byproduct of years of deliberate planning and training. The telltale signs of mobilization that Hezbollah had anticipated and even counted on didn't take place. A concept of initiating military operations with little or no warning, a process known as "Cold Start," was not an IDF brainchild, but they had perfected it to a level unseen anywhere else in the modern world. Southern Lebanon was a warzone in a matter of minutes, and the strikes in Beirut and the Beqaa Valley were nearly seamless with the initial raids into southern Lebanon. Reaction to the Israeli attacks on Hezbollah strongholds only added to the hysterical reporting coming in from all over the region.

*Hezbollah*

When the Hezbollah counter strikes began, even while the IDF was fully engaged in southern Lebanon, the results brought about the next level of panic worldwide. It quickly became apparent that Hezbollah's ability to survive an initial IDF onslaught was far greater than even the Israelis had anticipated. The massive increase in missiles available to strike inside of Israel had been a topic for the past several years, but the sheer volume of strikes, from multiple locations, was stunning. The events of a live CNN report from Tel Aviv froze the network. The broadcast was transmitted by cellphone, so it was impossible to edit the event. One second the young reporter was talking, and the next she was gone. The two strikes within a few hundred yards of her location showed the network and viewers how dramatic the attack was. With millions of people watching, millions who had been waiting for over eighteen hours nonstop, the words "we probably need to take cover" followed by a lost signal most likely created the highest level of panic witnessed by Western media. Somehow this singular event pushed the media off balance. Their collective reporting began to be inconsistent and confusing. So confusing that many who watched one network tried to switch to others in hopes of getting a better understanding of what was taking place. It didn't work. All of them seemed virtually lost in what they were witnessing. Comments on the air became unedited, and the fear that these comments created made an already bad situation worse.

When a BBC correspondent reporting from just outside

the Ramat David Airbase witnessed the three direct hits on the airfield's fuel farm, his words were heard throughout the world, live. "Oh, My God." What the public understood was the reality that Israel, for all her military might, seemed to be losing the conflict. At least that was the perception that the live feed from Ramat David projected to the world. Strikes into the heart of Israel were one thing, but strikes that continued for hours, strikes that struck targets that no one anticipated could or would be hit, drove the people of Israel into panic. For years just before the conflict, the IDF had worried about the concept of engaging an unconventional force with a mostly conventional force. It was a lesson that the US had taken years to learn in Iraq and Afghanistan, and the mistakes were documented. Collateral casualties were acceptable to the enemy, but not to the public that supported the IDF, or its allies. The concept of tanks battling tanks and aircraft engaging aircraft was not going to take place in the next war for the IDF, and they knew it. Pinpoint strikes of command and control and or communications would not be enough. Hezbollah teams were small, mobile, and slept with their weapons. The concept of "Zero Start" was just as ingrained in Hezbollah as it was the IDF.

What's more, Hezbollah was no longer a linear, fixed enemy. The conflict in 2006 had proven that. The IDF faced a new type of enemy in southern Lebanon, one that became known as "a fire ant mound." Hezbollah fighters could move into actions with the first signs of danger. Once struck, the response was as if the mound had been kicked, and the defenders of the mound spewed from the surface. Despite their efforts, the IDF could not place enough ordinance on the area to stop the missile attacks.

Something else had changed. A large proportion of the missiles in Hezbollah's arsenal were more accurate, easier to use, and far more mobile than in 2006. The ability to continue prolonged attacks into Israel was overwhelming. By late on the second day of the regional conflict, it was clear to the IDF that the only way to stop the attacks was to occupy all the land that could support launches into Israel. It was then the Zero Start concept fell apart. It was one thing to have the ability to generate a large part of the IDF's aircraft and missiles systems with little to no notice. They had proven that they could accomplish this feat only hours earlier. But, the idea of generating a ground force capable of moving into southern Lebanon, an area with an enemy force well-entrenched and fully engaged in combat, and doing so while all of Israel was under attack, proved to be a challenge too difficult for Israel to overcome.

### The Israeli Public

With the initial counterstrikes on the Israeli airfields, their Force Generation capabilities were degraded drastically. The defensive systems worked, but the sheer volume was the problem that could not be solved. Hezbollah had also deployed a brilliant plan. The initial strikes against targets with defensive assets, such as the airfields, were conducted using lower-quality expendable missiles. This tactic had been used against the US forces in Iraq and Afghanistan for years, e.g., utilizing an advanced weapon, a weapon that cost hundreds of thousands of dollars, to take out a fifty-dollar truck. In the case of Hezbollah, it wasn't the cost of the system, but depleting the limited number of defensive weapons. The first three rounds of attacks on the airfields were conducted within two hours. The plan was to do multiple launches against a single target repeated three times. By the time the fourth round of strikes was inbound, a strike that utilized far more accurate and powerful weapons, it was clear the tactic had worked. Israel had expended a significant proportion of its more advanced anti-ballistic defense weapons. The result was a reduction in aircraft attacking Hezbollah in southern Lebanon.

The IDF plan had been for the air assets to initiate the strike, but the real work would be accomplished when the ground forces moved into Lebanon. The success of the Hezbollah missile employment tactics was nearly crippling to the IDF mobilization process. Those strikes were carried out in the same manner, old missiles first and in large numbers. Then came the larger, more advanced systems, the same advanced systems that the initial IDF attack was tasked to destroy. Again, the issue became volume. Israel's air force was impacted, and that reduced the country's ability to not only attack the enemy but also to maintain the confidence of the Israeli people. Israelis understood the dynamics of how their military defended their nation. Seeing their airfields attacked made them realize, without the media telling them so, that their ability to continue to respond was being reduced. Their capability to defend the nation was being eroded along with confidence in their leadership.

Anyone who understood the concept of warfare in Israel was aware of air force plans to use the highways as operational airstrips. Again, the panic of the population following the events in the region made that operation far more complicated than the IDF planners had anticipated. The plan had been to clear and then close the roadways, but, like everything else in that period, it didn't work. The IDF decided to move air operations out of Israel, but that process was going to take time, and time was something Israel didn't have. The IAF had been generating missions from the Egyptian military base in Cairo West for over six hours when the first unofficial reports were made public. A few people near the airfield in Egypt had seen the activity and then noticed the markings on the F-16s. Contingency plans had long been made for such operations, plans that were even more secret than the agreements made with Saudi Arabia. The potential support missions in the Sinai had resulted in detailed agreements and prepositioned support equipment was vital to making that mission happen. What limited the effectiveness of the plan was the munitions on hand. The plan had called for a buildup period for any joint operation at that facility. There was no such period in this conflict. Although the US had some capability at the Egyptian airbase, it was not enough to compensate for what was lost in Israel. The idea of IAF "forward operating bases" would not impact the course of the conflict.

Reality had set in. Israel was not going to suppress the attacks on their country as quickly as anticipated. Hezbollah was too well equipped and also willing to accept tremendous losses on the nation they controlled, Lebanon. The region was in flames, and the most dangerous event was about to take place by the end of the second day.

*The Israeli Decision on Iran*

The nation of Israel was living the nightmare they had feared for over a decade. A Hezbollah force that was equipped and capable of inflicting severe damage on the Jewish nation. Israel had watched the Iranians, with the support of Russia, repeatedly attempt to supply Hezbollah with weapons that everyone knew were not intended for use in Syria. The few missions in which Isabel did attack these shipments were designed as a clear signal that Israel would not allow those transfers to take place. The real change occurred soon after the US attack on Shayrat. The Russians not only allowed the Syrian Air Force to operate from the Russian controlled base in Latakia, they also gave the green light for Iranian supply aircraft to operate from the facility, which signaled to Israel that the transfer of advanced weapons to Hezbollah was only going to increase. Israel knew the weapons flow was now unstoppable, and they realized that the Russians supported the whole concept. The undeclared and unofficial agreement between the US and Russia was not agreed to by Israel, the one nation that would not stand for any compromise that left Hezbollah stronger than before the conflict in Syria. At the end of the second day, the first day for the nation of Israel, the decision was made. Iran was responsible for what was taking place in Israel, and Iran would pay the price. Tel Aviv and Jerusalem were both being attacked, and for the government of Israel, that sealed the fate of Tehran.

Within hours of the decision, the strikes on the Iranian capital became the next "Breaking News" scrolling across the major networks. The war in the Middle East was a little over forty-eight hours old, but the world was collectively holding its breath. Israel was crippling the Iranian government and its military with a combination of weapons, but the most significant event was the realization that the most effective weapon was a keyboard. Israel showed the world the real destructive power of the feared cyber battlefield. History will show that this new form of warfare changed not only the course of that war, but it also changed the concept of war.

*The United States Response:*

As stated earlier, the details of the exchanges between the Iranian Navy and the US Navy off the coast of Yemen are vague. The communications and warnings that occurred are not a matter of record. It is also possible that no such communications occurred between Saudi Arabia's navy and the Iranians. What is clear is that the US Navy responded to being fired upon with overwhelming force. At the time of the initial attack, the US had four ships off the coast of Yemen, and one of them was the USS Cole, but the historical aspect was lost in the complexity of all the reporting that took place that day. Unofficially, it was Cole that made the first action of US forces in the conflict. The initial Saudi strike was against the transport vessel. The Iranian counterstrike was aimed at the Saudi naval vessel. The distance between the Saudi naval vessels and the US vessels represented a typical defensive posture used by both nations. The Iranian frigate that fired upon the Saudi ship was the initial target of the USS Cole. Less than five minutes elapsed between the strike on the Iranian flagged transport and the strike on the Iranian frigate. The US had very little time to determine what was taking place between the Saudis and the Iranians, and even less time report a clear picture of the chain of command. For the US forces, one order stood at all times, "defend yourself." The sequence of events will be covered in more detail later in this report, but in the end, the USS Cole did precisely as ordered. The commander of the USS Cole would not allow his ship to be attacked again. That lesson had been learned.

The reality of Iran's increase in operations in Yemen alarmed the US and others. The movement of support ships was not a surprise to the Saudis or the US. Both nations understood the dangers of this increased activity by Iran. Within the first week of increased Iranian operations, both the US and Saudi issued stern warnings to the Iranian government. Iran's response was the early indicator, or it should have been, that something was different. Tehran's reaction was just as confusing as the overt actions they were taking. Their first official statement addressed the issue of an "increased humanitarian mission." The Iranian statement once again accused the Saudi government of interfering with such aid missions. The difference was that this was the only statement the Iranians gave. There was no "The Iranian Navy stands ready to crush any actions of our enemies," or "our rockets will rain down on them." No retaliatory threats. No harsh speeches. That single statement caught the attention of intelligence organizations as well as those who followed the region intimately. It was not the typical Iranian reaction, and that alone made some speculate even further about what was taking place inside Tehran.

The US was well aware that the Iranians would not agree with the decisions that had been made about the future of Syria. Iran had been left out of the equation, and deliberately so. The US conclusion was close to the truth. Iran was going to create tension in Yemen and other areas in a desperate attempt to show the world they were relevant. Iran needed to save face, and that was the stance the US leadership anticipated. In reality, two things had taken place. One, the US underestimated the desperation of the Iranian leadership.

Two, the US failed to see that Saudi was intent on pushing Iran even further into a corner. But neither the US nor Saudi Arabia shared their true intentions. As had been the case throughout history, leadership's improper assessments would lead to conflict.

The amount of confusion during the first hours of the hostilities was anticipated and planned for by the US military. Military leaders at all levels were trained to deal with the "fog of war," but confusion at the diplomatic level became the issue. The US military command for that region of the world, Central Command, was fully engaged within minutes of the Saudi attack. Contingency planning was the trademark of the US military. The problem was not the US military's anticipated reactions, but the political response. Political leadership was not prepared to give guidance to military leaders at the speed required by this conflict. The civilian communications to the US military was a failsafe answer, i.e., protect our forces at all cost, and this was guidance for which US military leaders did not need approval. In a typical crisis, US military and political leadership would not require an immediate, large volume of interaction and coordination. But this was not an ordinary event. The US had exercised the concept of a conflict with the Iranians in the region for years. Few, if any, of these exercises prepared for a scenario in which the Saudis started a conflict with no prior warning to the US or others. Given this reality, the requirement for guidance to the US military was something that had not been built into the existing contingency plans. Which actions were the US commanders authorized to take given that the Saudi government had fired upon an Iranian naval vessel with no apparent warning to the Iranians or the US? This was not an ordinary event, and the political decisions that had to be made would not be provided at the speed required. Shock and Awe's impact on political leaders, in several key nations, paralyzed their governments at the wrong time. Defending themselves was a concept that many US commanders would logically push to the limit if the situation warranted. Neutralize the threat. That was the intent, and that is what the US commanders in the region executed with blazing speed.

*The Strait of Hormuz:*

The initial engagement off the coast of Yemen took place in less than twenty minutes. The Iranian response in the Strait of Hormuz began less than thirty minutes after the exchange off the coast of Yemen was reported. Iran had lost three naval vessels and two Iranian flagged cargo ships. The Saudis had one severely damaged frigate, and the US had locked down anything that moved by air or sea for two hundred miles. All of this had taken place in minutes, and the speed of the event took Tehran by surprise. The order to engage Saudi and US targets in the Straits was given after the initial damage assessments were communicated to the Iranian leadership.

The initial reports of the incident were more than alarming, and back in DC, they were confusing. The flash message from the US Embassy in Saudi stated that the Iranians had fired on a Saudi naval vessel. As that message was being processed, the United States Central Command (CENTCOM) confirmed that the Saudis had fired on an Iranian flagged ship off the coast of Yemen. Military leadership understood what had taken place, but political leadership was confused from the beginning. Reporting was a deliberate process for the US military, but many at the US Department of State were overwhelmed by what was taking place. Saudi's explanation of the origin of the conflict was not given until events in the Straits of Hurmuz were well underway, and the follow-up conversation at the US Embassy was disrupted with the Iranian attack on the Saudi coastline. US political leadership was confused with the initial impacts of the fog of war. What the US military had understood was clear. The Saudis fired first.

What took place in the Strait of Hurmuz started without the confusion of the events off the coast of Yemen. US naval operations had gone to full combat readiness as soon as the Saudis fired on the Iranian ships. Tracking of Iranian naval vessels was a constant process, and when the hostilities began, the location of any threatening ship was well known. The launch locations of the Iranian fast boats were also well known. Once the US had engaged the Iranian frigate, all US assets in the Gulf region were transformed into a combat status within minutes to include all land-based installations. The first incident in the Strait of Hormuz originated with an Iranian fast boat swarm team. This unit was already in the vicinity of US naval assets. The initial report was that three anti-ship missiles were inbound on a US destroyer, and the US was returning fire.

Within ten minutes, multiple reports were being processed at Fifth Fleet headquarters. It was clear to US commanders that the Iranians were engaging in an unrestricted response. The US battle plan for such an event was not only well known by all US forces in the region, but it was also a devastating plan. An escalating event was to be responded to in one manner, but an unrestricted attack would be met with a much different response. The US assets in the region were typical of a standard rotation. But what the Iranians did not understand was the potential of the US in the region. In less than six hours of naval combat, two-thirds of the Iranian navy was out of commission. The three primary Iranian maritime ports were categorized as "Combat Ineffective" by CENTCOM. What had taken place had not only stunned the world as it watched the reports flow in from the major networks; it created a state of panic in Tehran.

*Iran's Continued Response:*

As devastating as the US response was to the attacks in the Strait, the actions taking place away from the US Navy were even more frightening. In the middle of the naval conflict, the Iranians had launched a concentrated ballistic missile attack on Saudi refineries located along the countries eastern coast-line. Al Jubail was the location of a significant Saudi Aramco facility, which was the primary target of the first Iranian ballistic strike. Within minutes of that target being struck, three additional refineries in the United Arab Emirates were attacked. It became clear that the Iranian attack plan was not limited to engaging enemy naval operations in the area. The goal also included crippling oil facilities and fixed targets as well. As the battle on the water took place, the damage to the oil production capabilities of Saudi and the UAE were simply lost in the drama of the moment. By the time a significant net-work gave an update on what was believed to be taking place, it had become clear to everyone that the conflict was not limited to naval operations. The US Navy was doing its job. It was destroying what was left of the Iranian Navy. The British Naval operations in the region came to light three hours into the event, and these operations indicated that the British gov-ernment would be deeply involved in the conflict. The naval battle was being won and won decisively. The damage to the oil industry of the GCC members was just beginning, and at that time the Israeli operations were still hours away. The ability to produce petroleum products was being impacted by Iran, but the price Iran was paying was far beyond anything they had anticipated.

*The US / Saudi Communications Issue:*

Communication with the government of Saudi was diffi-cult, and that was not well received by the US President. The attempt to understand why Saudi had taken the actions they did, and, more importantly, what additional actions they may be contemplating became the priority of effort for the US Department of State. Military-to-military communications were taking place, but their priority of effort was to neu-tralize the Iranian attacks, not debate what had taken place and why. Iran's navy was being destroyed at the hands of the

US and Britain, but the crisis originated with Saudi Arabia, and the US needed to know their intentions. Was Saudi's intent communicated with Iran's primary ally, Russia? Who was aware of what was taking place, and what role did any of them have? Had the Russians been forewarned of the attack? Had the Saudis informed anyone of the plan? These were the questions that continued to occupy the US Department of State and the US administration as a whole. Answers were demanded, and within a few hours of the start of the conflict, it was clear that the Russians wanted an end to the destruction of the Iranian navy, and they demanded it without delay. It was also clear that the Iranians were talking to the Russians continually, and the irrational fear grew in the US that Moscow may have understood the events leading up to that point without any acknowledgment of the US. The US was desperate for information, and communication with Saudi was virtually nonexistent. The ability to deliberately develop a plan for the future was nearly imposable. The US was doing the only thing it could, neutralizing the enemy that was attacking them. The communication lines with the Russians and several others seemed to follow a similar pattern. Saudi had acted on its own and with no warning to anyone. At least, that is the way it appeared. The issue became one of credibility: Did the US believe any of them?

*Side Note: US / Israeli Communications:*

*Although this section addresses official communications between the US and Israel after the explanation of IDF operations in Lebanon and Iran, it is important to state that communications with key players in the region seemed uncoordinated and poorly handled. Both Saudi and Israel had become aggressors in the conflict, and the US was virtually unable to influence what was taking place or anticipate the actions of either nation.*

Before the initial IDF operations in Lebanon, the US received warning less than an hour before the operation began. The military was informed of the scale of the event, and the response was mixed at best. The Israelis were going to step into the conflict with or without US support. The issue of Hezbollah was going to be addressed before a desperate Iran could give any further instructions. The Israelis notified Moscow of their intent but only after the operation was underway. The same communications process precluded the IDF strike on Iran itself. Nations were acting faster than diplomats, and governments could even contemplate the ramifications or logic of such events. Crisis communication was not taking place, at least not with the two US allies in the region. The US and Russia were communicating, but what was taking place was lost in the emotional demands each nation made of the other. The region was spinning out of control, and the world watched as national leaders were paralyzed by the speed of the crisis.

*Russia's Role:*

Russia's strategic plan for the region was being altered, even destroyed. This plan was something the US and others had speculated on, but in the end, they were not aware of its inner workings. The US understood that the increased Russian involvement in the Middle East was a direct result of what had been taking place in eastern and southern Europe. NATO was the issue for the Russians, and the Middle East was a classic counter move in a never-ending game of international chess. The question was whether the events occurring in the Middle East were part of a deliberate Russian plan. By the time the Russians informed the US that an immediate ceasefire would be "demanded" at the United Nations, it was too late for the US to influence anything taking place in the region. The two powers that had been relied upon to keep balance amongst proxy nations for decades could no longer control what was happening.

Iran's situation had gone from bad to catastrophic in several hours, and the Russians knew it. The US intelligence community could see that Iran and Russia were talking, but the official communications between Moscow and DC had gone nearly silent as soon as the IDF opened their campaign in Lebanon. After the IDF actions began in Lebanon, Russia's demand for a ceasefire was the only "official" communication the US received. The two nations were talking, but the diplomatic process was not responsible. The "official" questions stopped, and the "hotline" phone was silent.

*US / Israel Communication Struggle:*

The US attempted to communicate with Israel on mutable levels, and as the situation became grimmer for Israel, the tension between the two only increased. The two nation's militaries were communicating, but diplomatic exchanges were far less productive. At the diplomatic level, emotional and often hysterical arguments were the norm. When the Israeli leader made the decision to attack Iranian sites to include the city of Tehran, the US objection was nothing more than a frank warning. If Israel attacked Iran, the US could not guarantee its continued support. Iran was not attacking Israel. Everyone understood that the capabilities of Hezbollah came directly from the Iranians, but that was not an acceptable justification for dramatically increasing the conflict that was already underway. The US was desperately struggling to keep this conflict contained, and entry by the Israelis against Iran would shatter any hope of containment. US intelligence had Iranian missile facilities under constant observation by that point, and it was clear that Iran was prepared to utilize its full capacity at a moment's notice. The strikes on the GCC members would only be the beginning of a much larger exchange if Israel entered the conflict with Iran. The US understood that they would not have the proper density of delivery platforms to eliminate the Iranian sites for several days, and Israel was aware of that shortfall. It was the US military that first learned of Israel's intent to strike Iranian soil. The fact that the US administration requested confirmation from the Israeli government was a luxury of time that the US and the world did not have.

*Russia's Support for Iran:*

The opportunity to de-conflict IDF targeted facilities was simply not available to the US given the speed at which the Israelis responded against Iran. The Iranian Air Force was not fully engaged in the naval conflict, but the US plan, given the scope of the conflict, called for the suppression of crucial Iranian airfields. As was standard US military doctrine, crisis planning was drawn directly from deliberate planning. In this case, crisis planning addressed the lack of a proper US strike package in the area of operations (AO). The course of action chosen was to utilize the air assets of the GCC members to augment the US's response. The Joint Contingency Plan had been exercised for years, and it would not be the first time that US and Gulf nation aircraft would perform operational missions together. This operation would have a saver twist that no one was prepared for. When the decision was made to execute against the Iranian airfields, the updated intelligence briefing stopped everything in its tracks. Multiple aircraft had been detected leaving the airfield in Latakia. The aircraft signature made it clear that they were Russian. They were flying east, and they were in a hurry. The entire region's skies were more than dangerous, and the ability to track what was flying was a dominant process the US was in full control of. The Russian aircraft communicated with no one. By the time the airfield strike package was ready for execution, the word had come in.

The Russian aircraft had landed at multiple Iranian airfields, the same ones the US had targeted. At that point, the conflict changed again. Any action against the Iranian airfields would be seen as a direct attack on Russian assets. It was now the US President's turn to demand answers from Moscow. The Russians gave no statement on the movements and even denied they were taking place.

*Coverage in the US:*

Word of the Russian aircraft movement was kept from the media and for a good reason. Back in the US, the public had watched this conflict unfold live. The significant networks in the US were receiving video clips from all over the Middle East, and editorial review was impossible. After the first six hours of the conflict, most of the significant networks resorted to making the generic statement that the clips could not be authenticated. It was the legal stamp the networks' leadership could live with. When the first pictures of the destroyed Iranian ships were shown by Fox News, the reality of what was taking place set in. A fishing boat had been in the area, and after the exchange was over it moved to see if anyone was in the water. Someone aboard the boat took the pictures and sent them back to a friend at the port. That was the method in the entire area. People were taking photos and videos at a fantastic rate. The communication networks were only partially targeted, and that allowed rumors to become unstoppable. To the US population, witnessing live conflict in the Middle East was not a new phenomenon. In fact, they had grown somewhat accustomed to this. What was new was that Iran was involved, and this gave the media a new sense of urgency. But the US population had yet to reach their highest level of panic.

In the early hours of the conflict, the people in the US were not yet in a panic to stock up on critical goods. When the media began to have "experts" address what this conflict would mean to the price of gas, they agreed that the cost of oil would "skyrocket." That alone did create somewhat of a run on local gas supplies, but panic was not a word being used by the US media at that time. That began to change with the transition from events off the coast of Yemen to the Strait of Hormuz because the US public got a sense that something more serious was taking place. From the time the networks gave their initial reports, the speed at which the situation was unfolding became the story. The first report was a verbal comment read by several networks that a US naval vessel had been fired upon in the Strait of Hormuz. The source was not the Pentagon or the White House, but a Saudi official at a refinery on the Saudi coast. As the networks tried to confirm this story, an Associated Press (AP) tweet was posted that showed what appeared to be an Iranian fast boat firing an anti-ship missile. Once again a local fisherman had taken the picture. The argument over whether the picture was authentic was also irrelevant. The world saw it, and the AP had posted it. The concept of fake news wasn't discussed. Within the next five minutes, multiple commercial ships in the area reported seeing a significant exchange taking place between Iranian, US, and British ships. Most of the networks accepted this information as accurate, and that is the point at which they began to lose the ability to control what was being reported. Soon after the events in the Strait started, the BBC read an email. It was blind copied on from someone at Lloyds of London. It stated that commercial ships in the Strait were being warned to make full speed out of the area as soon as possible. It was clear then that the Strait of Hormuz had become exactly what everyone had always worried it would be, a war zone. Panic now spread not only in the US but in many parts of Europe. The financial markets anticipated a major conflict, and the US government could do little to quell that theory.

*Events Inside DC:*

In DC, the news that Israel was about to enter the conflict almost seemed manageable when the issue was Hezbollah in Lebanon. When Israel's military notified the US military that they were about to strike critical targets in Iran, the US President's crisis team was already overwhelmed. What was not known was Israel's intent to strike locations where Russian operations were taking place. That issue proved to be the defining topic that resulted in the drastic reduction of Israeli and US support. The US informed Israel that it would not condone or support any actions in Iran that would impact Russian operations. The fact the Russians were the ones that moved into the Iranian installations seemed irrelevant. Israel would be on its own in a few hours, except for Saudi, Egypt, and Jordan. The only bright spot in the pending event was the fact the Iranian missile launch sites were, for the most part, not collocated where the Russian aircraft had landed. Israel's plan called for the total destruction of the Iranian air capabilities, capabilities the US had already begun the process of severely degrading. If Iran's missile capabilities were the primary targets of the Israeli attacks, then the US believed that they might have time to change and even prevent the attacks on the Russian assets.

Once again, the US was desperate to keep the events in the Middle East contained in the region. Critical communications with the Russians were necessary for preventing escalation, and it seemed apparent to everyone that the two were not communicating. By the time one of the US networks asked, "was the US talking with Russia," it was clear that the answer was no. Again, panic increased in the US, as well as in any other nation watching.

*The Russian Response to Iran's Support:*

The Russians decided that the future of Syria would not be

determined by the Iranians. The Russians also reduced Iran to a marginal role in the process of finding an end to the conflict in Syria. Moscow understood the Iranian commitment to Syria, but the future of Russia was far more important than Iranian dreams of regional power. To the Russians, Syria from day one was merely a bargaining chip, a pawn to be manipulated. Iran was allowed to listen to parts of the negotiations on Syria's future, but only the parts Moscow decided that they could hear. Speeches were given, and stories were posted on how the Iranian "partnership" with Syria and Russia had forged a peaceful solution. But, in the end, the Russians desired only one thing. The US had to bring the issue of NATO's continued expansion to the table. Until that happened, the pressure in the Middle East and elsewhere would not stop. All of this may seem overly simplistic, and yet it is precisely what took place. The Russians' decisions set into motion Iran's actions in Yemen. Iran would have an impact on regional events regardless of what Moscow decided. Russia would not dictate the future of Iran.

Russian intelligence was aware of the pending movement of weapons and fighters to Yemen weeks before the process began. When it became apparent that the Iranian actions in Yemen were going to have an impact on Russia's status in the region, the pressure to prevent the Iranian operations increased exponentially. That pressure only made Tehran more entrenched.

Western and Saudi intelligence had been monitoring this growing rift between the Iranians and the Russians, but no operational plan to leverage what was taking place was ever agreed upon. What was known was that Iran was becoming more isolated and more desperate. If there had been speculation that they would attempt to apply pressure somewhere else in the region, it never became an actionable item worthy of anything more than a sidebar statement in morning intelligence briefings. The US intelligence community didn't believe that the Russians would support increased Iranian activities in the region, but they would allow some level of additional verbal blustering on even limited Iranian actions. The short answer was that the US thought Moscow would support Iranian grandstanding, but not events that might jeopardize what had secretly been agreed to between the US and Russia. As it turns out, the US was correct, but the Iranians would no longer answer to guidance from Moscow, and the US didn't anticipate that change.

The Russians monitored the first movements from the time the teams and supplies were placed onboard Iranian flagged ships. The Israelis even claimed that the Russians had quietly notified Saudi Arabia of the event. Some in the US intelligence community speculated that this informal communication became the core deciding point behind the initial Saudi attack. The US and Britain discussed the theory that if the Russians had been willing to tip the Saudis to what Iran was doing, then perhaps the Russians would not take action if Saudi intervened in the process. If that assumption was made, it was one of the first events that drove the world into war. Had the Russians decided to warn Saudi Arabia, thus anticipating Saudi's action? If so, why? In reality, it seems that the purpose of the Russian warning was a feeble attempt to keep the Saudis from overreacting. As is often the case, war is based upon critical miscalculations made early in an event. Russia's actions most likely created the panic that Saudi Arabia was not prepared for.

*Russia Questions Iran:*

Even in Moscow, the discussion of the true purpose of the increased support in Yemen was a matter of considerable debate. Some speculated that the units were going as "trainers" or "advisors," two concepts the Iranians were already deeply involved with inside of Yemen. But, as the combat equipment was loaded, it was clear that there had been a change, and this set Moscow into motion. The Russian military advisory team in Tehran requested confirmation of the events in Yemen. The reply from Tehran was not well received. The Iranians informed the Russian senior military advisor that the team training units and gear were for instructional purposes only. This reply was insulting, and Iran knew it. What was even more insulting was that it appeared Iran didn't care about the Russian response. The relationship between the two was weakening, and this event only made matters worse.

*The Movement:*

It was estimated that three ships had successfully offloaded their cargo bound for Yemen. The process of changing a ship's identity as well as unloading at sea was known to both Russia and the US. After this third shipment, the Russians might have made contact with Saudi Arabia. Operationally, the US believed that the Russians were doing what many nations did by working for both parties in the event. For that reason, the US took a wait-and-see attitude. The US did request that the Russians provide any information they might have on the actions of the Iranians and increased support to the conflict in Yemen. The Russian response was predictable. They stated that they were monitoring the situation and would inform the US if any concerns became evident. It was an answer the US was not comfortable with, but again, the concept was waiting to see. Too much was now at stake with the Russians, and caution was the directed path.

*Russia's Initial Reaction:*

The Saudi decision to fire on the Iranian cargo ships caught the Russians by surprise every bit as much as it had the US and others. Moscow's immediate reaction was to contact Tehran in an attempt to clarify the actions taking place. Again, the speed of the event was overwhelming for the Russians as well. Only minutes passed between the first shot and the time it took to damage or destroy Iran's ships. Phone calls in Tehran were not answered, nor were requests to Saudi Arabia. Moscow was in the dark, and that was not a position they would accept. What the Russians did understand was that the Iranian ships had been fired upon by both the Saudis and the US. They also realized that this event ran the genuine risk of spinning out of control. What did the US know, and what would they say when asked? That was the priority.

*Russia's Decision Process:*

How should Russia react? That became the pressing question in Moscow. Iran's navy was under attack, and by the time its naval ports were struck by the US, the decision had been made: Russia would stand with Iran and demand an immediate halt of US hostilities. When word reached Moscow of the events in Lebanon, one assumption began to take hold. The US and its allies had put the entire event together. The informal, undeclared agreements between the US and Russia had been a hoax. Moscow had been tricked, and that theory ran like wildfire throughout the Russian military high command. The US's frantic attempt to convince Russia that the actions of the Saudis had taken place without DC's knowledge was slow at best. The US simply didn't have enough information to put forth a logical argument.

To make matters worse, there was a large group of "experts" in the US who believed that the Russians pressured the Iranians to increase their support in Yemen. Logic and factual evidence was nearly impossible to link on either side. Events occurred too fast to allow diplomats and military experts to figure out what was taking place. Extremely efficient weapons in the hands of incapable nations with poorly trained military leadership had changed the face of warfare. Saudi and Iran were at war, and modern weapons made this war unmanageable for both sides.

*Russia and Hezbollah's Actions:*

Hezbollah's ability to create a nationwide crisis for Israel stunned Moscow. The events in the Strait of Hormuz executed at a speed the Russian were unable to analyze with any logical, predictive support to leadership. Regarding the issue of Hezbollah, the Iranians had provided them with advanced missile systems, but the assumption had always been that any conflict utilizing these weapons would be "controllable." With the events of Yemen and then the Strait of Hormuz, the concept of control was gone. True to their word, Israel didn't wait for the next phase of a perceived Iranian operation. Moscow understood that Israel was preemptively striking Hezbollah, and, like the US, their hope was it would not expand beyond that level. As it became apparent that Israel was collapsing into a state of panic, Moscow realized that Israel was going to hold Iran responsible for Hezbollah's ability to do such harm. Israeli cities were under attack. Power was out, and the roads were clogged. Israel's nightmare had come true, and they blamed Iran. Again, the question was, what level of support would Russia provide? And still, Russia's answer was controversial inside Moscow's leadership. Many argued that Russia couldn't support Iran, given the circumstances. The actions were too fluid to predict the next event. A firm statement of support for Iran was one thing, but actual, physical support was a perilous road, and Moscow knew it.

*Russia's Scalable Support:*

After heated discussions, one course of action was chosen. They would move their aircraft. The movement of aircraft to Iranian airfields was a tactic learned in Syria. The theory was based on forcing the US and IDF to contemplate an attack on Iranian installations that would have Russian assets.

It had worked before in Syria, but this time around it was a calculated gamble. The Russians were only half right in their assumption. The US would later target locations given the Russian footprint. The IDF was a different story. The Russians were attempting to limit the conflict while showing a level of support for their regional allies. What they failed to understand was the level of desperation inside Israel.

*Restating the Russian Strategic Objective for the Middle East:*

From day one, the strategic objective of Russian operations in Syria was Europe. The expansion of NATO was a promise broken by the West, at least, that was how the Russians saw it. The Western response had always been "we didn't ask them to join; they asked to join." The West also argued that the Eastern European nations feared the Russians to the point they nearly demanded to be taken in by the European Union and NATO. The destabilization of Europe was the price they would pay if they continued to support the expansion process, and it would be accomplished by weaponizing the mass migration of displaced peoples. Syria was the source of these displaced refugees, and therefore keeping Syria in crisis kept the pressure on Europe. But what the Russians wanted was beyond what any one nation could promise. The "buffer zone" concept of Eastern Europe was more important to the Russians than many had anticipated. After the fall of the Soviet Union, Europe and the US somehow convinced themselves that the new Russia would abandon this concept. They had no idea how badly they had miscalculated. They failed to understand the psyche of the Russian president and the memories he had of being caught in the middle of the Soviet collapse. Russia had been humiliated, and the West was responsible. Eastern Europe was an all-or-nothing issue for Russia, and the West miscalculated this at every juncture.

The Ukraine issue should have indicated to the West just how determined the Russians were to stop the expansion. History will show that the Russians disrupted the Middle East as a way to counter what was taking place in Eastern Europe. In the end, Russia was willing to risk general warfare for the sake of regaining control of Eastern Europe. They could disrupt Europe with an immigration crisis. However, Europe's liberal leadership rejected the notion of the Russians manipulating that crisis. War was not the objective, but it was a price the Russians were willing to pay if nothing else would work. The final, secret agreement with the US on the issue of Syria and support to Iran was the answer the Russians had been driving towards. The US would freeze NATO expansion, and Russia would allow the issues of the Middle East to be determined by the West. It was an agreement that might have never held, but it was the best the two sides could come up with as the stability of Europe had come into question. Everything changed with the actions of Iran and Saudi Arabia.

*Turkey, Egypt, and Jordan:*

The events off the coast of Yemen caught the Jordanians, the Egyptians, and the Turks off guard. All three maintained constant contact with US military forces, and the explanations given for the attacks were simplistic and short. All three were notified by the US that the Saudis had fired on an Iranian flagged ship and that the Iranian naval escort had returned fire. The intricacies of the conflict in Yemen were well known to all three countries but declared escalation by the Iranians did not translate into believing that the Iranians were willing to risk a regional war. All three nations contacted Saudi within the first hour of the conflict, but nothing more than canned answers were given. The statement provided to Egypt was the verbatim statement provided to Jordan and Turkey. It was a communication between Jordan and Egypt that first addressed the theory of a faction inside the Saudi government deciding to attack the Iranian flagged ships. Rumors of a power struggle inside the Saudi royal family were not new, but it did help explain why the king's closest advisors seemed reluctant to defend the actions of their nation. All three nations understood the gravity of what was taking place, but they also understood that their ability to influence the events was extremely limited. Communications with the US and the Saudis were their best chance of being able to calm their respective populations. This was not their fight, and the course of events was out of their control. The Egyptian and Jordanian support agreements with the IDF would be honored, but public outcry against that support would become critical issues for both nations.

The initiation of operations by the IDF in southern Jordan was communicated, but not to all three nations. Israel informed Egypt of the pending action through military channels in anticipation of utilizing alternate airfield facilities. Israel believed that the events that were about to take place were far too important to communicate by normal political channels. Military to military was the best possible course of action that might prevent misconceptions. On the other hand, Jordan and Turkey received news of the IDF actions through normal channels. The typical verbal statements to IDF actions in the region were never released by Jordan, Egypt, or Turkey. Again, the issue became the speed of the events. Yemen, The Strait of Hormuz, and then Lebanon, in a matter of hours, not days, made it impossible to politically get out in front of the conflict for all three nations.

*Egypt's Involvement:*

Egypt had the most important task. The safety of the Suez Canal was critical to the crisis in the region. No nation understood this more than Iran, and the Egyptians had long been worried about Iranian plans to disrupt the US's ability to reinforce the area. The loss of the canal would not have prevented the US from moving additional assets into the region, but it would have impacted the overall effort to support the logistical aspects of a prolonged conflict. Regardless, the Egyptians' concerns over the canal were valid, which is the reason the Egyptian military was brought into the conflict.

The Sinai region had long been an area of contention between radical Islamic groups and Egypt. Confrontations in that area had occurred almost weekly, and yet Egypt had never truly committed a full-force movement into the area. The unconventional warfare in the Sinai prevented the Egyptians from reacting to the level necessary to truly neutralize the threat. The Sinai was also the reason the Egyptian and the Israeli militaries had a far better communications process than most in the region realized. Threats from that area were threats to Israel as well as Egypt, and a joint information and operations process had been in place for years. Both Egypt and Israel understood that the actions in southern Lebanon would result in threats from known groups and locations in the Sinai, and the decision to preemptively strike these threats was agreed to within hours after the initiation of actions by the IDF. From the beginning, the challenges of such a coordinated event were obvious to both the IDF and the Egyptian Armed Forces, EAF.

Combined Arms Operations was not going to be possible, and as a result of both nations quickly agreed to the division of labor and the priority of task. The objective was simplistic by description, but more than complicated in reality. The destruction of "hostile" forces in the Sinai was the intent, but like the operation against Hezbollah, the reality of that goal was not anticipated by either country. The events that took place in Egypt as a result of this joint operation between the IDF and the EAF caught the Egyptian people unprepared. For all the communication between the two nations' militaries, the preparation of dealing with a civilian population that was opposed to working with Israel was virtually nonexistent. As a result, the protest became violent within minutes of the cooperation being made public, and the anger many existing groups already felt towards the Egyptian government made the violence even more dangerous. Egypt's military was capable of working with the Israeli military, at least at the planning level, but the population of Egypt was violently opposed. Within hours of the IDF actions in Lebanon, the news of Israeli aircraft striking targets in the Sinai had reached all of Egypt. Shortly after the news of IDF operations in the Sinai was made public, word spread that the Egyptian Military was also conducting operations in the same area. At first, some Egyptians believed a rumor that their military was actually engaging IDF units, and social media quickly spread that story to the point that most of the world believed Egypt and Israel were at war. The facts in DC, by that time, were so difficult to come by that even the White House wondered what was really happening. It was a US Pentagon tweet that changed the rumor and also set into motion social strife throughout Egypt. The US stated that Israel and Egypt were conducting a joint operation in the Sinai and added that the US was not involved. It was an attempt to give the US population some sense that the government was aware of what was taking place throughout the region that inadvertently sent Egypt into crisis. Trying to stay in front of the events was difficult to impossible. Trying to counter the events on social media was even more impossible, and these attempts eventually made matters worse. Egypt's reaction to the violence was predictably harsh. Since the uprising of 2011, events in Egypt had a tendency to attract large crowds and turn violent. Who fired the first shots in Cairo was never determined, but the civilian deaths along with the news of Egypt supporting Israel's military set the nation on the edge of collapse.

*Jordan's Role:*

Jordan's reaction to the events in the Sinai was almost a moot point from the very beginning. What was already underway in the region was beyond their government's ability to impact in any proactive manner. Like the rest of the world, Jordan watched the live feeds and government reports on the hostilities. By the time the actions in the Strait of Hormuz unfolded, Jordan was unable to respond to questions pouring in from the public as well as their ambassadors. When the social-media-driven rumor spread of military actions between Egypt and Israel, Jordan's calls to the Egyptian ambassador went unanswered. Once again, it was the military communication between the two nations that gave Jordan some understanding of what was happening. They knew then that the events in Lebanon and the Sinai would create not only social unrest in their own country; they also knew it would lead to an increased threat to their border with Israel. They didn't fear actions from the IDF but from those who would strike Israel from Jordanian land. Fortunately, Jordan had a far more defendable border with Israel because of the civil war in Syria. Preventing an event that would provoke an IDF response was critical to Jordan. Making sure Israel understood that Jordan was once again a neutral party to the events in the region was the best way to keep the IDF from overreacting on Jordanian land. Jordan planned to stay out of whatever was occurring in the region. Their goal was to keep their own population under control, but even that concept was going to prove to be more than the Jordanian government could handle.

*Turkey's Frustration:*

Turkey's initial reaction to the events in the region was confusing not only to the outside world but more importantly, to the Turkish population. The Turkish ambassador to Saudi Arabia made a statement within an hour of the event that was most likely not coordinated with the Turkish leadership. He claimed that Turkey would stand by the government of Saudi Arabia after the events off of Yemen, but authorities in Ankara quickly retracted his statement. Turkey was credited with being one of the only nations that called on all parties involved to cease further action until an initial dialog could take place. The authorities in Ankara made their statement within minutes of the Turkish ambassador's statement, and, as such, the official stance of Turkey was a topic of discussion in the US as well as Iran. The level of confusion in Ankara was just as intense as in any other capital in the region. The Turkish government was concerned about the events and the reasons behind them, and they too wondered where the crisis was headed. Unlike Jordan and Egypt, Turkey's part in any potential conflict was vital for the nation to understand. As a member of NATO, Turkey could be called upon to support an increased level of the crisis. Military leadership found its own level of information, and that information was passed to Ankara.

When the Turkish military became aware of the IDF's actions, Ankara demanded answers not from Israel, but from the US. Communications between Turkey and Israel were formal, which meant that it was challenging to receive a timely explanation of military operations. An explanation of IDF actions would not come from Israel, and Turkey anticipated as much. What they did understand was that the entire region was on the brink of war much more extensive than anything it had witnessed in over fifty years. Turkey had a working relationship with Saudi Arabia, and Iran was seen as a regional threat to the dreams of another Ottoman Empire. Yet, the benefits of siding with a fellow Sunni nation had to be weighed against where the conflict might take the region. Like the other nations involved, Turkey looked at the events from a reactive position. But from the beginning, they were considering how to exploit the situation. No matter what happened, Turkey's goal was to position itself as a regional power. And they needed to figure out the steps necessary to make their goal a reality. Turkey had no idea what would unfold over the coming days, but their dream of capitalizing on the crisis soon evaporated.

Turkey had one true advantage over Egypt and Jordan, or at least they thought they did, and that was their NATO membership. The ability of their military to communicate at the operational level with other members of NATO was a daily process, and, as such, understanding what was happening with US forces should have been a key asset to Ankara. The realization that communications were not taking place angered Turkish leadership. At the onset of hostilities, all military communications with Turkey were interrupted. The tension that had been growing between the US and Turkey for the past several years, coupled with Turkey's well-proclaimed relationship with Russia resulted in a limited flow of information. The reality was that the US didn't trust Turkey enough to inform them of operational actions, particularly those that did not concern Turkey's security. When actions initiated in Lebanon, Turkey demanded that the US inform them of the situation. The US did not officially respond, perhaps due to the speed at which the events unfolded or because of a lack of trust. Ambassadors spoke, but most of the world's ambassadors had no idea what was occurring and simply watched the live feeds like the rest of the world. The region was a crisis that would quickly turn to chaos, and Turkey was powerless to change the course of the events and in the end, their own fate.

# CHAPTER TWO: ESCALATION AND NORTH KOREA

By the beginning of the third day of the conflict, the status of the three nations had the world fearing that global conflict was near. The action of Israel against Iran not only stunned the US, it shocked the rest of the world as well. The major cities in Israel were in a state of emergency, unlike any they had witnessed in their history. Hezbollah's missile operations had made an impact even beyond the hopes of their leadership. The decision had been made to strike the nation responsible for Hezbollah's capabilities, but the level of response was a controversial topic inside the Israeli government as well as in the US.

Israel's final decision to strike limited military targets was only achieved after extreme pressure from the US. The US's stance of non-support of an attack on Iran was traded for the Israelis "limiting" their actions. A controlled strike was not the choice of a majority of the Israeli leadership, and the preparation to quickly escalate their actions was in place from the beginning. Iranian naval facilities had already been targeted by the US, but again, the actions up to that point had been controlled. The Iranian Navy was the US's primary target, and the IDF would target the Iranian Air Force. Neither of these operations inflicted enough damage to significantly degrade Iran's ability to respond even though the IDF had targeted multiple Iranian missile sites. In the end, Israel and the US had opted for restraint. To many who watched the events of the first two days unfold, restraint was not a word the media mentioned, but, tactically speaking, restraint was the process followed. Iran, Israel, Saudi Arabia, the UAE, and Lebanon were battle zones, and the world now truly feared where the conflict was headed. The overarching opinion was that the conflict would escalate. And by the end of the third day, that opinion would prove correct.

*Iran and Israel's Unrestricted War:*

From the beginning, Iran prepared for what was doctrinally known as "total unrestricted warfare." A conflict with Saudi Arabia, Israel, and the US may have been underway, but the advisories of Iran were thinking in terms of limited escalation. The response by the Iranian government to the IDF strikes made it perfectly clear to Israel that they had made the wrong choice. Iran responded to a limited strike with devastating force. In the initial phase of the conflict, Israel had depleted over fifty percent of its anti-ballistic capabilities. US systems were limited in the region, which resulted in a perception of victory for Iran. Iran's ballistic response proved to be far more powerful than anyone had anticipated. Strikes in Riyadh and Jerusalem depleted the confidence of the civilian populations of both nations. The panic in Riyadh led to panic in the UAE, Kuwait, and in most of the member nations of the GCC. Once again, social media told the story earlier and less accurately than any nation's government. The total number of strikes in Jerusalem was unknown, but the number of photos posted on social media, along with the panicked messages of those who lived there, painted a picture of an Israel on the brink of social collapse. Kuwait City was not struck, but the sheer panic created by the Iranian response created an exodus that left the city unable to function. The memories of the Iraqi invasion in 1990 still lingered in the minds of many Kuwaitis, and the only thing they understood was leaving for the south. But this time Saudi Arabia was in as much, if not more, turmoil, than Kuwait.

Iran's response to the IDF actions created a conflict between the US and Israel, and the coordinated flow of military information virtually stopped after the Iranian counter-attack. Israel had done as the US had demanded, and now Iranian missiles had struck the heart of Jerusalem. The people of Israel were frightened to the point of losing confidence in the government, and the leadership of Israel had a very small window of time to alleviate public fear. The concept of limited response was dead. The IDF would have all restraints removed. The order was given, and the destruction of the Iranian missile capability and air force was to be achieved at all costs. The Israeli government had ordered total mobilization at the end of the first day of the conflict, but the process was severely degraded by the intensity of the Hezbollah action. Yet, Israel would not need a totally mobilized force for what it intended to do. The plan for the destruction of Iranian military capabilities would be executed, and it would not be ceased. By the end of the third day, Iran and Israel were officially in an unrestricted war, and the input or support of the US was no longer requested. Israel would go to war alone, and every weapon at the IDF's disposal would be used, if necessary. Israel might not have counted on US support at that point, but the world saw the conflict in a different manner. Iran was at war with Israel, the US, and members of the GCC; namely, Saudi Arabia. By the third day, the reason for the conflict was no longer a question anyone was addressing. People were simply watching events unfold at a speed they could not comprehend. Technology had made the art of war so simplistic and so accurate and so devastating that humans could not keep up.

*The Undeclared Freighter:*

Over the years, the US had responded countless times to the move of unauthorized items into the Middle East by third-party flagged vessels. The cat and mouse game of tracking a vessel from its point of origin and then deciding to respond at sea or in port was a common practice for the US. On several occasions, the vessels in question were known to have North Korean cargo, and the destination of that cargo was also known. The transfer of weapons technology was a very controlled program, and Iran had been the primary target of the US's efforts to keep certain items from their possession. This time, it was different. The attention that should have been given to an event of this nature did not take place.

Approximately two weeks before the conflict, US intelligence, confirmed by Japanese sources, noted that a vessel had left North Korea and had made a stop in Indonesia with an anticipated destination of Iran. The ship was reflagged and renamed while in Indonesia. Again, this was a tactic that was not new to the US or its allies. A standard tracking protocol had been executed against this ship just before the initial report. When the ship in question encountered another vessel off the coast of India near Mumbai, the difference came to light. Both ships stopped within 200 yards of each other, and a small boarding craft approached the ship in question. Within minutes, the meeting was over, and both resumed their separate ways. Speculation was that someone had boarded the ship. Again, if true, it was an event that had been observed before. And even though the event was odd enough to make the morning's higher-level briefs, it did not represent an alarm. Monitoring the Iranian operations in Iraq as well as the buildup in support of the conflict in Yemen took precedence over all other intelligence involved in Iranian activities. The ship in question continued its journey with little explanation of its actions. By the time the events off the coast of Yemen occurred, the package and its team were operational. Technology had allowed the US to detect what was not on the ship.

There was no indication of any nuclear material, and spending man-hours tracking its status was not worth the effort. It was all the intelligence agencies could do to keep pace with real-world events. But the US had been wrong about the importance of such ships in the past, and history was destined to repeat itself.

The undeclared North Korean ship had taken on four members during its meeting off the coast of India. All four were Iranian nationals, and two of them were senior officers in the military. The ship's new destination went unnoticed. The ship should have never been able to reach the port of Jeddah, but all the parties that should have been able to detect this movement had no time for such proactive attention. By the time the ship had moored in the port of Jeddah, nearly all the area intelligence assets were focused on Iran's strange, aggressive actions and not on a small vessel that had sailed from North Korea to Saudi Arabia.

The plan set by the Iranians called for weapons to be delivered, making it the seventh movement from North Korea. The plan could not have predicted the actions of the Saudis or the conflict that followed, but the Iranian leadership had derived a new mission for the package, a mission that would lead to the destruction of Iran as a functioning nation. As for the masking of nuclear weapons movements from North Korea to Iran, how that was accomplished is not addressed in this report.

The planning for the employment of these weapons was a clear indication the Iranian government was prepared to respond to an anticipated conflict that would threaten the future of Iran. They understood that their actions in Yemen could lead to a much larger event, and they intended to deal a mortal blow to their enemies. Advanced placement of these weapons would provide them with such a capability. In that regard, the Iranian assumption proved to be correct. It should also be noted that the nuclear signature of the devices ensured that North Korea was held responsible for the actions of the

Iranians, which sealed their fate as well.

*North Korea and Iran's Mutual Support Pact:*

Since shortly after US President George W Bush's axis of evil speech, many in the intelligence community entertained the theory of an operational pack between the Iranians and the North Koreans. The Israelis were more convinced than anyone, and their evidence of a joint nuclear weapons program was compelling. On several occasions, Iranian military and scientific members were identified at numerous North Korean nuclear weapons facilities. Although the US and its allies had more than enough evidence to bring this issue to the United Nation's attention, the practice went nearly unmentioned. Not only was there a joint nuclear weapons development agreement between Iran and North Korea, some speculated that the operational pack included a joint offensive / defensive agreement. Those who supported this theory had nicknamed it "You go, We go." The concept was based upon one nation supporting the other by creating a second crisis front for the US. If Iran were attacked, North Korea would conduct some level of military operation that would require extensive US response. If North Korea were attacked, Iran would do the same. If ether nation determined offensive operations were required for matters of national survival, the same support would be triggered only on a larger scale. This joint operation pack theory was not widely supported, and for that reason, the signs that such an event might be taking place were not deliberately monitored once actions against Iran were underway. In fact, the support pack was far more detailed than anyone in the West had anticipated.

Pyongyang was immediately briefed of the US strikes against Iranian naval operations in the Strait of Hormuz not only by North Korea's military but also by an Iranian advisory team that was permanently assigned to North Korea. United States Pacific Command (USPACOM) had been tracking that team for several years, and most of the support for the "You go, We go" theory resided in USPACOM. The validation of this theory occurred in a manner that not even the supporters believed was possible.

In April of 2017, the North Koreans conducted a missile test that was deemed a failure given the destruction of the rocket while still in its lift stage. A small group of intelligence individuals in several nations worried that the test was not a failure. Their fear was the rocket was deliberately detonated at a precise altitude. This fear was based on a byproduct of a typical nuclear detonation known as an Electromagnetic Pulse, or EMP for short. EMPs had been a popular topic during the Cold War and had come under discussion again with the US Department of Homeland Security shortly after the events

of September 11, 2001. The dependency on electronic devices was discussed during the Cold War, but the idea that an EMP would create the downfall of society was never considered. By the time the conflict in the Middle East started, the world had lived off electronic technology. By 2017, the impact of an EMP event was given the same level of analysis as the physical destruction of a nuclear detonation. Assessments of the impact that an EMP attack would have on modern-day society ranged from some damage, but survivable, to catastrophic. The argument about how to defend against such an attack prevented any true national-level program from being implemented. In reality, however, the damage from EMPs would prove to be cataclysmic.

Once North Korea understood that Iran's national survival was in question, its leaders designed a mutual support plan that called for multiple EMP events. Why North Korea signed onto a plan that would end with its own destruction, and all for the sake of another nation halfway around the world, will undoubtedly be a future topic of study among historians. In the end, North Korea was not the nation to implement such an attack. North Korea never had the opportunity to execute its plan.

## The Tipping Point

T
Throughout history, most major conflicts have been charac-
terized by a singular moment that pushed them past any possibility of de-escalation. Commonly referred to as the "point
of no return," such a moment occurred on day four of the
Middle East conflict. On that day, any hope of containing the
fighting to the region was lost. Events that had been happening too fast for rational governments to react to logically
became overwhelming. The loss of governance's ability to
communicate via the primary medium that most of the civilized world had grown dependent on was the breaking point
for public order. The breakdown of most societies takes place
in a cascading series of events. And Europe was no different.
The continent descended into what was later categorized as
anarchy, and this set the US on a desperate path to isolate itself
from the rest of the world at nearly the last moment before all
confidence in government was lost.

State and local governments in the US seemingly withdrew
its confidence in the federal government nearly as quickly
as the public. Communication between the federal government and the states was chaotic from the beginning and became worse with each event. The media became the primary
source of information, and state leadership would suffer from
the same uncoordinated action as the public. Every network,
every social media outlet, offered minute-by-minute information. What was real, what was rumor, states had no way
of knowing. Poor decisions at the state and local level were
unavoidable.

By day four, people not directly impacted by the war had no
idea how much longer that would remain true. Uncertainty
was the primary fear at that point in the crisis, and that fear

grew exponentially. Uncertainty was and is the fuel of fear. And fear, true fear, is the destroyer of rational thought. Day four showed the world that fear, uncontrollable fear, was the centerpiece of the expanding war.

*Losing the World Wide Web:*

For well over twenty years, countless stories have been written about losing the Internet and the impact this would have on modern society. As dramatic as these stories are, with each passing day in the Middle East conflict, the potential impacts of a collapsed Internet drew even graver predictions. Most people understood that the impact would be life-altering, but few truly understood the real ramifications of such an event. The idea that stores would no longer function, hospitals would fail, and banks would close were just some of the issues people were warned they would face. What actually took place was exponentially worse than anything anyone was prepared for. Once again, the "experts" were more than stunned. They were forced into a world of panic, panic that swept them up just as much as the common person on the street. In the end, the lack of information was the issue with which the public could not come to grips. Without information, people in every impacted nation did what they could to find some level of assurance. In the US, when information from the federal government was no longer available, or the public no longer trusted the information they were given, they turned to local government only to find that local government was crippled and thus could not perform even the most rudimentary functions of government. Without the visible signs of an organized response, confidence was lost, and, consequently, order. Local and state governments, like the federal government, could not function without operational

Internet support. The impact in the US was not felt all at once. The events that led to the loss of Internet support came in stages and was inconsistent, but it was the "on-again, off-again" events that degraded the public trust.

To make matters worse, the federal government initiated many of the actions that impacted the public's access to the World Wide Web with little to no warning or explanation. The attempts to "defend" the nation's networks were poorly communicated and actually increased the public panic. The actions taken to protect the financial markets were a prime example. Decisions were made by leaders in several nations that showed their lack of knowledge of cybersecurity. Several of these decisions made the situation worse. For all the briefings and studies, leadership did not comprehend what could happen.

How the World Wide Web was so severely degraded was not the product of some super virus or a single nation-state's actions. Nearly two years after the war, the explanation that was given seemed to be the most logical answer. The World Wide Web was attacked by multiple nations on multiple levels, but the targets seemed to be universal. The goal was to end each nation's adversaries' ability to mobilize its military forces and cripple their ability to conduct economic transactions. The actions taken to harm the World Wide Web were executed with little regard as to second- and third-order effects. Every country understood the strategic value of the World Wide Web, but none had ever anticipated multiple, uncoordinated events taking place at nearly the same time. All of this was more than enough to shatter the confidence of anyone who relied on the network. Having said this, it was the Chinese "kill switch," discussed later in this report, which brought the issue of the World Wide Web to a dramatic conclusion.

*First Cyber Event:*

It appears that the first verifiable attack originated from an organization known for web-disruption activities that were operated from inside the Iranian military. It also appears that the Chinese reaction to this Iranian-based event was designed to cripple the Iranian capability to continue their cyber offensive operations. Iran's ability to disrupt Saudi oil operations was known, but the level to which they would succeed could not have been predicted. Saudi was consumed with physically protecting their most vital resource, and they were losing that fight with each passing day. Production capabilities were at a standstill, and tankers had not been loaded since the first day of the conflict. When the Iranians attacked the information needed to operate these coastal facilities, it became apparent that information in correspondence about necessary actions was to be questioned. In other words, if the instructions came by electrons, they were to be questioned. The issue became the volume of information that now needed to be validated before decisions could be made. The Saudi Arabian oil industry did not function in that manner, and, worse yet, it could not function in that manner. The conflict itself had driven the price of West Texas Crude to over $150.00 a barrel in only three days. When word came of Saudi's inability to operate even its reserved storage facilities coupled with the news of disruptive Internet events taking place against Exxon, the US public knew one thing. They had to get gas and quickly. The oil industry was functional only as long as the computers that ran the industry worked. Attacking that link was not a new phenomenon, but together with the physical actions in the region, the flow of oil from the Middle East stopped.

*China's Reaction:*

China's dependence on imported oil was its Achilles heel. Iranian actions against GCC oil production were having a dramatic impact on China, and China openly warned the Iranians not to let their conflict with Saudi interfere with Chinese welfare. Iran was in no position to listen, and the attacks, both physically and in the cyber arena, did not stop. China's options were limited, given their desire to stay out of the shooting war in the region, but the loss of oil was a serious issue. Once it was clear the warning was not going to produce any actionable results, the Chinese decision was made. China would show the world its dominance in the arena of cyber warfare. Iran would be made an example of for the world to watch in amazement. The timing for such a response played right into China's strategic plans. The conflict in the Middle East was exactly as they had anticipated, and from their viewpoint, everything was going according to plan.

Iran's primary cyber teams were located in two small cities, and their presence was kept very low-key. But the Chinese had been Iran's tutors. The second critical issue for Iran was the fact they had a poor cyber defensive program compared to the capabilities of their tutors. When the Chinese decided to strike, the impact was overwhelming. Iranian banking systems completely collapsed. Many Iranians had already begun the process of withdrawing their funds from Iranian banks given the escalating situation. The event of their cellphone network being interrupted in Tehran was yet another warning from the Chinese. Most Iranians were well aware of the fact that the Chinese controlled the infrastructure of their cellphone network. The Iranians couldn't defend themselves from cyber attacks, but they could attack. And that is exactly what they did when the time came with Saudi Arabia. China had given the Iranians the tools that would disrupt the flow of oil from one of China's largest importers. How that potential could have been overlooked while support was being provided to Iran is still debated. It is also possible that this capability was overlooked, but it fell into the category of weapons capability transfer. A transfer the Chinese needed to ensure took place to move their plan forward. The Middle East was planned to be the point of origin for the required conflict. Giving key weapons, including cyber weapons, to both sides would have been a critical part of the process.

*Saudi Arabia's Cyber Response:*

Iran's cyber exchange with Saudi Arabia was centered on the ability of the Saudis to produce oil. Saudi Arabia's ability to respond was not anticipated by Iran. The intent was to show the world that Saudi Arabia had cyber capabilities and that those capabilities could be used against Saudi's enemies if needed. Both the Israelis and the US had utilized a very limited cyber campaign against the Iranian military, but the level of disruption Saudi Arabia could inflict was limited. The physical damage to the Iranian forces had resulted in an extremely degraded combat force. The impact of a cyber event by Saudi Arabia would have limited results. Even though the actions of the Saudis resulted in minimal impact, the level of sophistication indicated Saudi Arabia had "outside" help.

*Initial US Cyber Response:*

US cyber operations, in the beginning, seem to have been defensive in nature. What offensive operations the US did execute against Iran centered on Command and Control capabilities of the Iranian military. Even with that in mind, overall, US cyber operations were extremely limited and deliberately so. The US had no intention of showing its capability until the right circumstances arose. Even in the early stages of the conflict, the US was concerned the crisis might grow much larger, and capabilities should not be made known at the wrong moment in time. It was also clear the actions of the Chinese and the Saudis were completely uncoordinated with the US. The support the Saudis obtained was rumored to have come from the Israelis, but once the conflict between the Iran and Israel was underway, the issue of mutual support between the two was lost in the crisis at hand.

*Cyber Tools in the Hands of Iran and Saudi Arabia:*

Like the Iranian cyber teams, the Saudi units were allowed access to cyber tools that were far more capable and destructive than what they understood. Both nations, as well as others, had gained the ability for offensive operations through covert support from more advanced countries. They both also became very dangerous in the world of cyber capabilities, given the open market of individuals who could create such software. Like the traditional kinetic arms process across the globe, the cyber market was growing by the day, and the destructive capabilities were virtually unmeasurable and grossly underestimated. The concept of an Arm's Race had taken on new meaning, but few world leaders truly understood the danger of a race that could not be seen. There were no large parades designed around massive amounts of military firepower. World expos of weapons for sale didn't exist. Cyberwarfare was a popular topic that very few truly understood. In a region of the world where advanced weapons were sold to the highest bidder, cyber shared a characteristic flaw. Nations owned capabilities they truly did not understand.

*Israel's Cyber Operations:*

Israel's cyber operations took place at a level far more damaging than the actions of Iran and Saudi or even China. The loss of cell phone access for most Iranians impacted society on edge beyond what the Chinese had anticipated. Without the means to communicate on the conflict taking place with their nation, the Iranians didn't go to work. Even government employees had decided that staying home was the safest thing to do. Without the ability to communicate, the people of Iran became paralyzed with fear. When the power in Tehran was disrupted, the blame was quickly placed on the Saudis and the US, when in fact, it was the Israeli's preemptive strike. The Israeli Scada attack was the opening blow of what would prove to be a turning point in the cyber aspect of the war. Electrical power was the key to civilized life, and that made power the primary target for Israel.

*Cyber Operations' Unanticipated Impacts:*

The cyber events between China, Iran, Saudi Arabia, and Israel had unintended consequences all over the world. Most had always speculated unforeseen circumstances would happen in a cyberwar, but no organization or nation anticipated the level of disruption that took place. Governments and organizations around the world disconnected themselves from the World Wide Web. Countries frantically attempted to shield themselves from the cyber events that were taking place. The world had witnessed cyber-attacks in the past, but nothing on the scale of what was taking place. Frantic guidance was given by "experts," advice that was not based on fact but fear. Leadership had little understanding of what collective repercussions there might be from giving such drastic instructions. As the banking system in Iran and Saudi came under attack, the global banks took actions to ensure their customers were safe. It was the actions they took that created the correct level of panic, and the increasing fear drove the banking leadership into taking even more drastic measures. The cycle was a classic event in the sense that one event was feeding on the other. Within 24hrs of the Israeli attack on the Iranian power grid and financial industry, the world was in an uncontrollable withdraw from the world financial system. It was an event nobody had indeed anticipated, and no one had a game plan to respond to what was taking place. Some corporations and even some countries went as far as unplugging their computer systems completely; physically unplugging them from the wall.

*The Lack of Planning:*

In the end, there was no "global plan" for dealing with a

Cyber War. A war that had overt nation-state involvement and seemed to have no rules. For all the discussions that had taken place by just about every nation and corporations that relied on the internet, in the end, a cohesive plan did not exist. The world was utterly dependent upon the World Wide Web. Once again, fear of the unknown was the overwhelming factor in the reckless decisions that were made. The World Wide Web was redundant, but it was far more intertwined and fragile than any expert ever imagined. As nations quickly tried to distance themselves from what was taking place, the one causality they couldn't withstand became a reality. People who could no longer communicate had no alternative than to blame those whose duty it was to represent them. The government was to blame. Government and huge corporations, to include the financial organizations. The memories of 2008 were still in the minds of those who found themselves without access to funds, food, and gas. It was clear, the $21^{st}$-century society was fragile, and that truth was terrifying, more than anyone ever imagined.

*The US loss of Force Generation Capability:*

The process of generating a modern nation military was far more complicated than most civilians, or even military members understood. "Just in time" vending and transportation coordination were pillars of the mobilization process. Political leadership could declare war, but a nation must be able to produce the massive amount of requirements needed to have the commitment take place physically. Modern governments could respond to conflict, but the necessity to sustain combat capabilities required a much significant commitment by the countries involved and even the nations in support. If the ability to conduct Force Generation and Force Sustainment were disrupted, the country concerned would most likely have two options. It could decide to withdraw from the conflict, but only if their adversary chose to agree to end hostilities. The second option would be to escalate the conflict to a level where all existing capabilities, opportunities, must be used. The danger with the second option would be uncontrolled escalation. The disruption of the World Wide Web that took place crippled the US's ability to generate additional forces. Much like what had taken place with Israel, the US quickly came to the realization a sustained conflict might not be possible.

The other reality of this conflict was more dramatic for the US and its Allies. The speed of the panic brought on by the cyber events significantly impacted the US militaries' ability to mobilize even so-called "ready" units. The major US Seaports were technological marvels. Automated processes affected everything related to the military mobilization concept of operations. By the time the cyber events of this war were spiraling out of control, the civilian and private industry capabilities to support the mobilization process was for all practical purposes lost. The weak link in the US's ability to fight was the civilian support required to get a combat force into a position to fight. With that capability dramatically impacted, US leadership had to explore how to execute this campaign, but with much of its regular force unable to leave the mainland anytime soon. This reality held valid not only for the US but for crucial other nation's ether in the conflict or preparing to respond if needed. Unforeseen consequences continued to degrade the US governments' ability to be proactive.

*Withholding the Truth:*

In the world of preparation for war, simple was faster, and Combatants that did not have a complex mobilization process had a tangible advantage. Government controlled operations would make those nations or groups capable of responding with short notice. An example of this conflict was Hezbollah. They could step out of their homes and fight. They could drive to a "hide" and resupply for further contact. The inability to conduct Force Generation and Force Sustainment was a great equalizer. The playing field was altered and the citizens, who were already near panic over the speed of events in this war, didn't need to know their modern-day military was unable to leave the demarcation points. The US government went to great efforts to keep the public from realizing what was taking place, but it didn't work. Rumors were undeniable just before the escalation of cyber-attacks. Military member's text messages about the difficulties of getting ready-made their way to social media. By the time news networks began to asked questions, the damage was done. A large portion of the US population understood the US military was going to have a difficult time preparing for war. The government tried to explain to the public that US Naval operations in the region were fully combat capable. What was not functional was the ability to support those operations with "surge" support. The limitations of the US military were made known to the world, and the ability to answer the constant barrage of questions from the media did not exist.

The US and its Allies were experiencing something they had long trained for, disruption of the mobilization process. Countless tabletop exercises had been conducted at nearly all levels of government, but that did not alter the course of what took place. The United States military was unable to mobilize at a level that sustained Force Projection. As dramatic as that reality was to US leadership, the cyber events that impacted the civilian communities in the US were far worse. The United States military would have to rely on other means to guarantee the safety of the country. At the same time, the public continued to lose confidence in the nation's ability to function. The attempt to withhold information on the mobilization event did far more damage to the public's trust than the leadership in DC realized. In the public's eye, the US was in trouble, and their government was withholding just how bad it was becoming.

*State of Emergency:*

The specific event responsible for the US government declaring a National State of Emergency was never verified. The US was facing multiple, complex actions, such as the attacks on the financial networks and Sea Port Operations, when word came of the full-scale Israeli strike against Iran. Both the US government and the public understood the conflict in the Middle East was now unmanageable, and that meant the future of other actions was utterly unknown. Internet operations were interrupted to such an extent that many in the US were unaware of government guidance being given out. Even state-level leadership struggled to understand what the federal government was executing and how they should respond at their level. Coordinated press briefings from the White House had decreased substantially over the past two days, and the US public knew less by the fourth day of the conflict than they did on the second day.

*The power of Rumors:*

The National State of Emergency went out to all state Emergency Operation Centers, EOCs, but the guidance on what to do and why the emergency had was declared was poorly executed. State-level EOCs put into motion plans they had developed. The problem was, guidance for follow up actions was chaotic at best. The rumor of a pending nuclear exchange started in a conference call between the States of FEMA Region Six, Texas, New Mexico, Louisiana, Oklahoma, and Arkansas. Actions at several vital military bases, Ft. Hood, Ft. Bliss explicitly, set this uncontrollable rumor in motion. Two installation Commanders had chosen to prepare their locations for a possible attack, and doing so was their prerogative. The issue came about when the public became aware these two sites were taking such actions. In a healthier environment, a rumor such as this would have been handled with the Department of Defense's Military Advisor assigned to each FEMA district, DCO, Defense Coordinating Officer, but the crisis the nation found itself in prevented "normal" reactions at all levels. When the FEMA Region Six 1800 /6 pm (L) conference call was held, the rumor of the military preparing for a nuclear strike overtook the call. The DCO attempted to explain the standard process for military installations and stated the states had witnessed this action countless times in the past. That did nothing to calm the emotions in this case. Validation of the rumor was now coming from state officials that most local and county leaders trusted. In the minds of the public, the rumor was true. A nuclear exchange was possible. Within hours, the increasing interruptions to internet access and other social media networks ensured this rumor became a reality. The well-intended actions of two military installation commanders set into motion the panic the federal government had been fearing. Up until now, the US federal government could not control the message presented to the American public that was impacting the nation the most. Soon, state and local governments lost the ability to give the public any level of confidence. Weak guidance from the federal government resulted in the near-collapse of state and local government. The weight of a nation on the brink of war was far too heavy for state and local governments to carry. National level leadership was overwhelmed, and state and local government was powerless to help. A State of Emergency was declared for the US, but the government at all levels could not provide guidance or more importantly, reassurance. The result was a nation left to speculate what was happening and what would happen. The nation's ability to function virtually stopped within hours. Not only could the US military not mobilize, the nation's backbone, private industry could no longer function. The fragility of the US society had been dramatically underestimated. Rumors became a reality at an alarming rate and government, at all levels, was powerless to prevent any of it.

*Fallout:*

The United States' response to the crisis was not anticipated by its public or the governments of those nations that were allied with the US. The US's enemies were just as surprised by the speed at which the US became dysfunctional. Even more, concerning was the fact that what had impacted the US had also affected the Allies of the US. NATO nations had all initiated some level of preparation /mobilization given the gravity of the events taking place. Great Britain's direct involvement in the Strait of Hormuz pushed their nation into full war preparation. What had derailed the US mobilization process repeated itself in most of the NATO members. Turkey was somewhat of an exception given the support processes there belonged in large part to the Turkish government. Even with this advantage, the best Turkey could have hoped for was the ability to defend its borders. For them, becoming an offensive member against Iran would have to be limited to balletic and air support. Even at that point in the crisis, it was not clear Turkey would also enter the conflict against Iran.

The attacks on the World Wide Web along with a very destructive Scada operation that targeted the electrical grid in France and Germany was designed to place the people in Europe in the identical position of the US population. Runs on fuel and food were just as prevalent in Europe as they were in the US. As the people of Europe witnessed the US become dysfunctional, they suddenly realized the status of the EU was nearly identical. The disintegration of the European Economic Union was yet another example of the unpredicted consequences of what at that time was still a Regional War. People quickly demanded their governments to provide for their people and not respond to the needs of others in Europe. The fighting was taking place in the Middle East, but the damage was quickly becoming global.

*Impact of the financial market event:*

As fast as events were taking place, the speed of collapse for world financial markets was even more dramatic. Electronic banking systems stopped functioning with no warning. Those who relied on such systems found themselves unable to pay for goods that were already quickly disappearing. The resulting social unrest was mostly confined to cities, but as those who feared what was taking place in the cities moved to get away, the ability to control the violence became nearly impossible. Financial institutions it so frantically attempted to avoid the chaos taking place on the World Wide Web, they never seem to realize the chaos they created inside day-to-day societies. Even those nations with very controlled banking systems found it impossible to control what was happening to the financial status of their countries.

*The US National Guard:*

In the US, The National Guard was made up of Citizen Soldiers. They were not living in Garrisons or Dorms on military installations. They were at home or at work. Mobilizing the National Guard meant mobilizing a proportion of the same population that was finding everyday items such as gas and food disappearing at a rapid rate. The Governor's attempted to activate their National Guard, but the confusion over what units already activated by the federal government was a crippling limitation given the state of communications. The Deteriorating capabilities of all forms of communications greatly impacted the National Guard's ability to mobilize even at the local level. State Emergency Operation Centers had been the ideal focal point for National Guard request, but by that time, the process was dysfunctional. A Governor's historical backup force suffered the same fate as the active military. Force mobilization was minimal. In the US, the National Guard the public had grown so accustomed to seeing in times of crisis would not arrive in any functional manner that would have led to social stability. Other nations suffered the same fate. The activation issue was especially real for most of Europe.

*Impact on the Nations not involved:*

Those nations that were not directly involved in the conflict were still dramatically impacted by global reactions. Trade, ships moving goods, became chaotic. With the internet under attack from so many different parties and with a growing number of nations trying desperately to distance themselves from what was taking place in the cyber fight, daily movement of goods came to a crashing halt. Almost everything that moved by Littoral Lanes was accounted for by some form of networked-based process. Global trading automation had fallen apart, and nothing moved with any coordination, and this all took place in one day. Ships at sea suddenly had no guidance on what would take placed when they reached their ports of demarcation.

For all the emergency planning nations and groups of countries had developed, nothing could prevent international commerce from falling apart. Not only did it fall apart, but it did so in a matter of hours. Within days, raw materials, food manufacturing, and fuel production stopped. Just in Time Vending, a concept many corporations and governments had turned to for the sake of cost, guaranteed the whole process was fragile beyond comprehension. Nations like the US had stockpiles of certain items such as fuel, but the process for accessing them was just as dependent on the automation of information like everything else. Many governors had knowledge of these stockpiled items given their working relationship with their FEMA region, but when the answer became only limited items were going to be available, the relations between the states and the federal government became even more chaotic. Detailed plans at the federal and state level could not address what was taking place. Other nations that had no functional system of stockpiling emergency items suffered the same outcome.

*The Spread of Unrest:*

Virtually across the world, governments attempted to suppress social unrest with force. The word that these actions were taking place went almost unnoticed. In normal times, the pictures of people being shot by military members would have flooded social media within minutes. Some did make it, but no one was watching. The crisis was at all levels and those who did have time to watch folded that news in with everything else that was taking place. The attempts to suppress the social upheaval in other nations only increased the panic level of the US. Government. A change had taken place in many parts of the world, and the world didn't know or didn't care. Governments were now turning to force to keep their populations under control.

By this point in the conflict, most of the major cities of the world were near complete social collapse. It was the rural areas that seemed to withstand much of what was taking place, but that was only for a short period. When fuel, food, and medicine became the issue, even the remote communities in the world were impacted. Amid the global social crisis, the conflict continued. The civilian populations found it harder and harder to receive reliable information. That changed when the conflict escalated to the level everyone had been fearing. If there had been one topic most governments had estimated the impact of, it was nuclear war. The size and the duration of such a war were always the weighted factors, but in this war, even those benchmarks became unreliable. The world was on the edge of global disaster, and people everywhere felt powerless to do anything about it.

# CHAPTER THREE: THE IMPACT OF THE FIRST NUCLEAR EVENTS:

*Israel warns Russia:*

o

Once the Israeli government had committed to a full strike on Iran, the only option of the table was the utilization of nuclear weapons. Even then, the IDF stood ready to employ them if called upon to do so. Israel was at a full war footing, even with the limitations the conflict had placed on them. The ability of Iran to defend its airspace was nearly gone and had been so since the third day of the conflict. Iran's air force was combat ineffective, and the placing of Russian aircraft at Iranian installations had been the only thing that kept what was left of the Iranian air defense intact.

The warning the Israeli government gave to the Russians came only one hour before the strike. Russian lives could be saved, but Russian aircraft and support materials would be lost. Israel was now prepared to fight at any level to obtain victory, and the Russians were informed as such. Even with the warning given, within a few hours of the full-scale attack, Moscow placed the complete blame squarely on the US. Although the IDF strike had no nuclear weapons utilization, it did target the known Iranian nuclear facilities. The IDF strike package also included nearly all of Iran's primary communication nodes. The US had struck Iranian military facilities along with offensive cyber-attacks against tactical units, but Israel struck every key commercial location in the Iranian grid. Iranian power production was attacked with both kinetic and cyber weapons. What the Chinese had accomplished and what the US had targeted made this attack the final blow to Iran's ability to communicate not only with its military but with its civilization population.

*Iran Retaliates and Russia's Decision:*

Russian military units and Advisors in Iran reported the status of Iran's ability to function as a nation. It also advised that Iranian leadership had decided to target Israel with every ballistic capability they still had available. Moscow had a decision to make. Should they notify the US and Israel what was about to take place or not? Russian leadership was debating what to do with this information when the strike launched. Although the combat capability of Iran was an important issue for the Russians, their primary concern was the status of Russian service members in Iran. Iran's abilities had been dramatically reduced, but the Russians understood the capability to strike Israel was beyond what the US and Israel most likely anticipated. They were also convinced the entire event was continuing to spin out of control

Israel had been in a crisis for over four days, and the impact of the conflict was unlike anything most of its population had witnessed. When the retaliation strike reached Israel, well over seventy percent of the IDF's ballistic air defense assets had been expended. The US's ability to support Israel had been limited, and the result was dramatic. Israel's communication network was based upon a nation that woke each morning to the possibility of war. As such, the public was able to receive guidance and news when most of the world could not. That level of information let the Israelis know just how devastating the Iranian strike had been. Although media coverage was limited, people witnessed what had taken place. In a nation, the size of Israel, people could walk to spread the word. Take a picture on a cell phone and then send it to the next person. The Iranian strike did not come without warning, but the magnitude of the attack was something the nation of Israel had not anticipated. Several days of warfare should have left the Iranians nearly defenseless. It did not. Limited attacks with constraints had been the option taken as a result of extreme pressure from the US. That resulted in a massive Iranian retaliation, a retaliation the people of Israel could not anticipate.

*Israeli Sense of Security:*

Over a dozen warheads struck the nuclear power plant at Negev. The defensive systems there were credited with intercepting the most massive inbound warheads, and that concept worked well. The issue became un-vetted reporting. Just the news of the site under attack, an attack the Israeli people had feared for years, was enough to increase the panic across the nation. Leakage from the site was a report that was given and denied several times in the first few hours, but it was the strikes on Jerusalem that shocked the nation even worse. It was clear to the IDF almost everything that was left in the Iranian inventory was targeted toward the capital. Word of widespread damage, as well as strikes on precise locations, overwhelmed the Israel public.

In the middle of this unprecedented Iranian response, it was the chemical weapons rumor Israeli leadership could not control. Even the IDF could not confirm the use of such weapons for several hours. Multiple reports of large areas suffering from an unknown smell pushed the rest of the nation into an uncontrollable panic. Chemical suits and masks had been a way of life for the people of Israel, but they had never turned to these items in such a mass panic. The survival of Israel was now a reality to the people of Israel. Their ability to strike back was known to the world, and it was that response the world feared. What the IDF did know was that a large number of the missiles had launched from Gaza. How they had been smuggled into Gaza was not the question Israel had to answer. How many more was there, that was the immediate concern. The response coming out of Gaza nearly crippled Israel's military leadership. Gaza had been the scene of fighting for the four days leading up to this attack, but now, Gaza became a primary target of Israeli anger. What took place there changed the course of human history forever.

*The US Response:*

The shock of the Iranian response was overwhelming not just in Israel, but in Washington DC and Moscow. After four days of targeted destruction, the Iranian military was able to strike Israel in such a way as to shatter what was left of the Israeli civilian population's confidence. How would Israel respond, that was the question in DC and Moscow. It was more than a question; it was fear. From the very beginning, the US, Moscow, and the UN Security Council had some level of confidence; the conflict would have its limits. No one believed Iran or Saudi or even Israel would take this event to where it was at that moment in time. Within a day, the hope of limited, non-nuclear escalation had vanished. The US had had long believe they could anticipate an Israeli nuclear event. Preparation for such action had critical indicators in the IDF, and it was those indicators the US relied on to understand the depth of the crisis. When the US military reported they saw these indicators taking place, that word stopped every conversation that was taking place inside the US President's crisis team. The greatest fear of all sides was coming true. Nuclear weapons were going to be introduced into the conflict. The US "Hot Line" to the Russians became vital, and that attempt took place just as the Russian were attempting to do the same. The reality was, the fate of the Middle East and perhaps the civilized world no longer belonged to the US or the Russians.

*Israel's Nuclear Decision:*

Israel was incensed over agreeing to the US's 'limited" initial response. Israel sat in near ruins, and the US would never be forgiven. Iran was no longer a functioning nation, and the government of Saudi was in hiding. At the UN Security Council, who by this time was in constant session, the decision was universal. "All hostile actions must stop immediately." That statement had been made for the past four days, and it held no more validity after the Iranian counter-attack than it did four days earlier. One nation held the key to escalation, and that nation was not in the Security Council meeting.

The IDF's predatory processes for nuclear response was far more straightforward than the US had anticipated. The Nuclear option was given. The targets were chosen, targets that have been preset for years. Israel would inflict a killing blow on Iran, and the consequences would be dealt with later. As for Gaza. There was no nuclear option, but a full occupation with no limitations on operations was approved. The forces needed would be in place within hours, and Gaza would soon no longer exist. Israel was no not communicating with DC or Moscow. Israel was deciding what would happen next, and the rest of the world would have to wait to see what that decision was. That was the general assumption six hours after the Iranian strike. It was the wrong assumption.

*Placement:*

Not only had Iran been able to procure several nuclear devices from North Korea, they had been successful in placing three of the weapons in locations where a detonation would have cataclysmic results for its enemies. Had the Iranians anticipated an unrestricted conflict based on their actions in Yemen? That question remains today, but the placement of nuclear weapons in strategic locations may have been nothing more than their version of a "Doomsday Plan." Weapons that have been put into place could have been removed if needed and perhaps that had been the concept. Up until the time of this report, this discussion never had the opportunity to take place.

*Juarez:*

Juarez Mexico was a location the US government had conducting planning and exercises for based on potential Terrorist actions. The range of scenarios included nuclear events, and it was because of this planning, multiple detection systems were operational on the US border with Juarez. Preventing a device from actually entering the US from that location had been the primary goal, and that scenario had been reviewed time and time again. Part of that planning would prove to be helpful, but it didn't prevent the event from taking place. As some had speculated, the device didn't need to enter the US. It would achieve Iran's objective from inside of Juarez.

*Gaza:*

As impossible as it seemed to get a device into the US, successfully placing one in Gaza was even more remarkable. Like the US, the Israelis had practiced for such an event for years. Unlike the US, the Israeli objective was to do whatever needed to prevent a device from making its way onto Israeli land. There were no limits to keeping this act from taking place to include preventing such a device from even being assembled in Iran. It is assumed the Sinai area was the key to that device being put into place. The destabilization of the Sinai had been an ever-increasing issue for several years before the conflict. Tunnels into Gaza had been a significant point of contention between Egypt and Israel as well. One of the supporting factors behind the success of General Sisi's assumption of power in Egypt had been a quiet understanding between himself and Israel on the topic of the Sinai and the tunnels. Somewhere in the midst of all of this concern and all of Israel's efforts, the goal of prevention failed.

*Jeddah:*

If the goal was to destroy Saudi Arabia's ability to produce oil, Jeddah was not the most logical target. What Jeddah did mean to the Iranians was the ability to destroy the Muslim communities' perception that Saudi could protect the holiest of Mecca. Mecca was in the hands of the Sunni. The Persian Shia dreamed of that ending. The sectarian war that had been taking place in the region for the past several decades, much longer, in reality, would culminate with the rule of Mecca changing hands and that was the goal of this device. Far enough away from Mecca to not damage it, but close enough to destroy Saudi's ability to support it, that was the reason Jeddah was chosen. The other devices were never recovered or mentioned and to this day are still missing.

*The decision to strike:*

By the time Iran launched its total response against Israel, it no longer functioned as a nation-state. They had their Ambassador at the UN and at their Embassies thought out the world, but their ability to provide for their citizens as well as their ability to operate a functioning military were gone. It's the capability to interact with the world economy would not be able to return for decades. The people of Iran sat in the dark. They had no communications, no food distribution, and no functioning infrastructure. Iran was a testament to what man was able to achieve in the 21$^{st}$ Century of warfare. A nation-state wholly stripped of its ability to function with minimum losses to the civilian population. There would be no humanitarian effort to relieve the suffering of the people of Iran. No Non-Governmental Agency, NGO, would have the ability to come to the aid of what was left. As bad as it had become for the people of Iran, it would get much worse. Israel was about to deal a final, fatal blow to the nation of Iran and some inside the Iranian government and the public knew it was coming.

*Iran's government in hiding:*

Sabzevar was the location where the remaining leadership of Iran had set up what was left of the Iranian government. A facility there for such an event was nearly all that was left of the Iranian national government. It was from that location the Iranian leadership would witness the destruction of what was left of their country. It was at that location, the last of the Iranian leadership would be neutralized.

*The Iranian Program:*

The prepositioned weapons program was never assigned a code name. It was never officially spoken of outside of a vetted group known only to Major General Qassem Soleimani. No written history of the program was allowed. Discussions on what needed to take place or issues with the continued support for the weapons could only happen face to face with General Soleimani. The fact that these three weapons had made it into position even amazed the Iranians. The teams assigned to support the sites were known only to Soleimani. It is speculated that all the members had been assimilated into the communities where they would operate for several years. The concept of the "Sleeper Cell" may have been a Cold War relic, but the Iranians, for decades, had refined the skill craft through their operations with Hezbollah. The requirements and capability to set off the devices existed exclusively with each team. The actual requirement was based upon the Cell confirming a full-scale attack on Iran by Israel or the US. When Israel struck Iran in just that manner, Iranian leadership knew what was coming. As soon as the Iranian counterstrike was conducted, each Cell Team understood what the response from Israel would be.

The evacuation of a select group to the facility in Sabzevar was lost in the volumes of reporting during and after the conventional Israeli strike. Even if some indication were given of a Continuity of Government, COG, event taking place, it would not have seemed out of the norm given the scale of the attack. Realizing the Iranian government was preparing for something far worse never made its way to the intelligence briefings until it was too late. What Iran was preparing for was not detected by the US or its Allies. Although the link between the Iranians and North Korea's nuclear program concerned many, in the end, no one truly believed Iran had a functional device.

*First detonation:*

Gaza was facing the brunt of the IDF plan for neutralization of any future hostile actions against Israel. The fighting in Gaza had been taking place since the IDF actions in Lebanon, but the emphasis had been on Hezbollah and Lebanon, not Gaza. That changed after the massive Iranian retaliation. The people of Gaza were accustomed to IDF operations inside their city, but they knew this latest event would be much different. Hamas and Fatah's leadership knew from the moment the events off the coast of Yemen took place; they had a minimal window of time to convince the Israelis they had no intention of joining into the conflict. Phone calls were made within the first hour of the fighting to both Tehran and Jerusalem as well as Moscow and DC. Iranian operatives inside of

Gaza were well known to both Hamas and Fatah. Warnings were issued to all groups in the city who might try to take advantage of the latest conflict. Even with all the efforts of Gaza's leadership, the rockets still left from Gaza territory.

The IDF response was a forgone conclusion after the Iranian counter-attack. Clandestine teams from the IRGC utilized the cover of Gaza for a large part of that counter-attack and the leadership in Gaza was powerless to stop it. Within hours of the IDF operations in Lebanon, the first real attacks in Gaza began. The Israeli Airforce struck the typical command and control targets along with power production. The intensity of the strikes signaled the change in the IDF intent. Gaza quickly settled into a mode of operation. It had survived time and time again. The IDF was conducting above normal operations over Gaza, but ground operations were limited, and this meant Gaza could survive. By the third day, it was clear to everyone in Gaza, Israel was in a fight for survival. What would happen now in their city was no longer predictable. What took place in Gaza did not change. People stayed in the best shelters they could find. They avoided areas they knew military operations would take place, and they prayed. When the volume of rockets left Gaza, the people of Gaza had nowhere to run and no place to hide from what they knew would come next. Their fears would come true, but who brought them the destruction they feared was never anticipated.

The Iranian counterstrike into Israel had very little coverage in Gaza given the attacks on communications and power. Word of mouth was how most began to hear of the level of fighting. It was also clear the Israeli Airforce had shifted their priorities to the point that missions over Gaza had drastically reduced. The citizens of Gaza began to risk coming out, and that is when they learned of the ground forces poised at the edge of the city. Gaza had been used as a launching point for an Iranian counter-attack, and they knew it. The lack of IDF actions in Gaza shortly after the Iranian counterattack was puzzling to them. It was clear the IDF was preparing to enter

Gaza and enter with force unlike any they had seen in years. Gaza would be occupied, and resistance would not be tolerated. Up until that point, Israel's ground force operation had been limited to the campaign in Lebanon. The force that was tasked to neutralize Gaza was capable of sweeping most of the Sinai.

The Iranian weapon Cell for the Gaza package had a very well-rehearsed plan that ensured the proper execution of their mission. All four members were located within a few hundred yards of the weapon's secure location, and access was not an issue. Although the massive strike on Iran had taken place almost a day earlier and the Cell knew the parameters for using the weapon had been reached, they had decided to wait and ensure they received no last-minute guidance from Tehran. They knew there was no confirmation process in their training, but they did comprehend what they were about to do, and human nature seemed to set in. The word of a massive IDF movement into Gaza at any minute changed their mindset. The process was simplistic. The Cell had one hour to distance itself from the initial blast, and their plan had called for an evacuation route by water. The detonation took place at 930pm local time. It was seen throughout Israel.

*The reaction/ Assessment:*

As disrupted as the internet had become in the two days before the detonation, word traveled around the world in less than ten minutes. As had been the case countless times before, governments could not formulate a logical response to instantaneous press inquiries. Social Media was once again, the catalyst for governance seeming to appear incompetent. The shaping of the event was well underway before any official statements were released. Rumors of who was responsible included the theory if was Israel's final event to eliminate the people of Gaza. As irrational as that statement sounded, it resonated throughout the youth of the Middle East. The fact that nearly of Division of the IDF had been destroyed in the blast was the logical argument against the detonation being the responsibility of Israel, but that fact was unknown to those forwarding the photos and video clips.

The first official statements were all denials. The US and Israel were first, but that was nearly an hour after the detonation. Russia condemned the event and stated whoever was responsible was the enemy of the Human Race. Iran's statement was given at nearly the same time as the Russians, and their tone gave the world the answer they were looking for. The Iranians did not openly admit the device was theirs, but their closing comment on how a fatal blow had been dealt to the Zionist Nation gave the world the answer they were looking for.

The United States detection of the device's detonation was reported up the identified Chain of Command within the five minutes. *As a reminder, that is only five more minutes than it took for the news to spread around the world.* Confirmation protocols verified the site as Gaza, near the city of Jabalia. The estimated size of the blast was the second issue that stopped the US government in mid-thought. A 150 kiloton footprint was the initial analysis. It had been detonated at sea level, and there had been no indication of any inbound ballistics before the detonation. The ability of the US to determine the origin of the material was not classified knowledge, but the speed of being able to do so was not known to the rest of the world. The US knew the origin of the material first, and that knowledge confirmed the fears of those who wished not to accept the North Korean, Iranian program.

Informing the Israelis was a very emotional argument within the President's Crisis Team. It was clear Israel would lay the blame on Iran with or without US verification. Israel also knew the US would know before them the nuclear fingerprint of the device, but they had assumed for years that fingerprint would point to North Korea. Even when the US decided what to communicate to Israel, the issue of effective communications was made even more difficult given the Israeli's silence over the past day. What the US did immediately offer was the capability to assess the damage of the event. This process would take time, and predictive analysis known as modeling was an ability the US could make available to Israel in a matter of hours. Unfortunately, assessing how bad the event had damaged Israel was not a topic the Israeli's were interested in.

The communications between the US and Israel had been severely damaged over the past few days, but military to military interface was still taking place, and that is where the US would get their first indication of just how bad things were for Israel. The force that had been assigned to the pending actions in Gaza had been dispersed into their tactical positions and that somewhat reduced the impact of the event. Still, the Divisional losses were nearly 90 percent. On top of this number, the civilian population of Jabalia was estimated at nearly 90,000, and most were presumed to have been immediately killed.

*Reaction inside the US:*

The President's Crisis Team struggled with information on the detonation as well as the instantaneous inquiries from the media. Nearly two hours after the blast occurred, the White House warned the media a press conference would be held within the next hour, but, by that time, the people in the US had drawn their own conclusions. The existing rumors of a nuclear exchange had driven the nation to the edge of panic. When word of the Gaza event came, people were no longer willing to wait for the next delayed message from DC. What took place in the US was beyond anything the nation had ever witnessed. People believed only one thing; they had to get out of the major cities. For the past several days, order was a concept that continued to degrade inside the US. When the news of Gaza hit, order was all but lost. As the President's Team worked to calm the fears in the US, the real issue they feared was one they couldn't control, the response of Israel.

*The Status of Israel:*

Israel had lived this event countless times. Over the years, exercise after exercise addressed the issue of a nuclear blast on Israel's land. They knew a ground-level detonation was the best of all the bad options. Both physical and electromagnetic damages would be far less than an atmospheric event. Israel's real problem with a nuclear event was the size of the country. Both Israel and the Enemies of Israel understood it wouldn't take dozens of weapons to drive the nation into a survival crisis. In reality, it only took one. The devastating impact of the conflict with Hezbollah and then Iran had left Israel more vulnerable than at any point in their past and this event was Israel's worse nightmare come true. Power and medical support had all but vanished inside of Israel. A nation that was used to difficult times and times of war was pushed passed any possible point of confidence. The people of Israel were in survival mode, and guidance from their government was no longer of any comfort. The psychological damage was ultimately the greatest impact the weapon had. Up until that point, the IDF's casualty numbers were historically low for a conflict involving ground operations into Lebanon. Everyone in Israel knew of the force that was prepared to enter Gaza. Where their loved ones were actually located inside that force was yet another driving factor behind a state of panic.

A follow on event was the greatest challenge to maintaining social order. From the public's standpoint, the war had just taken yet another devastating turn for the worse. From the government's standpoint, the war was now without limits. Would Israel respond in-kind was no longer a relevant question. The only decision the government of Israel had to make was, what level of nuclear reprisal would they execute? Israel would not follow the nuclear theorem of Proportionality, but that decision was not made without a heated debate amongst senior leadership. At the end of the argument, the answer was clear. Israel would not just remove what was left of the Iranian military and its government. The intent was to, as quickly as possible, completely destroy the nation of Iran. Again, the size of the nation of Israel became the weighted factor. A series of escalating nuclear blast was a concept Israel could not survive. The fear of additional devices could only bring Israel to one decision. Any possibility of retaliation had to be dealt with in one, single event. It was an all or nothing conflict then, and the survival of Israel was now in doubt. Israel would strike a killing blow, but other events were already in motion, and no action by Israel would prevent them from happening.

*Iranian Reaction:*

Word of the first device detonating reached Iranian leadership via social media. As limited as communication had become in Iran, those who could access satellite links were able to communicate with the outside world. General Soleimani was not with the dispersed leadership group, and the process for communicating with them was based on couriers. Of the leadership that was at the dispersed site, only one knew of the program. The shock of hearing of the event was replaced by total fear as they were informed of what other actions would take place. The destruction of Iran had been guaranteed, and they knew it. The argument on why the plan had never been developed had the opportunity to be held. As for the people of Iran, they had only speculation as to what was the cause of the nuclear event. The prevailing rumor placed the blame on Israel, and that was an explanation the Iranians wanted to believe. The logic of why Israel would use a nuclear device virtually on top of its own land was completely lost in the panic created by the event. Official word from Tehran to the Iranian people was never provided. Structured communications in Iran was already gone. Fear of further nuclear events had the same effect on the Iranian population as it did in the US. People would leave the major cities and areas near military locations. How they would survive away from their homes was not even considered. The people of Iran and the US and most of Europe believed a nuclear war was imminent, and no one was going to stay in the major cities of the world.

*Russia Reaction:*

Word of the event in Gaza reached Moscow within minutes. The Russian ability to detect nuclear detonations anywhere in the world was not as advanced as the US's, but their capability did exist. From the very beginning, the Russians did not accept the Social Media based theory of Israel being responsible. How the weapon had entered Gaza was as much a mystery to the Russians as it was to the US. They knew of the plan to occupy Gaza, and they knew the forces were in place when the device went off. Iran was Russia's primary suspect, but the ability to communicate with Tehran had been lost for over a day. The only contact the Russians had with Iran, in the twenty-four hours before the Gaza event, was at the military, tactical level. Russia's assessment of Iranian military operations was categorized as "Combat Ineffective," and this assessment had been in place one full day before the detonation. Isolated and without national Command and Control, Iran's military was in complete disarray. Russian military Commanders in Iran were actually making preparations to remove their assets from the area when the Gaza detonation took place. That process took on a whole new level of emphasis as soon as Gaza took place. The Israelis would retaliate, and the location of Russian units would no longer matter.

The Russians accurately categorized the Gaza event as a strike of last resort, the Iranian "Failsafe." A final decision to support the Iranians was still hotly debated in Moscow when the news of the detonation became known. In the end, the Russians, like the US and others believed the Iranians were responsible, but admitting they had achieved nuclear weapons possession would have been a devastating admission to the world. Moscow's inability to communicate with the dispersed Iranian government meant Russia was left to speculate what had taken place and what other actions were planned after Gaza. What the Russians feared were the same fears the US had. Where there others? To what level would the Israelis respond? There was no Iranian government to communicate with. There was no attempt by Iran to communicate with Moscow. Iran was on its own, but the Russians had military assets in multiple locations, and the Israelis were bound to hit back.

*China's Reaction:*

China's engagement with the Iranians had been far less complicated than that of the US or Russia. As an example, no public acknowledgment was given by the Chinese of the cyber events taken against Iran. Publicly, China's opinion of the conflict was simplistic. It was a "regional" issue, and all sides should stop military operations immediately. Their statements at the UN were exactly what the world wanted to hear. China was opposed to everything that was taking place. That was their official position. In reality, what was taking place was exactly what China had anticipated and planned for.

As much as the US and Russia may have been caught off guard by Iran, obtaining nuclear weapons, the Chinese were not. The transfer of the devices had been monitored by the Chinese from the very beginning. Communicating that knowledge to others was deemed counterproductive not only to China's stance on North Korea but the transfer was vital to the overall Chinese plan. For years, the Chinese had advocated dialog as the only true pathway to peace with North Korea. To inform the US or Russia that functional weapons were transferred to the Iranians would place the blame squarely in the laps of Chinese leadership. Although China was aware of the weapons transfer, understanding Iran's intent for these weapons was China's real challenge. It was their estimation the final goal of the Iranian government was to declare themselves a nuclear power, able to defend themselves from any adversary. China's goal was to convince the US and the rest of the world would, in the end, to accept Iran's new status rather than face a potential nuclear exchange. How the Chinese miscalculated the resolve of Israel is not known. The concept of Iran utilizing the weapons as a last resort was the cornerstone of Chinese planning. The utilization of nuclear weapons in the Middle East would dismantle the economic system of the civilized world, and China would be the only nation able to rebuild the system. A system they would control completely. The conflict would be contained at a level where the damage to China was minim. That was the theory and the process of Iran gaining nuclear weapons was essential to the theory becoming a reality.

China differed from the US and Russia on one other issue. Their greatest fear was not the reaction of Israel, but the ability of the US to verify the point of origin of the nuclear material in the bomb. A retaliation against North Korea would be guaranteed, and the results for China and the region would be disastrous. Convincing the US that China would take responsibility for North Korea's actions was key to the overall plan's success. As this scenario unfolded, China's leadership suddenly feared an even greater threat. They too had gathered intelligence on the theory of the "You go, we go" concept. As impossible as it may have seemed, China found themselves fearing the worst posable outcome, a devastated Iran leading to a North Korean counterstrike. Assuming the blame for North Korea's support to Iran would be leveraged to convince the US to allow China to deal with North Korea. But, A North Korean attack on South Korea or other US Allies would be a very difficult scenario to control. The concept of forcing the US into a two-front war on either side of the world was the goal of the Iranian, North Korean plan, and it was that plan the Chinese now came to fear. China's leadership lived to see that nightmare become a reality, even after a blunt warning to North Korea's Leader. The concept of allowing the Chinese to deal with North Korea would not be well received by Israel, but the Israeli ability to strike at North Korea was extremely limited, and the expenditure of forces to do so would have only dawn away from a conflict they were already completely committed to. In that regard, China was not concerned with the actions of Israel. A regional war that would devastate the Western economic system was the goal. A lethal strike against the world's communications networks would ensure this goal, and if needed, a limited nuclear exchange between the US and Russia would guarantee the outcome China dreamed of. As for the US and its awareness of the origin of the nuclear material, it was understood that no matter who took action against North Korea, the impact on South Korea would be tremendous. What China would offer the US was the ability to limit the commitment to the two front war the Iranians and the North Koreans had planned for. Once again, the events that followed made anticipating this approach by the Chinese a moot point.

*Second Nuclear Event:*

The second nuclear event took place eight hours after the event in Gaza. It consisted of three separate targets all struck within thirty minutes of each other. If anyone not directly involved in the conflict, who still could receive any level of news or information, was not convinced the entire world was now in danger that doubt died after the second attack.

The first Israeli nuclear strike targeted Tehran. The detonations over the city was estimated to have been 100kiloton in size. The attack took place with no warning, and although a large percentage of the population had evacuated given the previous fighting, it was estimated that nearly 500,000 people were still within the impact area of the weapon.

The second event targeted Arak Iran, the central point of their nuclear program. It took place fourteen minutes after the strike on Tehran. The device was a ground-penetrating weapon that was estimated to be nearly 150 kiloton in size.

The third strike targeted the Iranian naval facility at Bandar e Abbas. It was an air detonation, and the device was estimated to be nearly 100 kilotons in size. The facility had been targeted by the Saudis, US, and Israelis over the past few days of the conflict, but up until then, the damage was limited to fuel points and dockside facilities.

Both the US and Russian militaries had detected the submarine-launched weapons, but the flight distance to the targets was minimal, and thus confirmation of what was taking place was lost in the crisis already unfolding from the Gaza event eight hours earlier.

In the hours after the Gaza event, the US and Russian governments did communicate if to do nothing more than assure each other that escalation between the two of them must not take place. The silence of the past few days was broken by the event in Gaza. Because of that communication, all third party air assets were not in the airspace of Iran when the Israeli response took place. Other Gulf nations were notified by the US of the events in Iran, but no official response was given by any of them. The events of the past few days had each of their governments executing whatever level of Continuity of Government plan they had. The time for speeches was over. The time to survive and limit the coming damage was their priority.

Every nation had a common concern. Did Iran have the ability to take further nuclear action? No one pondered this question more than Israel. The fact the Russians and the US had reopened direct lines of communications was a small positive on what was now becoming the worst possible fear for the Human Race, a nuclear exchange. Israel had not given the US, or any other nation, any warning of their actions and as such, it was fully anticipated that no future warnings would be provided.

*The Third Nuclear Event:*

The Iranian Cell Team in Jeddah had watched the event in Gaza, and even with that confirmation of what was required of them, the team leader was hesitant. Unlike the Gaza team, he and his men had no escape plan. Their distance from the devices' detonation would be measured in terms of a few miles. All the Iranian weapons were designed to trigger no more than ninety minutes after the devices were activated and that would have given them a minimum window of safety. As hesitant as the survivor of the team stated they had been, the news of the attack on Tehran insured their commitment to execute their plan as ordered.

The weapon positioned in the city of Jeddah was armed five hours after the nuclear strikes on Iran, and the team had decided they would face their future from the city of Mecca. The checkpoint lines were long that day as many had turned to faith in the face of the crisis. The team watched for the flash from inside their vehicle. They knew what to expect, but they were unable to give praise to Allah when the moment came. Their actions would kill tens of thousands of fellow Muslims in a blink of an eye. The flash dropped those in Mecca to their knees.

If the world had feared the escalation of a nuclear conflict after Gaza, they now had all their fears confirmed. It was not two superpowers attempting to destroy each other, at least not yet. It was one nation that was not suspected of having functional devices engaging a nation that had never admitted to having them. A little over twelve hours had passed since the event in Gaza, and the world had already witnessed five nuclear detonations.

Execution of "You go, We go":

A
s stated earlier, not everyone in the West had bought into the concept of " You go, We go." By contrast, the Chinese not only believed the theory might have been true, but many in their military were also convinced. Planning for the occupation and neutralization of North Korea had been a task given to the Chinese Military for several years, and the plan was not only complex, but it was also very dependent upon a few chosen members of the North Korean Military. It was one of those "chosen" members who first broke the news of the pending strike by the North in support of Iran. China's decision to not inform the US or any other nation inflamed the reactions of not just the US, but all the nations in the region. The cost to the Chinese for their decision to withhold what they knew was much higher than they had anticipated. They desired to have the US and Japan allow them to "deal" with North Korea. That desire went unfulfilled just as the US was deciding to allow China to solve the North Korean problem. What the US had not anticipated nor could they accept was the idea of allowing the Chinese to be the only responding party to the "You go, We go" agreement. On its own, North Korea could have been left to the Chinese, but after the failure to warn the US of the verified North Korean Counterattack and the event itself, the US and its allies were forced to take action.

*The Target:*

South Korea had been on a near-war footing since the beginning of the conflict. The "You Go, We Go" theory was not officially supported in South Korea, but many military leaders believed in it enough to plan for such an event. Unlike the Gaza event, it is known how the North Koreans were able to place the weapon. A South Korean fishing boat was utilized to move the weapon into position. How the South Korean fishing boat penetrated the stringent water checkpoints is still not known. The shielding of the device was key to slipping past detection points along the waterway. The Hangang Bridge, just outside of Seoul, was the planned point of detonation, and the fishing boat arrived right on schedule. The South Korean government had declared a War-Time State of Emergency after the Israeli attack on Iran, as their military had convinced the government the "You go, We go" theory was going to take place. When the attack in Jeddah took place, South Korea closed all traffic entering the city of Seoul. All inbound shipping was ordered to stay at the 10-mile buoy pending further instructions. River traffic was reduced to government vessels only. It was too late. The device was in place.

Seven hours after the event in Jeddah Saudi Arabia, the city of Seoul was struck by a nuclear device. The device was detonated at ground level and was estimated to be nearly 150 kiloton in size. The immediate loss of life was estimated at over three million. The nation of South Korea was crippled with just one device. Everything the South Korean government had done to anticipate such a day had almost been rendered useless in a single moment. The nation of South Korea would never recover. Seoul was placed in the history books as the greatest, single loss of human life.

*The US Decision:*

The response of the US for such an event had always been depicted as being overwhelming and merciless. What took place was anything but that. By the time the decision had been made as to what actions would be taken, it was determined the people of North Korea had been victimized enough. The Madmen who had ruled that country for decades would not decide the fate of the North Korean people. What would take place was the total destruction of the North Korean government and military. That decision was announced to the People's Republic of China, and it was not presented as a point of negotiation.

*The Chinese Reaction:*

The Chinese received word of the event in Seoul within minutes of the bomb detonating. The nightmare had come true, and China now had few if any options other than to wait to see the reaction of the US and others. The call from the White House came forty-five minutes after the attack on Seoul. The Chinese government had one option presented to them by the US; Do nothing while the destruction of the North Korean government and military took place. There was only one goal for the Chinese at that time, and that was to convince the US not to respond in with nuclear weapons. That goal was achieved, and that allowed the Chinese government to control events inside its own country. For the people of China, patriotism had been growing for well over two decades, especially for the youth. The idea that the Chinese government would not respond to a nuclear event on North Korean soil would have been unacceptable to the Chinese people. The one issue that the Chinese plan always called for was avoiding a direct confrontation with the US or the Russians. The Chinese understood the message from the US was one that had very little room, if any, for negotiation. A compromise may have been found, but the Chinese understood that at that moment in time, a discussion on compromise would be counterproductive. The only goal the Chinese had was the prevention of US nuclear weapons. That was their request, and it was not a demand. The fact that it was not a demand was the real message the Chinese hoped the US could understand.

*The Flaw with "You go, We go":*

"You Go, We Go" was designed to force the US into a two-front war with those two fronts being on either side of the globe. History will show that the goal was achieved. What North Korea and Iran did not anticipate was the US's ability to fight just such a conflict and to do so in an overwhelming manner. The actions of the US against North Korea shocked the Chinese beyond their ability to comprehend. Advances in both Kinetic and Cyber capabilities were completely revealed for all the world to see. Closed-door, emergency meetings were held in Moscow as well as in Beijing. The Paper Tiger concept of the US was destroyed in the actions of just five days. The US response in North Korea now had the Russians, as well as the Chinese, fearing the United States' capabilities more than at any point in their histories. The Chinese "Reset" plan and a baseline assumption that now was obviously flawed. Not only did the United States have the resolve to fight conflicts in multiple locations simultaneously, but they now could do so with weapons that had been unknown to their enemies. The Chinese plan was not dead, but drastic modifications would have to be considered. The Chinese goal of avoiding a direct conflict with the United States had not changed. What would have to change was, the acceptable level of warfare, on a global scale, to achieve the Chinese goal. Chinese forces will be placed inside of North Korea by the third day of the US actions in the fog of war prevented this event from being properly anticipated by all parties.

*South Korea's Response:*

South Korean forces entered the capital of North Korea five days after the attack on Seoul. When the South Korean forces enter North Korea, there was no power. There was no official communications network. The government of North Korea was gone. The North Korean military was fractured and unwilling to fight. The issue became what the South intended to accomplish after entering North Korea. The ability to provide support to the people of North Korea was impossible, and the intent was to do nothing of the sort. The South Korean military had one goal; the destruction of anyone responsible for the North Korean government. The South did not enter the North to rescue its people. They entered North Korea to complete the task of destroying its leadership and anyone associated with it. It was a concept the US did not agree with, but would not prevent. History was on course to repeating itself, and China remembered the Korean Conflict all too well. "You Go, We Go" insured the destruction of North Korea. Both nations who had planned the operation were destroyed. The Chinese anticipated conflict in the Middle East and led to the destruction of North Korea and the revealing of the US weapons capability like the world never seen. South Korea had lost the city of Seoul, but revenge was the order of the day South Korean military, and that to the Chinese government had not anticipated. China's worst nightmare had come true, and the future of the world they wished to restructure was now very much in doubt. The Chinese goal became to convince the South Koreans that a "joint" campaign between the Chinese and the South Korean government would determine the future of North Korea. China still believed and perhaps hoped that the US was dreaming of limiting the conflicts that were now taking place. The unpredicted events in North Korea seriously altered China's plan, but the ultimate goal, China believed, was still achievable.

*"You Go, We Go" World Reaction:*

The world had never witnessed what took place in Seoul. Nagasaki and Hiroshima were too far for the world to repair the events. Tehran, Jeddah, and Gaza amounted to a staggering causality number. The event in Seoul made the world forget everything it had just witnessed. Panic was already underway in most of the civilized world, but the attack on Seoul brought an end to all logical, coordinated efforts to keep any modern civilization functional. The conflict was a week old, and the ability of any nation to maintain a sense of governance was all but lost. The North Korean and Iranian pack had guaranteed the expansion of the conflict beyond the Middle East. The people of the world no longer attempted to stay up to date on what was taking place. Everyone was in some form of a survival mode and information, current information, was no longer relevant.

*The United States status after "You go, We go":*

In the US, nearly no one was aware of just how devastating the response was from the US. Those that were still taking the time to receive any form of news drew no comfort from the counterstrikes the US executed on North Korea. US cities were virtually ungovernable. Local leaders were powerless to instill a functional level of law and order. The desire to disperse out of the cities was chaotic at best. Nearly everyone who lived in a large city was convinced they would be the next target. As this was all taking place, the US government had one choice, and that was to defend the nation. The plan seemed to be to defeat the nation's immediate enemies and then begin the task of sewing the nation's social structure back together. As unbelievable as it seemed, the theory of, "Every man for himself," now applied inside the US. Communities and organizations banded together, and with that effort, some sense of order was maintained in isolated locations. Again, that did not apply to the major cities. They had become as many authors had always predicted would take place after a nuclear war. The fact that a nuclear event had not taken place on US land proved to be of no comfort to the nation. America was in a total war footing, and the people of the nation were preoccupied with a survival mode they had never experienced and never thought would take place. They were also preparing for what they believed was coming.

*Russia's shock:*

The detonation in Seoul was reported in Moscow within minutes. Russian Leadership's fist communication was to

China. Moscow understood the US would strike back and the Russians believed that retaliation would be nuclear. What Moscow needed to know from the Chinese was what they would tolerate? What level of US forces would be "too much" for the Chinese? This conversation was ongoing when the first US counterstrikes took place. What Moscow witnessed was not a nuclear event, and if any salvation was to be had at that moment in time, it was the realization the Chinese would not face a US nuclear strike on North Korea, at least not yet. To Moscow, this gave them time. Time to attempt to find a peaceful solution to what was taking place in the world and time to prepare.

The US strikes on North Korea were underway for several hours before the Russians truly understood something unique was taking place. Nothing electronic in North Korea was working, and the Russians had no idea how the US was executing such events. As the Russian military continued to report on what was taking place in North Korea, the alarm bells began to go off in Russian leadership. The US was utilizing weaponry the Russians had no concept of. It was clear the US was executing some version of "Directional Electromagnetic Energy," but the question of how was the issue they could not answer. As the reports kept coming in on the locations and the speed of the events, Moscow's leadership simply sat in silence. US weaponry had undergone some version of "Revolutionary" development, and it had done so without Russia detection. Panic was now not just based on current events. For Russian leadership, panic was shifting, shifting towards a feeling of complete vulnerability.

*The Russian People:*

The People of Russia lived a much more simple and dispersed life than in the US. The events of the past few days were disturbing and frightening, but the Russian people were used to hard times. Those that lived in Russia's modern cities may have been panicked, but the vast majority of Russians felt no overwhelming sense of urgency. The Russian government's ability to communicate with its public was far more simplistic than the West. The loss of reliable internet services was a dramatic event for the Russian cities, but the countryside hardly noticed. Russian people were for the most part, far more simple and far less prone to panic. What Moscow understood was the fact the Russian people knew hard times and pushing through what was taking place was not an impossible task. But, in the end, Russian simplicity proved to be a dual-edged sword. Those areas which were not dependent upon the actions of Moscow would grow to believe the commitment to Moscow was no longer needed or worse, enforceable. The news of the nuclear events stressed the very fiber of the Russian nation. Like the US, Russia became a place of isolated, independent support. Like the US and in reality, most of the word, loyalty would become inconsistent at best.

*Russian Prepares for the worst:*

Moscow had to prepare for what might happen. The events in Iran had cost Russian lives, but retaliation against Israel was not considered. What Russia understood was the reality the world economy would be virtually destroyed for years to come. How far would the conflict go was based upon China's reaction to the events in North Korea. Iran, Israel, and North Korea could only cause a finite amount of damage to the world, and that damage could be repaired. Keeping the US and China away from a much larger war was the most important goal Moscow was desperate to achieve. Phone calls were made, but assurance and confidence were not achieved. After the frantic talking was over, Russia did what Russia had to do. The war footing of the nation became its top priority.

*China:*

It is understood, but with no verification, the US had informed China the response to the event in South Korea would not be met with a nuclear option. China also knew that the statement was based upon no further actions by North Korea. They also understood something else, and they had to make it perfectly clear. They could not be told they would have no part in dealing with North Korea. It was the commencement of hostilities by the US that caught China completely off guard. Like the Russians, the Chinese could not comprehend what was taking place inside of North Korea. They determined the US was utilizing some form of Directional Electromagnetic Energy and as the Russians, the main question was, how? North Korean ballistic sites went dark. Their Airforce bases became useless at nearly the same moment in time. Reports continued to poor in with all of them having the same characteristic. Nothing electronic was working inside the North Korean Military. Military Headquarters became nothing more than powerless concrete bunkers. Field Units had no running machinery and no communications. Ammunition depots exploded with no sign of aircraft or ballistic activity. The Chinese looked on in complete bewilderment.

The movement of Chinese units into North Korea had begun shortly after the US, and South Korean operations began. Field Commanders reported the entire border with North Korea seemed to have no power and North Korean military members were simply standing around in the middle of the streets. Orders were given to proceed with all speed and assume as much territory along the border as possible. Everywhere the Chinese Army entered, the same scene was witnessed. If a North Korean government facility or a military unit was nearby, there was no power and nothing electrical worked. As the reports continued, it was clearly not just the Chinese leadership was shocked. Chinese units became unnerved with what they were witnessing. They had no sign of any enemy. They heard no aircraft, no artillery fire. The saw no destroyed buildings; no burned out armor. The North Korean military was defeated, and the government was standing around, just like the rest of the population. It was unnerving to Chinese military leaders. What had taken place was beyond anything they could understand. The US had neutralized the 4th largest military in the world in a matter of hours. Follow on actions would take the place of the next four days, but they mostly supported operations as the South Korean military moved north, a movement the US was attempting to minimize as much as possible. Where the South Korean and the Chines military would meet became the issue.

What China understood was this. If an object ran off of electricity and it was in the Battle Space the US was conducting, it simply stopped working. When a desperate request for coordination was presented by the Chinese, the US gave only one answer, "Stay out of North Korea." That was an answer the Chinese could not and would not accept. Diplomacy was a fading concept with millions already dead. Resolve was the US goal, but revenge was the Chinese perception and perception ruled any and all government actions, anywhere in the world.

*The Chinese Public:*

The people of China had the same fears as every other nation. Those who lived in the cities began to leave once word of the event in Seoul became known. The Chinese government advised their people not to panic, and they assured them the US and China were not at the brink of war, but the events of the past few days destroyed any confidence the people had and that included "official" statements. Chinese citizens were no different than the rest of the world. Fear and uncertainty ruled the day in China.

*Impact of "You go, We go":*

The alliance between Iran and North Korea was known to all the key nations involved in the current crisis. The decisions to avoid issues that were deemed too difficult to address in the open guaranteed the world would suffer the ravages of a much wider and destructive war. The Chinese may have anticipated the events in the Middle East and those events may have fulfilled the requirements for China's main objective, but in the end, China did what so many others had done in the past. They miscalculated. The Law of Unintended Consequences was the Achilles heel of China's vision for the world's future. The next event would set the final chapter of the war into motion, and the actions of that event would push "You Go, We Go" to the sidelines of history.

*Juarez:*

The Cell Team for the Juarez weapon had one true advantage over the teams of the Gaza and Jeddah events. They prepared their mission in the complete chaos the world had fallen into. All four members were Mexican Citizens. They had no history of interaction with Hezbollah operations in Mexico or any other group in Central or South America. The weapon had been moved in four separate shipments, and the sheer volume of cargo containers in Juarez made detection extremely difficult. Although the fear of such an event taking place was often reviewed, the reality of threat was overlooked. The concept had been discussed too many times and played out on tabletop exercises with senior leaders too often. The fear of failure had been lost.

Assembly of the weapon was completed on the day of the event in Jeddah, and it is most likely the team intended to execute their task that same day. Perhaps the events of Seoul disrupted the Team's timeline, but that is speculation. The fact of the matter is, the Juarez device did not detonate until four days after the North Korean attack on Seoul.

To say the US government was overwhelmed with the events in the world-leading up to the Juarez attack would be a complete understatement. Border Crossings had been closed since the event in Gaza. The attacks on Jeddah gave the US every indication Iran had some level of Cell Operations dispersed, perhaps outside of the Middle East. Where they were and what they planned to do was nothing more than pure speculation that flowed from the intelligence community and did so around the clock. It became clear the government's best efforts were nothing more than shots in the dark. Public outcry over detentions were nonexistent. Survival was the priority of even the most liberal members of society. The people in the US and other nations were too occupied with securing any level of safety they could obtain. If there was someone that was even slightly suspect, they were to be found. That was the concept. It didn't work. Not only were the cities completely dysfunctional, but many of the government agencies were just as bad. Even with fully operational federal, state, and local authorities, the task proved to be completely ineffective. The weapon had been placed in Juarez and not the US for a reason. The impact would be the same, but the ability to cross the border was avoided. Again, a concept of action the US had not overlooked, but the ability to monitor events in Mexico, with everything else that was going, on was simply not there.

The flash from the Juarez device was seen from the McGregor Range complex. Those that worked there knew exactly what the flash was and began the process of responding within minutes of the event. The estimated yield of the device was 150Kilotons. Its placement was within one mile of the Bridge of Americas Port of Entry. The immediate causality number was over 300,000. The secondary objective of the event was also achieved. Ft. Bliss was rendered Combat Ineffective. The loss of equipment and manpower to the United States Army's Air Defense Systems was devastating. The Infrastructure of El Paso and Juarez was destroyed, and the ability of the US government to respond was greatly minimized by the overall panic taking place in the nation before the event. Federal agencies that would have been tasked with responding were dysfunctional. People were simply not going to work and the disruption caused by the city's self-evaluating compounded the crisis that had now taken place on US land. El Paso was on its own, and they knew it. The locals of both nations did respond to the best of their ability, and no one worried about border issues.

*Word of the Juarez event:*

When word of the detonation reached DC, the crisis at hand was the US's response to the attack on Seoul. It had been four days since the Seoul event, and that event had only been seven hours after the event in Jeddah. DC was not only in full crisis mode, but it was also now in a total war footing. Confirmation had taken much longer than anyone anticipated, but it had been confirmed, the nuclear material of the devices in Gaza and Jeddah both originated from the same reactor in North Korea. The push to respond in North Korea with nuclear weapons was now winning the argument amongst the majority of the President's Staff. Although China had been given an unofficial guarantee of a non-nuclear response to the event in Seoul, confirmation of North Korea's hand in these two events changed everything. Iran's role in what took place was not debatable, and the process of destroying what was left of the Iranian government and military would not be altered. Israel had used the nuclear option on Iran and had done so with a dramatic and overwhelming impact, and for that reason, the nuclear option for Iran was not considered at that moment in time.

The news of Juarez and El Paso was read aloud to the President's assembled members after the word was passed to the President himself. Local news from the area was almost nonexistent, and for the first two hours, information came from satellite phones from inside Ft Bliss. Ft. Bliss's range support center called McGregor Range was far enough away from the blast and had robust communication capabilities. Solders from this location were the first ones on the scene. Also,

Holloman AFB flew an aerial survey mission over El Paso and Juarez three hours after the attack. With little media coverage surviving in the impact area, the media turned to the federal government for updates.

The US government had struggled to keep the confidence of the American public from the moment the event off the coast of Yemen took place. Gaza, Jeddah, Seoul and now one of the US's own cities had been stuck by nuclear weapons. How could it happen, and who did it? Those were the questions leadership in DC failed to answer. Although a large portion of the nation was in some level of exodus from population centers, the complete crisis point of such an event was still not at hand. That changed with word of the event in Juarez and El Paso. People no longer worried about receiving guidance. They were now in full survival mode, and anything that made survival possible was now a rational, reasonable act. Few even bothered to wait for the government's explanation. The United States civilian population believed they were own their own. What would happen next was no longer a question they asked of their political leadership. Social order in the US decayed past the point any level of government could control. Law Enforcement in the US was no longer a functioning process. The US government had one job then. Protect what was left of the US society and do so at all costs.

*US Notification to China:*

The President of the United States contacted the President of China four hours after the destruction of the city of El Paso. He informed the Chinese President the material utilized in both the Gaza and Jeddah weapons originated from North Korea and the US was confident the same results would come from the attack on Juarez and El Paso. The US President informed China the response of the US would be based upon the US's immediate intent to destroy the remaining capabilities of the North Korean military, and the option of nuclear weapons was now extremely possible. Although the North Korean government and its military had been devastated in the past four days, the desire to punish North Korea was now overwhelming. The Chinese response was based upon an argument that a nuclear strike on North Korea would most likely not impact the tactic these three events had been based upon. China viewed the US's intent as an act of revenge, and the revenge would be placed upon those who had little or nothing to do with the decisions of the North Korean government. The conversation was tense and yet professional. In the end, the US's primary concern was to signal the rest of the world that it would not tolerate such an attack on US land. North Korea would be an example for the rest of the world to witness. Desperation to maintain public confidence was a poor line of logic, but logic was no longer a concept used by many of the world's leaders. The US understood the Chinese had deployed units into North Korea, and the process of de-confliction was still be worked out when the event in Juarez took place. China's controlled crisis was now completely out of their control.

*Nations Prepare for the Worst:*

As devastating as the US's response to the attack on Seoul had been, the threat of a nuclear event set other nations in motion. The attack in Juarez guarantees a full US response, and everyone knew the Chinese would be unable to accept a nuclear event inside North Korea. China's defensive posture had been elevated since the attack on Seoul. South Korea was incapable of any additional support operations other than what it was attempting to accomplish in Seoul. What the people of South Korea and the people of North Korea had in common was the reality that both of them would be victims of the next level of warfare. In reality, South Korea and North Korea were no longer functioning nations. The Korean Peninsula was without power with food and water growing scarcer by the hour. The refugee camps outside the major US / South Korean military bases were the only locations that had any semblance of support, and that was minimum at best.

As the rest of the world watched the events in North Korea, the tension between the US and China was undeniable. This conflict was no longer centered on the Middle East. It was now a global crisis, and the survival of all nations was in question. Preparation for the worst was the top priority of all nations, and communicating with each other was no longer a requirement to make those preparations possible.

*The Russian's Response to Juarez:*

The Russian President's leadership team was in a crisis meeting over North Korea when the world of the detonation in Juarez came in. Russian military readiness, like the Chinese, had been on a war footing from the moment Israel initiated the nuclear option in Iran. When the news of the attack in Juarez and El Paso came in, the Russians were confident Iran was behind the event. The Russian President called the US President just as he was ending his conversation with the Chinese. Once again, the US made it's intent perfectly clear to the Russians, and the Russian President's Advisors let him know there would be very little room for discussion on the topic. It was agreed that both nations would immediately discuss the repercussion of a US nuclear strike on North Korea. This conversation was not as much based upon attempting to prevent such an event as it was an effort to minimize the impact on Russia. What would the US use? What was the plan, and what would that mean for Russia? Fallout patterns and potential migration of survivors, those were the two primary topics and that conversation, at all levels, went on for hours. Again, the Russians understood the ability to stop the US from responding to a nuclear attack was futile. Effort was to be spent on minimizing the post-event, but it was the conversation between the Russians and the Chinese that changed the course of pending actions. More importantly, it was a conversation the Russians and the Chinese had no idea the US could listen in on.

*China's Stance on North Korea before contact with Russia:*

From the beginning, the Chinese plan had been to invade North Korea to keep any US operation in North Korea limited in the scope of its objective. China had been asked to "control" North Korea for years, and that option was more desirable than to witness the West place a government in power on the Chinese border. All previous conversations and agreements between the US and China had been dependent on the US, not responding to the event in Seoul with nuclear weapons. An agreement to let China take the lead in physically occupying key areas of North Korea was poorly planned, and the operational flow of the events inside North Korea was more than dangerous. The "official word" had been for China to stay out of North Korea, but the US understood a tolerance of China's attempt to minimize the impact of a collapsed North Korea would have to be accepted. Informal communications attempted to make this process possible. What China did understand was the reality the US was going to strike North Korea with nuclear weapons.

It was the Chinese political leadership that received the phone call from the US President on the issue of a nuclear response. The drive to find a non-nuclear solution allowed a critical error to be made by the Chinese. The argument from the very beginning of a US nuclear response should have been based upon the advancement of Chinese military units inside of North Korea. In the panic, this conversation created was immediate for China's Military Leadership. The repercussions for the Chinese military units inside North Korea had been overlooked by Political leadership, leadership that did not understand military doctrine. The issue was made clear to the Chinese President just as soon as the initial conversation with the US was over. Military to military communications were quickly authorized as the Chinese were concerned the US action may have already been planned. As quick as the Chinese had been to realize their mistake, the US military had placed the same issue on their Commander in Chief's desk. Again, a heated debate took place with the US President's team. As events unfolded, a growing majority continued to ask if there was any tactical value in striking what was left of the North Korean leadership or military with nuclear weapons. Was the risk of escalation with the Chinese worth the intent of sending a "message" to the rest of the world? The vocal minority of the President's staff argued the US could not let the destruction of El Paso go unanswered. All of them knew Iran was most likely responsible, but North Korea had made the attack possible. Both sides agreed the government of the US was losing the confidence and the control of the nation. The Secretary of State and the Secretary of Defense were adamant the only real message was to their own people. "We are still capable of protecting you"! Both sides of the argument also understood the North Korean military was defeated, and its government no longer controlled any segment of North Korean actions. Units were surrendering to the Chinese military as the discussion in DC was taking place. The alternative for the North Koreans was to be captured by South Koreans, and they were not taking North Korean prisoners.

In the end, US leadership came to the conclusion a nuclear response to North Korea was simply not worth the risk of escalation with the Chinese. The losses to their units would be unacceptable to them. Their ability to disengage their military inside of North Korea would take days if not weeks, not to mention the South Korean forces that were on revenge raids throughout North Korea and in fact, several encounters between Chinese and South Korean units had already been reported. All sides were going to great lengths to avoid a true Chinese, US, South Korean confrontation. It should also be noted the fact the US ground forces had been ordered not to cross into North Korean territory had proven to be a major stabilizing decision. China now had to make a decision. Could they trust the word of the US? Would the US use nuclear weapons in North Korea or not? Finally, China had to have a clear understanding of where the Russians stood, and that conversation had to take place as soon as possible.

*The US Decision:*

The nuclear option for North Korea was off the table. There would be an enemy struck for what had taken place in the US, Mexico border and that enemy had already been devastated by nuclear strikes. Yet, the concept of sending a message to the rest of the world and the US population would be achieved. The Iranian nuclear development sites had been hit by Israel, but it was a single strike. The US would finish the task regardless of how functional the areas really were.

Once again, a critical error was made. In the confusion of the event in Juarez and El Paso and the ensuing heated argument inside the US President's team, a convincible and detailed explanation was not provided to the Chinese or the Russians. The US was not going to strike North Korea, but the Chinese simply didn't believe it. Events in the world moved too quickly. The lack of sound decisions were impacting not only the US but several other key nations as well. The message was to have been delivered to both nations within one hour of the decision. Six hours after the US had chosen Iran as the primary target, that notification had not been made. Unofficial verbal communications did take place, but the power of fear and paranoia proved to be too strong. In those six hours, the Chinese made a decision that would propel the conflict to the next level.

# CHAPTER FOUR: THE CHINESE "RESET" AND "KILL SWITCH" PLANS:

It is important at this stage and report to reemphasize what the primary cause of this conflict involved. The Chinese "Reset" concept was depended upon a predictable conflict in the Middle East. That confrontation would be manipulated into a limited and controllable global crisis with the outcome ensuring only the Chinese could reinstate calm and security to the global community.

*Reset:*

The Chinese initiative named "Reset" was the most complex and secretive program China had ever undertaken. Although the concept had been in the development phase for over three decades, the decision to implement the operation was dependent upon two factors that had to take place in sequential order. First, and most importantly, the Chinese had to have economic engines and technological capabilities in place. For decades many had made the comment the massive Chinese infusion of low-cost technological items was nothing more than a tool to build a powerful economic and military empire. As often as that theory was given, little action was ever truly contemplated. The US's reemphasize on military presence in the Pacific was an example of realizing what might be taking place, but even then the process was tempered by the overwhelming pressure to keep economic balance with Chinese. When the Chinese announced the new Silk Road project, the largest business investment program in the history of the world, people again begin to question China's true intentions. Simply put, the first phase of the "Reset" plan was based upon building a dominant economic engine the world depended upon.

The second phase of "Reset" was depended upon a practice that was carried out by not just the Chinese but prominently the United States and Russia. International arms sales on a massive scale ensured the Chinese that nations would acquire weapons beyond their capability to properly employ. No better region of the world existed to finance this phase of the plan than the Middle East. Not only did some of the nations in the Middle East have the financing to acquire such weapons, but they had a history of deep-seated conflict that would be needed to spark the initial confrontation. The Chinese had studied the long history of hatred between Sunni and Shia Muslims in the Middle East. They understood the artificial borders created after the end of World War I insured this religious rift would never heal. The difficult part was ensuring the required conflict would be severe enough to push the world into crisis, yet be controllable to the point the overall Chinese goal was not destroyed. All of this had to happen in a window in which China could not predict the exact timing of the initial conflict, yet every other aspect of the plan had to be ready. The decision to leverage the next major event in the Middle East had been made. China only had to wait for that next event to take place. Again, what China did not properly anticipate was what that next event would entail and the severity of the effects of that event. The goal of China's leadership was to place their nation where they believe that rightfully belong, as the leader of the New World. China would be the dominant power in the world, and the world order would be achieved. Those who always believed the Chinese were on the road to dominance were proven to be correct.

*Kill Switch:*

Reset was the strategic vision of China. Kill Switch was a central part of that operational phase. Kill Switch was based upon crippling the most complicated communication network in the history of the human race, the Internet. China's commitment to the topic of cyber warfare was known throughout the world. But, as much as the world had anticipated the threat of this version of warfare, most had completely underestimated China's resolve to the process. The modern world was utterly dependent upon the World Wide Web, and no one understood this more than the Chinese. By the time the conflict in the Middle East began, everyday life in the world simply could not function without access to the World Wide Web. Having a structured and sequential plan for destroying parts of the Internet and controlling the rest, that was key to China's vision of a reset of world order. The degree of preparation required for implementing Kill Switch was cleverly hidden in plain view, disguised as everyday business technology. Again, the fear many had of China's intent, never gathered enough attention to overcome the allure of doing business with the Chinese industry. The world suspected what the Chinese were doing, but it simply could not resist the economic opportunities the Chinese presented. In the end, the world financed the very process that brought humanity to the brink of destruction.

*China's Final Decision:*

The decision to implement Reset was made at the beginning of the conflict between Saudi Arabia and Iran. The decision to continue with their plan, after the events in South and

North Korea, ensured that there was no turning back for not only the Chinese but for the rest of the world.

*First Indications of "Kill Switch":*

The Chinese cyber events that targeted Iran were not only the first of their kind witnessed by the rest of the world, but they were also unknowingly and progressively destructive. Networks connected to Iranian systems were not effectively mapped by the Chinese before the attacks. Second and Third Order Effects were witnessed globally within hours. The global damage estimates were not only unplanned for, but they were also far more saver than the Chinese had anticipated. China's intent had been not only to warn the Iranians of taking actions that might have adverse impacts on China, it was also a message to the rest of the world what the Chinese were capable of. For the past two decades, multiple cyber events had taken place throughout the world, yet no nation had ever taken open responsibility for those events. Even in this instance, the attack on Iranian networks was not publicly claimed by the Chinese. China did leave certain fingerprints that made it clear they were responsible for what had taken place in Iran; fingerprints the US and others readily identified.

It was the Russians who informed the Iranians were the attack came from. It was also the Russians who informed the Iranians the event had taken place because of the potential impact on Chinese interest. Although the Chinese had anticipated a controllable event in the Middle East, they wanted to ensure that the parties involved understood there would be limitations. What Iran had suffered was only a small portion of China's Kill Switch capabilities, and the rest of the world feared just that point. The US struggled with the issue of why China responded to Iran's actions, but the answers were not convincing to anyone involved in the crisis itself. The reality was, the Chinese had anticipated the crisis, but it was clear they were concerned about unforeseen consequences. The conflict had to be manageable for their plan to work.

To some in the Chinese government, Kill Switch had already proven it was a cyber version of Pandora's Box. As a result of the unanticipated actions of Kill Switch, the confidence to move forward with the plan was in question. The decision to do so resided with only a numbered few inside the Chinese government. The repercussions of kill switches' impact on Iran and the rest of the world did not rise to the occasion of the Chinese doubting the outcome of their plan. Phase one of the kill switch had taken place. The Chinese would move forward, and the unknowns would be ignored.

*The US Listens:*

The conversation between the Russian and the Chinese was monitored in real-time by US Intelligence assets. It was a capability neither the Russians or the Chinese had any idea existed. Like the events the US had already implemented against North Korea, the capabilities of the US monitoring programs gave the US a strategic edge over any adversary. What the US heard put an already stressed government into a deeper state of panic. The Chinese informed the Russians they were about to initiate a total disruption of the World Wide Web. How they would initiate this act was not disgusted with the Russians, and in fact, the conversation appeared to be directive in nature. A few of the US intelligence Agency members picked up on the one-sidedness of the conversation, but that aspect of the event did not resonate with US leadership. It should have as it would be an indicator of how the Russians would react to the notification. Regardless of what should have taken place, what the US leadership understood was the very fiber of day to day life in the civilized world was about to come under an unknown level of attack. An attack most of them realized was going to be unlike anything the world had witnessed.

The analysis took over three hours to develop a Presidential level briefing. Initial notification of the conversation had been made to the President, but a full analysis of how the event might take unfold took several hours. Procedures to protect the most important aspects of systems that supported critical processes in the US were placed into emergency status. Many measures had already been executed, but what was categorized as extreme would now be ordered by the President. Many network systems were already in a disconnected status, but again, other systems such as those in the financial arena had been placed in this mode before the new, pending threat. Networks that controlled power, water, medical distribution, and fuel were ordered: "offline." Planning for such a catastrophic event had long been a concept the US government had attempted to prepare for. The prioritization of key aspects of the US economy and government had been identified, and the order to implement given procedures was carried out as soon as the detailed briefing was completed. The US would do everything in its power to prepare for what they now knew was coming. There was limited discussion on retaliatory options at that moment in time. The primary task was to mitigate the pending attack as much as possible. How this attack would take place was a topic that came back to the forefront of discussion as soon as the orders had gone out. When the issue of nuclear EMPs arose, the debate took on a whole new level of emotion. US experts insisted the Chinese would have to resort to EMP events and even nuclear strikes against known satellite clusters to achieve what they had stated. The Chinese were going to go nuclear, but in a way that would limit physical destruction. That fact did nothing to quell the recommendations of the US President's Advisors.

*China's Resolve:*

As much as it was true, the US had capabilities the Chinese and Russians were unaware of; it was also true, the US and Russia were unaware of the capabilities of the Chinese. The deciding factor that made a difference was the issue of resolve.

The Chinese not only had capabilities unlike any other nation, they now had the resolve to utilize their capabilities. Yet, their decision to implement Kill Switch had one flaw in planning. China did a poor job of masking its own defensive preparation. Protective measures were embedded in many of their critical operating systems and the awareness that this process had been developed helped the US understand some degree of Chinese capabilities. Network monitoring was a strong point of the US, and the implementation of certain events in Chinese networks allowed the US to anticipate some of what was going to happen. The US had observed China getting into a very protective mode, but this was not seen as terribly unusual given the events of the previous week as well as their actions against Iran. In the end, although China's potential flaw in Kill Switch's planning was observed, the indicators the US did saw did nothing to prevent the damage from Kill Switch.

*Missed Indicators and Miscalculations:*

As stated earlier, the one-sidedness of the Chinese, Russian discussion should have given the US an indication that was overlooked. There was no unity of effort on the part of the Russians. The reason the Chinese contacted the Russians and framed the conversation the way they did was not understood until several years later. The Russians were convinced they had received the notification as an attempt to keep the Russians from retaliating. What the Chinese had planned on was the perception in the US that a level of coordinated support was going to take place between the Russians and the Chinese. The US was to believe the pending conflict would be a Chinese / Russian event. China's follow-on discussion on the minimization of damage to Russian networks gave this perception all the validation it would need to set the US in motion. Once it was determined that a network-wide attack was imminent and all possible protective measures were put in operation, the issue of retaliation finally came into the conversation.

Again, the miscalculation by the Chinese would take the conflict in a direction the Chinese could not have anticipated. The US would not seek to limit the destruction given it was facing the Chinese and the Russians. The resolve of the US was finally coming into play, and that was something the Chinese simply had not planned on. The perception they had planned on was false. The consequences of that mistake would seal the fate of all involved.

*Background on US's Decision:*

In 2011, the US announced it reserved the right to use military force in response to a full spectrum cyber-attack. This doctrine was not clearly understood by the US population, and many believed it would be impossible to gain world acceptance for military action based upon an event that often proved extremely difficult to show the point of origin. In normal times, this argument may have carried some weight in the discussion over options for retaliation. These were not normal times, and the US was already in a very unstable status, a status that had not been seen since the beginning of its first civil war.

Eight hours had passed from the time the President had been notified of the conversation. Protective measures were being put into place, and the decision to form a retaliatory statement was finalized. The Chinese, as well as the Russians, were capable of observing the US protective measures once they were underway and the US knew it. The US also understood the topic of US retaliation was most likely being reviewed with both the Russians and the Chinese. The decision was made to deliver a grave warning to both nations. A warning that would leave no doubt of the consequences a deliberate attack on the US would bring.

*Another Chinese Misconception:*

The Chinese had no awareness the US had been able to listen in on the conversation with the Russians, and when the US defensive measures began to show up on US networks, the Chinese came to the only conclusion they thought possible. The Russians had warned the US what was going to take place. With that assumption made, China's primary concern now became how the US and Russians might retaliate? If they had communicated on the Chinese pending actions, would they work in unison against China? Did the US and or the Russians understand how the Chinese attack would come? Had Kill Switch been discovered? As this heated debate was taking place inside the leadership of China, the warning from the US was delivered.

The US Ambassador gave a written statement to the Chinese government, and it did not require a response. It was obvious the US was completely aware of the Chinese Cyber First Strike plan, and a clear and ominous warning had been given. To the Chinese, the message was black and white; the US was going to respond to any total network attack with the full force of its complete arsenal. The real message was one the Chinese understood. Kill Switch would lead to a US nuclear retaliation. Kill Switch, a plan that had several senior leaders of the Chinese government angrily opposing it, was now going to be responsible for untold damage to the Chinese people. The whole concept of controlling a global conflict seemed to have become a disaster, and there was no de-escalation option without total capitulation to the US and its Allies. The Chinese leadership came to one final conclusion. The final decision was made, and Kill Switch would go ahead as planned. Reset would be accomplished, and there was no turning back.

*Russia's response to the Chinese offer:*

Moscow's crisis mode was pushing the human tolerance of its leadership to the limit. The notification from the Chinese of the pending attack on the global network system was not well received. As one-sided as the conversation with the Chinese may have seemed, in reality, the Russians accepted none of what was announced to them. Even when a follow on conversation was held on the topic of impact mitigation, the mindset of the Russians was already set. They would not go along with the Chinse plan. They would not watch the future of Russia to be determined by the Chinese. Russia would not allow China to become the only functional world Super Power after their plan had taken place. Defensive network planning had been a topic in Russia for years, and the concept was well thought out. Within an hour of Chinese communication, the Russian were well underway with placing protective measures into place. They were well aware of the fact the US and others would see these measures taking place, but that was an acceptable issue given the consequences. What the Russians had not anticipated correctly was the perception of the US. Since the Russians had no idea the US was capable of monitoring Chinese, Russian conversations held at the highest level, it was not anticipated the US would perceive the Russians as working with the Chines. Explaining their defensive measures was not a topic they were ready or even capable of executing. To the US, the Russians were doing exactly what the Chinese allowed them the opportunity to do, protect themselves. To the Russians, they were doing what had to be done, protecting themselves. The long-feared, "Perfect Storm" was becoming a reality. The three global Super Powers were about to confront each other, and logic was nowhere to be found.

*China Moves Forward:*

Approximately nine hours after the Chinese, Russian communication, the Chinese leadership made the final decision to go forward with their plan. The dire warning from the US had only made a commitment to the severity of the event more resolute. A full Spectrum attack would be executed, and that called for an event that was the most dangerous of all. A series of nuclear warheads would be detonated in the Earth's Atmosphere that would result in the complete disruption of most commercial communication networks. The concept had been developed over the years by the Chinese, and the level of detail and preparation for such a capability had not gone unnoticed. Countless research papers had been written by multiple organizations and nations, and the outcome was almost always the same. The complete breakdown of global communications and economic trade actions.

Although a great deal of attention had been put into the analysis of what such an attack might mean to the world, very little effort had been placed into tracking Chinese preparation for such an event. The Chinese stockpile of ready to launch, replacement satellites was overlooked by Western Intelligence, to include the increased production. Their concept was simplistic but believable. The Chinese had prepared themselves to recover from a global event faster than any other nation. China would be the partner no nation could survive without. There had been rumors of this concept to the point that even the concept name had been spoken of, "Reset." Although these rumors were based more along the lines of Kill Switch, the idea the Chinese were contemplating a global event kept those rumors alive. Outside the realm of rumors, in the intelligence networks, the Japanese and the Russians had observed what some of their experts believed was a plan to win a race of dominance after some global event. Both nations had some level of concern over what seemed to be a drive for the Chinese to survive and then recover from an event faster than the rest of the world, but what might perpetrate such an event was the real unknown. In the end, both the Russians and the Japanese were worried, but not to the level of allocating resources beyond what normal intelligence operations.

As stated before, several of the Chinese experts knew full well; this concept was imbedded with assumptive flaws. In the time of Mau, China knew it had less to in a nuclear war, but that was long before modern China emerged. Times had changed drastically, and the risk of unrecoverable losses was a fear for several who were the architects of the overall plan. One other flawed perception sealed the fate of the modern world. China's leadership, in its final phase of decision making, believed the US and Russia would not commit to a total nuclear exchange. The Chinese had finally convinced themselves as catastrophic as a global network attack might be, the impacted nations would choose survival over a nuclear holocaust. History would record the Chinese were wrong, but not for the reason they anticipated.

# CHAPTER FIVE: RUSSIA'S "DEAD HAND":

For decades, the rumors and intelligence assumptions on the idea of a Doomsday process held by the Soviets and then the Russians had been well known to anyone who bothered to read about the subject. The premise was simple in concept. A series of sensors would be connected to a network of nuclear missiles, and if the right indicators were given, the weapons would launch to predesignated targets without human authorization. A concept that was seen as totally unacceptable in the West was seen as a necessity by the Russians. The idea was developed based on the Soviet's fear of a preemptive strike that would prevent Leadership from authorizing a counter-attack. Russia was a nation that for over a thousand years had witnessed countless invasions and betrayals, and paranoia was an accepted mindset in Russian leadership. It was nearly a requirement. After the events of World War II and the development of nuclear weapons, the idea of the "Dead Hand" couldn't have sounded that illogical to the Soviet Leadership. Yet, the Russians knew the only way the program would ever have capability was to execute total deniability. When rumors arose of such a concept being undertaken by the Russians, the only response was how outrageous the West was for insinuating the Russian contemplate something that reckless. Dead Hand, was denied year after year for decades.

As often as the Western Intelligence Agencies would bring the topic up, it would always lead to the same question from Western Leaders. "Even if it was true, what options do we have to prevent it"? From the West's perspective, the concept was not just a defense against First Strike actions; it was a revenge program. It was the Soviets and then the Russian's way of saying, "We will punish our enemies regardless of our fate"! Exposing such a weapon system was also deemed far too controversial for the public to contemplate and in the end, the West simply let rumors remain nothing more than rumors. It was a topic better left unaddressed.

Dead Hand, like any other War Plan, had been updated over the years. What was once a series of seismic sensors was now a very complex network of indicators? The ability to detect an attack on Russia was expanded, and in that expansion, the ability to communicate nationwide was now a key point of evidence a massive attack might be taking place. Like the original system, the core value of the process was the ability to execute a series of nuclear strikes if Russian national command authority was unable to interact with the program. That was just the event the Chinese attack would create. Upon hearing from the Chinese of their intent to attack the global network and thus, paralyze the world's ability to function, the Russians seemed to have overlooked what the Chinese might trigger. They simply didn't take into account the Dead Hand system. The Russian President and his Defense Minister may have been so shocked by the Chinese proposition; they didn't contemplate the impact of the Dead Hand program.

The US was overwhelmed with the task of preparing for what they now knew was going to take place. Their warning to the Chinese drew no response. Communications with the Russians appear to have taken place just before US actions, but it seems to have been more along the lines of statements given by each other and not a conversation based on interaction. The Russians were informed of the intent to strike the Chinese in such a way that a clear message would be sent as to the US's resolve, but limit the physical damage if at all possible. Actions to be taken against the Russians would be based upon any perceived involvement on their part. Those actions involved kinetic as well as cyber operations. The message was simple for the Russians to understand. The US would strike China first. The actions against the Russians were up to the actions of the Russians. Again, no reply was requested. The US would base it's response to Russia on hard evidence, not words.

Had the US given any consideration to the possibility of an actual Doomsday concept, the outcome of their actions may have been very different. In point of fact, it now seems the Russians did give an obvious hint to the concept of a Doomsday plan. In 2017, the US-based cable channel, Home Box Office, aired a four-part documentary interview with President Putin. At one point in the documentary Oliver Stone, the person conducting the interview convinced Putin to watch the movie, "Doctor Strange Love." This movie was a satirical play on an accidental nuclear attack by the US on the Soviet Union. Towards the end, the Soviet Ambassador admits the Soviet Union owned a Doomsday device. As the movie ends, the Doomsday device begins to detonate devices all over the world. When President Putin finished watching the movie, he made a statement about the underestimated dangers of a Doomsday network. That simple comment did generate informal discussions in the US, but again, the concept was simply allowed to be ignored by senior US leadership.

### THE EXECUTION OF "KILL SWITCH":

It took the Chinese hours to prepare their own networks for the event. Protecting critical aspects of the Chinese infrastructure and economic system was their priority. On just one occasion where part of the Kill Switch concept was tested, even the Chinese were stunned by order of disruption. The world had witnessed a reroute of South Korean banking networks for several minutes, and the impact of that event was far greater than the Chinese had anticipated. The economic tools of Kill Switch made up only part of what the asymmetric plan was capable of. The Chinese doctrine of Total Warfare was the foundation of Kill Switch, and as such, almost every aspect of critical infrastructure was targeted along with all major economic systems. Kill Switch was the Chines greatest weapon they had ever created. Its secrecy was the highlight of the entire concept. Many had long warned of a catastrophic attack on the World Wide Web, but few ever truly believed it would happen. They were wrong.

*The US Warnings:*

The US had warned key Allies of the pending Chinese attack on the global network. Isolation of key systems was a critical tool in defending networks, and many countries had already implemented measures given events that had taken place so far in the war. Most nation's protective measures required dramatic restrictions on financial processes. The world markets had already taken nearly a fifty percent plunge since the beginning of the event off the coast of Yemen. In fact, in many nations, financial transactions had already halted. ATMs no longer functioned and Banks themselves had been severely restricted. In the US, on the day of the government's announcement, half of the daily workforce did not show up to work. Satellite communications were restricted, and several key networks had their terrestrial stations moved for defensive reasons. The fact of the matter was, the world was already crippled in its day to day activities, so much so, some in the US government questioned what impact the Chinese event would even have on the nation. As chaotic as the world had become the Chinese set into motion events that would drive the world into near anarchy. The US had warned everyone what was coming. It was not enough.

*The Attack:*

US CYBERCOM detected the first phase of Kill Switch. The target was SCADA, Supervisory Control and Acquisition, that controlled key elements of the US and other nation's power grids. The fear had always been no matter how hardened the US government attempted to make SCADA for the power grid in the US; it would be the small, local and private programs that would allow entry into the primary network. That was just what took place, and the attack was far more advanced than anything the US had witnessed in the past. Because of the events over the past few weeks, many local networks were being manned by members of the US Federal Emergency Management Agency, FEMA, but their knowledge of the intricacies of those local networks was weak at best. Again, the issue of people no longer showing up for work was impacting the nation in ways leadership in DC didn't understand. It was impossible to backfill the key individuals at the state and local level, and that crisis was nationwide.

Within the first hour of the SCADA aspect of Kill Switch, nearly have of the nation's power grid that was still functioning was offline. Many of the control centers were physically damaged by bad command code execution. Cell Towers lost power, and unreliable networks became completely unusable. Those that had remote generators had been without fuel for days, and there was no one to refuel them. Communications in the US were degraded to the point that shortwave radios became the only truly reliable form of gaining information for local government. The first wave of Kill Switch was over in less than an hour. Power was key to the civilized world, and power was the target.

*US Government Assessment of Initial Impact:*

The US National Command Authority was dispersed, and the government had transformed into full crisis mode. The SCADA event was still being assessed when the notification of the second phase of the Kill Switch attack was given. Financial networks that were thought to be well protected, networks that were placed on standalone systems, simply zeroed out. It was not that the protected, controlled networks stopped functioning, they showed to be operational, but they simply showed zero-sum transactions. The records of transactions were gone. Accounts showed to be empty. It was an event that even the nation's best software minds could not understand. Within minutes, the US was informed by England and the EU the same thing had happened. Backup, hard copies were quickly loaded, and to the amazement of everyone involved, they too showed nothing. The best explanation the experts could come up with was the implanted hacks were accomplished and some electrical support level. As the experts explained what they believed may have theoretically happened, no one in government understood what they were saying. To them, it was nearly magic. A level of attack unimaginable even to those who claimed to understand the threat. In a matter of seconds, the financial transactions of even the most guarded networks were gone. The Civilized world had no reliable way to validate any of the financial transactions. Paper copies were part of the protection process, but they were not standardized, and many institutions had not been diligent in keeping such backups current. One agency did notice an anomaly. An obscure financial network showed to have gone offline just seconds before the second attack. Although the cyber community observed the network, no one had any understanding of what its purpose was. One fact was established. That network was owned by the Chinese. The global financial networks were gone. Every effort to protect them was based upon known threats. What took place was a complete unknown. The US financial system was the foundation of world trade, and it was gone.

*Russia Contacts the US:*

The panicked calls from other nations were too numerous for the US to respond to, but one line was always answered. The phone call from Moscow came within the first hour of the financial attack. Russian defensive measures based upon standalone networks had fallen victim just as they had all over the world. The Russian had also noticed the one network that belonged to the Chinese. As bad as the financial attack had been, the SCADA event had had less impact on the Russians. It was well known many parts of the vast territory of Russia were completely independent of any national network. What the Russian relayed to DC was a story much like the US's, major cities without power. Most of the Russian communication networks had been disrupted, but not all of them. The reality was, the Russians were letting the US know they were still functional but had suffered the same attacks as the US, and they held China responsible. The Russians then asked the question that was the real reason for the contact with the US. What was the US willing to do about it? It seems at that moment in time; the US decided to admit to the Russian they had monitored the communication between them and the Chinese. The US made it very clear the perception in DC was that Russia and China had executed these attacks in a joint effort. It was up to Russia to prove the US wrong, and failure to do so would propel the crisis to the next level. As the Russians were attempting to convince the US they were not involved in Kill Switch, the news of multiple Chinese Missile launches interrupted the discussion. The US informed the Russians that the Chinese launches were underway. The Russian stated they too were observing what appeared to be multiple Chinese launches. The Russian President's words were recorded. *"We are all about to pay a terrible price for the actions of a few fools in the Middle East"*! In the background, US intelligence members could hear the Russians arguing over how to interrupt the process. The Russian word that froze everyone on the US side was "Doomsday." The theory of Dead Hand was known to everyone in the room. The process of intercepting the Dead Hand network was the Russian top priority. The VTC link ended abruptly, and the US President's Crisis Team sat in stunned silence.

*US Defensive Measures:*

Trajectories were quickly plotted, and it was clear the number of launches did not indicate a full-scale strike. It was agreed that the cyber events where ether intended to disrupt the US's ability to retaliate or they were an indication the primary goal of the Chinse was not a ground targeted, nuclear war. US options were quickly addressed, but one response was automatically underway. The US's capability for ballistic intercept was almost as unimaginable as the Chinese Cyber Warfare program. Test that had been reported and even staged as "failures" had actually been designed to mask a far superior program. The US' ability to intercept a ballistic missile in Boost Phase with high energy weaponry was unknown to the rest of the world. The black hole projects that lead to this capability were so well hidden that only the President and a few trusted government officials were aware of the US's full capabilities. Not only could the US strike it's enemies warheads in Boost Phase, the US could intercept individual warheads on reentry. Even "Near Target Intercept, NTI, was possible. So disruptive to the nuclear balance of power would this information had been, it was decided, after several successful tests, the program would be declared a financial drain and thus drastically reduced. The US was cable of was dealing with a limited number of launches from any trajectory advantage, including Cruise Missiles, and the number of Chinese launched warheads was within the capabilities on hand. The readiness status of these networks was at its highest level ever since the first detonation in Gaza. US assets were in position to cover most of the anticipated launch locations based upon a perceived threat from North Korea, but they were easily relocated given the platforms were both airborne and mounted on recognized naval vessels. Deception was a key part of the US program, and it had worked beyond the US's wildest dreams.

The process of deciding on options was underway when it was announced that twelve of the eighteen Chinese missiles had been intercepted in Boot Phase. The reaming six were going to impact areas that had high concentrations of commercial satellite operations. It was clear then, the attack was not a ground target event, but an extension of Kill Switch. This confirmation quickly impacted the discussion of options for the US, and the decision was also made to not inform the US population of the pending strike. As the options discussion was taking place, the President was informed the first of the Chinese warheads were detonating. Other anticipated targets were much further out and the time to target was based upon how large of a device the Chinese intended on using. As the topic of options was continuing, the news of the first EMP detonation was announced.

*Hawaii and Japan's EMP events:*

How the warhead that detonated over Hawaii had gone unchallenged was a historical event. The fact was, the EMP attack took place with no warning in DC. Hawaii had been the target, and the effectiveness of the weapon was tremendous. When the President asked what this meant, the answer was numbing to everyone in the room. Hawaii would not be able to support the people who lived there. The EMP event measured beyond anything the US could have anticipated. US military operations in Hawaii were nonexistent. The Secretary of Defense informed the US President The US military in Hawaii was Combat Ineffective. As that description was being given to the US President, the status of Japan was announced. A separate EMP attack took place over Japan. The nation of Japan would be completely crippled. US military operations in Japan were now, Combat Ineffective as well. In less than ten minutes, the US was faced with the undeniable truth that they were now at war with China.

*Russia's Dead Hand Crisis:*

As soon as the Russian ended the Secured VTC with the US, every effort was placed on preventing the Dead Hand Program. Interruption or override of the network was not a simplistic task, and that was by design. What had made the issue even more difficult had been the cyber events that had taken place since the beginning of the conflict in Yemen. In the first few days of cyber warfare by the Chinese towards the Iranians, the Russians had feared the repercussion on their own networks. They had been particularly concerned about military and governmental operations given they had some network linkage with Iranian programs. Overreaction in the first few days of the conflict had led the Russians to harden as many of their networks as they could. How this impacted the Dead Hand program is not clear, but it is possible the ability to neutralize the program may have been addressed. The Russian may have grown so concerned about Chinese Cyber capabilities that Dead Hand had become unstoppable? What we do know is the Russians were panicked over the process of stopping the program.

When news of the US's interception of the majority of the Chinese missiles reached Russian leadership, they actually felt as if they could catch their breath. In the panic to prevent the activation of the Dead Hand network, the fact the US was capable of achieving the remarkable interception of the warheads seems to have been overlooked. The idea that a few of the weapons had made it past the US's capabilities was acceptable given the weapons were anticipated to be targeted against US locations and thus not able to activate the Russian Doomsday program. The Russians also believed other events inside of Russia, such as the SCADA and financial attacks didn't rise to the level of Dead Hand activation. What breathing room the Russians thought they had vanished when word came of the targeting of orbital communication networks. Russian satellites were placed in what was known as dense, orbital space. Key government networks were in less populated locations, but the vast majority of Russian civilian communications, both Russian owned and contracted were in this dense space. If that space were the target of the Chinese nuclear weapons, then the impact on the Russian government and industry would be dramatic. What networks were monitored by the Dead Hand program was not known to anyone outside of the Russian government, but the confirmation the Chinese were going to target clusters in that area was enough to keep the panic alive in Moscow.

The first detonation impacted several leased networks utilized by Russia. Some of these were already unreliable, given the events that had already taken place, and the actual impact on the Russian government was projected to be minim. The trajectory of several other warheads gave the Russian a clear understanding of what was going to take place. Two primary, government networks would be in the impact zone of these deeper strikes. If both of these networks were lost, Russian Naval operations would be degraded. Deep-sea communications with Russian Submarines would not be impacted, but the Russian Navy's logistical support operations would be. Again, the issue became, what networks would signal the Dead Hand program? It was remarkable how little the Russian Naval Command knew of this program. Some of their most senior leaders had no knowledge of the concept and were stunned when they were informed of the immediate crisis.

The EMP event over Hawaii caught the Russians by complete surprise. They had not tracked any warhead that would have lead them to believe an EMP was targeted towards the state of Hawaii. How this warhead had been missed was the topic of the Russian Command when the world of the second EMP event over Japan was announced. The Russian had one immediate question. "Where there more EMP events about to take place" How could they know if they had not detected the first two? How was it the Chinese were able to strike two targets without the warheads being identified in Boost Phase or Reentry Phase"? Their second question was not as important but addressed the issue of trust. "Did the US see these two attacks coming? Where they able to identify the warheads when the Russians could not"? During this phase of the crisis, someone in the Russian War room asked yet another question. "How did the US intercept the Chinese missiles at such a high success rate"? Again, this question and the pending answer was lost in turmoil at hand. Could the US intercept such a large percentage of Russian missiles that even a First Strike threat was now eliminated? In normal times, these questions would have created its own diplomatic crisis, but at that moment in time, the questions simply went unanswered.

The Dead Hand program was equipped with a notification process that was limited to the Russian President and The Russian Minister of Defense. The program did have a "Watch Desk," but the staff was only allowed to know it was responsible for alerting the Russian Defense Minister if an alarm took place. The Watch Desk was simply a backup for notification purposes only. The event itself was nothing more than an alert message stating the Russian President and the Russian Minister of Defense had a prescribed about of time to make a two-person notification disrupting the process. The Russian President devices were worn on his belt and were designed to look identical to the classified phones utilized by top Russian Officials. A Russian military officer was assigned to the President and the Minister of Defense for the sole purpose of ensuring that the device was on their body at all times. To the military aids, Dead Hand was only a Soviet Urban legend past on between Military Officers.

*Dead Hand False Alarm:*

Russia, like many other nations in the world, had initiated their Continuity of Government plan. The Russian President had the authority to keep the Russian Minister of Defense with him or have him relocate to a distant, redundant Command Facility. Directly after the Russian, Chinese communication took place, the Russian President ordered his Minister of Defense to relocate to a facility nearly 1300 miles away from Moscow. As the Russian leadership was debating the impact of the Chinese attack and what response options they should consider, the small cell phone looking device began to vibrate. The team that had been assigned to ensure the Dead Hand Option was not activated by the current Chinese attack was in constant contact with the Russian President's Crisis Team. As soon as the device went off, the Russian Minister of Defense contacted the President. The deactivation team could not explain why the device had gone off with the President and not the Minister of Defense. What they did know was the President and the Minister had three minutes to send a simultaneous, sequential code to override the process. By the time the VTC connected the two Russian leaders, one of the three minutes had already passed. As the President began to enter the required code, the Defense Minister was doing the same. Only a handful of people at each location understood what was taking place. The required codes were properly entered, and the Dead Hand Program indicated it was back in observation mode. The Russian Doomsday program had been activated, and no one in the Russian High Command knew why. The Russian President was said to have come to the conclusion that the entire program should be scrapped as soon as possible.

*US RESPONSE TO KILL SWITCH:*

The Chines Kill Switch attack had achieved the objective of completely disrupting communications, financial networks, and power distribution in the US. EMP events had completely disrupted the US military installations in Hawaii and Japan by design. The rest of the world's communications and financial networks had been drastically disrupted. Kill Switch had executed with the devastation the Chinese had planned for. The US was socially and economically unresponsive. Localized government and privately-owned power made up the majority of what was still functioning in the country. National programs like FEMA and the Department of Homeland Security were unresponsive to the needs of the nation. Communities were on their own. The cities of the US were without power, water, and sewer. The run on consumables had been taking place since the beginning of the conflict, and by the time the events of Kill Switch took place, the stores were empty of any basic necessities. In reality, the US was no longer functioning as a unified nation with one exception. Its military capabilities. Kill Switch attacked known networks of the US, but it did not address what the Chinese did not know.

The US President and his key staff had witnessed the impact of the Chinese attack. The decision had been made not to respond until the level of severity was determined. The concept of proportionality was still the preferred option at that time, but many of the President's advisors were pushing hard to strike back with every option available. The US may have been on its knees, yet options were still available. The President had decided to wait to see what a non-ground based nuclear attack would mean to the nation. He fully understood the consequences of escalating the event to a full-scale nuclear exchange. He also knew the impact of Kill Switch would not disrupt the capabilities of the US's nuclear options. On that point, the Chinese had been completely wrong. The loss of power and communications severely impacted the Force Generation capabilities of the US and in fact, those capabilities had already been greatly degraded, but the nuclear option was not impacted. In the end, the Chinese had gambled the US would not respond with a nuclear war. That was the reality the President of the US was facing. The cyber events of North Korea should have been the indicator of unknown US capabilities. The Chinese had witnessed the impacts of the US on North Korea and Chinese military leaders even warned of some new set of capabilities they were not aware of. In the crisis that was taking place, this concern was lost. China had chosen to move forward with its Reset plan, and the events inside of North Korea seem to have been overlooked.

*The Russian Explanation:*

Several hours after the satellite and EMP events, the US attempted to make contact with the Russians. The secured VTC network was operational given the satellite network's location and defense. The discussion only had one topic. Where the Russians working with the Chinese or not? The last conversation between the two had begun to persuade some of the US President's team the Russians had not sided with the Chinese, but they wanted to hear the explanation directly from the Russian leader. Their answer would determine the future for not only Russia but the rest of the world. The US President asked his Russian counterpart directly. The Russian President's answer was one the US was not prepared to contemplate. "Why"? Why did the Chinese execute this attack? Why did they risk the destruction of the civilized world for the simple sake of North Korea"? To the Russians, the US had to have had an explanation. The US quickly contemplated an important issue. Did the Russians not truly understand what had taken place between the US and China and the issue of North Korea? Did they not realize the US blames China for the North Koreans development of nuclear weapons; weapons that were used by Iran, weapons that were used against the US city of El Paso? Russia had been deeply involved in the issue of North Korea for decades. The chess match between the Super Powers had always seen North Korea as a pawn. A rabid dog on a short leash of the Chinese, that was how the West saw the relationship between China and North Korea. To the Chinese, North Korea was a weapon. A weapon the Chinese, and to some extent the Russians, had held over the West's head for years. Russia had been a member of this same chess match, but the real master was China, and everyone knew it. So, why would the Russians respond with, "why"? They understood what had taken place. Both nations had worked the rumors of a Chinese "plan," and both nations understood that China would someday leverage some other event to shape their own vision. What was vital was the understanding of where the Russians stood with that vision. But this theory had never been shared between the two nations. Not until that point in time.

The US listened to the Russian President's explanation of their question in all of its detail. It was then the Russian President revealed a concept the US had speculated about. China had long been preparing itself to win the "Reset" race! In the past three years, the Russians and to some extent the West had been witnessing a stockpiling of key items. Items such as communication satellites, production hardware, and automated manufacturing. At one point, the question of why it was even posed to the Chinese. The answer was one that was not met with complete acceptance, but it had just enough truth behind its explanation to keep world leaders from challenging the word of their number one trade partner.

The Chinse answer was the "Belt and Road Action Plan." The new Silk Road! A 900 Billion dollar investment program designed to incorporate the world's economic trading markets into one, centralized capability. Something the economic experts of the world sounded the alarm over, only to have political leaders see the dollar signs and not the danger signs. To the Russians, the New Silk Road project was nothing more than a cover story. A way to prepare the world for only having one trade option. The Chinese! The Russian President stated North Korea was only a tool in buying the Chinese time. Time to build a military-based upon technology beyond what the rest of the world was capable of. What leading technology the world did develop, the Chinse replicate. Stealing technology was the driving factor behind the early stages of China's cyber development. Buying time and staying ahead of your future enemy, that was the goal. To the Russians, allowing the North Koreans to arm the Iranians as part of the plan and the time had come for that plan to execute. The Chinese had begun a process that had only one goal, seeing China as the leader of the civilized world.

The US listened to the Russian President for over thirty minutes. The fate of the world was at hand, and the US President knew thirty minutes was worth Billions of lives. The US response to the Russian theory was encouraging to the Russians. What the Russian President had done was not based on deceiving the US and the US could since he was placing everything on the table, as he should. Now, the initial question was once again asked. "Are you with the Chinese on this? Is that what the conversation between the two of you was about? Did the Chinese offer you an out"? The Russian President gave the only answer he could.

Yes, the Chinese had offered the Russians an out. What the Chinese were looking for was to limit the destruction that might take place. They had gambled the US would not escalate into a full-scale nuclear war, but the Russians were a different story. Offering the Russians a way to limit the damage that would take place was the carrot the Chinese attempted to use. The Russian President gave this explanation, but he ended his statement with an emotional note. The fate of Russia would not be determined by the Chinese! The words came from the Russian President's mouth with conviction. His face told the story the US President needed to hear. If the Chinese had implemented this grand plan for the world, economic domination, then it would not succeed. The US President's response was a two-edged sword to the Russians. He informed the Russian President that he believed him. He went on to make a telling statement. He informed the Russians the Chinese had made a catastrophic error in judgment. The US's resolve and capabilities were unknown to the Chinese, and they would witness the destruction of their dreams. Records indicate, these were the precise words of the US President and nothing more was said to the Russians on what would happen. The conversation ended with the US President and the Russian President vowing to keep their staffs in constant communication until the situation in the world had stabilized. They both knew the road to recovery would be long, but together it was possible. The time of tension between the US and Russia was over. The future of the world was still unfolding.

*The US Strikes Back:*

The Chinese held the strategic edge in cyber warfare, and that was a fact the US didn't take lightly. The Chinese edge was twofold. One was the ability to steal data. The second was the ability to disrupt networks, and Kill Switch had proven that. What the Chinese had built their entire cyberwarfare concept on was the ability to defend themselves as they were disrupting everyone else. The key was called Quantum Networks. They had built their own day to day network that 90% of the Chinese government worked from. That included most of the major corporations run by the Chinse government.

Simply put, the Chinese believed the backbone of their ability to win a cyber-based war was the safety of their own network. It was complicated. It was based on groundbreaking math. It was not unique to the Chinese, and the US had once again made headways no one in the world was aware of. In the end, the Chinese's assumption of safety and survivability was a strategic error that would only be outweighed by their miscalculating of US resolve. The US had started the war with a level of caution, much like that of Israel. Like Israel, after the US suffered catastrophic damage from its enemies, the mindset of caution was gone. The US response to Kill Switch would leave China dysfunctional for decades to come. The repercussions of the US answer to Kill Switch would also lead to consequences no one had anticipated except for perhaps a handful of individuals in Moscow. Even they did not truly anticipate what was coming.

The US President was briefed on several options for response with each having a different level of impact on
China. Possible retaliation by the Chinese accompanied the
briefings. It was clear now the President was set on not following the Law of Proportionality. China's "Reset" plan, one they
had worked towards for decades was going to fail. Their dream
of dominance was now going to turn into a nightmare for the
whole world. The plan chosen and supported by all those who
were asked for input would be launched without delay and
without any warning to any other nation, to include the Allies of the US. Electromagnetic Pulse, "EMP," weaponry would
step from the world of futuristic weapons into the world of
reality. North Korea was just an example of what the US was
capable of. What China would suffer was unimaginable.

There was no ballistic launch for the Chinese to detect.
What took place was a slight course adjustment for a series
of satellites that had been placed into orbit over the past two
years by an experimental US military unmanned spacecraft,
capable of reentry. Speculation by the Chinese, Russians and
even the Allies of the US was based on these objects being a
new series of spy platforms. Their shape, their physical appearance, the way they were delivered to the launch site, all
indicated that was exactly what they were. They were not.
The deception plan executed flawlessly.

The first pulse was directed at Beijing. The intensity,
penetration, and duration were beyond anything the Chinese could have anticipated by a typical nuclear detonation.
Within seconds, a series of targets were hit across China.
None of them were Chinese Missile sites, and the hope was
that alone would send a clear message. What was struck
were communication nodes, major governmental facilities,
power production, air force bases, and naval facilities. In
only three minutes, nearly every electrical facility in over a
dozen Chinese cities were ruined. Chinese cell networks were
destroyed. Major transmission lines across the nation were

burned beyond repair. China was without power. China was without civilian communications. China was without a functional government.

As the EMP platforms were destroying the infrastructure of China, the US Navy was eliminating the Chinese nuclear-laden submarine capabilities. China had known of the US and Russia's anti-submarine programs as well as the development of small autonomous drones that could stalk and kill a sub upon command. What China did not know was the US had placed a much more advanced version of these drones into service within the last year. Chinese Ballistic submarines were known to operate in a predetermined location, and they had not deviated from that process for several years. Those areas were successfully infiltrated by commercial ships that clandestinely deployed the autonomous killer drones. The Chinese may have obtained the technical skills to build and equip Ballistic Subs, but the skill-craft of Submarine Warfare was the cornerstone of the US Navy. Within twenty minutes of the US retaliation on China, the Chinese Ballistic Submarine capabilities, that were at sea, were gone. Those that were still dockside were neutralized by the EMP attack on those facilities.

The attack on the Chinese submarine capabilities was inconsistent with the avoidance of the land-based nuclear sites. It was a decision the US made based upon the fear these ships had preset orders to attack if no communications with Beijing could be accomplished. The risk from the submarines was too high for the US to accept, but the message, "it could have been much worse. We have the opportunity to limit the destruction taking place", would be sent by not destroying the land-based warheads, at least in the first wave of attacks.

As the US response unfolded, the President and those assisting him received the reports in amazement. The EMP network had changed the course of warfare. The first nuclear weapon used in time of war had been delivered by the US in World War II. The US did not deliver the first EMP attack in warfare, but the concept of a non-nuclear weapon EMP capability went from theoretical to reality with the destruction of China's infrastructure. The long talked of, dominance of space as a weapon that now clearly belonged to the US. What this would mean to the rest of the world never had the opportunity to be debated. The first wave of the US's response to China was over. Now the decision had to be made. What to do next? Response from China was anticipated, and the US used the capability to contact the Chinese that amazed the Chinese even further.

A simple text message. The amazement of this feat was the fact it was sent over a network the Chinese had developed for one purpose; Nuclear Command and Control. A network that was closed and so closely guarded that even the electrical power utilized to run the program was a standalone system. The Chinese had been the world leaders in transmitting cyber-attacks through power transmission lines, or so they believed.

*China Responds:*

The Chinese dispersed government process was not unlike that of any other major country. The real issue was the delegation of authority. In the US, the law dictated who was responsible for the nation if the other key leaders were not able to make decisions. A recognized "Chain of Succession|" was a proven process for the US government. This concept of Continuity of Government had been practiced for decades, and the US was very good at making the process work. This was not the case in China. Yes, the Chinese had a version of continuity of government, but in practice, lower level, government officials were never truly expected to make a major decision. As the conflict in North Korea became critical, the decision to disperse the Chinese government had been made. Teams were sent to predesignated sites. Support processes were put into place. The problem was not the physical aspects of the plan. The problem was, the Chinese government never truly trained to run the county with anyone other than the Central Government. The crisis they now found themselves in was crippling not just in the physical damage inflicted by the US, but the issue of governance was immobilized. China found themselves in a position they never truly believed would happen. 1.4 billion people had no one to turn to.

The Chinese President and his key Staff were in a facility supported by the Chinese Army, and as such, information on the status of the military was received first hand. Reports of the EMP strikes came so quickly; they believed they had to be under a nuclear attack. Chinese early warning process was not on scale with the US, but their ability to detect inbound, ballistic events was complex enough that the question of how these EMP were taking place was immediately asked. How could major Chinese cities be losing electrical capabilities on such an asymmetric scale without the detection of a nuclear detonation? This conversation was taking place when the fate of their Ballistic Submarines was discovered. Communications with their ballistic submarine fleet was gone, all of them. Their fate was not known, but the Chinese had only two assumptions to work with. One, the subs had been attacked. Two, the communication network with them was lost. Like the rest of the world's Submarine fleets, the backup of longwave radio was the failsafe for China. When even that network showed no response, China's leadership came to the only conclusion they could. They had lost their limited, Ballistic Submarine fleet.

The issue of the Submarine fleet brought immediate attention to the land-based, ballistic program. Had it suffered the same fate? Communications were limited, but a redundant network, much like the ones they used for their Submarines, did establish contact with their Command Center. It became very clear to the Chinese that part of their nuclear program was still intact, but why? Several members of the Chinese President's staff realized the US intent. It was a message. It was possible to still limit the fighting to the current damage done to both nations. Now, the question became, how would China respond?

Assessment and estimates of just what had taken place in China was the topic of conversation when the US message was discovered on the Chinese Nuclear Command and Control network. The infiltration process was so precise; the message only showed up on the portion of the network that is directly linked to the Chinese President. His passcode was used to initiate the message, and the Chinese controller who supported the President was not sure what to say and who to say it to. Several Chinese Presidential Cabinet members were sitting next to the Controller, and it was they who brought the issue to the attention of the President. The US was inside the Chinese Nuclear Command and Control network, and they had done so with the Chines President's passcode. It was read several times by different members of the President's staff, and by that time, the President had asked his only question. "Do we control the network? Can we command our nuclear weapons"? The answer was given quickly, and with assurance, what assurance could be given at that moment in time. Launch Codes were hardcopy only, and no capability existed to execute an activated warhead without the proper codes. As soon as that answer was given, the next question became even more important. Was the networked required to transmit the codes to the Launch Control Facilities still secure? Yes was the answer given, but it was a far less assuring answer than the issue of the codes. The reality was, the network the US had compromised was needed to transmit the codes. Unlike the US system, Chinese launch capabilities did not reside with the Officers at the Launch Control Facilities. The ultimate authority to utilize nuclear weapons from China resided with the Chinese President. This same concept held true for their Ballistic Submarines. A government that was built around the concept of Centralized Authority was falling victim to their own philosophy. China's land-based warheads were intact, but they had no confidence in being able to control them.

Why had the US spared the land base program and yet, neutralized the Chinese ability to utilize it? What option was the US truly offering the Chinese? Survival! What the US was offering China was nothing more than survival. In less than thirty minutes, the US had won the long-anticipated war with China and had done so in a way, only a handful of people in the world knew could happen. China was defeated. After nearly fifty years of preparation for the next real war involving their nation, China was sitting on the edge of ruin. The Chinese President had only one option, and it was an option the US nor the rest of the world realized. What had frightened the Russians to the point of panic was the fact that somehow, their "Failsafe" program, Dead Hand, had been manipulated. How they had no idea. By whom, the guessed and guessed correctly. The Russian President had placed everything on the table in his conversation with the US President. Everything but Dead Hand. Everything but Dead Hand and the fear that somehow Dead Hand had been infiltrated. China's dreams may have been gone, but the future of the world would be determined by the Chinese.

# CHAPTER SIX:
# THE HOLOCAUST:

A joint conference call was held by the US. In that call were Russia, Great Britain, Germany, France, Japan, and India. Those where the major nations that at that time could hold such a call as they were part of a network the US had designed for just such emergencies. The status of the United Nations was unknown, and the US had not had official communications with the UN since the Chinese attack. The purpose of the call was to establish, to the best level possible, the amount of damage all the identified nations had received from Kill Switch. The collective picture was much bleaker than any of the parties had anticipated. It was clear that functional governmental duties were nearly impossible and would remain so for some time to come. The discussion of potential additional attacks was the most important issue, but the topic of recovery was already underway. All the nations involved in the call agreed that hostilities had to cease immediately and the question became, what answer had the US received from China. Iran and North Korea's ability to function as a threat was gone, and it was clear the only obstacle to the cessation of hostilities was China. The US notified the group they had made contact with the Chinese government, but they didn't reveal how. The Russians asked how much time had passed since the US communicated with the Chinese. They also relayed they currently had no contact with China at any level. Each of the other nations on the call also stated they had no communications with

China and had no means of doing so. It was clear the US was the only member of the group who could attempt to ascertain a status from the Chinese. The US informed the group they had no reply as of the time of the conference call. The group was informed the US had communicated with China nearly nine hours before the conference call. That statement brought an immediate response from the Russians. The question the Russians asked was supported by every other nation on the call. "Why had the US not attempted to reach out again"? To them, the concept of waiting nine hours was simply inviting a counter-attack. It was India that asked the next question. Had the US struck all of China's nuclear programs? Russia quickly followed with the issue of the Chinese Ballistic Submarines. Every nation on the call needed to know just how complete the US attack on China had been and what status was China left in? What options did they really have? For the US, those were questions that could not be answered with any level of detail and how the US framed their response was the next level of the crisis.

The Chinese had been left with their land-based nuclear weapons, but they couldn't launch them. How? How did the US do that, and what did it mean to the Russians and the others in the group? If the US was telling the truth, then they possessed a capability, the Russians had no counter to, and that could mean their ability to defend themselves from the US was in grave danger. How had the US defeated the Chinese Ballistic Submarine program in a matter of minutes? Did this same capability apply to the Russian fleet? These same questions ran through the minds of India's leadership. India had managed to stay out of the actual combative phase of the conflict, but the impact was just as devastating as it had been to nations who were involved. India's ability to defend itself was the question at hand. No one in the world trusted anyone to the point of assurance, and that included India.

The US had destroyed China's ability to function and every nation, friend or foe, wanted to know-how. What the US told them was guarded at best. China's confidence in its communication processes was unrealistic, and the US had taken advantage of the issue. That answer did not explain the EMP events. The Russians and several others in the group had First Warning capabilities, and none of them had observed a ballistic track anywhere near China. It was the Indians who made a comment on what appeared to be the repositioning of several satellites that were understood to be US communication platforms. The US did not acknowledge the utilization of EMP operations, but the spectrum of impact made it perfectly clear EMP was the weapon used. The question was asked by the Russians, where the satellites that were thought to be communication platforms, in fact, EMP weapons? The question was blunt, and the US answer was disastrous. "We are not prepared to explain how we defeated the Chinese networks"! It became the standard response for the US, and any confidence in the group continuing to work collectively was dramatically reduced. The US made a pledge to the group members; they had no intention of using whatever means they had at their disposal against any member of the group. They even made a pledge to defend them if needed, but that didn't matter. By the time that phase of the discussion was over, the Russians and the Indians understood what had taken place. The US had achieved a revolutionary, military advantage. One that very possibly meant both nation's nuclear programs were all but obsolete. Even the traditional "Allies" of the US were in a state of bewilderment. As the recovery from this new type of war took place, just where did the US see itself now? The group never collectively met again. Not only were the nations that took part in the conference call almost completely incapable of functioning as a national entity, several key members now believed they were unable to defend themselves.

*Russia's Misperception:*

From the moment the Russians believed their Dead Hand

program had potentially been compromised, they had been under the impression it was the Chinese who had done so. Their perception changed once the conference call with the US was over. It was the US that had been able to break into the network. The proof they needed came from what the actions the US carried out against China. Clearly, the US was capable of achievements beyond what Moscow had anticipated. There could be no other explanation. Based on the Russian change in perception, the decision was made to reach out to the Chinese in an attempt to validate Russia's fear. Some of the Russian President's key advisors failed to see the logic in the concept of contacting the Chinese. In their mind, did the Russian President believe the Chinse would say anything other than, "we had nothing to do with your Dead Hand event"? Regardless of the protest by some of the key staff, the Russians attempted to contract the Chinese leadership. A shortwave communique was sent to the Russian Embassy in Beijing with detailed instructions. The problem became, the Russian Embassy had no idea where the Chinese Central Government was located. Beijing was a city without power. Traveling the streets was impossible. The Russians had no way of contacting the Chinese leadership. Given the state of Beijing, the Russian Ambassador was not even permitted by his security detachment to leave their Embassy compound. Russia's attempt to contact the Chinese was left to the military of both nations. Russia would fly an aircraft to a Chinese Airforce Base and deliver a message from the Russian President. In all the confusion and panic Russia found itself in, that was the best answer they could come up with. It was an answer the Chinese were not prepared for.

China's Early Warning network was inoperable. The US EMP platforms had a set of follow on targets, and they struck them within minutes of the primary targets. China's key military and commercial satellites, ones that had not be impacted by their own Kill Switch event, were known to the US. These platforms were designed to operate in sequence and breaking a percentage of that sequences would render them useless.

The Chinese did have replacements on hand, but the ability to place them in the correct orbit was gone. The percentage of Chinese radar that had been impacted by the power loss was far larger than the US had anticipated. Between these two facts, the reality was, China had large sections of its border airspace that was unguarded. The approaching Russian aircraft was attempting to communicate on all open channels as it flew deeper into Chinese territory. The installation it was heading to was given, but there was no response. The Airbase had been struck by the EMP weapons, and no electrical capabilities existed at the facility.

Moscow received word the aircraft had been shot down thirty minutes after it had been launched. China was dysfunctional, and the only course of action the Chinese military was willing to take was to protect the country at all costs. One aircraft inbound could have been a US ploy. It may have been a nuclear Cruise Missile with a signature of a Russian aircraft. Logic was not in control, and the decision to down the object was given by the local Air Defense Commander. The Anti-Aircraft weapons platform was located in an area just outside the footprint of the Chinese Airbase. The argument in Moscow over the value of contacting China gained momentum. The Russian President decided to attempt to communicate with the Chinese openly. It was hoped the Chinese would have a process left that would allow them to do so. The Russians believed the US had to be responsible for the attack on the Dead Hand program. They also understood the US would be able to monitor the communications attempt. The US had capabilities no one knew about or understood, and that was precisely why the Russians felt they had to communicate with the Chinese.

The open-air transmission to the Chinese was sent to a known, emergency frequency monitored by the Chinese government. Upon notification to the Chinese leadership, once again, the authenticity of the message was questioned. What was agreed to was an escorted movement from the Russian

Embassy to a site determined by the Chinese escorting contingent. Once the Russian Ambassador was physically with the Chinese President, the follow on communications with Moscow was set. What was agreed to was simplistic, but it was the only way a confidential conversation could take place between the two nations. The Russian would immediately send another aircraft to Beijing and on this aircraft would be a video message from the Russian President. The message was straight to the point. The US had found the ability to manipulate Russia's Failsafe networked named Dead Hand. The Russians had taken the capability offline, but it was no longer confident the nuclear command and control of the nation were viable. The Russians had only one answer they needed a reply to. Was China going to retaliate against the US with nuclear weapons? If so, it was possible the US would mask their counter-attack by executing the Dead Hand network. Avoiding a nuclear exchange was Russia's goal. That was not the goal of the Chinese.

A return aircraft with a reply would not be necessary. The Chinese replied to Moscow in the open. "We are aware of your network, and we cannot influence what is taking place with your system. We urgently request you take all measures possible to prevent this system from remaining operational". That was it. That was everything the Chinese were willing to let the Russians know. The fact the US had been able to break into the Chinese Nuclear Command and Control network was not mentioned. The reality that China was incapable of executing its own nuclear program was also not mentioned. What the Chinese did realize was the fact that their dream of "Reset" was still not completely gone. A meeting was held as soon as the Russian Ambassadors departed.

The Russians had informed the Chinese they believed the US was responsible for the events that took place with Dead Hand. To the Chinese, this was the only good news they had received in hours. It was China that had developed a way to infiltrate the Russian Doomsday program, and it was China that still could control a limited part of the network. Chinese leadership understood their nation was crippled beyond all expectations and their dream of a "Reset" was nearly destroyed by the unexpected capabilities of the US. The argument that ensued was one that several of the Chinese Senior Leaders had favored from the beginning. Utilize the Russian Dead Hand program to retaliate against the US. Those who were opposed to this idea had only one line of logic to defend. If the Russian network were utilized, yes the Russians would be blamed for the event, but the retaliation by the US would leave the world unmanageable and incapable of achieving the Chinese goal. The concept of Reset was based on the impact of Kill Switch, not a potential, total nuclear exchange between the US and Russia. China's nuclear weapons program may have been crippled, but the Russian and US programs were far more autonomous than China's. As such, the number of weapons that might be utilized was unacceptable to those in the Chinese leadership who were against the idea. The debate came down to one issue. Was the utilization of the Russian Dead Hand program a window to still achieve China's "Reset," or was the use of Dead Hand the beginning of the end of civilized man? The decision was not put to the vote. The Chinese President would decide the fate of not only China but of the modern world.

Not only had the US observed the Russian flight into Chinese airspace and the subsequent downing of the aircraft, but the second aircraft and then the open communications between the two were tracked as well. Given the frank and open discussion the US President and his Russian counterpart had held that same day, the idea the Russians were now reaching out to the Chinese without notifying anyone was alarming. Trust was an issue that no longer existed between any two major nations, and the concept of trust between the US and Russia was no exception. The reference to the Russian "System" by the Chinese was more than alarming. The idea of a Doomsday program with the Russians was never far from the minds of the US leadership, and it had only been a few hours prior that they had heard the Russians in a near panic over such a process. With the level of activity that was taking place and the sensitivity of the concept, it was decided the US would not bring up the question of such a program during the joint conference call. The task of validating what the US had heard had fallen to a lover level assessment group, and they were to report on their findings at the next Presidential update briefing.

Almost everyone aware of the conversation understood what was being discussed. The Russians had a Doomsday program, and they didn't have control over part of it or all of it. The Chinese answer was such the only logical conclusion the US could come to was that Russia was asking the Chinese if it was them that had penetrated the program. The US knew it would be insane for the Chinese to admit such an issue, and they also knew the Russians believed it had to be the US that was inside the network. Did the Russians know the US had compromised the Chinese Nuclear Command and Control program? If so, how? Did the Chinese tell them? If the Russians believed the US was responsible for the breach in their Doomsday program, what were they contemplating? The US President gave one order. He wished to speak to the Russian President immediately. It was time for the US to be perfectly honest with the Russians.

*US Full Disclosure:*

The secured VTC link was once again provided by the US Ambassador to Russia. It had been less than an hour since the US President decided to speak with his Russian counterpart again. The conversation was blunt and exceptionally clear. The US President informed the Russians the US had gained limited control into the Chinese Nuclear Command and Control network, but the US had no capabilities with the Russian Dead Hand program. The Russians responded as many in the

US predicted, with skepticism. In the past week, the US had consistently presented capabilities the Russians had no idea of. Now the US wanted the Russians to trust their word on the only program that might ensure Russia's survival. It was time for the Russian President to be honest, and the statement was going to be met with just as much skepticism in the US as the US statement had in Russia. The Russian President informed his US counterpart the Dead Hand Program had been effectively disconnected from the Russian Nuclear Command and Control network. In short, Dead Hand was no longer functioning. Belief was not the answer the US was willing to give. What the US said in reply was once again, even more, alarming to Russia. The US believed it was the Chinese who had infiltrated Dead Hand, and they also believed the Russian confidence in the network being deactivated was an assumption they or the US could not rely on. The Russians had lost control of part of their Nuclear Command and Control program, and it was impossible to convince the US otherwise. The US attempted to gain some level of assurance the Russian had been successful in deactivating the program, but that required yet another level of trust. How did the program work? What was it connected to? How was the program disarmed? A technical follow up conversation would follow the call between the two world leaders. What both of them needed to know was if they could trust each other? The Russians had reached out to the Chinese after the Chinese had reached out to them. How was the US to know the Russian posed no threat to the US? How was Russia to know the US posed no threat to Russia? Trust was all the two world leaders were looking for, and neither believed they were going to find it. The follow on, technical conference call would determine the level of real trust. Before it would end, the answer as to who was responsible for the infiltration of Dead Hand would become a reality. One final argument took place with the US President's team. Was the Russian story a hoax? Was Dead Hand really disconnected? Trust.

The concept was lost to 21$^{st}$ Century governance.

*Launch:*

The US Early Warning Program had been degraded by China's Kill Switch, but the capability to detect launch plumes still existed. It was trajectory and target confirmation that had been damaged, but redundant sensor platforms could give the sixty-five percent solution, and that was good enough for the US to make strategic decisions. The first plume indicator alert was reported near the known mobile ICBM site in North-Western Russia. Within seconds, multiple plumes were identified from the same area. The notification process for the US was still intact, and the alert reached the US President within thirty seconds of the initial alarm. Confirmation procedures were underway when the next set of alerts came upon the watch screens. Plumes were being identified from three sea-based locations with all three being in an area just north of Japan. At the same time, more plumes were being tracked originating from Western Russia. After less than one minute since the initial alert, over sixty plumes had been identified. Based upon the location of several of the Western Russian launches, the assumption was made US military facilities in Europe would be the probable targets. The President was notified these sites would have less than ten minutes until impact. A process that had been practiced thousands of times over decades was not going into operation for the first time. The US was under nuclear attack, and every second would mean countless lives could be saved or lost.

The President was receiving a briefing on the status of the nation's power grid when the notification of the launch alert was given. The words were exactly as they had been rehearsed time and time again. "Mr. President, we have confirmation of multiple inbound ballistic missiles with a high probability they are armed with multiple, nuclear warheads"! The first words out of the President's mouth were recorded.

"Dead Hand........The Russian's lied to us"! The protocol was automatic for a staff that had drilled this event to perfection. The US President would be connected to the Russian President within seconds by a phone network that was hardened and supported by a satellite network in deep orbit; far beyond the area impacted by Kill Switch. The Russian President was put on the line within seconds of the call being placed. Each of them had been in their "war rooms" for days, and access to the Red Phone System was never in doubt. The phone network had one purpose, and that was to save the world from nuclear destruction in time of war.

The first statement came from the US President. "Did you deliberately launch these Missiles"? The answer was given before the question was finished. "No,"! The Russian President was clearly shaken, and the conversations in the background told the story of confusion, panic, and surprise. The Russian President stated their Dead Hand program had initiated a partial response and they had no idea how it could be happening. The Russians had disengaged every known process that allowed Dead Hand to respond autonomously. They could not explain why part of the network had partially activated. The US asked if there was a way to disarm the inbound warheads. The answer was no. What the Russians could tell them was that it appeared the segment of the program that had generated launches had a common backup communications process. A variant of Very Low Frequency, VLF, was one of multiple, redundant networks used in the segment of Dead Hand that controlled mobile weapon's platforms. All of the technical information was too much to comprehend with minutes to work with, but the US knew it was Dead Hand that had been activated. What other parts of the Dead Hand program might have the ability to activated? The questions from the US came too quickly, and the Russians were now looking for their own answers.

How would the US respond? The Russians knew what systems had fired, and they knew the targets of those systems.

That information was provided within the first minute of the conversation. It appeared all the inbound weapons were going to target US military facilities. San Diego and the Ballistic Submarine facilities on the West Coast were on that list. As soon as the Russian provided the target list, the question was asked again. How would the US respond? No answer was given, and the only agreed-upon topic was the need to limit what happened next. As the President was talking, he was informed the first targets in Europe, were inside of five minutes of an airburst detonation. Europe was about to be struck by multiple nuclear warheads. The size and types of detonations were given by the Russians, and that helped everyone anticipate the aftermath.

The US and Russian President had been talking for over five minutes when the Russian President finally made a comment they both knew was true. China. It was China who had infiltrated Dead Hand. Russia was aware of China's Reset plan and activating the Russian Dead Hand was their last attempt to make that plan possible. Reset was a concept the US had anticipated the Chinese would never truly implement given their economic status in the modern world. Again, resolve had become a concept governments had underestimated. The US President had little time to contemplate the concept of the Chinese attempting to execute their plan. A nuclear war was now underway, and the decision had to be made. Did the US respond in kind? Would the US take the path of "Proportionality," or would the US strike a blow that would ensure China's Reset dream would never come true? No US President had ever compromised in the face of an Enemy, and that fact held true in this war as well.

In all, over one hundred warheads were inbound to their designated targets. As the US and Russian Presidents had been talking, the US antiballistic sites in Europe had activated and begun the process of identifying and targeting the missiles and the warheads that had already separated from their platforms. That was a process the Russians were aware of. What they did not know was the process that was taking place in close orbit around the Earth. A series of Low Earth Orbit, LEO, satellites, much like the ones that destroyed China's infrastructure, began the task of identifying those warheads both in boost phase and in reentry. Attacking these targets with the speed of light was a capability the US had placed into operation only eight months before the war. Those warheads targeting the US mainland held the highest priority, and as such, the network of interceptors reacted to them first. The process would not only shock the Russians but every other nation that had held its nuclear weapons program as their ultimate safety net and yet, it proved not to the absolute answer to the concept of ballistic attacks. The idea that one nation, who had violated the international treaties on Space Weapons, was now able to defend itself and others from Ballistic attacks by utilizing space-based platforms would have been far more impactful had the world been able to return to a normal state. The accusations of treaty violations would never have the opportunity to be discussed.

*Impact:*

Sixty-three of the estimated one hundred warheads launched by Dead Hand were intercepted. It has not been determined how the thirty-seven that did make it to their targets were able to do so. Speculation centered on them not being targeted in time, but no identifiable evidence has been produced at the time of this report. Eighteen of the thirty-seven stuck their targets in Europe. Seven locations in England were struck as well with two of them being high altitude, EMP events over London. Six warheads reached their targets on the West Coast of the Continental United States, not including three weapons that impacted Ballistic Defense locations in Alaska. Two warheads struck the US military facilities located in the State of Hawaii. One weapon reached it' target of the US military facilities on Guam Island. Within an hour of the initial warning of plumes being detected, an estimated thirty million people were dead. An additional twenty million were said to have been critically injured in what was to be the first wave of the nuclear exchange.

The Russian and US President was still speaking when word of the first target's being struck came in. Several European Leaders had been warned, but the warning did not impact their ability to absorb what was going to happen. What was being discussed at the time of the first impacts was not recorded, but the discussion of just how limited the Russian Early Warning had become was thought to be a major topic at that moment in time. The Russians were almost completely limited to actual radar signatures as their satellite-based networks had been devastated by the Chinese Kill Switch event. A discussion was known to have taken place between the two leaders on the issue of the US providing launch notification to the Russians in the event of a Chinese attack. That topic was part of a larger conversation that addressed the US's response to the Dead Hand event. The decision had been made to allow the anti-ballistic network to execute before the US made a final decision retaliation, but the Russians understood the US now firmly believed China was responsible for the nuclear attack. Just how successful would the US defensive network be? That was the answer the Russians were told to wait for. The Russians believed they had little choice as it was clear that any strike against the Chinese would be a joint operation. The Chinese had attempted to place the blame of a limited nuclear war on the Russians, and if they were retaliated against, how could China not see such an event as a US / Russian joint response? That was the prevailing thinking of both the US and Russia and in fact, it was indeed the perception of the Chinese.

The European detonations took place only ten minutes before the first two on US soil. The launch locations that targeted Hawaii and Guam meant they were the first to be struck. The Pacific LEO platforms were reprioritized as soon as the confirmation came several of the missiles were targeting the

West Coast of the US. The theory had been, localized capabilities within the US Navy would be able to counter the limited number of warheads set to impact Hawaii and Guam. The US Navy was successful in intercepting nine inbound weapons for Hawaii. The issue was the anti-ballistic capabilities of the US Navy were a generation behind what was operational in the LEO platforms. That LEO technology was Revolutionary, not an Evolutionary. The US Navy did all that it was capable of doing to save the state of Hawaii and its own Fleet Headquarters.

Word of the impact on Hawaii and Gaum was given to the US President, and it was at that time he informed his Russian counterpart they would have to end their discussion and agree to speak within the half-hour. The size and type of weapons that struck Hawaii and Guam were being briefed when the President asked the status of the intercept of the Weapons bound for the West Coast? The answer started with a muffled conversation. The Secretary of Defense and the President were in separate locations, but the President was keenly aware there seemed to be an issue with answering his question. Nearly a minute later, it was stated the Platforms had experienced a short-term targeting error due most likely to a change in atmospheric conditions, changes that required a recalculation of the targeting system. In that amount of time, several of the high-speed reentry warheads had passed the optimum window of interception. The reality was, those warheads would most likely make it to their targets. The President asked where they were headed, and he was informed San Diageo and Los Angeles. He then asked how long until they were struck. When he was told, his words resonated and will do so in US history. "I've waited too long. I've waited long enough"!

Three warheads each struck San Diageo and Los Angeles. Two near ground detonations, approximately one thousand feet above the cities. The third impact stuck both cites three minutes later, and they were considered mid-altitude detonations, nearly ten thousand feet above each city. The people of both cities and the surrounding areas had been notified of the pending strikes by traditional notification methods such as the air raid sirens and radio statements from the National Emergency Broadcast System. For the past several days, many of the people of both cities had been in the process of moving out into the countryside. The issue had become, the areas outside the two cities were not capable of supporting the influx of the high volume of people, and in many cases, local authorities were not willing to take on the additional burden. Regardless, the population of both cities was estimated to have been reduced by nearly fifty percent at the time of the nuclear strikes.

The US had lost four major cities, El Paso, San Diageo, Honolulu, and Los Angeles. The primary military facilities for the Pacific were not operational. The mainland was without a regulated and structured power grid. The US had a minimal communications network, and transportation was paralyzed. The flow of commercial goods had virtually stopped, and all local inventories had been nonexistent for several days. The US President understood confidence in the government was all but gone, and the only thing he could do now assured them the perpetrators of this attack would pay a terrible price. It would be a price the rest of the world would pay as well, and that was the issue that haunted him to the end of his life.

*US Prepares A Nuclear Response:*

Over thirty minutes had passed since the US and Russian President had spoken, but the conversation took place none the less. The US President received the condolences from the Russians and then informed them of the US's intent. The US would strike the Chinese in a disproportional way. The US President intended to neutralize the Chinese military to the greatest extent possible. What this meant to the Russians was a critical part of the conversation. The use of nuclear weapons along the Russian border had been only one concern. The retaliation of the Chinese was the focal point of the Russian reaction. US nuclear weapons were cleaner than both the Russians and the Chinese. The ability to recover from such an exchange had been factored into the US's response, and particular data on the impact of US weapons would be provided to the Russians as soon as possible. The Russian stance was less complicated than that. Was the US capable of preventing the Chinese from responding to both nations? Was the US able to stop the Chinese nuclear weapon's threat? The infiltration of the Chinese Nuclear Command and Control network gave the Russians hope. The new reality this capability would mean to the Russians was a topic for the future, but at that moment in time, survival was the goal. The US was retargeting weapons, and that process took time, but far less time than the Russians anticipated. Weapons that had once been programmed for Russian targets were now being retargeted to Chinese locations. This retargeting had already been underway before the events off the coast of Yemen, but that was something the Russians were not aware of. The reprioritization of China was nothing new to the US, and the time it would take to set known targets to new weapon systems was only a matter of hours, not days or weeks. The end state was clear to Russia. The US intended to strike China with a devastating counterstrike. The US would also make it known to the Chinese people and the rest of the world the reality of the Chinese interfering with the Russian nuclear weapon's program. The US President then asked his Russian counterpart the question both of them feared. Where the Russians confident Dead Hand was completely offline? Was there any possibility the Chinese could still influence Russian warheads? The Russians had an answer prepared for just that question, but the Chinese would not allow them the opportunity to prove their answer.

*China's Control of Russia:*

The decision to implement their control over Russia's Dead Hand program was made for one reason and one reason only. The amount of capital expenditure and time invested in the Reset concept was based on China's leadership's vision of not only their country but the world. The time for the Chinese people to instill order over a destabilizing, Western, Capitalistic landscape had come. The future of China was not going to be determined as it had been for the last 500 years. Western, Caucasian dominance was coming to an end. Asia would set the course of the new world, and to China, they were Asia. Reset was not just China's vision, it was the Human Race's future, or so the Chinese believed. The Chinese were convinced the US and Russia would not throw away everything they had achieved. The Christian faith was based on compassion, forgiveness. The leaders of both nations would not bring destruction upon the world when, in reality, all that had happened up to that point was less than the total destruction of ether previous World War. The US was on its knees, and the Russian had lost control of their nuclear Doomsday program. Yes, the US had struck back, but the damage was nothing they had not anticipated. It was still possible for China to achieve Reset! What the use of the Dead Hand program had provided them was a clear advantage to restart the economic engine of the rest of the world. Africa and South America were the least impacted areas, and as such, they would be the new center of gravity for world trade. The old world was gone. The new world was beginning. That was the dream. That was the perception. The Chinese had executed the first step to a thousand-year rule of the world by Asia. All that had stood in the way was gone. Those who would not follow had been beaten into submission. The next morning would be the first day of the new China. They would now rule the world, and that world would gladly accept their new Leader. In reality, they were right. The world had changed. To the Chinese, it was the dawn of a new age, but the age of the new China would not come to pass.

The Chinese control over part of the Dead Hand program was a reality. The greatest fear both the Russians and the US had, was based upon China's ability to control additional sections of the Russian nuclear arsenal. All remaining weapons in ready status had been physically removed from any form of electronic connectivity. But again, even those who were recognized as "experts" on the issue of data manipulation and infiltration, commonly called, "Hacking," simply didn't understand the level of complexity the Chinese had obtained. Like the US processes, power and the connection to power was the unrecognized enemy. The concept of interrupting future instructions would not guarantee the safety of any system that relied on coded data. Dormant commands were the enemy, and too little was understood about the process to keep every operational item functional. The world had simply grown too technologically complex for governments to have any form of assured security. If a device had been on an electrical grid at some point in its development and that device needed coded data to function, then the ability to influence that device's operation was there. Many governments had gone to great lengths to keep so-called "secured networks" in a standalone environment. The flaw was almost always in the assembly process or the support equipment, especially during processes such as quality control and review. Activation of embedded commands was the complicated part of the process, and that was the real magic of what the Chinese had been able to achieve. In the end, how this impacted the crisis that gripped the world was the fact the Chinese had control over other aspects of Russian infrastructure, not just Dead Hand.

US countermeasures had been a policy for many years, and the fears of what was known as Y2K had opened the US's eyes to imbedded threats. An elaborate, corporate supported, Cyber Command had also allowed the US to defend against what had taken place with the Russians. The ability to infiltrate US corporate research and development, given the US's reliance on the World Wide Web, had been the preferred track of the Chinese. The effort the Chinese had used towards the Russians was based upon dormant, imbedded infiltration. Stealing trade secrets was not the reward the Chinese had been seeking with the Russians. Being able to control what the Russians could and could not do at a critical moment in time that was a vital part of the Chinese plan. Although the infiltration of Dead Hand had been a resounding success, to the Russians, the next phase of Chinese manipulation was just as horrifying.

*Russia total loss of communications:*

The Russian and US presidents completed their conversation. It was clear Russia had to prepare for the actions the US was going to take, and they had to give the US a clear answer. The Russian President asked for an hour, and the US President agreed. As soon as the conversation was over, the Russians began their meeting on the issues at hand. At that very moment in time, every secured communications system they relied upon simply stopped! The networks simply turned themselves off. The satellites that had survived the Kill Switch event stopped communicating. Any communications device that had any part of its Motherboard made outside of Russia was no longer functioning. Even the backup, High Frequency, and Ultra-Low Frequency networks were dead. Commercial networks that supported Russian operations that had survived Kill Switch were dead. Not only could the Russian President not communicate with the rest of his government or military, he could not talk to the room next to him. He had one line that might still work, and it was his only way to communicate with the US. When his aid picked up the line, it was dead! The Russian leadership could not communicate with anyone electronically. Communications had been severely impacted all over the world, but this was different. Nothing worked. No network based on electronic operations was functional. Russia was without a voice and without leadership in the middle of a nuclear war. The Chinese could not communicate thanks to the actions of the US. The Russians could not communicate thanks to the actions of the Chinese. The US was preparing to respond to the Chinese manipulation of the Russian Doomsday program, and the Russians could not speak to either side. The US was waiting for an answer from the Russians, and the Russians could not provide one. Panic ruled Russian leadership. Russia was without a functional government.

*The US Strikes:*

The US counterstrike on the Chinese initiated with yet another set of EMP events, but this time the number and types of targets were far greater. Not only had the US mastered the weaponization of directional EMP, they had refined how to fire these weapons in consecutive order with only seconds in-between salvos. A feeble attempt was launched by the Chinese to intercept these platforms with an older generation of anti-satellite weapons, but none of the US assets were disrupted. They either moved or the inbound missiles were struck by defending High Energy platforms designed to protect the EMP grid. The simple answer was, the US had perfected space-based weapons, and the ultimate advantage of the "high ground" had been archived. China was defenseless as the counterattack from the US began, and they didn't even know it.

Twenty minutes after the US EMP counterstrikes began, the Chinese were unable to detect the inbound, ballistic warheads. Some had been launched from the sea and were approaching their targets just above the water's surface. Others were racing towards their targets after separating from the booster platforms. All of the warheads had been preset to give maximum detonation, but all of them were also considered much cleaner than any weapons in the US's inventory. The blast zones of these weapons would be their greatest impact. The amount of persistent radiation was designed to be at an absolute minimum. In five years, the areas impacted by these devices would be habitable. Yes, the US was responding with nuclear weapons, but the lasting damage to the ground in and around the impact zone would allow for the future use of those locations. For the Chinese, five years would be too late for them to attempt to execute their Rest program. In five years, China changed beyond their wildest dreams.

China lost every major Sea, Land, and Airport facility on the mainland. Locations were the stockpile of Satellites, and other highly technical equipment was maintained were not struck. The theory had been, the government of China would change hands, and those assets would support the whole world's recovery process. To the US, there would be a Reset concept, but the Chinese would not control the program. The US and its Allies would. Three hours after the US counterstrike had begun, the War with China was over. An estimated 150 Million Chinese were dead. Another 200 million were in grave danger of dying within weeks of the war. All total, the Chinese losses were nearly 350 Million people. China had 1.4 Billion citizens, and even in their eyes, the cost of Rest was going to be nearly what was lost in the US counterstrike. It proved to be the only concept of Reset that would become a reality.

*Russia's Shot in the Dark:*

The Russians had no indication the US response was underway. The remaining capabilities of their Early Warning System had been neutralized by the nationwide communications event. They could not detect the US response, and more importantly, Russia could not detect what response the Chinese were taking. The hysteria created by the loss of all communication networks had left Moscow powerless. Russian leadership could not communicate with its own military or its citizens. Russians were on their own, and Moscow was not responding.

The Russian Strategic Rocket Forces Headquarters was without communications with Moscow. What had taken place in the US was known to its leadership. It was also known the Dead Hand program had been manipulated. The fact this manipulation had taken place at the hands of the Chinese and not the US was not known to the Command. For decades the standing orders had never changed. If the Senior Commander of the Russian Strategic Rocket Forces could not communicate with Russian leadership and the Commander knew the nation's survival was in question, then the option of defending Russia at all cost and with all means necessary was within his authority. This is exactly what he believed, and no one in Moscow could tell him otherwise.

As degraded as the US Early Warning System had become, the launches from Russian locations were still easily detectable. The counter strike on the Chinese had been completed for over an hour, but the US President's attention, along with all of his key staff, was solely on the Chinese event. Amid the US counterattack, no one had bothered to inform or even state the fact they had not received a reply from the Russians. The question of a Russian response to the US plan was immediately followed by the comment, "we have not heard out of them at any level." It was then the early warning notification began. The first plume analysis indicated over 300 launches from locations all over the Russian mainland. Seaborne launches were being reported, but the degraded US detection networks were making the analysis of how many extremely difficult. It was at that moment in time the US President stated, "I fear we have the Russian's answer"!

The US was able to determine nearly 200 hundred of the Russian missiles were targeting the Chinese. The rest were inbound to US locations across the world. Final estimations place forty-five of the missiles targeting the US mainland. The types of missiles were identified within the first minute of the attack. All of the weapons identified for the US mainland had multiple warheads with decoys mixed into each attack.

The US could detect the decoys, and that part of the Russian attack plan proved to be ineffective. The concern expressed to the US President was based upon how depleted the US Space Defensive platforms had become. The attacks of both Kill Switch and Dead Hand had consumed nearly fifty percent of the Defensive capabilities of the US's capabilities. The interception of ballistic targets while still in boost phase was already underway. Within twenty minutes, the US had an estimate of just what percentage of the warheads would be neutralized. The real vulnerability came from the Map of the Earth weapons. Those that had been launched by Russian Ballistic Submarines or could be launched by aircraft were much more difficult to counter. The US President had also informed the bulk of the US's Space-Based Defensive network centered on events originating from the Pacific region. Assets had been reprioritized in the past few days, but acquiring the optimum intercept position was going to play in the Russian's favor. The most important question the President had was the one that ultimately took the longest to answer. "How many warheads would reach the US mainland"? The answer was on the conservative side, but the number still forced the President and his key staff to realize what was about to happen. If no follow on launches were to take place, and Aircraft weapons were not utilized, the US mainland was going to be struck by over 100 warheads. The yield and type of detonation was pure speculation. The locations were less difficult to determine, and the list was being complied when word of the first detonation came in.

The Russian Strategic Rocket Force's Headquarters was able to communicate with their remaining Nuclear Forces utilizing a technique replicated by the US. A 1960's era network based on vacuum tubes and pre-microchip technology. A network developed long before the Chinse began to lay the groundwork for Reset. An era where parts and designs of parts came from the Russian, German, and Japanese industries. Nothing had been influenced by Chinese commercial programs. In the late 70s, as more advanced systems came into operation, it was decided to keep the original network. It would be placed in protective storage and would serve as the "Failsafe" if anything would happen to the more modern programs. It seems some did not trust the future of commercial based technology, and they were proven correct. The US had followed this same concept and had done so only after discovering the Soviets taking this course of action. In the end, Russia's Strategic Rocket Command was able to communicate, and the Chinese had overlooked a network they had forgotten about. It seems the parity they perceived they had achieved over the past few years had made them less observant. They simply didn't realize the simplistic approach the Russian would take. Not every Russian Commander or political leader believed in Dead Hand, and the Commander of Russia's Strategic Rocket Forces was one of them.

*Russian Commander's Assessment:*

The Chinese were defenseless after the US counterattack. They had no idea what was about to happen, and they had no way to prevent any of it. Russian warheads were cleaner than many of their older models, but the fallout was still far more persistent than what the US had utilized. The follow on the attack from the Russians would impact the Russian mainland, and they knew that. Russia understood that it was a fact the Chinese had always counted on. The Commander of Strategic Rocket Forces had determined to place the emphasis of his strike on the Chinese given his limited understanding of conversations that had taken place between the US and Russia before the loss of all communications with Moscow. It was clear to him the start of this war was based upon the relations between the North Koreans and Iran. The ability of the Iranians to arm their Cells with the weapons to attack Saudi, the Israelis and the US could only have come from the North Koreans. He knew the North Korean program could not have taken place without the support of the Chinese. When the decision was made to launch the nuclear strike, his beliefs were made known to his staff. The Russian nation had two known enemies in this war, two enemies that could have been responsible for the Dead Hand event. Of those two, only one had set a clear course for war shortly, and that was China. As such, the majority of the Russian effort would be against the enemy that shared a common border with Russia. The Russian Strategic Rocket Forces Commander would have no confirmation of his weapons striking their target other than the retaliation he was certain would follow. It was for that reason; he now readied his next option. The use of the Russian Airforce. Time was short and his window to be successful with his next attack was very limited.

*US's Decision on Russia's Actions:*

The US discovered the impact of the Chinese Communications attack on Russia just before the US counterstrike on China. The US intelligence community became aware of the event, but the size and scope were not fully analyzed by the time the US strike was underway. Once that strike was taking place, the ability to get information in front of the National Command Authority was extremely limited, if not impossible. The issue did make its way into the discussion within minutes of the Russian launch. The probability the Russian Strategic Rocket Force Commander had made the decision to launch was very high, given his inability to communicate with the Russian Command Authority. His awareness of who was truly responsible for the Dead Hand event was the real question. It was obvious he had placed a greater degree of responsibility on the Chinese given the targeting that had taken place. The fact the US also targeted lead the US to believe the Commander was doing everything in his power to protect Russia. How much of his force he had available after his fist attack was the question posed to the experts. Between the impact of the Chinese Kill Switch attack and the expended assets in both the Dead Hand event and the Russian launch, it was estimated the Russians had only about thirty percent of their ready arsenal available and most of that belonged to the Russian Airforce. If Russia were going to have a follow on attack, it would most likely come from Aircraft delivered platforms. If the US were going to limit the impact of the second round of nuclear detonations, it would have to neutralize the Russian Airforce capabilities as quickly as possible. The time of restraint had passed for the US. The only chance the nation had was to act decisively from that point forward. That is exactly what the US did.

Up until the US's decision to attack Russian Airforce installations, their mainland had suffered the least amount of physical damage from the war. Nuclear warheads had impacted, Europe, China, the Korean Peninsula, Japan, England, the Middle East, and the US, but they had not been delivered onto Russian land. The US's decision to prevent a Russian response was not going to be based on solely a nuclear option. The US had advanced to a level the Russians did not anticipate. The EMP platforms were moved into position within an hour of the order to do so. The refueling of the platforms had to be accomplished to execute the orbital changes, but that process only added to the event by under an hour. The prepositioned fuel points were accomplished, and the EMP platforms were prepared to execute with the precision that had destroyed North Korea and China. The Russians had no concept any of this was taking place and in fact, most of the Russian National Command Authority, if not all of it, had no idea they had struck China and the US.

Over two-thirds of the Russian Airforce locations that had the mission of loading and delivering nuclear weapons were struck within thirty minutes of the attack. The EMP events were so devastating each base found itself unable to generate a single aircraft. Follow on strikes on the same targets took place thirty minutes after the first attack with the theory being any machinery that had been shielded was now out in the open as the quest to generate aircraft would be the top priority. In reality, only a handful of the installations even received the communications from the Russian Strategic Rocket Command Headquarters. Individual bases had not given the attention to keeping the original communication network safe or maintained, or at least not nearly as much as the Ballistic locations. Russia was a nation of remoteness, and that mindset often resulted in a lack of attention to details. That was especially true for something as mundane, redundant as an antique communication network. The Commander of Russia's Strategic Rocket Forces had placed his plans for a follow on attack with the Russian Airforce. The Russian Airforce was already dysfunctional before the communications event. Russia's last option resided in its Ballistic Submarine fleet. The status of that force was unknown to Russia's Strategic Rocket Forces. The status of that force was not unknown to the US.

*Russia's Ballistic Submarine Fleet:*

The US made a conscious effort to limit the destruction of Russia's ability to defend itself. The US President was convinced if he could communicate with his Russian counterpart, they would be able to find a way out of the conflict. The EMP attacks did not target the Russian industry or what was left of Russian infrastructure. Kill Switch and the follow on communications event had left everyday life in Russia unmanageable. The US understood the Russians had not started the war and the Russians had decided not to side with the Chinese at the moment in time when they could have limited the war's impact on Russia. In the US President's mind, Russia and the US would form the backbone of the recovery process. A process that would take decades if it could even be achieved. Utilizing nuclear weapons against key Russian cities to reduce Russia's industrial capacity was not an option.

The US needed Russia and Russia needed the US. Keeping the conflict between the two from becoming completely out of control rested now with preventing the Russian Ballistic Submarine fleet from utilizing what weapons they had left. They had expended a portion of their weapons in the Dead Hand event, but their capabilities could still be extremely damaging to the nation.

The ability of Russia's Strategic Rocket Forces' Headquarters to communicate with Russia's Ballistic Fleet was virtually nonexistent. The antiquated communications network that made up the Failsafe concept was not built into the Ballistic Submarine concept. They were too new. The equipment was simply not part of the required inventory. The Commander of Russia's Strategic Rocket Forces knew this. He also knew what the US knew. The Commanders of the Russian Ballistic Submarine Fleet had the same authority he did. If the Commander of the Submarine believed the survival of Russia was in question, he had the power to launch. It was for this reason; the US had to deal with the Russian Submarine issue as quickly as possible. The US Navy had been training for just such an event for decades. The process would be different than the one used against the Chinese, and so would the outcome.

The first Submarines the US attacked were the ones that had been utilized in the Dead Hand event. Their location had been compromised after they launched, and the US Navy did not lose track of them after that point. Within an hour of the order to sink all Russian Ballistic Submarines, the ones that took part in Dead Hand were destroyed, and the rest, whose locations were known were under attack as well. The process for dealing with them was far different than the system utilized against the Chinese. That system was successful beyond the US's expectations, but their numbers were limited as the program was only in its first phase of deployment. The US relied on a tactic many believed had been discontinued for over twenty years. The Russian Submarines were destroyed by the American version of the Russian Status-6, a nuclear-armed torpedo. The Americans were thought to have discontinued a nuclear torpedo program, but when the Russians placed an updated version into their inventory, the US reentered that phase of the arms race. The known Russians Submarines stood a very slim chance of survival. The issue became the ballistic submarines whose location was not confirmed. The Russian inventory of such submarines had been depleted over the past twenty years, but those that were in service had modern weapons on board. The newer models were also far superior in cloaking their movements and locations. The bottom line was, the US estimated five such Russian submarines were unaccounted for.

The US President was informed of the actions against the Russian ballistic submarines, and that briefing update included the concern that at least five were unaccounted for. The US was aware of their general location, and that gave them some idea of what the target areas could be. A conversation on how to reestablish communications with the Russian government was taking place when the President was informed the Early Warning System had detected multiple, boost-phase events from three sea-based locations. All were located in the Central Atlantic where US and British Naval counterstrikes were already underway. The three Russian submarines were struck within twenty minutes of their initial launches, and it appeared they were all three in a phased attack sequence. None of them were able to sequence a second launch process as the nuclear detonations in their immediate area were more than enough to disable all three. The US President was informed that at least forty more warheads were inbound to the continental US. The US's Eastern Coastline defense network was as robust as the one placed in the Pacific. Interceptions of Boost Phase weapons from LEO platforms tasked with protecting the East Coast began within one minute of the early warning event. The US President was informed twelve of the weapons were Map of the Earth and the odds of intercepting all of them were low. The US Coastal Air

Defense network was equipped with Fighters that carried anti-Cruise Missile capabilities and if that processed failed the Fighters were trained to intercept the missiles with their automatic weapons if needed. Of the twelve Cruise Missiles fired, three made it to their targets. Two of the weapons struck Norfolk Virginia and one detonated over Andrews Air Force Base in Washington DC. The NEO platforms intercepted a total of twenty warheads. Eight warheads reached their targets along the East Coast of the US. All of the missiles had military-related targets. Unfortunately, most of these were generally located within very close proximity to major population areas. The US's attempt to neutralize the Russian Ballistic Submarine fleet had greatly minimized the potential damage to the nation, but it had not prevented the attack entirely. The Russian Submarine Commanders had not been able to communicate with Russian leadership, but they were able to monitor communications that were taking place in the open. All of the Commanders understood what was required of them given the circumstance before this phase of the war. When underwater, nuclear detonations were detected; every one of them took the only actions they were trained to do.

*THE DECISION OF PARITY:*

Seven hours after the destruction of the Russian Ballistic Submarine fleet, the final decision was made to neutralize several Russian facilities that would ensure greater parity between the two nations. The US President's hesitation in striking Russia and the Russian's ability to launch a limited number of its Submarine based missiles had left an unbalanced level of physical damage. The US land-based nuclear program was, for the most part, intact. The US's Ballistic Submarine fleet was virtually untouched. The Russian nuclear program was crippled. The issue became the speed and ability to recover economically. The damage inflicted by the Russian weapons had severely degraded the US's ability to recover at a speed that could match that of the Russians or India. India had gone virtually untouched by the conflict. The US had defended itself far beyond the expectations of the government. It was the people of the nation that would have no idea of how to recover or the cost of attempting to recover. In their eyes, the government had failed them, and that would limit their desire to follow any future guidance. In the eyes of the US President and his key staff, the US had won the battle, but now faced the real fear of losing the war! They had to ensure the future of the economic recovery for the US didn't rest in the hands of some other nation. China would not be an economic function engine for years to come. Russia was physically better off than the US or China. India was not yet capable of leading the world out of an economic disaster. Europe was severely impacted by the limited nuclear attack. England was crippled by the events of Dead Hand and the nuclear strikes. Africa and South America were not even considered as possible economic recovery threats. Russia, with its vast, industrial capability, spread out over a large landmass that was the real issue. The Russians would not be the recovery partner the US had planned upon. The Russian industrial capabilities would be the leading partner in any worldwide recovery, and the US would be depended upon Russia's capabilities. The US had only one option. That option was debated, but in the end, the final decision was made. The US would strike a limited number of key facilities and locations to place the US and Russia as close as possible to economic parity. The US President had one condition for that plan. He wanted communications with the Russian President as soon as the strike was over. If the world were going to have an economic "Reset," the US would not allow its fate to be in anyone's hands.

Twenty-five targets were approved for the US strike. They were all based upon their impact on Russia's industrial and military future. The strikes took place within a day of the decision being made. Contact with the Russian government was established through a growing network of shortwave radios that had been kept in a shielded environment by many nations. Those devices that were more than forty years old were trusted. None of them had any Chinese based hardware or technology. Conversations between nations began to take place, but none of the discussions was in the format of a unified effort. Nations were not interested in establishing the status of other nations. They simply want to know who could help them and how soon. A collective effort to assess where the world stood would not take place for over two years.

### *SECESSION OF HOSTILITIES:*

The communications between the two would be reestablished based upon an emergency satellite network the US had not activated yet. Eight US aircraft would be launched within that same hour, and from those aircraft, a network of small communication satellites would be placed into orbit. This network would guarantee the ability of the two governments to talk without interruption. The conversation between the US and Russian President was tense and was interrupted on several occasions by the Russian President's Staff clearly arguing in the background. With the damage that had been achieved, both leaders had realized the fate of the Human Race was already in jeopardy. What was understood was the fact the exchange of nuclear attacks had to stop immediately. It was clear to the US the Russians were not fully aware of the targets struck by the US. Situational awareness of their own country was limited at best and to some extent that held true for the US as well. What had taken place as a result of an irrational dream implemented by the Chinese, and that fact alone gave both nations the commitment to disengage in a conflict that had already altered the course of history. Both leaders spoke of how they had allowed nations to acquire weapons that none of them were capable of understanding the ramifications of using them. It was agreed that both nations would immediately freeze all military operations. A joint announcement would be given to the world within a day, and that announcement would place the blame for what had taken place clearly on Chinese leadership. The risk of further destruction was over, but the loss of life would continue for several years to come, with the total being immeasurable.

Salvaging what was left was the goal of both leaders and that required both to sacrifice their plans for the future of their nations. The future of civilized societies was now the goal. Thoughts of reconstruction and reconstitution of the world's economic systems were completely premature. Not only did both nations not understand the state of their own counties, they had no idea the state of the world.

SUMMARY:

The Chinese had designed a plan to become the World's Dominant power. A select few in the Chinese government and industry had repeated the same fatal flaw that so many others had done in the past. When the leadership of a nation believes the time has come for them to decide what the future of the world should be, they begin to plot the pathway to make that belief a reality. The Romans, The Ottomans, The Persians, Nazi Germany, were just a few examples. Power was the first tool of world dominance, and power came from two weapons in the Chinese plan. Trade and Technology. Both were designed by the Elite of China to drive their nation to the top. Forcing their enemies to become involved in a catastrophic conflict, while not being identified as the instigator that was the core of the Chinese plan. But, like most visons, the plan had a flaw. The Chinese underestimated their enemies. They miscalculated. They interpreted a weakening public support in the US for conflict to mean the US would no longer stand and fight thousands of miles away from their homes. The manipulation of the issues in the Middle East, particularly Iran and Saudi Arabia, was to be the catalyst to the start of the downfall of Western dominance. The world would suffer a war. A war the Chinese had believed they could manipulate.

At the end of that war, only China would stand ready to "Reset" the world order. Only China would be able to restart the economic engine of the world. Throughout history, miscalculation is the word that has cost the Human Race millions upon millions of lives, and this war was no different. What was different was how far the Human Race would fall. What had been achieved since the beginning of the Industrial age was now standing idol. The world's advancement had stopped. There would be no great recovery period as there had been at the end of World War I or II. Modern-day life had become completely dependent on the Electronic Era. It had become far too fragile. This time, when the war-damaged the world, others would not profit from the war. The Human Race was not destroyed, but it had been changed. The future would no longer be based upon advancements in science and technology, at least not for decades to come. The near term was based on survival, and the concept of minimizing the further decay of the society was an effort that would not take place for over two years. To stabilize global societies, balance would be critical. Balance was what held mankind together, and balance is what the world no longer had. Finding a way to ensure the people of every nation that some sense of normality would someday be achieved rested with them believing "balance" was returning to the world. The problem became, one other key factor was now gone from the day to day language of just about every nation. Trust. The concept of trust was something that only resided at the family, friend, or local level. Trust was a concept that would be foreign to any group calling themselves, "government" at any level above what people could see or touch on a daily bases. Trust became based on localized, small group thinking. Governance depended on trust, and few had trust in any form of government. This reality would prevent the world's recover even more than the weapons that were used against the innocent. The world had changed. The Human Race had changed, and the ability to shape the future was a concept that was not even spoken of for several years after the war. The weapons had stopped. The dying had not.

The deterioration of society had just begun. The 21$^{st}$ Century's repeat of the "Dark Ages" was upon mankind and in ways, no one had anticipated.

## SECOND REPORT

## POST CONFLICT

*An Analysis of the Impact of World War III.*

*This report intends to capture the impacts the Third World War had on not only the United States, hereafter referred to as "U.S," but the Human Race in general. As in the first report, my analysis is based upon both interviews of relevant individuals, as well as my own experiences of living through the aftermath. Given it has been five years since the start of the conflict, one that lasted less than a full month, I have once again attempted to address key issues in a sequential timeline. As such, topics in this report will begin with events that took place during the conflict and may address follow on items that continued for the five years afterward. Finally, I will end this report with my analogy of where the world stands, five years after the war. This report is my opinion, and I have no intention of this document being considered a formal review for historical records. I am sure a far more in-depth analysis will be developed over time, but as I began this journey, I was only aware of my attempt to capture what took place. "Lest We Forget."*

## OVERVIEW:

Daniel steiner

*Predictions vs. Reality:*

On the day hostilities ended, the US had been struck by over eighty nuclear warheads. Analogies of how the nation would be impacted by a nuclear war had been based on as many as 300 detonations striking almost every major city in the nation. Such depictions were easily anticipated. Topics such as Nuclear Winters and Global Fallout all created apocalyptic predictions that allowed those who studied the repercussions of such a war to avoid having to give a truly detailed analysis. The easy answer had always been, "Everyone dies"! Many knew that would not be the case, and some even attempted to predict what might be needed to rebuild the modern world. Those reports were ether highly classified or never accepted by governmental authorities at the proper levels. The fact of the matter was, the US and all other nations did survive, but many of the changes were not anticipated.

**Panic:**

As stated in the first report, the issue of losing confidence and trust in governmental authority began early in the war. Panic and poor communications were the fuels that accelerated those losses. By the time the World Wide Web became nearly inaccessible to the public, the ability for federal, state, or local leadership to provide information and guidance was realistically gone. People began to make decisions with little or no factual support. As the war grew more intense and the US population began to believe their own safety and survival was at stake, what little guidance the government attempted to provide proved to be nearly worthless and in many cases, counterproductive.

For over a hundred years, the US was the most stable nation in the world. In the first few days of the war, as the news reports and social media postings increased, it became clear to the rest of the world the stability of even the US was coming into question. Panic became a global epidemic, and social media became the foundation of perceptions. Perception became a reality, and the government was powerless to change any of it.

*Speed:*

The speed of the war was a factor no government had anticipated. Their ability to execute a protracted war was all but neutralized by the sheer speed of the conflict. Events took place faster than world leaders could react. Even China, who had prepared for this war for decades, could not comprehend and react promptly. The pace of events didn't just shock world leaders; it froze them. Decisions were made with little to no consideration of their possible impacts, and these decisions were on a global scale. On the day the fighting stopped, few people in the world understood why the war had even taken place. The decision to stop had been made by two world powers, but both powers no longer controlled their own nations.

In the end, what had taken place was beyond any rational thought. For all the predictions, for all the billions of dollars spent on preparation, nations could not continue to function. The world was not destroyed in a nuclear storm. The predictions of the Cold War did not come to fruition. The reality was, the world had changed, and the new world was unlike anything anyone could have predicted.

# CHAPTER SEVEN:
# PRELUDE TO
# YEAR ONE:

*The Beginning and the Reactions of the Public:*

The news of hostilities off the coast of Yemen was dramatic and major networks such as CNN, BBC and FOX were overwhelmed by the initial reports. Social Media coverage allowed a much larger audience to observe in real-time what was taking place. Again, the speed of the crisis made logical reporting nearly impossible. Yet, by the end of the first day, although governments were in full crisis mode, most of the world went along with their business with only a slight feeling of alarm. The prevailing thought was the issue would be, as usual, an isolated event. When word came of the increased activity in the Straits of Hormuz, those who had a decent understanding of the Middle East began to realize this was more dangerous than many had anticipated. It was then, the first real impacts of the fighting were observed. In the past, a sustained conflict in the Middle East had resulted in fuel shortages, and for that reason, the lines at gas stations began to form. News of those lines resulted in even more people attempting to fill their tanks. As the lines grew, the news increased, and like so many other events that would take place in the war; one event inflamed the other.

Fuel remained the issue until the actions of Israel became public. It was a noticeable change for the media broadcasters, and enough time had passed that each major network had assembled their group of experts. Comments by these individuals resulted in the next level of concern for the public. The concept of Israel, the US, and Iran are in conflict were understandable even to those who paid little attention to the region. Fuel was no longer the primary concern of most US citizens. People began to head to the stores and pharmacies, and it was noticeable to the press. Again, the media's coverage of this next level of public action only exacerbated the process. Live stories of events at home and away only made matters worse.

It had been decades since the American public had felt truly threatened. The attack on September 11th, 2001, had been the closest example of feeling afraid in their own homes, but even that event was quickly recognized for what it was. It was not a war in the traditional sense. It was an act, an act of Terrorism, and in the end, people understood they were safe. This event was different. It felt different. It was handled differently by the media. People began to realize the US was quickly being pulled into a conflict they had always been told could spin out of control. Simply turning on their TV's did not give them a feeling of relief. The US population, like many around the world, we're fixated on what was taking place. Something the public had been told to fear was actually taking place.

### The Second Day:

In the US, the morning of the second day started with the nation watching exhausted reporters urgently attempting to keep pace with a crisis only one day old. As dramatic as the events seemed to be, most people in the US still went about their daily lives. Fuel was now an issue, and the stores were compensating for the increased panic buying. The good news was, most of the nation was not yet in a real panic mode. Stories of runs on supplies were taking place on the local news, but those who were spending the time to keep up with the event were concentrating on national networks. Coverage of local panic buying simply was not the priority for the major networks, at least then. The perceptions of what was taking place in the Middle East was far more dramatic in other parts of the world. The people in Israel understood what their government's actions might lead to. The people of the other nations in the region understood the severity of the event as well. The US and other Western nation's citizens may not have been in a crisis mode, but they were closer than they had been in years.

Within hours of the reports of the conflict now taking place in Lebanon, the Western Media was beginning to comprehend the gravity of the event. Israel's actions in Lebanon were far more dramatic than any recent incident. Even the conflict in 2006 paled in comparison to the level of military operations taking place. It was clear media coverage was losing the ability to depict what was unfolding accurately. Events in Iran, Saudi Arabia, and the United Arab Emirates were still taking place and doing so at a pace even more dramatic than on the first day.

By noon of the second day, two major networks in the US, CNN, and FOX had grown increasingly more impatient with official news from the government. A press conference that was intended to provide the American people an update on the crisis was postponed three times in five hours. By 2 pm Eastern Standard Time, both CNN and FOX were openly ridiculing the White House for not speaking to the American public. The answer given for the continued delays was even more unnerving for the nation than the actual delays. FOX News reported the White House was in consultation with the "key" nations on the crisis and the decisions being made needed to be verified before speaking to the public.

As the US population waited to hear from its leadership, the counterattacks from Hezbollah began. Within an hour, reports of the impact these attacks were having on the nation of Israel occupied every Western media network. Video clips and photos were being sent around the world. Israel was under attack, and the level of violence had not been seen since the 1967 war. All of Israel's major cities were being struck, and the level of violence seemed to be increasing by the minute. As the US public watched these events in Israel, it had still not heard any official word from the White House. Day one had seen several short statements, but they were lacking in detail and painted a picture that was obviously not true by the beginning of the second day. By late in the afternoon of the second day, those who had not reacted to the issue of fuel and supplies were now joining the growing numbers of those who were. Panic was growing at an alarming rate, and every level of government in the nation knew it.

As dramatic as the events in the conflict were, the coverage of what was taking place in the US now became the story. The percentage of the US population that was now taking part in panic buying was creating just the consequence every level of government feared. Violence was easily covered by any level of network news. Bloggers were posting actual riots taking place outside major stores. Many of these events were even being streamed live on several social media sites. Local authorities were asking people to stay home until the events in and around their areas could be brought under control. As the sun began to set on the East Coast of the US, it was clear matters in the nation were getting dangerously out of hand. Local Law Enforcement was unable to suppress what was taking place. The number of locations that were reporting looting and violence was far too numerous for any agency to respond to. US cities were sliding into an unprecedented crisis as the rest of the nation looked on. As the media coverage continued, the news that many locations were now without fuel, and most stores were without food pushed the panic even further. The US was quickly approaching a perception driven crisis, and the federal government was going to be compelled to react in some manner.

At 6 pm Eastern Standard Time, the White House warned the networks the President would address the American people in thirty minutes. This time, the White House did not deviate. At 630pm, the President spoke. The message was short and precise, and when he was finished, there was no opportunity for questions from the media. The US President stated the crisis in the Middle East was the responsibility of the government of Iran and as such, the time had come to remove the leadership in Tehran. The US was working in conjunction with its longstanding Allies in the region, and the threat from the Iranian government would be neutralized as quickly as possible. The President then addressed the growing unrest in the US. He stated the US government would be releasing a percentage of the national stockpile for fuel and that this would be taking place within the next twelve hours. He told the American people the panic buying in the country was a byproduct of unprofessional media reporting, and he strongly urged the nation not to take everything they heard from the media as the truth. He then warned those who are promoting violence and taking advantage of the crisis that their actions would be met with a stern response. The US President spoke for less than five minutes and ended by telling the American public he and his administration would keep the nation informed: "As needed"! That was it. He was finished, and the feed from the Oval Office ended.

The major networks were stunned. The President had not allowed any form of questioning. He had spoken for less than five minutes. He had ended his message with a promise to keep the people apprised, "As needed." It was the "As needed" statement that put an already shaken media on its heels. As CNN and FOX both struggled to shape what had taken place, one thing seemed clear to both. The leadership of the US was struggling to comprehend this crisis overseas as well as inside their own nation. If the President's message to the people was not disturbing enough, the opposition party had no typical response. No word came out of the House. No one commented on what the President said or didn't say. The silence from the rest of the US government was remarkable. Even the Pentagon media office was nearly unresponsive. A few generic statements were released, but again there was no opportunity for questions to be asked or answered. The message was over, and the American people knew nothing more than before the President spoke, other than the release of fuel. Within an hour, the issue of why he seemed so vague was falling off the public's radar. The issue of the fuel, that was what the people wanted to know. How would it work? Would it actually have an impact? If anyone was going to leave areas that now seemed unsafe, how would they do so?

When the IDF attacked Iran's capital, the now exhausted news outlets slid into a whole new level of panic. The nations of Europe demanded Israel halt all hostile actions inside Iran immediately. Statements were confusing and unrelated. The unified front of Europe had collapsed, and media networks in Europe seemed lost on what topic to cover. Panic was now taking place in all of Europe's major cities. Not uncontrollable panic but panic never the less. No one took to the streets to demonstrate against what was taking place. People were fixated on any news from the Middle East they could find and simply didn't have time to organize a protest at any level. Europe was faltering under the fear of where the conflict could lead and Europe, as well as the US, were not alone.

China had one huge advantage. Key leaders had prepared for just such an event. The people of China were not aware, but those who made decisions on China's future knew. Messaging to the public was deliberate and reassuring. China was not part of this conflict, and the people of China need not fear where the conflict was heading. With a population of over

1.5 billion at the beginning of the war, communications only really mattered in the more modern cities and townships. For most of the Chinese people, nothing had changed, and that was exactly what their leadership desired.

Japan and others in the Pacific region understood the gravity of what was taking place, but like most, they felt powerless to impact the event. The on-again-off-again political process between North and South Korea had been the primary concern of most Pacific nations. Actions in the Middle East would impact fuel supplies, but the criticality of conflict there was limited to matters that didn't pose a threat to life itself or so most believed.

In South America, at first, news of yet another conflict in the Middle East did not gain the attention of the public. When stories of what was taking place in the US began to air, the effect was the same. People who lived in large, modern cities or towns began to look for fuel. The quest for fuel was followed, as it was in the US, by the hoarding of other supplies. By the second day of the war, the people of Central and South America may not have been convinced the dangers of the Middle East would come to their lands, but the ramification of the war would. The results would be the same. Populations that received little guidance from the government began to make their own conclusions. By the time any level of guidance was provided, most were past the point of listening to officials they already perceived as corrupt.

In Russia, the events of the Middle East were just as stunning as they were to the US and Europe. The Iranian's relationship with Russia had been severely damaged by the events in Syria. Permissions were not asked for, and notifications were late or nonexistent. By the time the Iranian ships had been involved, Moscow was only able to watch what was unfolding. Communications with the US and Israel took place, but once again, the speed of the conflict was overwhelming. Russia's cities were aware of the events in the Middle East, but the countryside saw little need to stay glued to a TV or phone. Life was hard, and time could not be wasted on things that didn't put food on the table or money in a pocket. Of the nearly 8 billion people in the world, the events of the Middle East truly impacted less than 10%. The so-called "modern world" was worried, scared. The rest of the world always lived in fear, and worry was a given. By the end of the war, even those who didn't know or didn't care would have their world changed forever.

### *The Internet:*

The verifiable order of cyber events in the war is impossible to show. Who did what first is a matter of speculation, and the exact timing of each level of attack is unknown. What is known is the reality that cyber events created more damage to public trust than anyone on any side would have ever imagined.

The Israeli attack on Iran was the breaking point for communications in the US. The public that had been consumed with the constant flow of official and unofficial news suddenly saw that flow interrupted. The cyber events between Israel and Iran created an uncontrollable series of issues throughout the world. As stated in the first report, networks were pulled from the World Wide Web with astounding speed. The attempts were simple in their logic. Everyone was trying to distance themselves from an unknown level of danger. As word spread of cyber events taking place at levels never witnessed before, nations and institutions enacted the most failsafe protocols they could think of. They turned off or disconnected everything web-based. Detailed planning, planning that had been years in the making, was disregarded as fear was once again the number one response. Even the warnings of overreacting had no impact on this new level of the crisis. Social media platforms became unpredictable. News outlets continued to air their programs, but the information they had was dated by hours and by this point in time, information that was hours old became useless to the public. The war had entered an unprecedented phase, but the American public could not grasp just how bad it was becoming. Without viable information and with little to no guidance from any level of government, only one result was possible, panic.

If the lack of Realtime information on the war, something most of the modern world had grown accustomed to over the years, was not damaging enough, the sudden stoppage of most electronic banking infuriated just about everyone that relied on such a system. It was one thing not to be able to find fuel or common supplies, but to no longer have access to funds, that was a true breaking point. Not every financial network was removed from the web, but the rumor spread that it was taking place, and that was enough to create the run that dropped the remaining financial networks. The financial crisis of the war was a global event, and news of this taking place worldwide only made the event worse.

Within hours of the first round of cyber events, even those social media networks that had been working became overloaded and then failed. Reliable information became nonexistent. Yes, some level of the web was functional, but nearly no one knew it. The US was in a long-feared conflict in the Middle East, and the repercussions of that conflict now had a global impact. Life had changed and changed dramatically in the US and in many parts of the modern world, and it had only taken three days. It was not the nuclear war many had spoken of for decades. It was not the Super Powers that had decided to come to blows. It was something different, something that was never truly expected by the everyday person on the streets. The US had been pulled into a conflict much like in World War I and World War II, but it happened for reasons no one really understood, and it happened in hours, not years or even months. The sun had come up in the US on the fourth day of the war, and nothing was the same. Nothing would be the same for a very long time, if ever.

*The Shutdown:*

By day four, it became clear to the US government the nation was quickly becoming dysfunctional. The events of the war were more than overwhelming for DC to cope with, but the unraveling of day to day life was the real crisis. Governors had received little guidance, and the public was demanding answers, answers they were not getting from the federal government. Understanding where the conflict might be heading and anticipating how to be prepared for that fact left DC unable to provide guidance to the states. The concept of addressing the nation had been attempted early in the crisis, but the message was poorly prepared, poorly presented, and poorly received. Sound communications within all level of the US government was the weak link in the chain, and from the perspective of the public, that chain had broken. By day four, most of the nation was staying home. What information they could find was enough to keep them from doing anything else. A physical threat was not the central element of fear, but uncertainty had a paralyzing impact. America was not going to work, at least enough of it that common processes ground to a halt.

Federal, state, and local governments had always anticipated a major event would disrupt the school systems first. Issues such as pandemic outbreaks or major natural disasters had been planned for, and those plans anticipated the issue of children and schools. It had even taken place on several occasions with major Hurricanes and Earthquakes, but nothing compared to the events of this war. Children were not kept at home because their parents feared their exposure. They stayed home because the parents had no idea, no confidence in where the nation and the world was heading. Children at home meant parents stayed home from work. That had been the normal planning process, but this war was not normal. Those that didn't have children stayed home as well. What the government anticipated as a scaled event, happened all at once. Not just schools, but entire businesses closed and closed abruptly. As networked-based communications began to fail, many businesses' only recourse was to shut down. Key employees that did not show up for work compounded this process even more. By late in the afternoon of the third day, the rumors of shutdowns were important enough that major networks began to cover the story and this was true not only in the US but in Europe as well.

Information was sporadic, but the perception was formed. The US population was confused, scared, and unwilling to go to work. Emergency Responders and other critical operations such as hospital staff continued to function, but that was because they had been trained. It was their duty to keep serving, and they were ready to do so, to the best of their ability. The problem was, day to day life in the US and other modern nations relied upon more than just First Responders and government agencies. The concept of a modern society being dependent upon a chain of processes was not new. How complex this "chain" had become had been completely underestimated. Day to day life in the US fell apart at speeds and at locations no one was prepared for. Children were home. Businesses were closed, and none of the detailed plans the government had designed for such events were working. It was once said; a modern nation is three meals away from anarchy. No one in the US had any idea how true that statement would become.

The State of Emergency was declared on the National networked designed for just such an announcement. The public was informed of the declaration, but the threats to them were stated in such a way, few people understood what was facing them. There was no mention of pending conflict on the US mainland. The fear of a wider war was not addressed. What was said addressed the panic the American population was creating for itself. To most, it seemed the federal government was blaming the people for the crisis, at least at home. The people were asked to stay calm while the government reestablished reliable communications as well as the flow of essential items. Some mention was given to the nation's emergency communications capabilities, but the problem stemmed from state and local government not being prepared to switch to this level of communications. True or not, it didn't seem to matter to those who were listening. What did matter was the reality the nation was now under special guidelines, guidelines the public did not know. The interpretation of a National Emergency seems to have been quickly confused with Martial Law. This misinterpretation spread so quickly; the national networks began to give definitions of what Martial Law meant. The federal government had addressed the nation, and the perception was, the government was drastically changing what the public would and would not be allowed to do. It had happened before. September 11<sup>th</sup> of 2001 had seen the nation placed in a National State of Emergency, but this was different. Perceptions were being formed by rumors, rumors from not just people on the streets, but from major media networks and rumors spread by state and local authorities. The questions asked by the public were not being answered, at least not to a level most would believe, much less follow.

*Unrest:*

The violence that had been taking place in the US had been based on the lack of fuel and essential items. The level of unrest had been predominantly in larger cities. Most people still understood the value of the order, and as such, they were reluctant to take part in what they were witnessing. That began to change after the declaration of the State of Emergency. People who were opposed to violence decided that public discourse at the location of state and local government was their next acceptable option. Marching for answers seemed harmless at the time, but that to would change.

Crowds gathered at public offices, and it was only then they became aware of an even more frightening reality. Many of those very people they were there to demand answers from were gone. Faces could be seen through windows, but no one came out to address the growing crowds. Overtasked law enforcement was slow to respond to such events, and often when they did arrive; the situation only became worse. Reports of such events were lost in the confusion that gripped D.C, but soon, states were reporting these events were turning violent. The federal government knew the difference between a riot in a major city and a violent protest in a rural community. What was taking place now was uncommon. When the bigger picture began to become known, it became an event the federal government had never prepared for. Governors had requested support, but it seemed DC was unable to respond. Mutual Aid concepts had been planned for, but the problems were so widespread, event that the concept proved worthless. The National Guard became the next option. Each Governor had his or her forces, and each one could activate them if they desired. Several had already taken this step, and they were the first to realize, besides the Pentagon, the process was not working. Citizen soldiers were Patriots, but patriotism could not provide fuel for those who could not find it. It could not provide a reliable level of communication that allowed the force to mobilize. Many of the Guard members knew they were needed, but this event was different. The threat was unknown, and the extent of the threat was undefinable. Members who did show up at their unit locations found leadership that was unaware of what was required of them. The National Guard was a force designed for such an event, but that was not their primary mission. Their funding was based upon support to the Active Duty War Time Task. By the time some Commanders were able to determine their capabilities, secured networks had sent out the warnings of possible mobilizations for a federal mission. The nation was in some level of conflict, and the requirements for the National Guard were unknown.

These forces belonged to the Governors, but the authority to mobilize them for a national mission took priority over any state's wishes or needs. In the end, the National Guard had little impact on the early stages of unrest. What did take place was the rapid spread of even more ominous rumors. The National Guard members informed their families and friends of what they had heard or been told. The result was rural communities believing the force they had always counted on was not going to come to their aid. The validity of those rumors no longer mattered. People continued to fear the worst at ever-increasing speeds.

The Federal Emergency Management Agency / FEMA / was designed to help state and local governments in times of crisis. The nation was divided into regions, and each of these regional teams had a representative for each state. Interaction between these teams and the state leadership had been taking place from the moment the crisis began. Early on, both the states and the FEMA teams understood the reality of how limited guidance would be. The speed of events took everyone by surprise, and that held true for federal agencies as well. Questions were asked, but few answers were given. When the President announced the intent to release National Stockpile fuel, questions began to flow from state government. The problem was, the FEMA teams didn't have the answers. On a normal event, it would take a few days for the process of fuel distribution to begin, but again, this was no normal event. The promised fuel never arrived. The support of FEMA became vital for communications, but the ability to support the public was minimal. States waited to hear any information FEMA could find, but that did nothing to ease the emergencies across the nation and to make matters worse, major cities were no longer the only locations of unrest. The suburbs of the larger cities had their own level of trouble. State and local Emergency Responders had reached their limits, and that was the last line of defense the public had.

Daniel steiner

*Law Enforcement:*

From the beginning, federal, state, and local Law Enforcement suffered from the same lack of information as
everyone else. Preparation and planning had always been
based on information. If some event was coming, a storm, a
riot, it didn't matter, Civilian Law Enforcement was at it's
best when they had time to prepare. The speed of this crisis
was unlike anything they had trained or planned for. Once the
issue of fuel was obvious, some anticipated further problems.
Agencies at all levels began to prioritize their efforts. It soon
became impossible to defend each store and in many cities,
ones that had similar riots in the past, the effort became containment. If problems were going to take place in given areas,
then containing those who were creating those problems
would become the priority of effort. That had been the theory
for every typical riot most agencies had experienced. Again,
this time, the normal way of responding did not work. Violence broke out in multiple locations in almost every major
city. Law Enforcement and other First Responders could not
concentrate their efforts on a few city blocks. Where there
were gas stations, there was some level of response required.
Traffic jams paralyzed intersections and soon the desire or
ability to respond to something as simple as a traffic jam disappeared. The continuing process of prioritization could not
keep up with the reports. Mutual Aid pacts between agencies
collapsed under the weight of events. Again and again, plans
that states and cities and counties had made did not work. By
the third day of the crisis, many parts of major cities were simply not covered. Law Enforcement had to do what any combative force is trained to do. They had to pull back and try to
regain a stance at a different location. This was the mindset,
but in actuality, many parts of the cities where the events had
taken place were no longer the issue. Once it was known that
fuel and essentials were gone, the issues became that of simple
looting. In normal times, this would have been the point

THE SECOND DARK AGES

where Law Enforcement would have regained the upper hand. The problem was, Law Enforcement was not capable of moving back into areas that had been impacted. Like a wild brush fire, they had moved to the next location. What was no longer useable to those looking for fuel and other items, became irrelevant to overtasked responders. The crisis was spreading with each passing rumor and with every broken statement from some level of government. To make matters worse, First Responders were citizens as well. They also worried about their families and friends. This crisis was different. No one knew why it had started or where it would end. The reluctance to stop their sworn duties was crushed by their desire to take care of their own loved ones. By the time the major departments began to run out of fuel and other essential items, it was clear to their leadership, the crisis was going to get worse, much worse. Israel had attacked Iran in an unprecedented way. Iran, in turn, had struck Israel in a fashion that shocked the world. Most of the men and women of the First Responder community knew what that could mean. Anything was possible now, and that is what they believed

By the third day of the crisis, it was becoming clear the whole concept of law enforcement was faltering. The ability to detain individuals and the processes typically involved no longer functioned. Detention centers were attempting to operate with skeleton staffs. Networks were so inconsistent proper documentation could not be maintained. Decisions on who should be detained degraded to the point only those who were responsible for personal injury were taken into custody. Even that concept soon became impossible to execute. Across the US, what began to take place was nothing more than disbursement. That tactic quickly devolved into one based upon bruit force. Reports of shootings from both sides of these events reached DC and the number grew by the hour. Governors were without a key tool, their National Guard, and that was the issue that was consistently reported to D.C. by FEMA regional offices. Several states were successful in utilizing a portion of their National Guard Force, but in the end, it was too little and too late. Somewhere around the evening of the third day, the concept of Law Enforcement melted away. The federal government understood the position the states were in, but the events in other parts of the world remained the primary concern. One quote given by an unknown federal official to the State of Texas was, "do the best you can." By the morning of the fourth day, the absence of any viable Law Enforcement process had led to complete lawlessness in most major cities. The glue that held any society together was law. The ability to enforce those laws had degraded to the point, the glue inside the US was gone. Those who still believed in the rule of law continued to follow as best as they could. Those that did not were not tolerated by those that did. As had always been depicted by movies and books, people began to ban together, and this was especially true in remote areas. Families, friends and people and others that were trusted formed defensive groups based upon a common location. Everyone was still looking for information, but the need for basic survival was growing stronger and stronger.

### Infrastructure:

One issue had always been identified by every level of government planning. What would it take to keep critical infrastructure functioning in a true crisis, a nationwide crisis? Hundreds of billions of dollars had been spent on this issue, but in the end, the real answer was people. It took people who knew the systems and people who would continue to come to their jobs, regardless of what was taking place, and that didn't happen. By the time of Israel's full-scale attack on Iran and Iran's counter strike, the issue became the next crippling event in the US. Automated systems for large scale processes had been moved over to manual operations. The fear of what was taking place in the cyber world had activated the protocols designed to keep everything functioning. Some had always feared it would be the humans that would fail, and those fears came true. The first dramatic event was the loss of power on the US East Coast. It happened somewhere on the third day, and twice the attempt was made to restart the power grid. Nothing impacted the confidence of the American people more than this event. The power was lost a few hours before dark, and when the sun went down, over a hundred million people had their fears reach uncontrollable levels.

The US government had executed the national disbursement plan, known as Continuity of Government. Critical government members were in locations that were designed to keep the nation functioning. That theory had one flaw; the only people who were able to maintain some level of normality where those moved into designated sites. The rest of the nation was left to fend for themselves or at least that was the perception from coast to coast. With the loss of power in over half the nation, the already unstable communication platforms became even more unreliable. Those in areas without power relied on FEMA transmitted AM broadcast. What the federal government had failed to realize was just how few people could listen to AM radio. Vehicles were the best choice, but the lack of fuel made that option limited at best. What little information the federal government was providing was heard by a very small percentage of the civilian population. The US government was in survival mode, but the American people were left in a position where they felt abandon. Over the past two or three decades, the civilian population had grown accustomed to a federal government that tried it's best to provide anything the public desired. Hurricanes had been the prime example. People were always told to be prepared for no support for up to 72hrs. The demands for food and fuel and electricity typically began as soon as the winds died down. A very large percentage of the American public was dependent on federal, state or local government and that fact had been completely overlooked by those who now found themselves in secured, survivable locations. Huge reinforced doors had been closed, but the public was on the outside of those doors.

### *Military Installations:*

The speed of the conflict took everyone by surprise, and that included the US Military. As the situation in the US deteriorated, people saw military bases as possible safe havens. Many of these installations were within several miles of major population centers. By the time people realized they should seek support at these facilities, every single one of them was in a wartime posture. Gates were heavily armed, and roads were closed. Installations had anticipated the possible influx of civilians, but the process was not developed to any level of effectiveness. Families of service members were the first to arrive, and they were taken in with little hesitation, but by the time the public became aware of this option, there was limited support available. Many of the major bases had a great deal of self-sufficiency. Major Army locations had huge supplies of deployable, combat meals / MREs/ as well as medical supplies. What was not known was the possibility of deployment.  As maddening as the first two days were for these installations, it was not until the third day the crowds began to gather. By the third day, secured communications had allowed all major commands to understand the true danger the nation was facing. The possibility of deployment of combat forces was practically a given and as such, supplies had to be set aside for this task. Besides, Installation Commanders were reluctant to take legal responsibility for civilians, especially in large numbers, but the need for some level of assistance was undeniable.  Once Commanders were notified of the status of civilian law enforcement, they began to ask for legal guidance. The regular military had long understood the limitations of Posse Comitatus. The National Guard was lead on such matters, and it was not until the major commands understood the status of the National Guard, that the legal issues needed to be addressed. The President had declared a National State of Emergency, but did that free up active duty military units? Could the President authorize such an event? The question and the answer had been given in countless training scenarios, but this was different. The concept of civilian Law Enforcement being overwhelmed seemed surreal. Some Commanders didn't wait for guidance. Units were tasked to secure the area surrounding their locations, and that would become the area where the military would provide some level of support. It was said an area of over 400 thousand people was established near Lackland Airforce Base in San Antonio Texas. In the end, the concept of "safe-zones" did take place, but they didn't last.

### A Deeper Panic:

The official notification of the detonation in Gaza came to the public by AM radio. State Emergency Operation Centers were notified given each of them had a FEMA team attached, and each team had a closed communications network with D.C. The public had only one question on their minds, was this the beginning of a larger attack? That was the question everyone wanted an answer to. Up until that point, people had some sense of safety. Yes, the situation in the US was bad, but the fighting was only in the Middle East, and the major nations of the world seemed to be avoiding a larger conflict. But with this event, no one was sure of anything. The fear had been a conflict involving Israel and Iran could lead to the use of nuclear weapons, and that fear reached a fever pitch once Israel and Iran exchanged long-range missiles.

The camps that had been set up outside major military installations heard of the attack by way of rumors spreading from the installation. Alerts were heard broadcast over base-wide intercom systems, and the sudden movements on the bases caused a flowing wave of panic throughout the camps. Many understood that if a nuclear war were starting, military sites would be a primary target. People began to leave the only way they could, on foot. The bases themselves were far too occupied with the information to react to what was taking place in the camps. Within hours, most of the camps were empty, and the US military was powerless to provide any level of support to the people who had left.

In the camps, people had a feeling of safety. Those that had gathered in them were from every walk of life. Wealth knew no value in a nation that had all but stopped financial transactions. Weapons had been secured, and those that would not agree to this requirement had been asked to leave. The level of panic in the nation had not been matched by an equal level of violence. As bad as things had become, many still understood the value of order. Cities had been the exception, but the geographical areas of cities meant the higher levels of violence were confined to small areas. Up to that point, to avoid real violence, people had to avoid large cities. With the news of the nuclear detonation, people became far more desperate, and desperation quickly turned to violence. People were no longer looking for help. They believed they were trying to survive an event they felt sure was coming. It was only a matter of time before the nuclear strikes took place in the US, and that was a perception that spread faster than any form of official communications. Day to day life had fallen to an even lower level. Those that had tried to live by what they believed were acceptable became consumed with thoughts of survival. Nothing was for certain anymore, and hope seemed a lost dream.

### Cyber Events:

The impact of the larger cyberattacks came without any official word. Announcements from the US capital had slowed to the point some of the FEMA teams began to question if DC truly had and understanding of what was happening. Suddenly, those that had been able to utilize the sporadic internet found no connectivity at all. All commercial wireless networks no longer functioned. Social Media workarounds were gone. Many of the AM radio transmissions had stopped. Power across the nation was minimal and typically localized to smaller areas with privately-owned power grids. Remote parts of the nation had power, but those that lived there had no capability to distribute what they had. Drinking water and wastewater plants were shut down. Those that could run them no longer came to work, or the lack of power made operating them impossible. Potable water became a real issue across the nation, and that issue alone resulted in immeasurable violence. Without the consistent flow of any level of information, people simply quit looking for any guidance. Most began to understand they were on their own, truly on their own.

### *The Saudi Event:*

The nuclear event in Saudi Arabia went nearly without notice. People were too occupied with finding a manageable environment, and as such, they paid little attention to more bad news. Those that were still near the military installations were aware of the second event, but the information was useless to them, and they had decided it was better to risk the military site being attacked than it was to try and find support somewhere else.

### *Korea:*

It was the event in Korea that created the next wave of panic. Up until that point, the war had been confined to the Middle East except for some actions in locations the public was not aware of. Seoul proved the public's greatest fear. The war was spreading. How and why the event in South Korea took place was unimportant. The reality was, the war was no longer just in the Middle East. Activity inside the military bases reached a new level. All across the country, units were seen leaving, but the process looked much different. Those who lived near these installations were used to seeing large convoys of commercial trucks hauling heavy combat vehicles. People used to seeing trains pulling into the base and large lights illuminating marshaling areas all night long, as units loaded their equipment onto the trains. That did not happen this time. Some of the units quickly departed aboard military aircraft. These units were capable of deploying with minimum civilian support. The large majority of the US Army could not move in such a fashion. For the first time in their lives, people observed combat vehicles leaving the bases on their own. It began nearly twelve hours after the nuclear attack on Seoul, and once it started, it lasted for hours. Where were they going and why? Those questions would not be answered officially. Again, rumors played a major role in making the public's perceptions become a reality. The US Military was deploying, and those units that could not be loaded traditionally were going to convoy to a designated location on the coastline. All of this could only mean one thing to the civilian population. The US was going to war, a war much larger than they had ever thought was possible. The process of moving the military to the point of demarcation had been lost. The forces of the US would have to execute this process on their own, and that was something they were not prepared for. The reality was, their attempts would never factor into the fight.

*Juarez:*

By the time of the nuclear detonation in Juarez, some level of emergency broadcasting had been reestablished, at least at the FEMA Team level. State government had been reduced to a few key and essential members and just about everything at the state level was taking place inside their Emergency Operations Centers. What situational awareness they had was limited to the communities with the ability to communicate with the state Emergency Operations Center. Shortwave radios had been a critical asset at the local level of government. Organized violence was responded to, but only to the level of dispersing those that were taking part. When word of the destruction of El Paso came in, it was no longer just the public that believed a nuclear war was at hand. State and local government believed a larger war was taking place.

The description of what had taken place in Juarez and El Paso matched what had happened in the Middle East and South Korea. It was verified those attacks were ground-based detonations and the National Command Authority was sure they were not the work of a major world power. The states were informed it had been Iran that was responsible, and the nation of Iran, no longer existed. Many states began the process of informing the communities they could contact. The message was simple; the crisis was nearly over, and the fear of a larger nuclear war was gone. Not everyone believed that the statement was true, but they desperately wanted to. What the states were not told, was how Israel had reacted. They were told Iran no longer functioned as a nation, but they were not told why. An explanation as to the event in South Korea was not given, and that was because the states didn't care. The questions of why and how didn't matter to the states. What mattered was how soon real, tangible help would arrive?

### From Bad to Worse:

In every part of the US, the events of the past several days seemed to destroy all sense of time. People were no longer sure if it was Tuesday or Sunday. What day of the week it was no longer mattered. Time was now divided between daylight and darkness. During the day, people continued to search for the essentials, but at night, that became a time not just of desperation, but fear. All anyone knew, was that sometime after the fourth day, all communications once again disappeared. Battery operated radios had gone dead. Most had not thought of the concept of conserving battery life and had listened to whatever news they could find for hours at a time. Many people observed the atmospheric detonations over parts of the US, and the fear of the war growing worse was undeniable. Some had heard the Iranian story given by the government, but most had not. What people did understand was that things were getting worse, much worse.

In large areas of the US, electrical-based systems stopped with the onset of the EMP events. People were not aware of the devastating impact of China's "Reset" attack. All they knew was those that had functioning electrical devices, suddenly had nothing. Organizations that had been able to provide some level of support were now as helpless as the people who relied on them. The war was raging, but to the civilians in the US, it could not get much worse. Even the FEMA Teams assigned to states saw a large portion of their communications capabilities become inoperable. Although plans had been developed for an EMP event, and this resulted in large quantities of replacement equipment being stored in protected casings, the ability to communicate with the American people was ineffective. Other federal networks were hardened for such an attack, but the distribution was limited to governmental operations, predominately at the federal level. The result was a general population that was now completely without news or guidance. China had entered the war, and its primary target was the US's ability to communicate. Even the US military had a temporary, limited network.

By the end of the fifth day, the overall health of the US population was in question. Some had gone more than two days without water, and those who were dependent on medical treatment had no idea where to find such resources. Many local hospitals were still functioning but at a very reduced level. Supplies of common medical items, especially medications, were running extremely low. Most major medical facilities kept an average of five days of fuel. Without any organized resupply process taking place, even the large Hospitals began to falter. Patients in Intensive Care status were the first to die. People removed their children from maternity wards as word spread the Hospitals were losing power. They didn't know where to take their children, but they had to try.

Hospitals' staffs were powerless to control who was seeking help. Local Law Enforcement had initially given these locations priority, but as other locations became the target of unrest, the little protection the Hospitals had, left.

It is estimated that over 100 million US citizens were displaced in the first week of the war. Where this estimate came from is unknown, but it seems to have been attributed to some level of FEMA reporting shortly after the conflict's end. As bad as the situation had become, almost everyone understood that without ample food and water, the number dead would rise dramatically. People were completely unprepared for the visual shock of what was taking place. In the first few days, the dead were limited to areas where violent clashes had taken place or individual acts of murder. Attempts to collect the dead had taken place mainly in the areas where large scale violence had occurred. The US public was accustom to seeing death on the news or the internet. School shootings had been one of the most emotional events the nation dealt with, post-September 11th, 2001, but no one in the US was prepared for what they would encounter. The sick were dying, but in locations that were not visible to most of the public. It was the sight of the dead and knowing there was no intention of dealing with them, that was impossible to comprehend. Incidents that had taken place at stores or gas stations became so common; the local government was unable to respond to every event. If anything caused a higher level of panic, it was ordinary people seeing the results of raw violence. The visual impact of the unattended dead was catastrophic to everyone who encountered the nightmare.

Those that chose to leave their homes were limited by what mode of transportation they had available. For the first several days, many had vehicles, but the major roadways had become so congested after the first nuclear event, many simply ran out of gas sitting in line. Some had found ways to avoid major roadways, but the fuel along those routes was extremely limited, and again, it resulted in many of them running out of fuel. The dispersed population of most major Cities never made it more than twenty to thirty miles away from where they began. The concentration of people needing food and water was instantly overwhelming, and without drastic federal support, the situation became just as bad as the areas the people had left.

### Nuclear strikes in the US:

Few if anyone was aware of the attack on Hawaii. Again, states were made aware of what was taking place, but the information passed by the FEMA teams did nothing but create a new level of panic. From the state's standpoint, Hawaii proved the federal government was wrong. The War was not limited, and the threat of a true nuclear war was real. When the next series of nuclear events took place, no warning was given by the US National Command Authority. Again, states learned of the second series of attacks, but this time, the level of information was even more ambiguous. Who was struck? What cities, and was it over? None of these questions were answered. Several of the states that had locations attacked were not informed. Hawaii, Texas, California, Missouri, Virginia, New York, and Washington, were the states that had suffered the brunt of the attacks. Other locations of strategic value had also been attacked, but the population density near them provided a limited human impact. The issue that the state's leadership could not get an answer on made everything that had happened seem far worse. The question of, " Was it over," would go unanswered.  For those who were near the impact areas, the nightmare was far more real than the rest of the nation realized. The so-called, "Walking Wounded" numbered in the tens of thousands and there was little support for any of them. People understood the danger of being near the struck locations, and they also knew the danger based upon the prevailing winds. As bad as things had become, going towards the blast zones was exactly what many people did. Those who had little or nothing to offer the injured attempted to do something, knowing full well the reality they faced.

At the time of the strikes, the nation's roadways were unmanageable, and areas that were close to population centers were so littered with vehicles, open movement was nearly impossible. With the news of the nuclear attacks, those that had not fled the areas they lived in, who still had vehicles with fuel, began to form another exodus. Their confidence in the ability to ride out the event where they were, was gone. This segment of society was more prepared for what had taken place, but once they began to move away from areas they had been secure in, their advantage was greatly reduced. Most were armed, and most had supplies. Supplies that were in high demand and the visual impact of others seeing them with vehicles that worked made them prime targets for desperate people. Local officials, especially Law Enforcement members, made up the nucleus of many of these new groups. Some level of order was maintained inside the groups, but the ability to take in additional members was extremely limited. Many of these more capable groups relocated to chosen remote locations. Locations they had decided upon. Locations that they knew would provide them a far better chance of survival. Trust was a difficult topic for anyone that was not known to the groups before they began their movements. This phenomenon of "grouping" had actually been underway even before the conflict's start. The reality was, the nation had divided along the lines many had feared would take place in a true national crisis; those that could fend for themselves to some extent, and those that did not. That became the new normal for most of the US population. The ones that couldn't predominantly came from large cities and nearby rural areas. Those that had some level of capability came from the more rural areas and locations most considered, remote.

# CHAPTER EIGHT: THE FIRST SIX MONTHS / POST CONFLICT.

*Estimating the damage:*

The war had been over for days, but most of the people in the US had no idea. Most had no way of knowing and word that the fighting had stopped took time to spread. Many who heard the news didn't believe it. The whole event had taken place so quickly, trying to understand information coming from any form of government was overwhelming for most. The essentials for survival were far more important than receiving information about a war no one understood. The US population was in survival mode, and issues were getting worse. The reality was, news the attacks had stopped had little impact on a stunned and demoralized population.

The US government had developed a complex plan for Initial Assessment Operations, more commonly known as "IAO." The initial concept IAO was designed for was a post-nuclear attack. The purpose was to give the federal government a snapshot analysis of the severity of such an attack. Because it was developed as an "initial" /Snapshot/assessment, a great deal of detailed information would not be collected. Critical issues such as power, roadway accessibility, water, and food supplies were given priority. Radiation levels and contamination based on weather patterns rounded out this initial assessment. This collection process was based upon several levels of support from both federal, state, and local organizations. FEMA was the government's lead for this process, but the military had been tasked to conduct the same level of analysis as an alternative. It was the military that was given the task of conducting, IAO. Military installations had maintained a robust communications capability and the geographical disbursement of these locations made them the priority for getting the needed information back to DC. This proved more difficult on the East Coast, given several military facilities were struck.

It was not just the US population that doubted the conflict was over. Although the agreement had been reached with the Russians, both the nation's militaries had to remain in a war footing for weeks to come and because of this, it took several days for the order to conduct the assessment process. Twenty Teams were formed based upon their location and capabilities. Team makeup had been a very detailed process, but that had been in the development phase. What was actually put into operation was regular military members who may or may not have had some level of expertise in the areas they were going to evaluate. That decision was made based upon the fact the evaluation process had been simplified and placed in a checklist format. Locations that needed to be analyzed had been mapped by the US Department of Homeland Security in great detail. The whole IAO process became a matter of going to those locations as quickly as possible. The military was still able to provide team members with subject matter expertise in the areas of power production and water production, so when the initial reports on these two areas came in, the concern inside the federal government grew dramatically.

Within five days, the military initial IAO reports were completed. Hope had been based upon the fact a limited number of warheads had struck the US. That hope was crushed once the reports were compiled. The electrical infrastructure of the US had been devastated. Between the EMP event and the cyber-attacks, less than 10 percent of the nation's power production was operational. Several teams had reported seeing signs of electrical operations but on a very limited level. Most were thought to have been coming from portable generators. Two days after the reports were reviewed, a satellite mapping process took place over the US. That image confirmed what the teams discovered. Most of the US was in the dark.

Without power, the capability to produce potable water was nearly impossible, and in fact, the IAO teams found no working water production. As the government had always feared, the lack of power had led to the lack of water and the lack of food. The US was incapable of providing the two most basic functions, food, and water. FEMA contingency stockpiles could not be transported, and even if they were, it was enough for an estimated five million people, for less than ten days. The process had been designed to rely upon Just in Time Vending after several days. That vending process could not take place.

Each IAO team was given the additional task of making contact with state leadership, with a priority given to those states having the least amount of contact. Team movements were conducted by rotor-wing support and the arrival of such assets at state emergency operation centers was a dramatic event. After several days of executing this task, it was decided more robust packages would be sent to conduct these contact missions. Assessment was still the primary goal, but the process was taking too long, and request for communications support was overwhelming. Within a week of these additional contact teams being sent, a much better picture of the status of the US began to take shape.

States had varying levels of awareness of their status. Some states, such as Texas had a working communications process that was robust. One advantage the military assessment teams discovered was the coordinated usage of shortwave radio networks. Texas was one of the states that had developed a detailed Shortwave radio program that allowed the state emergency operations center to have communications at a level the federal government had not anticipated. Another real advantage that several states had tapped into was the Army Military Auxiliary Radio System or MARS for short. This concept had been around for decades and is centered on providing greater capabilities to states and state agencies. The equipment was military hardware, and the program had been adopted in many states. The concept of shielding this equipment had been supported by many of the assisted agencies, and that proved to be critical to all involved. It soon became clear; some states had a much more robust ability to assess their overall status than the federal government realized.

### Shelters at Military Facilitates:

It was quickly discovered how sensitive the initial contact process would become. Within a few days of the end of the war, people once again began to gather at major military installations. It was there they learned the war was over and it was also there they believed the US government would provide them with whatever they needed to survive. Major military organizations were still in a war footing, and the amount of additional supplies that could be distributed to the large gatherings was extremely limited. These facilities were not designed nor equipped to become large shelter operations for the American public. Again, the idea of keeping these civilians in some level of shelter support was a concept most Installation Commanders knew they couldn't support effectively, but the alternative was against everything they stood for. Discussions with their higher headquarters centered around two topics. What was the individual unit's capability, given the environment they all were in, and what was the status of the civilian camps at their location? This phenomenon of people gathering at military sites was taking place down to the individual National Guard Armory level. The federal government had been virtually nonexistent since the beginning of the war, but the American people never gave up on the one institution they knew would never give up on them. Two weeks after the war was over, it was clear, the US military would make up the backbone of the nation's attempt to stabilize.

After the initial IAO task was complete, the federal government began to put together a plan to address emergency issues such as food and drinkable water. Many of the standard plans developed by the US Department of Homeland Security, FEMA, and the states, would need to be adapted, based upon the status of many support functions. States were provided guidelines on processes to create drinkable water. As this guidance was taking place, the federal government began to realize, states were capable of verbal guidance, but limited physical support. In reality, people understood what needed to be accomplished. As an example, boiling water from streams or other water sources produced some level of relief. The federal government had underestimated the resiliency of the US public, and that would not be the last time that situation became evident.

### Support issues in the First Month:

Nearly a month after the war, the US population was still completely dysfunctional. Production of just about any item was not taking place. The stabilization of the civilian population was the priority, but that task was still overwhelming. The nation's power grids were not functioning, and the reality was, it would be years before regional power was possible. The mortality rate was climbing at an uncontrollable speed. The elderly and those dependent upon advanced medical support continued to make up the bulk of the deaths. At first, the process of managing the number of dead was too complicated. Traditional funerals were impossible to achieve. Not only were the numbers too high, but the resources required didn't exist. Dedicated areas were numerous, given the transportation of the dead was not possible. People understood the dangers of decaying bodies, and in many areas, burning became an acceptable process.

Those pockets that had found some level of stability became more and more reluctant to take on additional members. Limited resources meant limited capabilities. Some of the largest shelter camps continued to be located near military installations. As the federal government began to accept the risk of taking the US military off of a war footing, the ability to expand support operations increased. The wartime reserves of items such as military-grade fuel provided the ability to maneuver into locations that had not been evaluated. Movement of these fuels was accomplished internal to the military and in some cases, adaptable fuel was provided to locations that had functioning electrical output.

The problem became the size of many of the shelter camps. The more people showed up, the more difficult it became to support the location. The process of turning people away was then designed to educate them on the location of the next camp that would be made available. Coordinating the expansion of these camps was under the control of the military by order of the President. The plan called for a controlled handoff to FEMA and other authorities as time went on, but the final decision to do so was completely up to the senior military commander on scene. Law Enforcement inside the camps was under the control of the senior, civilian law enforcement officer, but the military was in direct support to that civilian. As bad as things continued to be, the shelter camps supported by the US military were peaceful for the most part.

*Impact Zones:*

The areas around the impacted locations were made

off-limits to the public. Enforcing that process was completely based upon the US military's ability to allocate forces and equipment to the task. For the first few weeks or months, the military's primary task was the stabilization of the population. If people wished to enter the "Hot Zones," then they most often could. The major cities were uninhabitable. Without power, food, and water, those that traveled into the cities were there to scavenge. People understood the value of US currency was nearly worthless, but they also realized that it would not hold true forever. Those looking to find items of value inside not only the large cities but any location that had been abandon were met with a stern response from authorities. Holding facilities for those that had been caught breaking the law were basic in design, but attempted resistance was met with brute force, typically at the barrel of a gun. A vast majority of the public understood the need for civil order, and those who didn't follow that order found little sympathy. Feeding and providing water to those who were willing to break the law was very unpopular.

Simply put, the American public was short on sympathy for those who broke the law. Cases were heard by a senior law enforcement official or typically someone with a criminal law background. Hard labor was the most common form of punishment, but any offense that resulted in death typically resulted in a quick execution. Documentation of this level of the judicial system was ad-hock at best. The nation was no longer in a position to perform in-depth legal processes. The amount of effort to watch over the abandon areas was minimal. The task of feeding and sheltering people was far more important.

*Winter Concerns:*

The War had begun in late Summer, and the pending Winter was on the mind of all levels of government. FEMA had designed plans for major events that would require the movement of large segments of the population. Possible events such as the New Madrid Fault had required extensive planning based on the loss of infrastructure in a large area. It was this plan the federal government adopted to provide a baseline plan for the pending Winter. Nearly 100 million people would have to be told to move, and some had to begin within a week of the notification. Again, the federal government underestimated the American Public. Those who had lived in the Northern Tier States understood what it would require to stay there for the Winter months. The evacuation process had originally been given as an order, but the federal government soon understood, they had no power or capability to enforce such an order.

The Shelter Camps near military installations would become the processing points for movement. The problem the government did not have a sound answer for, was where to move them? The theory had always been to relocate the required numbers into Southern tier states, but that assumption had been made upon those states being in a position to support such an event. That was not the case, and the Southern States let that be known to the national authorities. The task of moving the US population away from the harsh impacts of Winter could not be accomplished. Within two weeks of the process starting, it was officially stopped. Many people chose to leave, but they did so utilizing their own plans. Groups would move together, and military support was provided if possible. The reality was, most of the people in the states impacted by Winter were going to be there when Winter came.

*Leveraging:*

Manufacturing had stopped at all levels, but the government had begun to gain a better understanding of what materials and equipment were still usable. Items such as fuel in storage, other than storage programmed by the government for emergencies, were identified and the process for making this stored fuel usable was quickly developed. Employees who had worked these locations were requested by the federal government, and it was the state and local government that found many of them. Fuel production was not going to be possible for several years, but the use of fuel that was stored became critical to the nation's ability to find stability. EMP events had destroyed a great deal of the electronics in the nation, but the sheer volume of such items meant that many had survived. A basic list of items was developed, and the process for finding them was put into action.

Power production was the primary goal. Any power producing facility that was still capable of working would be potentially tasked as a shelter location. In essence, the US government had begun a nationwide scavenger hunt. What was out there that could still be utilized was enormous, but the process of getting any of it working again proved to be too much so soon in the struggle to survive.

At first, nuclear powerplants had been identified as potential starting points for power. Most of the plants across the nation had been shut down just prior to the nuclear attacks. The problem became, understanding the right sequence of events required to start the plants and the electricity to do so. A "Cold" nuclear powerplant was not designed to be completely without power. What sounded logical at the conference table turned out to be far more complex than anyone anticipated. The areal survey of all the US nuclear plants had been completed within the first two weeks after the war. The actual assessment teams completed their analysis nearly two months later. It was determined that none of the plants had an acceptable process for a complete restart. The cooling systems were too complex and required very clean power. Secondary electrical starts would be tested on two sites, and both proved to be unsuccessful. The nation's nuclear power capability would not be useable for years to come if at all.

One concept that had been contemplated for years was based upon utilizing the nuclear reactors onboard US military Naval vessels. The idea had even been tested, but in very controlled operations and with limited requirements. The stockpile of fuel for these ships and submarines would ensure the process could continue for years. The issue became how far inland the power could be sent and what systems were in place to actually execute the plan. The Naval facilities in California and Virginia had been destroyed, but several ports were considered usable for the first attempt. Cape Canaveral in Florida was the first location utilized, and it was considered a controlled success. Within a week of this attempt, a Shelter Camp of over 35,000 was established. Many had already been near the facility, given its military support operations, but others were moved to that site with a priority given to unaccompanied children and military family members. The concept was deemed a success, but a more refined plan of where and how to use this capability had to be developed.

Providing power to areas that had limited support capabilities was not the answer. In several instances, the Naval asset was required to supply power to critical military locations. Any area that could utilize this limited power supply had to be close to the coastline. In the end, this concept of power projection had a marginal impact on the crisis at hand.

***Continued Evaluations:***

The evaluation process continued, but the priority remained the stabilization of the civilian population. By the time Winter had taken hold, it was clear the death toll would continue to rise. Satellite imagery showed the vast number of areas where fires were being utilized for heat, but it was also assumed many of the fires were a continuation of dealing with the number of dead. Although it had been three months, the nation was still struggling to stabilize.

***Flu:***

Winter of the first year saw the US living on under 500 calories per day, and the government knew what that would lead to. Starvation had already been taking place throughout the nation, and pandemic disease would not be far behind. Those that became sick with what had once been common events, such as flu, now faced life-threatening issues. Again, the very young and the elderly made up most of the fatalities. The federal government could account for the population status only based on satellite data and information provided by the military locations with shelter camps. Some states had a level of awareness, but that was true of less than a quarter of them. By the end of the third month, many state Emergency Operation Centers were now nothing more than communication relay networks. Their ability to provide or coordinate support was ineffective. Most operations were taking place with little or no knowledge at the state level. The disbursement of military response units had become very refined, and the communications between these units and local pockets of civilians developed its own rhythm.

In the Northern Tier States, Winter provided a new source of drinkable water, Snow. The purification of water sources had limitations, but the large snow levels provided abundant drinkable water. Winter had another advantage over the Southern Tier States. The spread of diseases was greatly reduced. Locations were people became sick with flu-like illnesses, were quarantined. A process called "Social Distancing" had been developed by the Center for Disease Control, CDC, in preparation for pandemic events. This Social Distancing process was understood by many in the medical community, and the implementation of this event was utilized effectively. The problem arose from the fact that communal living had become the norm. Most of the US population had gathered into camps that ranged in size from a dozen or more, up to thousands. The largest camps were the ones near military facilities, but others nearly as large had formed in remote areas. By Winter, data gathered by satellites and overflights had been compiled into a working map of the population, and that allowed the government to focus support. It was this camp process that became the health issue the government had feared. Identifying those with contagious diseases could not happen in a timely enough manner to stop the spread of the illness. Flu was the most common event, and it was later estimated the flu killed over 30 million people that the first year. The global impact of the Flu is still unknown.

### The Health of the Population:

Medical stockpiles were depleted within a month. Contingency kits from CDC were expended supporting the shelter camps near military facilities. Although the US military was no longer on a war footing, a designated percentage of the war trace medical supplies had to be kept aside. The fact the US was no longer in conflict was no guarantee that would hold true soon. The process of Triage became standard practice for any medical event. The individual's age and overall health were the weighted factors in determining the amount of medical resources expended.

Non-prescription drugs had been pillaged in the early days after the nuclear strikes. Even with that limiting factor taken into account, the availability of this level of medication far exceeded prescription products. Simple items such as aspirin, alcohol, and bandages made up the bulk of what was available, but after months of demand, even those items ran out. By the end of the first Winter, any injury would potentially be life threating. Other than the Flu, infection was estimated to be the greatest cause of death.

Food items brought on a new challenge. In the first few weeks, stores and warehouses were the leading suppliers of non-perishable foods. As these locations were depleted, the search for food became an issue of life and death. Some of the smaller gatherings were unable to protect themselves to a level that guaranteed their supplies. People were moved to violence, not because they chose to, but because they felt they had no choice. Rumors of these limited violent events distorted the truth. Paranoia was the cornerstone of daily life, and just the hint of a violent group being near resulted in the smaller shelter camps questioning anyone they came in contact with. Isolation from the rest of the population meant smaller groups had fewer capabilities and limited communications.

One impact the federal government could influence was information. As the shortwave radio networks began to stabilize, the government executed an information operation plan that would prove to relieve the fear of the spreading violence. The message was given the US military was rapidly spreading out across the nation, and anyone that was found to be breaking the law would be dealt with "severely." All communications had this statement embedded, regardless of the topic. The federal government was not able to physically protect everyone, but the perception had the desired impact. That impact seemed to influence those who were truly out to create violence. The sound of aircraft let the people know someone was out there; some level of help was coming.

As encouraging as this plan proved to be, it did not provide relief to the issue of food. The American population had a very small percentage that understood how to find food or prepare it. Few understood what was consumable and what was not. The government did attempt to distribute this information to the public, but in the end, most learned by listening to those around them that did understand the concept. Those that did have the skills to produce food became vital members of any group.

Despite the best efforts of the government, starvation became a reality. By the end of the first month, those that had not consumed more than 200 calories a day, became too weak to travel and susceptible to sickness. As smaller groups found it harder and harder to survive, they began to ban together. The larger groups made up of people who had left; the larger cities were still dysfunctional. The fact they had not traveled far from the major cities made the process of finding them easier for the military. Guidance was given to these groups on how to find food and what level of consumption had to be maintained. The expectations of these larger groups were often dramatic, and this was especially true on the issues of food and water. The Assessment Teams were not able to provide physical support, but what they did provide was hope and reassurance. Instructions on how to survive were effective, but only after the shock of realizing the government was not going to feed and care for everyone they came in contact with. Information was a powerful tool, but reality had to be faced. The US was going to lose millions of additional lives before stability could be reached.

### The Military:

The United States Military became exactly what the American public expected the minute the nation began to sense they were in trouble. It became the backbone of hope, the organization that would calm the nation's fears. When the nuclear attacks took place, the public lost hope. The fear of the war spreading, and the anticipation of further detonations was overwhelming to nearly everyone. Within the first day of the strikes, people across the nation began to hear and see the military moving. Where they were going and what they were doing was not as important as just knowing they were there. The nation would not fail as long as its military was standing.

As invincible as the public believed the military to be, in reality, it was made up of people just like them. Sons, Daughters, Husbands, Wives, Mothers, and Fathers, that is what made up the military. They were citizens in uniform, and they had the same fears as anyone else but, their dedication to duty prevented them from collapsing into the same state of panic that gripped the rest of the nation. Most members were not from the areas where they were stationed. Most had family and loved ones far away. As the conflict grew worse, it was a new experience for everyone in the military. In the past, threats they faced took place far away from home. The concept of loved ones being in danger was new to nearly all of them. When word of the nuclear attacks reached the services, every member had the same questions as the rest of the nation.

Service members were some of the first to know what cities had been struck. New York, DC, Las Angeles, San Diego, and the list continued to grow. Families were being lost. Loved ones all across the nation were in danger, and the process of preparing for war had gone terribly wrong. Units that were accustomed to mobilizing and moving into the fight were sitting still. Members understood the attacks on the World Wide Web had paralyzed most of the units across the country. The nuclear strikes in Europe were directed at US Joint military installations, and that news only added to the fears inside the rest of the nation's military. Preparations for pending strikes had many locations dispersing their equipment and manpower. That act alone began to convince the service members the war was going to get much worse. Families that were stationed at military bases were given instructions on what they should do, but that only inflamed their level of panic. Confusion and hysteria had gripped the nation, and that included the service members. There was one huge difference, discipline. Service members were schooled in the art of discipline, and that would make the difference, but not without challenges the US government was not prepared for.

Within a few days of the nuclear strikes on the US, most units began to realize they were not going to mobilize for some conflict thousands of miles away. They had been told the war was over, but the requirement to maintain a ready status was not lifted. They began to realize they were not going to be called upon to fight, at least not anytime soon. Without the task of preparation for war, the service members turned their minds back to their own issues, family. Family, loved ones, and hometowns, that is where their attention turned to. All had been trained in Nuclear, Biological, and Chemical, NBC, warfare, and they all knew the dangers of the strikes even if their homes had not been directly impacted. Commercial communications had been gone for days, and the status of hometowns and families was impossible to obtain. Those that had loved ones stationed with them were better off, but even then, other family members were far away, and in an environment, they could not control. This was a drastic change not only for the members but for the military as a whole. Loved ones had been killed or were in real danger. They had not truly been trained for such an emotional challenge. For years, the primary enemy was Terrorism and not the threat of nuclear war. Yes, military members knew Terrorism could impact the lives and safety of their loved ones, but the reality was, most never truly believed such isolated events could impact the people they cared for. The realities of nuclear war were simply not embedded in their minds. In the end, the American People were not mentally prepared for a nuclear attack, and neither were the members of the United State's Military.

The War had been over for nearly a month when the first official reports of desertion began to be reported. Although the issue had been taking place from almost the beginning, most Commanders were reluctant to report such events officially. The number of assessment teams was large, but in comparison to the total number of service members, less than 20 percent of the military was actually responding to the event. Deploying large numbers created a logistical support environment and given the limited supply of items already in demand, the missions were tasked to specialized units. Army Rangers, Special Forces, and other smaller organizations were responsible for the initial assessment process. Military Police and highly mobile combat units such as Infantry units, made up the bulk of the follow-on support missions. Units with organic air assets also played a huge role in the response, but again, this was a very limited percentage of the combined force. By the time Winter began to take hold, the percentage had increased dramatically, but the issue of desertions was already taking place.

The events inside the US Navy drew the most attention, and the government knew drastic decisions had to be made. Naval members who had been at sea since the beginning of the war knew two things. One. Without logistical support, their ability to stay at Sea was limited. Two. If they could not stay at Sea and their homeports had been damaged beyond repair, where were they going to go? They knew the country was no longer at war. They knew the US had taken multiple nuclear strikes, and they had no idea what the status was of their families and loved ones. Going home was not just the desire of the crews.

Leadership began to ask when they would be returning home. There was no enemy to prepare for. There was no ability to stay at Sea. The US Navy may have been made up of advanced ships, but the ships were manned by the men and women of the United States, and they could only think of what was taking place back home. They could only imagine what the fate was of those they loved. Keeping these dedicated Warriors away from their crippled homeland was not the answer. Finding a way to bring the Navy home, that was a much more difficult issue. This was the predicament the Senior Military Commanders found themselves in. It was the Commander in Chief that had to give them an answer.

The decision was made. The US Navy would fall back to within 100 miles of the US coastline. Ports were designated for support operations. Twenty-five percent of the US Navy would be left at Sea to protect the nation from the coastlines. The Ballistic Submarines would maintain their positions until they were within twenty percent of their supplies. This plan was full of complex problems, but the decision had been made by the Commander in Chief. The fact of the matter was, the bulk of the United States' intercontinental missile capability was operational, and that was how the nation would protect itself for the immediate future. Every nation in the world was given this warning, but none of them were in a position to threaten the US. The US Navy was coming home, and its resources would be leveraged in the struggle to stabilize the nation.

### Coming Home:

The discussion of the status of the Navy brought about a much larger and far more strategic decision. The United States Military would be utilized to bring home as many US Citizens as possible. Those elements of the military overseas that would not be tasked to support the repatriation of citizens would depart as soon as possible. Equipment that could not be returned to the states would be made inoperable. It was determined that aircraft were a priority, and the amount of fuel utilized from the national stockpile would be allocated to ensure this priority took place. Getting the US citizens and service members home where the mission and all avenues of making that task take place were authorized. Stockpiles of vital supplies would be returned as well, but the priority was the people. Power Projection was no longer a priority for the US. Repairing the nation was the goal, and it would take as many able body men and women as the nation could gather. This process would take months, and the failures were too numerous to track, but at the end of the day, the mission took place.

The leadership of the nation understood one critical issue. A military manned by angry, disgruntled members was a military that would not follow orders. To save the nation, the men and women of the United States Armed Forces had to know they could still do what they had sworn an oath to do, protect the ones they loved. For the first time in over 200 years, the United States would not have a military contingent on foreign land.

By the time the order had been given to return home, the US military communications network was nearly restored. The European Command had the most difficult challenge. Not only had they suffered the greatest losses in the nuclear strikes, but the number of US citizens in Europe was far beyond anything the command could handle. The crisis in Europe was far worse than in the US, and England was just as bad. The decision was made to commandeer any seaworthy vessel in every European port. The goal was to put as many US citizens on those ships and sail them for the US as soon as possible. The crews of these ships were promised US citizenship if they would support the mission. The number of military members who were capable of operating large seagoing vessels were extremely limited, so the support of these ship's crews became vital to the success of the operation.

Contamination and sickness were weighted factors on deciding who would be allowed on the ships. People were informed there would be limited supplies and medical care would be leveraged towards those that had the best chance of survival. These were not encouraging words to the civilians, but the chance to get home was worth every sacrifice they had to make.

Word of this operation spread quickly, and the marshaling locations became an issue. Locations were determined based upon the ability to transport civilians and military members in mass. The identification process was easily accomplished, but the task of turning away those who were not US citizens became the issue. The military had set up processing lines, and once someone was identified as not being a US citizen, they were forcibly removed. There was no room for compromise, and in many cases, these processing locations had violent events. The goal had been to evacuate as many

US citizens as possible and to do so with a sense of urgency, but within a week, the evacuation operation was canceled. It was decided the second round of evacuations would take place sometime in the next few months. This decision was made based upon the inputs of the local commanders at the processing sites. After several days, the number of US citizens was minimal compared to the huge crowds of people simply wanting to go somewhere that might have some level of help. The US military could not save the people of Europe, and they knew many US citizens were still on the continent, but the risk of the whole operation collapsing was too great. European Command estimated that nearly 250,000 US citizens and military members were evacuated. Where they would be taken upon returning home was not decided until many of the ships were already underway.

Yet another crisis arose during this event. The word had spread the US had survived the war. The concept of commandeering ships was not limited to US military operations. Satellite imagery indicated vessels from not only Europe but from the Pacific were heading towards the US mainland. The US was most concerned about the ships coming from the Pacific and the threat of a Chinese event. Communications from the US warned them to stay out of US territorial waters. All of the ships that could reply stated they were transporting refugees and that many Americans were on board. It was decided a processing location would be established at the Mexican port of Ensenada. A contingent from the US military executed this mission, but the goal was to identify any US citizens simply. All others were ordered back onto the ships and advised to sail for some location on the Pacific side of Central or South America. The US was in no position to supply support to anyone other than their own.

By the end of the first six months, the US had accomplished one primary goal; the repatriation of as many citizens as possible. The leadership of the nation also understood an even more important issue, the preservation of loyalty from the United State's Military. Now the question became, how to stabilize the nation. It was the middle of Winter, and the number of deaths was still climbing.

# CHAPTER NINE: END OF THE FIRST YEAR:

*Coal Power:*

Six months had passed, and the US government finally realized just how fragile the nation had become. All the planning for survival and rebuilding that had taken place for decades proved almost completely ineffective in a world that was totally dependent on technology and the World Wide Web. The capability to restart even the most basic manufacturing could not be achieved. Electricity continued to be the crippling issue, and raw materials were not being produced. Several coal-fired powerplants had been the focus of a restart concept, but the loss of integrated systems proved to be the hurdle the government could not overcome. The retooling of these plants would require them to operate without integrated electronics. The parts that were destroyed could be salvaged from other storage locations or manufacturers' previous inventory, but the decision was made to avoid making these plants dependent on equipment that would most likely not be reproducible for years. An older, simpler version of a coal-fired powerplant was the goal, and if successful, the transformation process could be repeated in as many locations as possible. Again, processes that were taken for granted became the stumbling blocks of hope. The level of coal at the plant chosen was estimated to last less than 60 days. The ability to deliver further shipments depended upon the railroad network, and that network was completely inoperable. The ability to load the coal from the mine onto the coal cars was also impossible. The plan became loading and transporting the coal with military engineering equipment. Other trucks were found to be in working order, but the availability of commercial-grade deasil fuel became an additional issue. Even once all of the transportation issues were developed, the long-term reliability of such a plant came into question. The nearest coal mine had a little over one year's supply of deliverable material and the processing of restarting the mine would require a whole new approach. Mining had become a very technological process, but technology was now absent. Again, the concept of mining as it had taken place 100 years ago was the goal. The drills in the mine were shielded from the EMP events, and most were not connected to the internet, and as such, the Chinese cyber events had not impacted them. The problem became the automated removal system in the mine. That was completely dependent on computer technology, and those networks were above ground and plugged into the internet. In the end, the concept of producing power from coal-fired plants was several years away at best.

### Priority of Effort:

The government came to realize most complex processes would have to be redesigned backward to the days of simple human action. The nation would not be moving forward for decades to come. A holistic review of where the nation stood was completed by the end of the first year, and the answer was far worse than even the most pessimistic members of the government feared. The nation was not going to stabilize as a unified body. The ability of the federal government to maintain its geographic boundaries was not possible and would not be for years. Just the issue of retooling a power-plant was going to be limited to certain locations. Delivering such capabilities to areas like the North West or Alaska would not happen. National leadership had concluded all efforts to restore some level of stability would be concentrated into the areas with the highest population density. The East Coast had been struck harder than any other region of the nation, and the issues of contamination made the major cities in that area unlivable. In fact, large cities, in general, were not targeted for any effort by the federal government.

Where the people had fled to became the benchmark. Some of those areas were logical choices to attempt stabilization, but some were not. The most current maps of population locations became the primary tool for decision making. Locations that were far enough South and close to large bodies of inland water were reviewed first. The population within 150 miles of Dallas, Texas had become home to over 20 million people. That is where the government made its decision. A primary effort for stabilization would take place inside this zone. The intent was not to abandon the rest of the nation, but state and local governments would be tasked to take the lead on providing for their locations. The federal government would support them as much as possible, but in the end, most of the rest of the nation was on its own. The federal government would concentrate on the "Dallas Zone" with the concept of building out from there. When this decision was made known to all the states, the response was predictable. Several of the Northern Tier States had no response. The East Coast States protested the loudest, and a few brought up the fact their locations had been where the federal government had sheltered during the war. That was a true statement then.

The reality was, the federal government had moved to other predetermined locations three weeks after the war was over. The was another reality, those who could leave the East Coast region had already done so. Winter and contamination had made much of the countries Eastern Coastline virtually unpopulated. Many smaller pockets of Shelter Camps had been established in the Northern sections of the East Coast, but the Winter there had been so harsh, most had perished. Satellite flyovers confirmed this fact and any additional discussion on the topic of priority of effort was limited. The area that would become, "The Dallas Zone" would receive the maximum effort of the federal government. To most of the nation, the concept of a "Federal Government" was becoming irrelevant to survival.

## *Division:*

The Dallas Zone concept allowed the federal government to maximize its efforts, but even then, just about everything was a challenge. Military facilities were reinforced with most of the forces that had been brought home. Bases that were West of the zone were reduced to a level of support that allowed them to maintain organic operations. In a sense, the US went back to the Outpost mentality. These remote military sites were a combination of all four services. They became critical to state and local authorities, but they were predominantly there to provide support to civilian order. To the greatest extent possible, service members, who were from these areas were selected to cover these locations. This was another attempt to keep the military committed to the concept of serving the nation, but as time went on, this decision proved to be a major factor in the divisional struggle inside the nation.

The commitment to one area of primary effort was controversial not only with state government but at the federal level as well. Although the decision had been made, the efforts to provide greater assistance to other areas never stopped. Federal political leaders were still local in their commitments, and it became apparent assets where being diverted without the proper chain of approval. The unity of effort by the federal government came into question at the highest level. Decisions were not only being ignored, but the falsification of authorization was growing by the day. Four months into the Dallas Zone response, an open challenge to the project was legislated requiring the President to sign an Executive Order. This Order required all support operations to be reported immediately and limiting the authorization for any support mission to the President, The Vice President, The Secretary of Homeland Security and the Secretary of Defense. This decision created a rift inside the federal government, unlike anything any member was prepared for. It was not the recognized Chain of Authority, and both Houses demanded the Executive Order be withdrawn.

Since the end of the war, several Special Temporary Laws, STLs, were enacted, with all of them granting special powers and authorities to federal. At first, the states had little understanding of many of these STLs as they were completely overwhelmed with responding to the ongoing crisis. As the months passed and what seemed to be " The New Normal" began to take hold, some states and local governments began to question many of the emergency laws openly. Virtually none of the STLs had been reviewed by any level of state or local government. Although the argument was made the Council of Governors had been involved from the very beginning, that statement was never verified. The reality was, the federal government had taken possession of all stored fuel as well as control of any interstate support agreements. If a state had something that another state had requested, it had to be approved by a federal review process. Those states that could conduct state to state support were outraged. Between the discourse inside the federal government and the resentment at the state and local level, the seed of a much larger crisis was now planted.

### The Dallas Zone:

As stated before, it had become obvious to the US government the ability to respond to the entire nation was not possible. It was also going to be impossible to rebuild the whole nation for decades to come. The Dallas Zone was the starting point, and the outcome of even that attempt was in doubt.         Once again, the Law of Unintended Consequences became a factor the government was unprepared for. Word had spread of the Dallas Zone. Anyone who could find a way to get there began to try. Within months, the estimated population inside the zone had reached over 35 million. The area had been unable to support the basic needs when it was first discovered, and the increased population made the possibility of managing the area unachievable, and yet, people continued to do everything possible to get there. When the decision was made to control all major roadways into the zone, the issue grew even worse. State governments had no authority over who could and couldn't enter. The zone concept had a huge, geographical issue. The landscape made approaching the zone possible even with avoiding known roadways. Where people were stopped, violence became a reality. At first, the US Military was the enforcement support, but that changed when it became clear people who had risked everything to get to the Dallas Zone were being told they could not enter. There was no recognition of any Federal Law Enforcement Agency by citizens who had not been supported by the federal government for months. The definition of, "Authority" was no longer universal. What people did accept was the guidance of the military. The approach changed when the military leaders tasked with the area around the zone came to the conclusion no one would be turned away. If needed, the zone would be expanded, and the ability to support the expansion would be figured out. This decision was enacted without prior approval, but commanders were authorized to do whatever they needed to keep the people safe. This broad-brush authority was leveraged to the greatest extent possible. The Dallas Zone would become unmanageable until the military came up with a compromise, a compromise that again, was not developed with state or local leadership.

FEMA employees and assets had been placed under the authority of the Regional Military Commanders, and this worked well given many of FEMA's planning teams were made up of retired or prior military members. The change to the Dallas Zone operation was to move its physical location away from a circular, geographical concept; a concept most had no idea where it had come from other than someone drawing a ring around Dallas. The new Dallas Zone was based upon Highway 20 and Highway 35, with the Northern boundary set at the Red River. It's Sothern boundary was set at the city of Waco. Its Eastern boundary was set at the city limits of Dallas, and it's Western boundary set at the city limits of Ft Worth. This new zone would have logistical operations at DFW Airport, Carswell Naval Air Station in Ft. Worth and Ft Hood to the South. The Shelter Camp that had been supported by Ft. Hood would remain, but its priority would change.

The statements about the Dallas Zone would now be controlled by a reviewing group headed by the Secretary of Homeland Security who reported directly to the Vice President. A public information campaign was developed that would spell out the requirements for traveling to the Zone. It was clear the government had to ensure the rest of the nation understood the extreme limitations this area would have, and life might have been just as manageable where people were currently located. Information Operations was a concept the US Military had grown far more capable of performing than their Civilian Leadership. Managing the expectations of anyone who would hear of the Zone became vital to controlling the operation. The government was making an attempt to stabilize a slice of the nation, and if that process failed, the survival of the US, as a truly unified body, would be lost. What never was realized or at least accepted, was the fact that in the process of setting up the Dallas Zone, much of the nation had given up on the very concept the government was trying so desperately to save, the "United" States.

### Government to the Zone:

The US government had been in an emergency configuration two days before the nuclear strikes. The plan had called for a dispersed government, with key members in predetermined locations. Initially, none of those locations were within what would become the Dallas Zone. By the time the decision had been made to make the zone the priority of effort, it was also decided all key government operations would be relocated there as well. As the states became aware of this decision, the perception of abandonment became even more widespread. No amount of assurances was able to ease the growing tensions between the federal government and those states that believed they were on their own. Western States made up the majority of those who accused the federal government the most, and that trend continued as the Dallas Zone concept matured.

### Tension inside the Zone:

How people would be provided for, and what resources would be made available to them became a point of contention inside the zone not just with the public, but between federal and state leadership. Although the nation had been placed under several federal emergency laws, state and local governments still felt obligated and authorized to be involved in the process of providing support and guidance. The ability to ensure every level of leadership was constantly made aware of decisions inside the zone was not possible. Communications had been restored to a level where most government agencies could coordinate activities, but what was communicated and how became the weak link.

As the Dallas Zone became sectorized, local leadership increasingly complained about the lack of prior notification or coordination. To them, the federal government was deciding key issues and simply notifying state and local leaders after the fact. The "Joint" decision making bodies that had been agreed to, was not taking place, or at least that was the perception from all the non-federal government actors. Communities, Cities, and Counties were being changed, and their local leaders seemed to have little input. To them, they had held their own after the attacks and the overwhelming authority of the federal government was becoming troublesome not only to state and local government but to the people who had lived in the area before the war. Everyone understood the goal of establishing an area the nation could rebuild from, but the decision-making process seemed one-sided. The influx of people only exacerbated the issue. As the government began to gain control of the process of moving people into the zone, state and local leaders, especially local leaders, simply observed where they were placed.

The land was designated for Shelter Camps, and very little notification was provided. The event at Lake Benbrook was not the first incident of confrontation, but it was the issue that became the rallying cry for those who did not wish to bend to every command by a federal government simply. The area around Lake Benbrook had become an ad-hock shelter area shortly after the war. By the time the Dallas Zone concept was developed, nearly 50,000 people were already sheltering around the lake. The government's advanced party that was sent to the lake had made contact with what they believed to be several smaller camps in the area, but they incorrectly determined the complex network of camps that had been coordinated by local authorities and landowners. The first real indication the government was beginning to move over 150,000 people into the lake area, was the installation of a water purification unit from the US Army. When the unit was approached by a group from one of the camps, they were informed the government was building a camp at the lake. The unit commander had little information other than what his task was, but he did provide the group with a point of contact. It took three days for the locals to get in touch with the federal authority provided by the commander. What they were told became the point of contention. Everyone in a designated area around the lake would need to be properly identified and vetted prior to being allowed into the "Benbrook Section." This Benbrook Section had been developed with no input for those who had been living near the lake. The local group advised the federal officials it would be difficult to get the word to everyone in the area. That was when they learned the plan called for a form of identification. A federal identification process would be implemented throughout the Dallas Zone. If anyone were found to be without the proper identification, they would be removed to a marshaling area and processed back into the zone. To the federal government, this was the only way they could account for what part of the population they were attempting to support. The other reality they were attempting to address was the loss of the US border with Mexico and Canada. Identification had become not only a priority but a necessity. The process not only confirmed US citizenship, but it identified the overall status to include health and capabilities. What the locals inside the zone understood, was the fact the federal government was categorizing the civilian population. This process would lead to events the federal government was unprepared for.

### Violent Outbreaks:

The public's trust in the federal government was at historic lows even before the war. Areas such as the counties around the Dallas Zone were known for their independence and distrust of the government at many levels. When the process of reidentifying those around the Lake Benbrook sector was in its fourth day, a clash took place that sent shockwaves through federal leadership. The teams that were assigned to make contact with identified camps were fired upon and the aircraft they were in, an Army UH60, was shot down. Word of these teams had been making its way across shortwave radio and by word of mouth from the moment they began. The government was not able to monitor the inter-camp communications, and so the fear of resistance to what they were trying to accomplish was not realized until it was too late. The attack on the processing team changed all of that. A few reports of violence had been reported, but nothing like the attack that changed everything. For three days, an attempt was made to make contact with as many of the camps as they could, but this was accomplished by radio. The government even dropped pamphlets in an attempt to explain the process and why it was taking place.

In many cases, it worked, but the configuration of the pro-cessing teams changed, and it was that changed that spread an even more destructive rumor. Each team now had an armed escort. Even though many of these camps were organized to the point of having local and state law enforcement members assigned to them, the teams continued to be armed. The num-ber of people who refused the federal ID process grew, and the rumors of those resisting grew even faster. To those who had always warned of a federal government attempting to take control of the population, this identification process was all the proof they needed. To a federal government that was a shell of its former self, the idea of the population resisting what needed to be done was unfathomable and in the end, un-acceptable. As exhausted as the civilian population was after the war, the federal government was just as exhausted. Over-reaction was to be the mistake both sides made, and it would lead to a federal government in an even deeper crisis.

Word of the events of Lake Benbrook spread not only throughout the Dallas Zone but throughout the nation. West-ern states who were all but ignored became even more con-vinced they were on their own, and that led to a general feel-ing that they had no accountability to a federal government. Other states in the North and East were coming to the same conclusion. Buy the time the stories of further conflicts with what would later be named as "Resistance Groups" became widespread; it was clear the federal government was going to take a hard line on such events. Those state and local law en-forcement members who were still attempting to keep social order at their level notified federal contacts of large groups leaving their camps. It was understood those that were leav-ing were unwilling to abide by the identification and process-ing programs. What this meant to the federal government was the fact that "Resistance Groups" were forming around the Dallas Zone, and that was unacceptable. The issue became, how to deal with this growing crisis. Again, it cannot be emphasized enough just how dysfunctional the federal government had become. Not a single federal agency was operating at any level even close to the prewar era: the FBI and the National Intelligence Agencies where hollow shells of their former selves. The ability to properly anticipate and calculate the impact of these resistance groups was not within the capabilities of the US government. The result would be an over-reaction to the problem, an overreaction that would make the issue far worse. The military was tasked to track the major groups in and around the Dallas Zone, but that task was far more difficult than even the military could execute. As word spread of these groups being tracked, the definition changed to "hunted." It was this rumor of people who simply didn't want to be part of the identification process being hunted that made things go from bad to worse. The vast majority of the people in the Dallas Zone complied with the government's program, but they were also sympathetic to those who did not. The majority believed, if someone wished to opt-out of the program, they should be allowed to. The problem became when those same people were unwilling to leave the Dallas Zone area. The government's heavy-handed approach made even its supporters angry. What every functional resistance movement needed was a base of support, and that was exactly what took place. Within a month of the Lake Benbrook event, a full-fledged resistance movement was underway, and it had a national following. What the federal government was not aware of, was the level of support this movement was provided, even by those who the government counted on the most.

### Insurrection:

The federal government's concept of how to salvage the nation was far from perfect, and the ability to have an inclusive development team was nearly impossible. Communications had been established with every state in the nation, but the needs of each state on their own were overwhelming. The priority of effort would result in many parts of the nation feeling left out or abandon, and everyone who developed the plan understood that reality. It was this lack of inclusion that created events even the federal planners had not anticipated.

The US Military had reestablished multiple locations west of the Mississippi River for the primary purpose of providing confidence to state and local authorities as well as the general population. These locations were not capable of offsetting overwhelming requests for support, but they did provide a central point of coordination for processing those requests. When the Dallas Zone concept was made known to other locations in the nation, the leadership of these military facilities became the central point of anger from civilian state and local leadership. Most had not been briefed on the concept. The nation had decided on a plan, and that plan could not provide for everyone that was still alive. The military installations had their own questions as well, and the answers did not come promptly. The priority of effort being the Dallas Zone led to other military locations receiving less support than anticipated. This was a universal concern of all most all of the commanders. They understood the concept of sacrifice, but what level of sacrifice would be made? The lack of planning on the government's part prevented a comprehensive plan from being implemented in the rest of the nation. It was soon clear, even large parts of the US Military had developed the same perception as many of them civilians. Support was going to be limited at best. That perception only made a bad situation worse.

The US had gone to war, but not like any war its members were prepared for. The actual number of troops who were engaged in the conflict was less than 10 percent. Other than the forces in South Korea, the US Army was not involved. The mobilization process was just underway when the ability to do so became impossible. A military that was equipped to go to war and sustain itself for months was not utilized. Some of the primary installations where these resupply materials were stored had been lost in the nuclear strikes, but the vast majority of it was still available. Many of these sites received the order to transport critical medical supplies to the zone. It was this reprioritization issue that brought the whole topic of abandonment to a boiling point. Areas that were receiving little support were now informed that many of the key items the US military had at their disposal were being tasked to move into the Dallas Zone. From the public's view, what little they were getting from the government was being taken away. This perception was the strongest in the Western and Midwestern states. Although many of the people in this part of the nation were able to find a new level of existence, their ability for long-term survival was still very much in question. Just the rumor of the military taking assets away,\ became more fiction than fact. Rotor wing support was one of the most visible items the public become comfortable with seeing. For months they had been used to transport vital supplies to areas that had sprung up as Shelter Camps. Because of the fear of attack, many of these Camps were in remote areas and once they had been identified, supporting them was a challenge. Just seeing the military flying in gave the public a feeling of calm but, by the time the Dallas Zone project was underway, the inventory of these assets was less than half. The process of keeping such a large fleet operational was not duplicated at all military locations.

Phase maintenance was a concept that required most of the fleets to be transported. Those maintenance locations were in areas that were severely impacted by the war. This fact was compounded by the reality that the electronic items needed to service the fleets of Helicopters were mostly inoperable. By the time the analysis of what it would take to support the Zone was completed, it was understood what would be tasked for reassignment. Each military Main Operating

Base, M.O.B, would be left with three rotor-wing assets. This formulary was not based on any level of operational analysis. It was simply an arbitrary number the government came up with given the projected lifespan of the remaining aircraft. With no manufacturing taking place and limited functional military flight facilities, once again, prioritization became the primary issue. In many areas, the decision was made to move the remaining assets without prior notification. Rotor wing support would be drastically reduced, and the shelter areas were given no explanation.

The process of reallocation didn't just take place inside the military. FEMA and several other federal agencies were equipped with support materials that would also be moved. The nation had gone a year without the production of pharmaceuticals and the shelf life of many items were coming to expiration. Contingency plans had provided for temporary production of vital drugs such as penicillin, but that concept was extremely limited as well as based upon only a short-term disruption of day to day production processes. The capabilities of temporary production were moved into the zone as well. The rumors of other, non-military assets being moved to an area where they would not support the people who were hearing of the event continued to make matters worse. Not only was this shifting of national assets not well received by the public, once it was actually underway, the government discontinued briefings on the whole process. The struggle was to establish the Dallas Zone, but the impact of accomplishing that struggle became a much larger issue.

The first identified report of violence came from the MOB near Ellsworth Airforce Base. That area had been given a much higher priority given the location of nuclear assets. The nuclear leg of the Triad had become the primary defense of the nation and as such, assets were provided above what was allocated to other facilities. Ellsworth had not been struck during the war, and the population around the base had increased to over 200,000 civilians. The installation had a very good working relationship with the appointed civilian leadership, but the flow of information seemed to be the incident that set events into motion. Nearly half of the military's medical assets were tasked to move by air, but the movement would be what the military termed, "unaccompanied." The Ellsworth MOB Commander notified the civilian leadership that medical support would be greatly reduced. That announcement resulted in a large protest at the MOB's main gate. Civilians were still required to live outside the actual installation, but accommodations were such that up until this event, no one there seemed to mind. When word was given that medical patients would be moved from the installation out into the facilities that had been built in the civilian section, the protest turned violent. It was reported that shots were fired from the civilian groups at the team that was sent to address the protest. That team was made up of both military and civilian leadership. By the time the situation report was sent to leadership in the Dallas Zone, the event had gone on for several hours.

In the months after the war, events like the one at the Ellsworth MOB had taken place all across the nation, but the severity and frequency had dropped off dramatically after the first few months. This event was different, but what made that true was not clear until several days after it had taken place. As hard as both sides of the event had tried to stop the violence, the event continued to spiral out of control. The initial report indicated that shots had been fired by several unknown members who were mixed in with the civilian protestors. Three officials on the de-escalation team sent to address the crowd was killed. The next report stated the three that had been killed had been shot from a distance and the attack seemed planned. It had been the policy for all such events to be dealt with locally, and the ability to do otherwise was unrealistic. It was for this reason the next several reports on the event received no reaction. The national event log that was kept by the government showed the event taking place, but it had not risen to the level of true concern. Two days later, a follow-on report provided input that did gain the attention of the national government. Not only had the event taken place with what seemed a deliberate attack on the de-escalation team, but a day afterward, two joint, civilian and military patrols were ambushed inside the civilian Shelter Camp. This had happened before, but again, it had been several months and not with the level of coordination this event seemed to have. The casualties were brought back to the main base with five killed and three wounded. Again, the attack came from a distance, and the actual attackers were never identified. This event resulted in a much larger sweep of the area with the intent of disarming the Shelter Camp. The law's government had enacted after the war had not changed. Civilians were allowed to own and carry weapons, but they could not do so inside the camps.

All of the Shelter Camps in the US had their own mix of cultural and demographic differences based on the region where the camps were set up. This held particularly true in the North West. People in that region of the nation had a long history of independence, but a deep commitment to the US Military. The day to day life in the Ellsworth MOB was one of the more stable in the nation. The fact that an event took place, such as the one that was reported, worried those who had long feared the stress placed upon the public would once again manifest itself in violence or worse, resistance. After the war, most violent events were based upon desperation or fear. Few were based on anger or resentment of the government. Some in the federal government had warned that resistance would become a real threat as the people began to realize the nation would not be able to return to any level of acceptable life. When the decision was made to implement the Dallas Zone, those that had been predicting resistance once again made their thoughts known. When the event at the MOB took place, their theories became viable, and options for response had to be reviewed.

### Ellsworth MOB Event:

The event at the Ellsworth MOB may or may not have been the first, but it was the first of its kind the government reacted to. Up until that time, the struggle was so overwhelming, being proactive at any level above local or state law enforcement was not documented. This one was different in that enough time had passed; the government was beginning to believe a proactive stance to stabilizing the nation was underway.

Local authorities and the military had come to the conclusion the attacks were the work of a group that had moved into the area from an unknown location. Again, the concept of nomadic armed groups was not new. It was the follow-on analysis that alarmed both the leadership at the MOB and the federal government. Rumors throughout the MOB spread the group was made up of military members. These members were said to be a few who had been ordered to relocate to the Dallas Zone in support of the equipment being moved from Ellsworth. The ability to validate if this rumor was true or not was not possible. The people had spent a year simply trying to survive; they didn't have the energy to question rumors. With that, the rumor of military members revolting at that location grew for days and weeks afterward. The fact of the matter was, the US Military estimated they had over 25 percent of the force that had simply walked away after the war.

Two weeks later, a convoy delivering a generator to a local school that had been set up as a hospital was attacked. The results were dramatic. The idea that an organized armed

group was operating in the vicinity of one of the nation's remaining nuclear sites was unacceptable. The plan for dealing
with this event was poorly developed and included a minimal amount of support or input from the locals. This was
attributed to the continuation of rumors. Intelligence assets
were assigned to the area in an attempt to identify who the
group was and their location. These assets were not from the
MOB, and the integration with local assets was minimal. It
seemed enough time had passed that those not from the area
were seen, to some extent, as outsiders. When the Intelligence Team brought up the issue of what they perceived was
a lack of local cooperation, the decision was made for the
mission to continue with limited interaction. That decision
resulted in the local support becoming even more skeptical.
An exhausted federal government made a bad decision, and
that decision was compounded by an even more exhausted
local leadership. Even the military leaders at the MOB began
to question what actions the federal government was taking.
Having operations inside of the same area where one was assigned was nothing new to commanders, but this was different. This was an event they felt responsible for solving, and
when they couldn't answer the questions of their civilian
counterparts, the situation decayed even further.

Rumors spread not only amongst the civilian population in the MOB. Military members began to hear stories of
fellow service members leaving. The military was made up
of civilians, and they had families and loved ones. The Dallas
Zone concept created more than just a civilian climate of resentment; it impacted the members of the US military as well.
Those that had been sent to the Dallas Zone for the movement
of equipment returned to the MOB. Stories spread based on
what they saw and what was available to the people inside the
zone. Those that refused to be reassigned without their families were punished, and that didn't go over well with the rest
of the members. The overall climate of the service members

continued to come under great stress. By the time the rumors of the Intelligence Team became known to them, even that story was completely distorted. Word spread the "Team" was there hunting down deserters. What they were seen as was exactly what they became. They were outsiders coming from a government that had set up its own survival zone. A zone none of them would be allowed to live in. The fear of discontent inside the military was, once again, a major concern. Members had been moved in an attempt to satisfy desires to be near loved ones. Now, the fear was those same service members would believe what many in the civilian population already understood. The federal government was only attempting to save a portion of the nation, and that portion did not include the MOB at Ellsworth.

The nuclear weapons at Ellsworth were vital to the nation, and the idea that some level of insurrection was forming in the area was totally unacceptable. The Installation Commander had been doing everything in her power to keep a lid on the situation, but trust with local authorities was damaged with the issue of the Intelligence Team and the rumors they were there to kill the attackers. When the orders were given to the commander to restrict all essential members of the nuclear program inside the base, the situation only grew worse. The result was the base remained in complete lockdown, a status it had been put in right after the initial incident at the main gate. Civilians were no longer allowed in, and although that was not a day to day event, the perception the military was separating itself from the general public could not be avoided.

The order was not well received by the members of the installation as well. They had survived the war along with the public that now lived inside the MOB. They had made it with little to no support from the federal government. Now, that same government was setting up a survival operation that didn't include them, and at the same time, they were dictating to them where they could go. The expectations became un-realistic, but few inside the government understood that fact. Within the month, the MOB at Ellsworth was seen as a high-risk event, and a disastrous decision was made.

The order to move the Civilian encampment was not sent to state authorities. They were sent directly to the In-stallation Commander, and it became her job to coordinate the event. The MOB was to be reestablished in Cheyenne Wyo-ming. How this location was chosen is unknown at the time of this report. Notification of this event was the responsibility of the commander. Guidance as to how to execute this move-ment was left to her. Requests for support would be limited to an increase in military fuel for limited movement support. The commander was given two weeks to execute the closure of the Ellsworth MOB. Her questions and concerns went un-answered. She was to coordinate the mission with the locals, and to her, it seemed the government was more concerned about the movement taking place then how actually to make it happen. The sensitivity of the federal government suddenly giving orders to an area of the nation that had seen limited support was the deciding factor on how to execute the mis-sion. The military significance of Ellsworth was more import-ant than the people who lived there, at least that is how the news was received.

The Ellsworth Commander requested a meeting with state authorities who were located in Sioux Falls South Da-kota. She traveled there and informed them of the mission she was given. It was beyond the state's ability to refuse what they were told, but the event had unforeseen consequences as a plan was being developed on how to execute the movement and closure of the MOB, the word spread of what was going to take place. Two days after the initial meeting in Sioux Falls, a report was sent to the government that a riot was tak-ing place inside the Ellsworth MOB. The event had spun out of control in a matter of hours, and an attempt was made to notify the population the MOB closure had been stopped, but it didn't matter. The sequence of what took place next was not verified, but by nightfall that day, Ellsworth AFB was in complete lockdown. Incidents involving gunfire between the US Military and US Citizens were being reported, and the casualty numbers grew higher by the hour. The Shelter site became unmanageable, much like the events inside the US cities just after the war. Civilian law enforcement requested support from the installation, but the orders were to stay inside the base. The number of people actually fighting was small, but just the sound of gunfire created an area-wide panic. The orders to the commander changed. She was to defend the installation, and it's surrounding silo sites at all costs. Deadly Force was authorized, and a response force was tasked to be on location within twelve hours. The MOB / Shelter Camp would be evacuated and order restored at all costs.

The Response Force was tasked out of Fort Carson and was supported by the US Army's 10th Special Forces Group with attached units from 4th Infantry rounding out the mission. The mission was poorly designed, and the units had no prior knowledge of how to execute such a task. The requirement was to be to Ellsworth within 12 hrs of notification, but it took three days for the operation to actually show up. To make matters worse, the coordination on what the requirements were came from Ellsworth and not the government. Air assets had observed the situation had de-escalated by the second day, but the base and its silo sites were still considered unsecured. The visual impact of the Response Force showing up was dramatic. Not only did the civilians still in the area of the MOB not realize what was taking place, but many of the military members on the base were caught off guard as well. The information the Response Force was coming was not well communicated and that only added to the confusion. What the leadership back in the Dallas Zone understood was the situation at Ellsworth was still not under control, but in fact, the violence had been reduced to individual acts of theft and robbery.

The arrival of the Response Force sparked a whole new level of fear. Their Commander was not under the operational control of the Ellsworth Commander, and his orders were clear; secure the area in and around the missile base. Their first priority was the silos, given the base was secured by organic forces. It was the additional order that was given that changed everything. The weapons-free zone around the base would be extended to twenty miles, and that included any armed individual, civilian or military. When this order was challenged by the Ellsworth Commander on the issue of civilian law enforcement, the answer was clear. The weapons-free zone included civilian law enforcement. The reality was, the government had lost what little confidence it had in the locals to keep the situation under control. Rumors had continued to spread, and those rumors included the story that many law enforcement officers had agreed to resist the closing of the MOB. Their families were reliant on the MOB operations just like everyone else in the area. Closing that operation and moving it miles away was not acceptable to many of them. That was enough to convince the government they could not trust the very officers who had been keeping the peace since the end of the war.

The nation had witness violence in the early days after the war, but the deployment of this force was something far different, something far more dangerous in the eyes of the government. What had taken place was unorganized and based on desperation. What had taken place in South Dakota was a revolt, or as it was later called by the locals, "The Resistance." The government's fear had been the fragmentation of the nation, and the events at the Ellsworth MOB proved those fears were valid.

Within a week of the Response Force being deployed in the area, several violent contacts had taken place. The word spread quickly. The force was tasked with disarming those they came in contact with. Most wanted to know part of this event and those that were armed simply left for other locations. The issue became much worse when yet another rumor began. People all across the area were hearing stories of other units being deployed, other units with the same mission. To those that believed the rumor, it was no longer an issue of being within 20 miles of the base. This rumor was exactly that, a rumor, but local authorities were no longer confident of what was a rumor and what was reality. The communications on where the Response Force was working, and what they were doing was completely ineffective. Perception became a reality. People in the area had begun to fear their own military. To the federal government, their only hope was that word of what had taken place near Ellsworth MOB would not reach the rest of the country. Their hopes were short-lived.

For the most part, rumors of the actions in the area of Ellsworth MOB spread thanks to Ham Radio Operators, but that was not the only source. Members of the military knew of the deployment, and they had heard rumors other such units had been pushed into several parts of the US. State governments heard enough about the event that they began to ask questions. The information provided was not coordinated, and soon several states realized the version they had been told didn't match from state to state. What they did understand, was equipment and supplies were being moved from all across the nation into the Dallas Zone, and they were not given a vote on the process. They also understood the MOB at Ellsworth had resisted the movement of these items, and that resulted in the US Military attempting to disarm the whole area. Fear was a daily norm in the nation, but fear of the federal government was something new. Those states that didn't accept the answers they were given by the government began to talk amongst themselves as to what this all would mean to them. What they didn't realize was the reality the federal govern-

Daniel steiner

ment was listening. The end of the first post-war year saw the nation struggling to stabilize, but it also saw something else. The nation was dividing. Those that felt left behind not only saw the federal government as unwilling to help them, but they were beginning to fear that same government.

# CHAPTER TEN: YEAR ONE FOR THE REST OF THE WORLD.

*Europe:*

The impact of the war on the European Continent was far more devastating than in the US. Not only had the nuclear damage been more severe, but the ability to stabilize was extremely limited. The whole concept of the European Union had never amounted to much more than a unified currency and market system. Emergency preparations and response capabilities were underfunded for decades. One EU nation's ability to aid another after the war simply didn't exist. Even more, telling was the unwillingness to attempt such support. With the collapse of the World Wide Web, commerce had stopped days before the nuclear exchange, and this set every nation in the EU into a mode of self-preservation. Germany and England suffered the worst of the nuclear strikes, but the ability to respond to their citizens far exceeded any other nation in Europe. Borders became a thing of the past as there was no viable force to enforce them. Most of the people of Europe reverted to a social environment they had not been that far removed from, the local village. Much like the US, Europe's population had to rely on those that lived near each other, as no one had an organized national government that was still functioning.

As of the time of this report, the death toll in Europe is

still not officially known, but the estimated loss of life in the initial war was over 25 million based upon satellite data. That estimate was from a year after the war was over and no valid data has been released since that initial figure. It has been estimated the death toll climbed dramatically after that analysis, but again, no official figure has been released.

Power production was accomplished in several locations, mainly in England, Germany, and Russia. The level of production was mostly attributed to all three nations' Emergency Management programs, and as such, the ability for the public to utilize this limited resource was simply not there. Power production should have been utilized for shelter operations, but that theory didn't hold true in Europe. The concept of sheltering in Europe was far different than in the US. In the US, the decision had been made to avoid major cities, but in Europe, cities became the primary source of shelter. People near the major cities stayed or tried to stay as close as possible, given that is what their authorities told them to do. What the US understood that Europe did not, was the reality that cities were too complex, too dependent upon common utilities such as power, water, sewer, and gas. Large cities were also unmanageable from a law enforcement stance. As the people of Europe banded together, protection became their primary concern. Cities may have provided physical shelter, especially in Winter, but humans could no longer survive in dead modern-day cities. Like the US, European Nations had to learn how to prioritize. Not everyone could be supported, and that especially held true for those who tried to stay in the larger cities. The countryside was the best chance of survival, but the nations of Europe realized this fact too late for millions of people.

Violence took on many forms in Europe. As stated earlier, people's desire to be safe created protective bans. Like in the US, these groups were made up of all segments of society. When members were identified that had law enforcement or military backgrounds, they became the primary leadership for issues of day to day safety. Territorial issues became a critical topic and that usually revolved around the issue of fresh water and food sources. The ability of these bans of people to move was far more limited in Europe. The ownership of cars and other vehicles was minimal compared to the US. The consequence of this immobility was the concentration of groups.

The desire to survive was strong, but the basic humanistic value of compassion was not lost. What many governments had always feared and predicted, a Mad Max type of world did not appear. People were willing to help each other as long as they felt safe and could provide for their loved ones as well. Unity of effort was the key to survival, and that unity was not lost in Europe. Those that looked to exploit others were responded to most severely. The groups that looked to take advantage of others were always vastly outnumbered, and as such, they seldom deliberately approached bans they encountered. Stealing was a far easier method for the criminal element. Stealing without confrontation was their goal. In reality, Europe was much like the US. The threat to survival didn't come from people. The threat to staying alive came from the harshness of day to day life. People feared the unknown, but that fear drove them to band together and like in the US, those that threatened the safety brought on by that banding were not tolerated.

The people of Europe did not realize it at the time, but the governments of Europe survived the war, all be it with extremely limited capabilities. The US had always depended on a robust Continuity of Government, COG, concept. FEMA was funded beyond any of its counterparts in the Western World. Europe was also made up of many smaller nations that had very limited emergency options. Membership in the EU had not prepared any of these nations for what took place. Local government was even less capable. In most areas, they simply folded into any of the small groups that formed. Governments in Europe had survived, but with nearly no ability to support the public.

It was the British government that began an actual process to stabilize their nation. Although several nuclear strikes had destroyed key facilities, the ability to rely on other parts of the nation for stability did exist. Communications between England and several other nations continued with little interruption. The assessment of England's status was relayed to the US as well as Canada, Germany, and France. Slowly, the communications between European Nations began to return. Within the first few days, most of the nations had made contact with each other, but the process of assessment would take months. It also became clear they had not heard from a key member of the conflict, Russia. The US had communicated with a lower level of Russian leadership, but the President of Russia and his key staff were not on any communications network, not even Shortwave. In the first few days after the war, the US military and Russian military had contacted each other, but the formal government of Russia was nowhere to be found. Russia's military leadership was attempting to locate the emergency site they had evidently changed locations to, but their equipment was badly damaged.

By the end of the first week, Europe was beginning to understand just how much damage the war had done, but they didn't know the real status of the most important nation involved in the war, Russia. The fear that someone would believe the war was still taking place consumed the nations that were now communicating. Russian leadership had agreed to the cessation of hostilities, but the additional strikes by the US were communicated to the only part of the Russian leadership that was unaccounted for. The Russian military leadership that was in contact with the US had been told of the "parity" issue, but they remained silent on their approval of the event. They, like the US and Europe, were overwhelmed attempting to establish the status of their nation, and they had been assured by the US that no further hostile actions would take place. Russia was the nation Europe worried about, and Russia was the nation that seemed the most dysfunctional.

Nearly one month after the end of the war, Russian leadership had been reestablished. What had taken place was not known, but the rumor was a new government was formed without explanation. As tense as this first month had been over the Russian issue, almost every nation in Europe had begun the process of evaluating where they stood. Like the US, the priority was based on two issues. 1. What was the status of the population? 2. What resources could be utilized to help stabilize the country? Power, fuel, food, and freshwater were the priorities. Medical support was a key issue that every government understood had a limited window of effectiveness. Like the rest of the world, Europe lost its ability to produce pharmaceuticals, and the advanced equipment needed was not going to be functional for years if not decades. Locations that would typically house such items had been plundered by the public days before and after the war. In Europe, stockpiles of such items were far less than in the US. The military had the largest contingency of such items, but this was insignificant for what was needed. Europe's military organizations were not configured for protracted deployed warfare, and as such, the items they did have would not even meet their internal needs. It took Europe nearly a month to develop its first collective snapshot of resources available, and it became clear, Europe was going to be much worse off than the US.

*China:*

China had suffered a devastating blow, far beyond what had taken place in the US or Europe. The impact of the US EMP weapons and Cyber events left China with no functioning government. Areas that had been impacted by nuclear weapons were completely destroyed, yet communications with sections of the nation took place within hours of the announcement that hostilities had ceased. Determining the status of China's overall capabilities was a priority for the US government. Could China still execute further attacks? That was the question that had to be answered as quickly as possible. Attempts to contact established Chinese military channels were unsuccessful until ships of the Chinese Navy were located. They had safely moored where satellite imagery detected them. Their ships were incapable of operations, and the crews had left, with only a few Officers staying onboard. The information they provided was very limited but did give the US an idea of just how dysfunctional the Chinese military had become. None of the Naval Officers had any means of communicating with any segment of the Chinese government and even requested such support from the US military. For them, the war was over, and their only concern was how to get home. By the end of the first week after the war, the US had come to a conclusion, China was incapable of further hostilities. An even greater assurance of safety was obtained when the US determined that well over fifty percent of its defensive orbital networks were again operational. The time to fear further conflict with China came to an end.

The next several months saw Chinas remote areas attempt to establish a new level of order. Providences such as Yunnan and Sichuan had a history of agricultural independents. Life had always been hard for the people in those two areas, and the war had not changed that reality to the point they did not find ways to survive. Yet, gone was the idea of a capital city. Gone was the concept of a centralized government. Beijing was nothing more than one of the thousands of dead cities throughout the world. The people of China who had relied on rivers and wells for water, who had relied on farm animals and crops to survive would become the future of China, at least for decades to come. China had been a fragile collection of cultures before the war. Afterward, China became what it had been for thousands of years, a land of villages and clans. The dream of the Dragon was gone, and few in China knew it ever existed. Intelligence estimates indicated over 600 million Chinese had died either during the war or in the first year after the war's end.

### India:

India had not been an actor in the war, and as such, its infrastructure was very much intact, but only in the physical sense. The nuclear exchanges had some impact, but the loss of commercial goods and communications led to the complete collapse of its society. China's cyber-attacks had struck every level of India's infrastructure, just as it had for the rest of the world. Panic and the rapid loss of daily items created the same results as everywhere else. Again, like China and several other nations, a large percentage of the population of India was somewhat self-sufficient. The standard of living was such that a new normal for day to day life was found.

By the end of the first year, India was a nation without a central government. It was a nation without industry, medical support, and only limited power. Those that had lived off the land continued to do so. Those that relied on the cities found life unmanageable. Starvation was not unique to any one nation, but in a country of over 1.4 Billion people, starvation became the leading cause of death. India was an example of what the rest of the world had become. India was a victim of war, and as such, it was completely dysfunctional.

### Central and South America:

No nation in Central or South America had taken part in the war, but every nation suffered the same outcome. Economies were gone. Vital support issues were no longer available at any level. Brazil's entire power grid had been destroyed in the cyberattacks, and just like in every other corner of the world, cities in Central and South America were dead. The governments of several nations were able to establish contact through a variety of networks, and again, shortwave radio was the common denominator. Brazil and Argentina's militaries formed the backbone of response, just as had taken place in the US. Communications with the US were established within a few days after the war, and it was clear both nations intended to keep order at all costs. Military facilities would become the center of the government of each nation, and within the first few months, both Brazil and Argentina began to find an acceptable level of stability. The two nations also formed a working relationship that was centered on the two militaries' mutual aid agreements.

The climate of Central and South America became the biggest advantage they had for survival. Rainfall and near steady temperatures allowed many civilians the ability to live in an exposed environment. Within months, large population groups formed along the coastlines of many of these nations. The ability to harvest food from the sea was an advantage the coastal nation always maintained. Yet, the problem was universal in every corner of the world. The amount of food that could be produced was not even remotely capable of sustaining the population. Central and South America were trying to find a balanced survival and like many other nations in the world, borders no longer mattered.

### Mexico:

By the end of the war, the border between the US and Mexico and Canada did not exist. The US Border Patrol was gone. With virtually no functioning command and control, the mission of the organization was lost. Travel between the three nations was unobstructed, but the volume of people moving to and from Mexico far exceeded anything taking place on the Canadian border. Mexico's government had been barely functional before the war. Almost all the Northern territories had been under the control of the drug lords for decades. Local government to include law enforcement was corrupt beyond the level of public acceptance, and with the outbreak of the war, virtually no one in central or Northern

Mexico relied on the government at any level.

Family ties along the US Mexican border were far more integrated than any government realized. As the crisis deepened, families and loved ones on both sides of the border ignored the day to day laws. By the end of the war, to the people who lived near the border, there was no longer a boundary between the three nations.

Like many less capable countries, Mexico's government virtually disappeared. Mexico City's huge population left within a matter of weeks. Without power, water and any resemblance of law and order, Mexico City suffered the same fate as every other large city in the world. Like others, Mexico's agricultural community provided some level of capability, but only for those in the localized areas where agricultural development was prevalent. Food was the issue that drove the stability of the nation, but it was the perception that things were much better in the US that resulted in a Mass Migration.

The process of distinguishing between US and Mexican citizens was finally settled upon, but it took nearly two months to become functional, and those two months were marred with violence. The fact that over 10 million people had migrated to a city, Juarez, that was the site of one of the initial nuclear attacks was somehow lost. The damage to the city of El Paso was substantial, but what was left of the city and Ft. Bliss was better than anything the people moving up from the South had encountered. The operational part of Ft. Bliss had been relocated to McGregor Range Complex with White Sands Basecamp as the Headquarters for all military operations. The Mexican citizens who entered the city of El Paso found Ft Bliss uninhabited. Information was provided as to the dangers of staying in the area, but to a large mass of desperate people, the city of El Paso was the only hope they had.

Three months after the war, nearly everyone who had traveled to Juarez and El Paso was gone. How many perished from the radiation is not known, but the military estimated there were over 300,000 dead. For that reason alone, the entire area was declared a "No go zone." In desperation, a large portion of the Mexican population had traveled to Juarez in hopes of finding help in El Paso. In the end, that decision had led to an untold loss of life. Nearly two years after the war, the story of a very similar event taking place in Southern California was discovered. Mexico, as a nation, was gone. Mexico, like so many other countries, became a land of small agricultural towns struggling to create enough food to survive.

## Canada

By the end of the war and like the Southern Border, the Northern Border of the US disappeared. One huge difference between the US's Southern and Northern Border was the movement of people. In the south, people predominantly migrated north, at least initially, but in the north, the movement was into Canada. The volume of people taking this northern migration path took place mainly in the Eastern US. The East Coast of the nation had taken the brunt of the nuclear strikes and those that could travel, even by foot, believed moving north provided a greater chance of survival than heading south or west. The Canadian government was in no position to either help or prevented this event.

Like several other nations, Canada had a large population who lived an independent lifestyle. In its Northern Territories, the concept of being without power was a hardship, but it didn't result in the inability to survive. Yet, those that had created an environment they could live in were limited in the amount of support they could provide to outsiders. In the end, the influx of people from the US was confined to the southern portions of Canada, and this reality allowed those that could continue to function the opportunity to do so.

The first Winter after the war saw a dramatic increase in the number of deaths. Those that had made the journey to

Canada from the East Coast of the US were already impacted by the fallout. Radiation sickness had so compromised most of the East Coast population's immune systems, their ability to survive a Canadian Winter was nearly impossible.

Canada's population suffered from the loss of medical items and power, but overall, it was far better off than most. The strikes along the East Coast of the US had resulted in a very high level of radiation that impacted Quebec City, Toronto, and Montreal. Prevailing winds and front patterns made these areas too dangerous to live in. The same was true for most of the East Coast of the US, and it was Ottawa that became the first real Shelter Base for anyone in that region. Winnipeg and Calgary made up the final two locations the Canadian government concentrated its efforts on. These three cities became the foundation of Canada's attempt to stabilize the nation.

The interaction between the US and Canada increased dramatically over time. An agreement of mutual support between the two nation's militaries was easily expandable based upon the day to day relationship between the US and Canadian forces working inside of Northern Command/ NORTHCOM. As positive as this partnership may have seemed, again, word of limited US supplies being sent to Canada, when most US states had little to no support, was not well received by state and local leadership. What most of them didn't realize was the fact this aid was based upon a large number of US citizens that had migrated into Canada.

Canada would stabilize over the first year, but the new normal was not much different than many other nations. Rural areas that could produce food and had abundant water, whose people understood how to continue such processes, would find a survivable level of life. The resentment of support going to Canada would become an issue the US government didn't anticipate, and that resentment only added to a growing divide in the US.

*Summary of Year One for the Rest of the World:*

The initial few months were far more chaotic than the experts had ever imagined. In the days of the Cold War, the model was based upon a full nuclear exchange, and the loss of life was so immense that no level of response was ever anticipated. This war was much different than anything those experts imagined in that the total loss of life was not beyond being manageable. What was lost was the complexity of response. Nearly every society on Earth had grown so dependent on modern technology, that when the time came, they could not use the tools and assets they owned, at least not at a level that would prevent the further loss of life. A large percentage of the world's population had survived the initial impact of the war, but the destruction of day to day life made staying alive far more difficult than anyone imagined. Year one ended with every nation in the world unable to function, unable to provide the most simplistic requirements of governance and with very little to recover with. Life in the 21$^{st}$ Century had become far more fragile than the world was prepared for. By the beginning of the second year after the war, the number of people dying had slowed considerably, but the number lost in the first year was incalculable. Without medical care, those that suffered from the most simplistic illnesses were far more likely to die than at any time in the past 200 years.

By late in the first year, nations began to gain awareness of the world in general. Manufacturing was limited to agricultural events, and no one had the ability nor the desire to export food products. Stockpiles of critical items such as medicines, batteries, building materials were gone and gone was the ability to replicate any of those same items. By the end of the first year, the world was in a universal status, survival. The idea of rebuilding even the most simplistic capabilities was still years away. Nations could communicate, but they could do little to help each other. All over the world, people were dying at an unmeasurable rate, and yet the priority was the survival of those who stood a chance of living. It was a new world. At the end of the first year, the world had only one goal, to survive.

# CHAPTER ELEVEN: THE FEAR OF SUCCESSION:

The beginning of the second year witnessed the US federal government becoming aware of the division that was growing inside the nation. The perception of those states that were receiving little or no support had come into the open during a national conference call. The topic had been the continued reallocation of critical resources to the Dallas Zone. After months of hearing of how important the project was to the nation, it became clear many states were no longer willing to support the process. When the state governments of Kansas and Colorado were informed that additional medical resources would be moved, both states stated they would not support the movement. As the discussion continued, New Mexico, Wyoming, Arizona, and Montana announced they would no longer authorize the reallocations of any items in their states. The federal authorities reminded the states that special laws enacted after the war gave the federal government the authority to take control of any items or resources in the nation for the sake of national survival. It may have been the way this statement was made, or it may have been the reality that several of the states were no longer willing to hold conversations with a federal government, but the result was over twenty states signing out of the call. This was not the first time the emotions of state leadership had resulted in terminated conversations, but it was the first time such a response took place in a unified event.

The discussion of why this had happened and how to react to it was nearly as emotional as the event itself. Many federal officials had the opinion the states were becoming less committed to a federal governmental construct, and these opinions had been gaining support for months. Inputs by regional military commanders supported this perception even further. Reports of physical resistance to the realloca- tion process had been coming in on continuous basses. The federal authorities saw something even more ominous. This mass departure from a critical conference call was more than just localized resentment. In their opinion, it was the most dangerous sign, yet the nation was beginning to splinter.

Within an hour of the disrupted call, a meeting was held to determine what actions, if any, needed to take place. Two schools of thought divided the individuals who were tasked to come up with Courses of Action, COAs, for the President to review. The first group would recommend the government simply do nothing and reach out to the states that had signed off. They also recommended delaying any reallocation move- ments until further conversations could take place. Simply put, their stance was to not overreact. The other group's opin- ion was nearly the opposite. They suggested the movements take place as scheduled, and the impacted states should be notified as such. The requirements were too important to lose time attempting to reconcile with the withdrawn states, es- pecially given most of them were not on the list tasked for re- allocation operations. When the President was given the two options, he chose to delay the movements. As important as the Dallas Zone was to the US's survival, the concept of losing the unity of the nation was even more important. The federal government would reach out to the states who left the call. They would be assured their needs would be met, but they had to understand the most immediate task was to secure the Dal- las Zone project. Only then could the government begin to rebuild the nation.

The decision to talk to each state individually was not as important as how soon those conversations would take place. The goal was to start that same day with the priority placed on the states that had shown the most resistance. The ability to communicate with each state had been regained at the state level. Prior to that, all communications had been supported by federal assets, mainly military satellite equipment. What that meant was the states now had the option of answering the call or not. Wyoming was the first state called, and there was no answer.

Because the communication network the states utilized was based on satellite operations, the federal government was able to monitor any and all communications. This is exactly what took place after the twenty states' departure from the conference call. When Wyoming did not answer the call, a team of federal officials was dispatched from the military outpost at FE Warren. When they arrived at the alternate State Headquarters, they were met by a security detail who stated they had instructions not to allow anyone into the location. When the team notified the federal authorities, the reaction was predictable. A series of phone calls were made to the state headquarters, but only lower-level staff members responded. It was then; the federal government learned the team they had assigned to Wyoming's Emergency Operations Center had been asked to leave. They had been gone for over an hour when the team from FE Warren arrived, and that team was not permitted access. As the conversation was taking place on how to handle the event in Wyoming, the President was informed several states had been communicating with Wyoming and the discussion was Wyoming's decision to expel the federal support team. Colorado, North Dakota, South Dakota, Arizona, Kansas, and New Mexico had held a conference call, and each state's federal support team had not been allowed to take part in the call. What was said was then briefed. The states on the call had agreed to limit communications with the federal authorities both inside their states and at the Dallas Zone. The President was then informed, eleven additional states had agreed to take part in a follow on a conference call later that evening.

Two hours after the team from FE Warren was denied access, the President was informed federal support teams assigned to the state headquarters in New Mexico, Kansas, North Dakota, South Dakota, Colorado, and Arizona had been asked to leave. By this time, all the communications taking place between the states on federal networks were being monitored. In total, 41 states utilized the network. The rest were located in areas that had been evacuated due to the dangers created by nuclear strikes. The eleven states that were scheduled to talk had already agreed to not communicate with the federal government, at least until after the conference call was held. Nearly half the states that made up what was left of the US were contemplating ether limiting their interaction with the federal government or discontinuing it altogether. By late that night, the President began to realize; the United States was in the early process of no longer being, "united." The price the nation was paying to support the Dallas Zone concept was too much for the rest of the nation to accept. The US was a Republic, and it was the laws that founded that Republic the states were intending on utilizing to stop the federal government's plan.

The eleven states' conference call was held, along with the states from the initial members. In total twenty-one states took part. As the federal government listened in, it was clear what the overall objective would be. They would reach out to the remaining states, excluding Texas, to gain enough support to demand an Article V Convention. Its use would be to revoke the Emergency Powers Laws that were enacted after the war. The states were out to limit the authorities of the federal government to implement the law, even emergency laws, that would negate state authority. States would have the right to deny the movement of any item or materials in their territory that might endanger the lives or welfare of the citizens in their state. Simply put, the federal government would be denied the ability to place demands on any of the states.

If anyone had doubted the nation was in a crisis of government event, that doubt was now gone. The group who advocated talking to the states did not change their position. They had to let the states know the federal government was only doing what was best for the nation. They recommended another immediate attempt to communicate. This time, the decision to respond did not come from just one meeting. The President called for a conference with a select group of experts, and that event did not take place until late the next day. As the list of who would attend this meeting was being finalized, those who continued to believe the best course of action was to speak with the states, grew more convinced the other school of thought would win out. Overreaction was the fear, and that fear was so prevalent, a small group decided to make contact before the President's meeting. The federal support team that had left Arizona was contacted by an old associate, and it was decided two members of that team would reach out to friends inside the Arizona Headquarters. The two team members were told the state's conference call had been monitored and the President was holding a meeting the next day to determine a response to what had been learned. That conversation set into motion a series of events that neither the federal government nor the states could control. People who were attempting to prevent a bad situation from becoming worse created a crisis that would change the course of US history.

The Arizona Emergency Management members who met with their federal friends were stunned to hear of the monitored calls. The information was not provided deliberately but was simply used as an example of how bad things were becoming. The damage was done. Soon after the meeting ended, Arizona's leadership was made aware of the issue. A decision had to be made. Should Arizona notify the other states, or should they openly confront the federal government and demand an explanation? The decision was made to do both. The governor of Arizona initially requested a conversation directly with the President, but when the question of the topic was asked, the Governor refused to answer. His stance was that he insisted on speaking with the President as soon as possible. The fact the Governor would not state the topic resulted in the President's staff delaying the answer to the request. That response only solidified Arizona's concerns. The Governor was informed the phone call would take place later that evening and that it would be helpful if some indication of the topic could be provided. The Governor's answer was simply, "trust," and he discontinued the call.

As a meeting was being held to discuss just what the Governor of Arizona meant by, "trust," there was still no knowledge of the discussion between federal employees and Arizona Emergency Management members. What the President's Staff did understand was the tension that was rising by the day between many of the states and the federal government. Arizona had taken part in both monitored calls, and their stance was undeniable. If the US government were not going to support them, then they would not support the government. It was assumed Arizona was one of the chief proponents for an Article V Convention, and somehow this requested phone call had something to do with that topic. The President's Staff was wrong.

Arizona had made a decision to communicate with several nearby states, but they did not do so with electronic devices. Couriers were dispatched, and they traveled by private aircraft. The war had destroyed most aviation capabilities, but some of the most simplistic, privately owned aircraft were optimized by several states. They had been used to transport state officials to shelter sites or to disperse limited medical assets. The fact of the matter was, several states could travel without federal support. Arizona dispatched aircraft to New Mexico, Colorado and Wyoming. Three aircraft, all of them carrying the same message. The states needed to know communications supported by the federal government were being monitored, and it should be assumed all other forms of electronic communications were monitored as well. After months of tension as well as the disastrous conference call, the states had to consider any interactions between them was a critical issue to the federal government.

Except for the area around the Dallas Zone, interior US airspace was virtually unmonitored. Although radar coverage didn't really exist, most functional aircraft had been centralized at identified airfields. This allowed for coordinated support and optimization of fuel expenditure. Any civilian aircraft that wished to operate had to have proper approval from state or federal authorities. The allocation of aviation fuel was so critical, the only missions that were authorized involved at least state-level emergencies. The three aircraft launched by Arizona had state-level approval and the federal footprint at the location they departed from was limited to military aircraft maintenance crews. This led to the state of Arizona launching the mission without anyone knowing.

Two hours before the scheduled conversation between the Governor and the President, the President's Chief of Staff called Arizona and stated he wished to review what the topics would cover. The Arizona Emergency Operations Center answered they were not aware of their Governor's agenda, but they did know he intended to be on time for the call. The President's Chief of Staff then asked if the senior members of the support team would be allowed back in the facility for the conversation. Again, the answer was no one knew. The tension inside the federal government grew.

When the call was placed, Arizona's Emergency Operations Center stated their governor was requesting the call be moved until noon the next day and the states of Colorado, New Mexico, and Wyoming be added to the discussion. The President and his staff had no choice, given the Arizona Governor was not at his Emergency Operations Center. Why the other three states were invited into the conversation was the first question asked. Again, the answer from the Governor's staff was the same as before. They didn't know. It was agreed the call would be moved, but the rift between Arizona and the federal government was now approaching a crisis point.

How had the additional states been added? How did Arizona communicate with them and the federal government not know? The initial theory was shortwave Radio / HAM / operators, but that was soon ruled out. A large part of the world was communicating with this system, and the US had established a very sophisticated monitoring process for just that reason. If Arizona and the other three states had talked, they did it without electronic support. The topic quickly changed from how, to why? What was the issue the four states were wishing to speak about? Arizona's Governor had used the word, "trust," but what did that mean?

By the next morning, not only had the states in questioned communicated, but Kansas, Nebraska, North Dakota, and South Dakota had all been informed. Colorado had sent a messenger to Kansas and Nebraska, while Wyoming had done the same with North and South Dakota. Careful attention had been made to ensure the governors of each state were informed without the knowledge of any federal support officials. All of them would be on the call at noon, and all had agreed to let the Arizona governor ask the key question. Did the federal government listen in on the state conference call over the topic of an Article V Convention? Every state had agreed if the answer was yes, then they would discontinue any activity with the federal government until they collectively decided to reengage.

The conference call took place at noon the next day. The President started off by thanking the Governors for being on the call and wanted to ensure them he was going to do everything he could to address any issues that came up in the call. The Governor of Arizona waited for the President to finish and responded with one question. "Mr. President. Did you listen in on the state's call that took place after your last conference call"? The answer was blunt and to the point. "Yes." The President explained to the group the nation had no choice but to monitor transmissions taking place all across the country. He then explained this was done not as a matter of trust, but as a way to stay ahead of any potential issue that might jeopardize the stability of the US. It was the governor of Kansas who asked the next question.

"Why didn't you inform us that all communications were monitored"? The answer appeased no one. The President replied, "We didn't think it was necessary." The Governor of Arizona then asked, "Mr. President, are you aware of our desire to call for an Article V Convention"? The reply to that question set the tone and indeed the fate of any future conversations. "Yes, and I can tell you the idea of such a process taking place now or soon is out of the question." Those were the words that ensured the crisis the federal government had feared would now become a reality. The President tried to explain why he believed the timing of such an event was dangerous for the nation, but his words had no impact. The final question was again asked by the Governor of Arizona. "Mr. President, is it your intention to prevent the states from executing their Constitutional Rights"? Still, the President's answer stunned the Governors who were listening. It was his opinion and a majority of the surviving House and Senate, the Emergency Laws implemented during the war superseded "Normal" Constitutional law. What the Governors heard was clear. The federal government was overriding Constitutional law on the pretense that it was a temporary necessity based on national survival. The Governors did not respond. Silence ruled the call, and then suddenly, without warning, the Governor of Wyoming signed out. The Speaker of the House had been invited to be with the President on the call, and he was in the middle of explaining how these temporary laws would be removed when the other Governors simply signed off. And with that, the call was over.

The President and his primary staff sat in silence. No one wanted to speak before the President commented. They had been through a war, and the struggle to hold the nation together had taxed them relentlessly, but this was a new crisis. This was a crisis they had believed they held the answers for. From the early days of the Cold War, plans for an Enduring Government had always been ready. How was it the Governors did not realize the dire condition the nation was in? How could they not understand the hard decisions that had to be made? The answer was one federal officials never understood. Governors had one primary responsibility, their states. To those who had spent their whole life in DC, the US was a singular body. To the Governors and the States, the US was what the founding fathers intended it to be, a Republic.

The fear of being monitored kept the Governors from immediately talking about what had just taken place, but the perception was clear to all of them. The federal government was not going to allow the states to attempt an Article V Convention. It would take two days before the collective opinions could be reviewed, and when they were, this opinion was confirmed. What would happen next was the universal question. As much as the Governors wanted to address this issue, day to day challenges remained far more critical. Except for Arizona, preparation for the coming Winter was the primary concern of the states that had been involved in the call. How the federal government would react was worrisome but staying alive was still the most significant challenge. What the states did prioritize was the ability to communicate with each other.

They understood this was an obstacle that had to be addressed, and each state went to work on finding options.

The federal government was not prepared to label the identified states as subversive, but the decision was made to monitor their actions as closely as possible. Three days after the call, none of the states had been detected communicating with each other. Normal daily activity was present, and that activity even included coordinating with federal authorities. On the surface, everything was as it had been. If there was the knowledge of division in the country, it was limited to those on the call. The President had decided to let the whole issue rest for several days, and then he would attempt to talk to each of the Governors. In his mind, this entire event was a byproduct of unrelenting stress, stress that had impacted all of them, and even a year after the war, that pressure had not let up. He would attempt to defuse the situation before entertaining any other options.

Despite what had taken place between the states and the federal government, Joint Assessment Teams, JATs, continued to map out the condition of the nation's infrastructure. Word of the controversy spread both inside the states as well as in the federal government, but the members of the JATs had agreed their work was too vital to allow the division to creep into their level of cooperation.

As the nation entered the second post-war year, the assessment process was less than thirty percent complete. Identifying usable items and then tagging them for movement or refurbishment was an undertaking much more massive than anyone had anticipated. Priority was still based on power production and available fuels, but secondary assessments were providing a reasonably accurate snapshot of the nation's ability to restart many levels of production. Farming machinery was also given a higher than normal priority, and it was this issue that created the next contentious moment between the states and the government.

Even though the acceptable levels of radiation standards had been changed, the residual levels were still too high in most of the Midwestern States. Illinois, Missouri, Indiana, Iowa, and Ohio had been massive crop-producing states before the war, but it was these same states that were now unable to receive supported farming assistance from the government. As such, much of the equipment that was still functional in those states had been identified for assessment and movement, movement into the Dallas Zone. Every square inch of the zone that was not tasked with housing or potential housing was slated for agricultural production. Assessing the equipment in the Midwest States had been taking place when the incident with the Western Governors occurred. Those identified Midwestern States had been notified of the assessments, but the decision to relocate the equipment had not been made public, at least not officially. The federal program managers had decided to hold off on making the relocation issue known until they could give a precise picture of what needed to be accomplished. Although no official discussion had taken place, rumors grew by the day. The population of these states had been significantly reduced as people moved away from the higher levels of radiation, but many locations maintain enough people, especially farmers, that the word spread. In one instance, a confrontation took place in Southern Illinois, and several members of a JAT were killed or injured. JATs had a standing order to be nonconfrontational if possible but to defend themselves when required. The result was an event that spread the fear of the JATs throughout the farming communities within hundreds of miles.

The issue of relocation plans for farming equipment came to a head with the State of Missouri. The Governor had requested a review of the current residual radiation standards based upon scientific data collected by his members of the JATs. The state's argument was based upon a faster than predicted reduction in the radiation levels, especially in

Central and Southern Missouri. A change in Missouri's status would allow them to received seed from the National Strategic Stockpile. Much of the crop seed that had been stored in local granaries had been damaged our expended in the first year after the war. Without power and fuel, all most all of the farmers were unable to maintain their privacy or local reserves properly. The other factor that significantly reduced seed crops was the issue of food. Any stored corn was almost wholly exhausted in the first year in an attempt to feed as many people as possible. Most storage facilities had been picked clean by groups looking to survive. The fact the Mississippi River had become unregulated with the loss of the lock and damn networks, resulted in the inability to move seed crops from the areas that had ample storage, but small populations. The simple answer was, the Midwestern states would need the government's help to restart any level of food production.

Missouri's request was granted, and that resulted in their functional farming equipment being removed from the relocation list. When word reached the other states in the Midwest, they immediately requested a review of their status. To the federal government, it became clear the entire process of collection from the Midwest was going to be in jeopardy. The reality was, Illinois and Ohio's radiation levels were still too high for any form of support. When the denial was given, Ohio and Iowa's Governors demanded an immediate discussion with the President. On the day that request was made, the President was involved in an issue taking place in another part of the world, a fact that was serious enough that he had to give it his full attention. Although the call had been scheduled, it was canceled several hours later and just one hour before it was to have taken place. What the President's Staff was not aware of was the fact a delegation from Kansas and Colorado had arrived in Iowa the day before. The discussion of the Article V Convention was the topic, and that same day, the Governor of Missouri and Illinois had sent delegates to Iowa as well. When the word came of the canceled call with the President, Iowa and Illinois informed the government, they would let them know when they would like to attempt the conversation again. The next day, Indiana and Ohio attended the meeting in Iowa. The decision was made. None of the Midwestern States would support or allow farming equipment to be moved. Each state informed the federal government of their choice by way of their members on the JATs. It was not long before word made it back to Federal leadership. The crisis of governance was growing, and the options for addressing the event were minimal.

The President didn't change his approach, and the results did not vary as well. The Governor of Iowa received a request to speak with the President. The time was set, but the call didn't take place. The Governor's staff requested the conversation be moved to a group discussion with all of the impacted states. Personal communications were preferred, but it became clear that the approach was ineffective.

The conference call took place, and the discussion became heated. The movement of farm equipment may have been the catalyst of the request, but the real overarching issue soon became evident, and it was a topic the federal government had heard time and time again. The Midwestern States understood the concept of the Dallas Zone. What they could not accept was the lack of support they received. In the early days after the war, the expectations of states were minimal as everyone struggled to stay alive. The extent of damage the nation had suffered was unknown to state and local leadership, and that helped reduce expectations, but as time went on, it appeared the country had fared far better than many states thought. The visual impact of the military being seen gave people hope, and that is what it was intended to do. Hope quickly turned into a request for help. The initial support, all be it limited, gave the states the impression the process of healing was underway, and in fact, many of the initial conversations revolved around the concept of rebuilding the nation. It was not until the Dallas Zone concept was made known that states began to worry about their future. Over time, that worry manifested itself into paranoia, and by the time the Midwestern States were briefed on the farm equipment issue, that paranoia had turned into defiance.

The federal government went into the meeting with orders not to be confrontational. After an hour of very emotional statements, the President decided the farm equipment from the Midwestern States would not be repositioned. The topic of seed crops was not resolved, but the President's Staff committed to reviewing the residual radiation issues, and that could impact the seed crop question. The call was completed with the Governors thanking the President and his Staff for listening. The President's answer was telling. "We are all doing the best that we can, and we all realize hard times are still ahead of us." The President's staff knew they had lied to the states. The federal government had no intention of reevaluating the radiation issue. The limited about of seed crops would be utilized in the Dallas Zone. The farm equipment was vital to the Zone, and it would be collected. The survival of the nation was still at hand, and additional sacrifices would have to be made.

It was Illinois that first became aware of the government's real intent. Nearly two weeks after the Midwestern State's call, a large convoy of empty military heavy transport vehicles, Hetts, were reported to have assembled just outside Springfield Illinois. Rumors of such vehicles being spotted on highway 72 had been reported for several days, but when military authorities were asked, the answer given was that they were passing through the location. State officials had no idea what the real mission was until the rumors of collection units being seen on several large farms near the towns of Dawson, Williamsville, and Salisbury began to come to the state's attention. The lead federal authority for Illinois' JAT operations was called to the governor's office. When the individual didn't arrive, the rumors became a reality. The collection process was underway, and it was being accomplished without notification.

### The Dawson Incident:

All National Guard units had been activated shortly after the war had begun and there had been no official deactivation message sent to any of the states. From the Governor's perspective, they had no National Guard assets under their control. Guard units had been tasked to support many of the states, but they did so under federal authority with limitations on what support missions could be authorized. Even though the units had been placed on Active Duty, the members themselves still had deep loyalties to the states their units came from. When word reached the Illinois Governor's Office that their units were part of the movement process, it was decided they would be approached for answers. When locals approached the collection processing areas, they were told to move away without explanation. The unit patches identified the Illinois Guard members and several of the locals realized many of the members involved in the process where Illinois Guardsmen. At one collection point, the Military Police Unit assigned to secure the operation was made up mostly of Illinois members. Two State Troopers asked the MPs whose authority were they operating under and who had authorized them to enter several of the local farms? The answer was the standard given by the federal government since the end of the war. The military operation was being conducted under the authority of the Special War Powers Laws, the same laws that had allowed the federal government to execute any mission deemed vital to the nation's survival. This collection point near the town of Dawson became an incident that changed the future of the country.

After a heated exchange between the State Troopers

and two senior Officers from the MP unit, several members of the Illinois National Guard refused to continue with the mission. Most were from an Army National Guard Truck Company, but several of the members were from the MPs. The members who refused to take part in the mission walked away. A small number of them who had been at the scene of the altercation asked if they could leave with the party accompanied by the State Troopers. No one from the military side of the event attempted to stop them. Once again, the locals were told to leave. The Troopers later stated, they chose to leave rather than risk a physical confrontation.

The event that would become known as, "The Dawson Incident" had not been the first altercation between state, local and federal authorities, but it was the singular event that set far more critical decisions into motion. These decisions would have disastrous impacts on the continuity of the US. A reoccurring fear would take hold of the most senior leaders inside the federal government. Again, the issue was the loyalty of the military. Accommodations had been made. Troops were allowed to be stationed as near to their homes as possible. By the beginning of the second year, the US military had lost an additional twenty percent of its force. Members from all branches continued to leave at every opportunity they could find, but tracking them down and punishing them was a process that required resources that could not be spared. Incentives continued, but a new issue had come to light. The reallocation missions had been controversial from the beginning, but somehow the federal government overlooked the reality of what forces were being utilized. The mixture of National Guard units had not been identified as a potential issue. The assumption had been those forces would do what was required for the nation, even if that meant going against the wishes of their states. These men and women were members of the US military, a military that had become far more seamless in their integration between the Active and Reserve

Components. The stigmas of the past were gone, at least at the operational level. What the Dawson Incident proved was that leadership was once again worried about the division. It would prove to be a perception crisis born out of ignorance and extended fatigue, but in the end, the fear of loyalty inside the military was once again a primary concern to the President's Staff.

The collection process was stopped, at least in the state of Illinois and the federal members of the JATs were told to relocate to the federal facilities at the Great Lakes Training Center. Illinois has informed the federal support to the JATs would be placed on hold until further notice. Within a day, Missouri, Ohio, Indiana, and Iowa were all aware of the JAT event. Each state also realized that all electronic forms of communication between them were being monitored. Couriers were the only form of communication, but the process of staying in contact with each other improved quickly. Within a few days, all the impacted Midwestern states agreed on a critical point. The relationship with the federal government was changing dramatically.

The federal government came to the realization, and they were now facing a crisis on two fronts. The States were openly resisting the directions given to them, and the loyalty of the US Military was in question. The President called an emergency meeting to address the most recent facts related to both issues. When the comment was made the Midwestern States had been communicating, just as the Southwestern States, the President asked one question. Where they monitoring all communications with all the functioning states? Most of his staff understood he had been briefed on this process, but no one made a comment. The answer was given by the Secretary of Defense. It was then the President made a comment that was not only recorded but understood by everyone in the room. "If we are concerned over the fear of succession, then it seems we have fired the first shot."

Another crisis meeting lasted over two hours, and it ended with the President giving an order as the Commander in Chief to the Secretary of Defense. He was to head an action group that would determine the ability of the government to keep the states from breaking away. The President wanted two specific issues answered. Was the country capable of preventing succession? Where there states that must be kept in the Union at all costs? The group was to meet with him in one week to provide him with answers and options. It was not the first time the staff had reviewed the question of succession, but it was the first time the President had tasked them to produce a working plan. The US was well into its 'second year after the war, but the ability to survive as a nation was still in serious doubt.

### *The State's Respond.*

The Courier process had been the safest and most reliable form of communication between the Southwestern and Midwestern states, but it was prolonged, and every state understood time was a critical issue. Colorado was the first state to submit a concept that would change everything. A code system was developed by a group of Computer Software Engineers, a group that had formed in an attempt to restart an academic level of education in Colorado. Since the beginning of the war, Universities all across the nation had been closed. After the war was over, the ability for any of these centers of higher education to continue didn't exist. Some of the brightest minds in the nation had been taken in by the federal government, as that concept had been part of an existing plan, but the country was still rich with knowledge, and it was that richness that would lead to what would become known as, " The Colorado Code Team."

It took a little over two weeks for the courier process to reach each of the identified states. The fear of someone learning of the code concept required only the Governors and their chosen coding experts were allowed in on the event.

Two weeks later, the first test message was sent between Arizona and Colorado, with all the others listening in. The message was short and had no real meaning. The purpose was to validate the encoding and decoding processes. It was assumed the government would detect the event and what reaction it would create was unknown.

No state had brought up the topic of succession, and it was unknown to any of them the government was concerned over such an idea. What the states had spoken of was an Article V Convention. It was the President who assumed the issue was going to ultimately lead to a question of succession and his guidance set the rest of the federal government into the motion of preparing for such an event. When the President was briefed on the detected message event, he became convinced his fears were coming true. One week from the day he gave the review orders to the SecDef, the President received the information he requested.

The code development team asked for permission to send a second message with the purpose of attempting to see if the federal government had broken the base-code. This request was not without risk as it required the movement of several state representatives to a set location. The reps would also be given a false reason to hold the meeting, an idea they hoped would force the government to respond. The movement and meeting took place without incident. The topic of the meeting was supposed to be how the states could work together without the federal government. There was no real discussion, as the whole process was a test. The test was considered a success, and as soon as that decision was made, the federal government detected transmissions taking place from every state they were concerned with.

### The President's Briefing:

The Secretary of Defense opened the meeting with a

simplistic map. It depicted critical military locations that were currently being utilized. The top of this priority list was made up of the nuclear missile sites. The nation had only one operational military installation that could support the nuclear submarines and that had been developed in Houston. The city itself was not inside the Dallas Zone, but the federal facilities that had been established there were also on the top of the list. The nation's ability to defend itself was considered to be the Center of Gravity for survival. The briefing then showed what locations were deemed to be vital to the potential rebuilding process. This included key mining facilities as well as critical manufacturing sites that were outside the contamination zones. Items that were critical to the Dallas Zone project had been identified, but the next phase, the concept of rebuilding the rest of the nation was not mapped out and as such, anticipating further critical issues were not reviewed. After being able to defend the nation, the Dallas Zone was the priority.

Before the President's second question could be officially addressed, the discussion pulled the topic onto the table. What was it going to take to secure these identified locations? The military facilities were a simple answer, but what of the others? That was the emotional topic at hand. Many of the identified items, sites, were in states that now seemed to no longer support the federal government. How would these sites be secured without the state's approving? How could the states be forced into supporting the government? The question then became, could the states be forced? Legally, they had not threatened succession, but that was no longer the prerequisite for action by the federal government. The Emergency War Powers Laws that had been drafted gave the President the authority to do whatever was required to ensure the survival of the nation. In reality, the Senate and Congress had given the Commander in Chief Absolute authority the overall functions of the government.

The SecDef's recommendations for securing the non-military sites were terrifying to everyone in the room to include the President. The most critical locations on the list would be secured by combat forces without warning. The initial " Hold Teams" would be airdropped with a full follow on security force arriving within a week. The timeline for conducting this series of operations was just as stunning. It would take an estimated four months to prepare for the missions and then nine months to complete the task. Each site would be accomplished with a 400 person Combat Team, and the SecDef's working group had identified over 122 sites located within the states in question. With support requirements, the entire mission would call for over 110,000 military members.

As the discussion continued, someone asked a question that brought silence to the room. "Could such a mission be put together without the states knowing? That question led to the topic of giving the states an ultimatum, but what would that ultimatum be based upon? The federal government was anticipating succession from multiple states, and sites inside those states had to be secured for national survival. Would the states truly resist such an event? Federally declared locations had been set up in the states after the war, so why was the government so concerned about the state's reactions now? Was this concept really necessary? Would the state care? Even if they did care, could they do anything to stop it? People were tired of uncertainty, and two years of merely trying to make things work for one more day. The idea of rebuilding the nation was still a distant dream to just about everyone, but the fear of the nation disintegrating into undefined Territories was more terrifying than anything they could think of. Up until the event with the Southwestern states, the concept of the nation falling apart, as much of the rest of the world had done, was a concern, but it didn't rule the daily thoughts of those in charge. The Dallas Zone had changed everything.

To many in the federal government, the state's fears of

being left alone were justified. When the farming equipment event took place, people in both state and federal government became convinced the nightmare of dissolvement was coming true. They were unsure what reaction would come from the states, but the defining question was clear. What was the federal government willing to do?

The President's guidance was seen as a compromise. The operation would be limited to the immediate sites required to support the Dallas Zone. All others would be addressed and reevaluated at a later date. The states would not be notified of the operation, but if they inquired as to any rumor, they would be told some sites were, "under consideration for protective support." It was agreed the states would learn of this program and it was also agreed some level of resistance could be expected. In reality, many of the identified sites had already been occupied for just that reason, but that concept had been a joint project. Areas that had been designated as "vital" had been secured by the joint efforts of the state, local and federal authorities soon after the end of the war. What the states would come to realize was the fact these identified locations would no longer be jointly controlled. They would now be exclusively under federal authority. The decision was made. The federal government would take measures to ensure the survival of the Dallas Zone and then reevaluate any further rebuilding concepts.

The mission to secure critical sites in the states had been decided, but two issues had not been addressed, and everyone knew what they were. Was the loyalty of the US Military in question and what did the federal government intend to do if some of the states began to approach the concept of succession? Again, the President asked the SecDef for his analysis on the issue of loyalty, and again, his answer shocked the room. He started his response by informing everyone in the meeting what the current combat readiness was for the US Military. Most understood the impact of the war, but they also had no real concept of what the damage meant to the countries fighting force. The nuclear capability of the nation stood at forty percent of the post-war readiness. Even worse, the ability to maintain the nation's nuclear posture would degrade dramatically over the next ten years.

The estimate was the capabilities of all nuclear programs would be exhausted within ten to fifteen years. At that time, the US would not have a reliable nuclear option. The nation's space-based EMP platforms were currently at sixty-five percent of post-war readiness. Their lifespan was projected to expire in less than five years. This short operational time-frame was based upon the nation's inability to conduct maintenance missions as well as technical replacement items on the ground. The US Navy was at sixty percent, but the drop off percentage was dramatic. The issue was the same, but the impact was exponentially worse than nuclear or space operations. The ships were immensely complex networks, and maintenance was a process that never stopped. The decision had been made to keep the US Navy inside territorial waters, but their combat readiness was going to degrade rapidly. The Army was at sixty percent, due mainly to manpower. The fact there had been virtually no ground fighting events in the war resulted in large stockpiles of equipment items, and that would result in the US Army being a capable fighting force for the foreseeable future. That statement had one tremendous caveat. The US Army would have minimal deployment capabilities. Without a commercial support network coupled with a very limited Navy, the Army had lost its power projection capability. This limitation was forecast to grow even worse over the next ten years or more. In the end, the picture the SecDef painted was one of a US military that was still capable of defending the nation but would lose that capability rapidly over the next five to ten years.

The President's initial question had been one of loyalty, but the SecDef stated he had to give everyone in the room a holistic snapshot of the force before addressing the President's question. People had to understand the status of the force before they heard the status of the members who made up the force because no one understood better what the future held more than the US Military members.

The first attempt to address the Presidents question was based on the topic of Morale. Shortly after the war was over, it had been decided military members who wished to be closer to their homes would be transferred to locations that were still functional. The East Coast did not support this concept due to the damage from the nuclear strikes. The states of New Jersey, New York, Delaware, and Maryland had no organic military support, but members from that area were stationed in Ohio, Virginia and West Virginia. In the initial period after the war, morale was a great concern as the military had estimated that nearly twenty-five percent of the force had walked away. The fact that most military locations became centers for support prevented this number from being much higher, and providing for military member's families was a priority. Much of the equipment had survived the war, at least the items based in the US, but it was the manpower, the members who made the whole agency work. Taking care of the members was second only to securing the nation. What the services had not accomplished was an accurate analysis of overall morale. The struggle to help the civilians survive the first post-war year had been overwhelming to everyone, and the issue of confidence was only thought of inside the federal government's senior leadership. It was not until the incident with the Southwestern states that regional Commanders began to voice their concerns. Those military members who had asked to be reassigned to areas near their homes became sensitive to the issues brought up by the Dallas Zone project. Rumors of state leadership being told they would have to sacrifice even further did not go over well with military members whose families were trying to survive inside those same states. Commanders began to report their concerns of the perception issues the Dallas Zone was creating, not just with civilians, but with their members.

Simply surviving from day to day was still the number one challenge in the nation and hearing that the odds of your family members being left out of any possible support was not well received. The reality was, reports of desertions were increasing in the Western locations even before the Dawson Incident. Everyone understood the short answer the SecDef gave the President. Yes, he was concerned the US Military had a moral issue, and that issue would be directly tied to loyalty. Most of the nation was going to be left to fend for themselves with limited support as the Dallas Zone became the priority for the federal government. The concern of the military's loyalty was confirmed, but the logic behind the affirmation was understandable. The Dallas Zone was going to leave out a massive percentage of the military members' families and loved ones, and everyone in the government understood that would impact the future of the force's loyalty.

The President's next question was one the room was not prepared to hear. " What is the most dangerous scenario we need to prepare for"? Someone in the meeting made the statement it was apparent the National Guard held the highest threat of disloyalty. The President quickly challenged that statement and reminded everyone in the room, and the National Guard was the founding military force of the nation. The SecDef challenged the comment as well. All of the members of the military were volunteers. The country had not had a draft in decades, and the only difference between the Reserves and the Active was their fulltime commitment and not their loyalty to the country. That answer didn't put the issue to rest. Several others in the room spoke of how the National Guard was state assets, and the issue at hand was preventing the states from working towards succession. It was then the issue of succession finally came up. The Vice President asked, "Has anyone heard any Governor talk of succession"? No one in the room answered. He went on to say the only conversation he was aware of was based on the issue of a possible Article V Convention. It was the President who replied that one was the prelude to the other. It was his opinion the states would have no option than to push for succession if the Article V topic was denied. Succession was an assumed issue, but the perception was once again reality, and the impression was succession was a threat to the nation, and if the country had a known threat, could the US Military be counted to protect the nation?

The President decided succession was the nation's primary concern now. If states began to work towards leaving the Union, then the options of how to prevent such an event would become the top priority, even over the continued development of the Dallas Zone. In his eyes, stopping the threat while it was still nothing more than a conversation was going to be far less costly than dealing with it once it was underway. If the SecDef was concerned about morale and thus, loyalty, then the President wanted to know what part of the force would remain loyal. If his intent had not been made known before, it was made very clear by the end of the meeting. The SecDef was to determine who in the force could be relied upon and then devise options for dealing with the threat of succession. The meeting ended with the guidance given by the President, and all agency heads were told to support the SecDef in any way required. To many in the room, it seemed the nation was sliding into a new crisis, and one they feared had no answer.

The topic of coded messages being sent between states never came up in the official meeting. The President kept the staff answering questions at a pace that no one felt they could start a proactive topic. It was decided the issue needed to be tabled with him at the right moment in time, and that would allow the IC to determine what was taking place.

The states had communicated on daily issues along with the federal government, and from that perspective, nothing had changed. What had changed was the fact that all communications were now monitored. The encrypted messages came at random times and random lengths. It was impossible to know who the messages were for, but it was assumed any of the states or civilians that had shortwave radio equipment could receive them. It was decided the IC had to discover how the decryption process had been sent out and who was the receiving party. It was assumed the messages were strictly between state governments, but the IC's ability to gain access to whoever was sending and receiving the messages was not working.

After three weeks of working this issue, it was decided the President had to be informed. His displeasure with the topic was easily seen. States were talking, and no one inside the federal government could break the code. It was the issue his staff knew would push him into action. The President had become convinced the states were now openly maneuvering against the federal government. The SecDef was not ready to brief the options on dealing with succession, but the President was prepared to hold the meeting to make a decision. Unlike the previous session, this one was short and not open to discussion. The SecDef had one more week to give his Commander in Chief options, but in the meantime, the states would be informed, not asked, of a mandatory All States conference call and the Governors were to be told there would be consequences for those who decided not to attend. Every functional state was to be in on the call, not just the Midwestern and Southwestern states. The request was set for three days after his meeting, and with that, the President ended the session with his staff. What was the topic, and what groundwork was his staff to prepare was utterly unknown. That same day, the Vice President asked those very questions, and the reply was not to be repeated. " We are going to see if this nation remains a Republic."

For two weeks, the list of states utilized the coded messages to grew. Georgia, Mississippi, Alabama, Tennessee, and South Carolina had received couriers from both Arizona and Kansas. Not only did they believe the federal government was monitoring them, but their JAT members had all heard the same rumors from their federal teammates. The traffic between the states was almost exclusively over the issue of an Article V convention. Working on details had proven to be more complicated than any of the states anticipated, and a group of constitutional scholars had been chosen to frame the concept.

The process of holding these conversations was always wrapped with concerns for security. At least once a day, false messages were sent in an attempt to determine if the government had broken the code. A few of the states struggled with the fact they still had their federal support team members in their EOCs. Friendships had been established even before the war and suddenly excluding them was not the right answer. What the federal team members did begin to realize was the distance that was developing between the Governor's key staff and the federal team members. Reports of perceived changes were sent back to their higher headquarters, and those reports only reinforced the fears on the President's staff.

### Reactions to the Call:

Every functioning state attended the All States Call except for Michigan, Utah, and Alabama. Michigan and Utah's downlinks had technical problems, but that was verified by the federal support teams at their locations. Alabama's support team could not confirm why the Governor wasn't able to attend, but they did state they had been asked to leave the state's emergency operation center earlier that morning. Several of the states had been operating under a federally supported location and had no living elected Governors. The war

THE SECOND DARK AGES

had so badly damaged them; federal authorities conducted the only true form of government.

The discussion began with a statement by the President, and he wasted no time getting to the issue at hand. Afterward, many of his staff believed his approach was the primary reason the event took such a dramatic turn. The President's message was unmistakable. If the states could no longer see the value in being united, then the nation was not going to survive. As he was making a point about the legality of succession, the Governor of Georgia interrupted him with a question. Where had the President heard the states wanted to secede? As soon as the Governor of Georgia asked the question, several others began to make comments, and the discussion became too confusing to continue. The President had the network muted and paused for a moment, then he replied with a statement that set the tone for the rest of the call. He stated it was apparent the states saw more value in working with each other than with the federal government, and that was the reason they had been talking about an Article V Convention. Again he was interrupted by a Governor who asked, " Do you listen to everything we talk about"? Many of the states on the call had not been part of the events with the Southwestern or Midwestern states, but they had all heard the stories. The President's answer was, yes. He went on to say his number one priority was the survival of the nation, and everyone had to continue to make sacrifices. The Governor of Florida then commented on how everyone in the country was making sacrifices every hour of every day, but it seemed the federal government was in a far better position sitting inside the Dallas Zone. Again, the call broke down into multiple states speaking at once and again, and the President had the call muted. When the mute was lifted, it was quiet for a moment, and then the Governor of Kansas said, " Good God, we are not even allowed to speak." In what seemed to be an attempt to defuse the tension, the Governor of Oklahoma informed the President the states do talk of an Article V Convention and those conversations were held without the federal government's knowledge-based upon the President's previous reaction to the topic. The Governor then spoke of why many of the states wanted the convention. The federal government was making decisions about the future of the nation without the inputs of those that were holding the country together. Yes, the federal government was providing vital support and had been since the war began, but the bulk of the effort was being accomplished by state and local government as well as ordinary citizens. The President didn't reply.

As soon as the Governor of Oklahoma was finished, Tennessee stated they had a question about the Dallas Zone concept. They wanted to know why the states had never reviewed the criteria for moving to the zone. The President's answer only made matters worse, "There wasn't time." Every Governor on the call knew the concept of the Dallas Zone had been developed over several months. They knew this because of the rumors their JAT members had heard. The answer given was not only not accepted, but it also resulted in yet a third round of jumbled discussions that led to a third muted reaction. This time, when the line was cleared for input, the Governor of Arizona spoke. His question had nothing to do with the Article V issue or the Dallas Zone. His problem was about the future of his state and every other state. What did the federal government expect them to do? Where they to give the government the equipment and resources they needed to survive, yet not attempt to travel to the Dallas Zone? If any answer the President gave sealed the fate of the nation's future, it was the one he gave the Governor. "You need to lean on each other. You need to combine your resources. We will not strip any one state of all the critical items they may need soon, and we will provide as much support as we can. As the Dallas Zone grows more stable, we will begin to increase our support to the rest of the nation". Georgia's Governor was the first to respond. " We need to lean on each other? Then why do we need you"? As soon as he made a comment, he signed off the call.

The All States Call was a complete disaster. The response to the Governor of Georgia's statement could not be heard. The uproar was from nearly every state on the call. The mute action was ordered again, but this time as soon as it happened, states began to sign out. The last three states on the call were states that were already under federal control, California, Oregon and Washington State. They had no input, and nothing was asked of them. The call was still muted for several minutes, but they could see the President and his staff were talking amongst themselves. After a few minutes, all three states were told they could sign out. The call was over, and the future of the United States of America was now officially in doubt.

The topic of the critical locations and the government's intent to secure them never came up by design, but it was clear the plan would need further emphasis given the climate that now officially existed between the states and the federal government. Not only had the relationship changed between the states and the government, the President had changed. He ordered the SecDef to draw now up plans to secure the entire list of sites. He then told his staff they would convene the next morning to review what took place in the all state's call and what course of action may be needed.

When the call was over, several states sent messages to each other on the topic of how to discuss what had just taken place, without the federal government gaining knowledge of such an event. It was decided several states would draft a message and then sent it to the rest for input. This message would be based on options the states could consider, mainly, how to interact with the federal government soon.

# CHAPTER TWELVE: CRISIS

Within a month of the, all states call, a majority of the Governor's had agreed. They would hold an Article V convention without the knowledge or support of the federal government. It was to be held in Missouri, and each state that had voted for the convention would send three members. The topics to be reviewed were the Special War Power Laws, and the authority of the federal government to commandeer state, local and private property. There was to be no discussion of succession. No topic addressed any state leaving the Union. What the states wanted was a less intrusive federal government, and that was it. How to arrange this convention without the government becoming aware was an issue that had not been ironed out, but as soon as it was, the date and location was set.

It had been anticipated the news of this event being planned could not be kept secret. All communications between states took place over the coded network, and that coding was changed every three days. The states were confident the ability to keep this information away from the federal support teams inside each state was impossible. If it was for that reason, only a few people on each Governor's staff were allowed to know the plan. An Article V convention was going to take place, but only if the federal government didn't become aware of the event.

Several states had Constitutional Experts advise them the very process they were counting on was not being correctly followed. The procedures for such an Article V Convention required an internal state voting procedure, but that was not possible. The Governors, like the President, had been acting under their own set of state Emergency Powers laws that were designed to be temporary in duration. In a typical legal environment, this procedural flaw would allow the federal government to declare the whole process invalid, but everyone understood the nation was not in normal times. Just as the federal government had determined, "Extraordinary" measures would be required to keep the nation functioning, the states adopted the same viewpoint. They were not following Article V requirements by the letter of the law, but they were executing the state's rights to the best of their ability. The nation had been ravaged by global war, and that gave everyone room to justify their actions, right or wrong.

### Crisis in the Zone:

The federal government was dealing with two pressing issues inside the Dallas Zone, and that took the day to day attention off the topic of the states. The ability to prevent people from entering the zone had been nearly impossible from the very beginning, but the problem came back into focus with an event near Lake Ray Hubbard. With the loss of border continuity, the flow of people seeking a safer environment was relentless. Stories of the Dallas Zone had been spreading as far away as Central America and people risked everything to get to the zone. A group made up of El Salvador and Columbian military members, along with their families, had made it into the zone and set up camp near Lake Ray Hubbard. They were only discovered when several of their children came down with Measles and had shown up at a local clinic. When it was found they were not US citizens, the children and the adults who brought them to the clinic were detained. Within a few hours, a team was sent out to the campsite to determine who was there and who else had encountered the infected children. The team was fired upon, and three of the members were killed. The inspection team radioed what was taking place, and a reaction force was sent to the location. It was not the first time an armed group had been responded to, but this group was more capable than most.

By the time the reaction team arrived, the campsite was empty. Where the enemy had gone and how many of them there where was not near as concerning as who had come in contact with the force. Measles without effective medical preventive care in the area would become a killer, and just the rumor would send shockwaves throughout the zone. The search for the group started immediately, but the military members were good at traveling undetected. Word of the incident was spread both by authorities and by word of mouth. Coming in contact with the group was a danger both because of their weapons and because of the measles. The area clinics were warned, and additional security was assigned as well. The assets needed to track the individuals were not immediately tasked, given this was not the first time such an event had happened, but when leadership was informed of the measles issue, those assets were freed up. It was assumed the group was on foot and the members already in custody stated they were made up of El Salvadorian Special Forces as well as Columbian military members. They estimated there were over 50 people in the group, including family members. Priority was given to the task of locating them and many of the locals banded together for safety.

Five days later, a report from Fate Texas indicated a medical convoy heading into that town had been attacked. The convoy was escorted by three military vehicles operated by six military members as well as two Texas Highway Patrol Officers. Three US military members were killed, but four of the attackers were shot. One was taken alive, and he was moved to the MP /Civilian/station in Rockwall. The individual stated they were only trying to find medical support for their sick members, but one of their members fired on the convoy as it was pulling over. He stated that over 20 of the people in the group were sick. By the time this story was relayed to national levels, the decision was made to have a maximum effort in locating the group.

That same week, a child was brought into a clinic near Forney, Texas. It was apparent the child had measles. The Mother was asked where they could have had contact with anyone in the past five days, and she stated a woman had dropped off a sick child at her home. She asked the Mother where she was from, given she had heard of the incident from a few days earlier. The child's mother said she was Mexican and had seen a group of people several nights before and their children had played together. No one knew if the story was true, and no one cared at that point. What mattered was a US citizen, and her children had been exposed. The Center for Disease Control, CDC, arrived at the clinic and began the tracking protocols required to map a possible contamination area. To the government, one thing was clear. The group was contacting civilians, and the fear of another outbreak in the zone was now a reality.

The zone had seen two outbreaks in the past year. One was a flu event that killed over 15,000 people. Three months later, a stronger variant of a different flu virus killed over 25,000. Vaccines from the National Strategic Stockpile were utilized, but many of the items had been destroyed after going months without power. Antibiotics from Military mobility sites were recovered, but again, significant quantities had been rendered useless without refrigeration. Tablet medications were the bulk of what the zone had, but the protocols for using them were stringent. What the government was facing was a large-scale epidemic with few resources to combat the outbreak. The one real advantage they had was the typical distance between large gatherings of people. Although the zone was home to over 40 million, the area where this event took place was one of the least populated locations. The hope was this group would be found soon, and the spread of the illness would be controlled by nothing more than Social Distancing, a concept the CDC had developed years earlier.

When the updated report was given to the President, he responded by asking just what improvements could be made in securing the perimeter of the zone? The answer he was given did not give him a level of comfort. The task of securing the area was mostly restricted to public roadways and water-ways. The truth was, a clear majority of the zone's perimeter was simply wide open. The President then asked for options. How was the nation expected to start the rebuilding process if it couldn't protect the area that the goal would begin? The best option his staff came up with was to increase the patrols, but when the calculations were made on the expenditure of fuel, that option was not approved. Fix observation post, much like the Border Patrol, became the answer. The zone al-ready had such a network, but the increase in numbers would be dramatic. The President then asked about, "National As-sets," satellite assets. He wanted to know if it was possible to cover the zone and the area around the zone 24/7. It was possible, but the concept would mean pulling them off pri-mary locations, such as Russian and India and what was left of China. There was also an issue with fuel. To move the assets would burn limited fuel, and the ability to conduct refueling was now gone. It became clear if the assets were transferred, the nation would be assuming the risk from other parts of the world. The President's orders were clear. The satellites would be moved, and the zone would be covered to the greatest ex-tent possible. Without the zone, the need to observe other lo-cations in the world was a moot point.

By the end of the next week, eight more cases of Mea-sles were confirmed. The group from Columbia and El Sal-vador had not been found despite intensive search operations. Then an event near Lake Tawakoni caught the attention of the government. Four bodies had been found, and they had been burned. Three of them were adults, and the other was thought to be a young teenager. Their identity was impossible to determine as all four were burned beyond recognition. There was nothing else with them, but the team sent to investigate reported a small, temporary campsite had been located near the fire. It was decided this had to be the people they were looking for, and the bodies were most likely burned because they had died from the infection. The search for the group was intensified, and the authorization of rotor-wing support was given. Two days later, a thermal image was identified just West of the city of Emory. A response team was lifted into to verify that group. Many small pockets of citizens were still living in camp environments, and it could not be assumed they had located the group in question.

A report of a firefight was up channeled, and a Quick Reaction Force was flown into the area with an hour. When the fight was over, twenty-three prior members of the El Salvadorian and Columbian military had been killed, and twenty unarmed non-US citizens were taken into custody. The Situation Report from the Reaction Team set off even more alarm bells. The group had no children with them. When interviewed, several of the women stated they had left their children with families they had encountered because they were sick, and the group couldn't support them. When asked how many children, the total answer was fourteen. They were between two and seven years old, and that was why the families they came across agreed to take them in. As the CDC team was talking over the issue with the President's staff, more news came in from the team. The survivors stated they had actually moved into the area with two other groups, and all were about the same size and that they had all been staying in Dallas. Glendale Park had been their campsite for over two weeks. One woman stated they only decided to split up when several of the children became sick. She and the other survivors of their group had no idea where the other two groups had gone. It was determined, all three groups were made up of El Salvadorian and Columbian military members and their families. The other two groups were heavily armed, and all had made the Dallas Zone their destination point. Their ability to blend in was based upon their everyday language with the Hispanic population in the zone. The captured members were transported to a facility located at The Naval Air Station Joint Reserve Base in Ft. Worth.

An update on the situation was given during the President's morning brief, and the reaction was predicted by his staff. The security of the zone was a top priority, and it was even more evident that priority was not being met. The plan to increase security post was reviewed, and a concept the State of Texas had been using for years was given as an option. On Texas' Southern border, a series of low-cost cameras that were linked back to an operational center for surveillance had proven to be very effective at detecting intrusions. These cameras were modified game cameras that had solar packs. Their signal was based on a standard cell network. Texas had employed thousands of these cameras in combination with the more advanced systems operated by Border Patrol. The bottom line was, it was a very effective way to monitor known areas of approach without having to commit vehicle-based denial. Several other options were given, but it was clear the ability to secure the movement into the zone was a task most of them had underestimated.

When the issue of the three groups that had entered the zone came up, the President's question was straight forward. "How do we find them"? Someone at the table then made a comment, "can we find them"? Since the end of the war, the nation's largest cities had been unusable. Without water, electricity, and food, most became ghost towns. Over the first two years after the war, organized operations were sent into most cities, but the goal was to retrieve essential items. In every case, people were found living in them, but the federal government had made it very clear, these sites would not be supported. In some situations, states and city governments attempted to organize some level of community operations, but the large percentage of cities were unregulated. In the case of Dallas and Ft. Worth, Lines of demarcation were based on on-street locations. Patrols were assigned to monitor and identify who was inside the unusable areas, but they were minimum given the expenditure of limited resources such as fuel. The zone identification cards were somewhat useful, but the number of forgeries was nearly uncontrollable. Everything about the event with these three groups formed one perception. It was not only impossible to control the influx into the zone, but it was also impossible to find people who were already inside. To the President, the concept of the zone had to change. They would do the best they could to control entry, and that would mean harsher measures for those attempting to enter illegally, but the concept of how the zone operated would need to change.

Securing the Dallas Zone would now have three levels. The perimeter security would be drastically increased. Assets inside the zone such as food and medical support would be centralized, and finally, the movement inside the zone would be restricted with an emphasis placed on who came out of the closed areas.

The President gave the SecDef knew orders. The primary mission of the US Military was the security and survival of the zone. Any assets located outside the zone needed to fulfill this task would be moved as soon as possible. The nuclear sites would keep a priority, but only until it was clear the systems would no longer function. The survival of the nation became the zone and only the zone. Preparation to execute the critical assets mission changed. The priority was now the zone's security and resources required for the assets mission would be re-tasked.

Daniel steiner

*The Convention:*

The crisis in the zone had one dramatic, unintended impact. The issue of the states, although not forgotten, had fallen off the President's Staff's radar for over two weeks. Morning briefs mentioned the ongoing communications, but nothing out of the ordinary had occurred. It was noted that four states had denied the federal support team members to attend parts of their governor's briefings, parts that they had been allowed to participate in the past, but the sense of urgency had been overtaken by the event inside the zone.

By this point in time, the movement of individuals out of state was still not a common practice, but it was taking place at a level that could go undetected. Checkpoints along significant roadways at strategic locations were predominantly utilized to keep people out of highly contaminated areas. States had their own "Safety Checkpoints," but they were limited to major highways at state lines. In the end, it was easy for the states to send their delegates to a meeting.

The initial meeting location had been changed to Tulsa Oklahoma for unknown reasons, but all the states that had committed to attending at least the initial meeting arrived. They were scheduled to meet for two days and to have no communications with their home states during the discussion. Their guidelines were specific, and none of them were authorized to speak of additional topics. Their job was to begin the process of addressing the changes to the US Constitution that would prohibit the federal government from enacting the very Emergency Warpower Laws they were living under.

The question at hand was not a new one. Three times in US history, the President had declared "Emergency Powers"; Abraham Lincoln suspension of habeas corpus, Franklin Roosevelt with the internment of Japanese Americans on the West Coast and Harry Truman when he nationalized the steel mills. What the collective body came to realize was the fact they had not been provided the legal explanation of the federal government's actions. No state had seen an actual copy of what these laws stated and how they were justified. No one was aware of what limitations these Emergency Warpower's Laws were operating under. It was clear. All the states in attendance, thirty-eight in all, would openly challenge the legal status the federal government was operating under. The issue became, how to change the US Constitution to make this action illegal. There was no discussion of succession, and that fact was made a matter of record.

From the time the states sent their delegates until the time they returned was less than six days. No state reported anything unusual with their federal support teams, but they had heard them talking about an issue inside the Dallas Zone that appeared to have become an emergency. The Draft changes to the US Constitution were briefed to the Governors, and the discussion was already underway as to when and where the follow-on meeting should take place.

Since the end of the war, every state had attempted to gain the status of their federal representatives who had still been in DC when the nuclear strikes came. Many had traveled home before that, but a large number of them were never heard from again. Over a year after the war ended, the federal government attempted to identify how many members of the House and Senate were still alive. The process of replacing them was not even approached given the status the nation was in. Most states assumed many members of both the House and Senate were in survival facilities when the nuclear attacks came, but that fact was simply not worthy of validation, at least not until the issue of an Article V convention came up.

It was decided that instead of following the normal process of questioning the federal government's authority to enact the laws they were operating under; the states would concentrate on changing the constitution and then inform the federal government of the changes. The 10<sup>th</sup> Amendment of the US Constitution would be changed, and that change would invalidate the federal government's, to include the President's authority to operate under the current Emergency War Powers Laws. State's Rights would also be reviewed, but those changes proved to be far more difficult for the states to address. Changing the course of government proved to be more complicated than many of the states had anticipated.

The follow-on meeting was set. The states would meet, and each of the thirty-eight that attended had signatories authorized by their Governors. Again, this was not the exact process spelled out in the US Constitution, but the "intent" was followed, and that was the consensus of each of the states that attended. A group of constitutional scholars were chosen to review the final draft, and there were no objections. The states then faced their most challenging task. How would they go about informing the federal government? A list of options was developed, but in the end, the only acceptable choice was to request another All States Call. When asked what the topic would be, the answer was a statement. An Article V Convention had been held, and changes to the US Constitution had been ratified.

The Governor of Missouri was elected to make the official notification, but his formal request would have the endorsement of all thirty-eight Governors. The Missouri federal support team most senior member was called to the Governor's Office. The Governor was straight to the point. He handed the team leader a written request and asked her to submit it as soon as possible. The meeting was short but professional. Thirty minutes later, the written request was received by a secured email network. Now the states had nothing more they could do other than wait for a reply.

*Impasse:*

The message from the Governor of Missouri was read

by the President with the Vice President and the President's Chief of Staff standing in the room. The President's first words were, "how did they meet and when"? after a short discussion between the three of them, a meeting was called with a very select group to attend. The Chief of Staff prepared the list and acknowledged no one else was to know of the meeting. The federal support team in Missouri was also notified they were not to mention this event to anyone until further notice.

The primary members in the meeting were the President, the Vice President, the Chief Justice of the Supreme Court, The US Attorney General, and the Secretary of Defense. These were the members sitting at the table, but others were in the room as observers or subject matter experts. The flow of the meeting was very structured. The group had two topics. Was the action taken by the state's legal? What options did the President have? The first comment came from the Vice President. He asked the President if he intended to hold the All States Call? As far as options went, the Vice President believed not holding the call was one they should consider. The Chief Justice then stated the legal procedure requirements for an Article V Convention could not have been met. The states couldn't hold state legislative assemblies to gain a majority vote. The question of procedure became the topic at hand. The President asked the Chief Justice if it was his legal opinion the states executed an invalid process? His answer created even more confusion. After just questioning the state's procedures, he stated they would need to see the process the states actually utilized, and that would require an extensive review of the whole event. It was the Attorney General who made the next comment that dragged the group even deeper into confusion. If the process the states had undertaken was going to end up in some form of legal review potentially, should the Chief Justice be part of this initial conversation?

Simply put, if this issue was going to go through the judicial review process, should the highest court in the land be involved now? It was decided the Chief Justice would give his opinion on how to proceed and then excuse himself from the meeting. The Attorney General agreed, and both he and the Chief Justice advised the President to hold the All States Call to determine what process was followed? The first tasked had been achieved, but only in part. The call would be made to gather facts, facts that were needed to determine future courses of action.

The President reframed his second task. "Let's assume it is decided the states followed a legally defendable process. How would their changes to the constitution impact the nation's future"? The problem with the President's question was, no one knew what changes had been made. They were aware the states had been openly against the Emergency War Powers Laws and most believed that was most likely what had been addressed, but what actual changes had been made? That is what they didn't know. It became apparent; the All States Call had to be held. Each state was notified of the date and time. The topic would be the state's "attempt" to conduct an Article V Convention. It was the word, "Attempt," that ensured the call would end in failure.

15 states would attend the call, and only three had any level of input. The President ended the call after only ten minutes and thanked the states that did attend. Only two questions had been asked. Did any of them know why the other state chose not to participate in the call? Could any of the states provide feedback on how the convention was held? Florida's Governor gave the only answer the government could work with. It had been decided the changes to the US Constitution would be hand-delivered to the federal government by a delegation chosen by all the states. When would this take place, and would it include an explanation of how the convention was conducted was not known by any of the Governors on the call. After the call was over, it was decided the Governors did know but had agreed not to divulge any in-

formation other than what the Governor of Florida provided.

The concept of the call was a failure. It was also seen as a gesture of good faith that had not been returned. The Vice President made a comment, despite their best efforts, the states seemed to be determined to pull away from the Union. It was the SecDef who responded. "I don't believe they are trying to pull away. It seems they're just unwilling to live with the impacts of the Emergency Warpower Laws. Perhaps that is how we solved this"? The President and others in the room didn't agree. What they were trying to do was hold the nation together. The states could not be allowed to break the Union, and whatever they had come up within their convention could not be honored. The SecDef was ordered to continue the planning process for securing the critical sites list as well as increasing the security of the Dallas Zone. Both could not be accomplished at the same time, and the SecDef and his staff knew one task was far more dangerous to the nation than the other.

Feedback from the All Sates Call was provided to every state. The delegation was tasked to depart for the Dallas Zone within the week. Three Beechcraft C-12 Hurons would move a ten-person delegation to inform the federal government of the approved changes to the US Constitution. All ten were aware of the procedural actions in the Article V Convention, but they had no documentation and no intent of justifying the convention process. Their mission was clear; the signed changes to the US Constitution were to be implemented immediately. The states fully anticipated there would be reluctance, but that was why they had agreed upon a team who were all recognized constitutional law experts.

The aircraft all requested flight approaches to the military airfield in Ft. Worth Texas. One aircraft departed from Tucson, Arizona with the other two leaving from Columbia Missouri and Montgomery Alabama. All three arrived within four hours of each other. That same evening, the delegation met with the President and key members of his staff. Approximately five hours after the beginning of the meeting, the delegation was scheduled to depart. The exchanges had been professional but very tense. In the end, the President informed the delegation the federal government would review the proposed changes, but only after the states gave a detailed explanation of how the convention was executed. The delegation was given a set of questions that would require answers for the federal government to consider reviewing the process further. The departure took place, and as soon as the three aircraft had left, the President called a meeting of his key staff.

Upon return, the delegates all insured they departed the aircraft with nothing they had on them during the meeting. Trust was gone, and the capabilities of the government were unknown to the states. The members were even required to change their clothes. Within 24 hours, the conversation with the government and the stipulations they gave were known to all the states. What the government could detect was a large volume of traffic between the states and that it lasted for well over three hours. The states would provide a legal review of the Article V Convention process, and it would have the signatures of every state involved. That document would then be given to a designated federal support team with the instructions to deliver it to the President. The response was finalized and executed just as it had been agreed upon.

If anything from the meeting had surprised the President, it was the reality that all the governors of the functioning states had signed the document. Not only had they agreed on the changes to the US Constitution, but they had all supported the processes taken to validate those changes. To the President and his staff, it was clear the states firmly believed they had met the requirements to amend the US Constitution, and the states now waited for an official reply.

The state's legal review of the Article V Convention

was transmitted to the government by the Kentucky support team. A legal analysis was immediately called for, and DOJ was given three days to brief the President on their findings. One issue stood out from the very beginning. The states based their actions on the same grounds the President had used when the federal government enacted the Emergency Warpower's Laws. The nation had been in "Unprecedented Times" when the Emergency Warpower's Laws were signed by the President. These "unprecedented Times" were also the cornerstones of the state's actions. Just as the federal government was not able to follow standard procedures to institute the new laws, the states' argument was, they too were not able to follow standard procedures. The short answer was, "if it was acceptable for the federal government, it was acceptable for the states.

DOJ's findings were mixed. The review had been conducted by seven constitutional experts, with five of them coming from the department and two coming from members of Congress who had spent years studying the US Constitution. The briefing to the President showed that three members of the review board concurred with the state's process, and four did not. At face value, the majority of the board non-concurred with the states, but the arguments from the minority were so compelling; the President decided to hold a more significant forum for a final opinion. The functioning portion of the US House and Senate had been advised of the situation from the beginning, but the President had decided to limit the involvement given his confidence in getting the states to understand what was best for the nation. That changed when the Couriers arrived at the Dallas Zone. The DOJ was asked for a legal review, and when that review was given, the President knew he had no choice but to address both houses with the issue. Based upon the powers given him in the Emergency Warpower's Laws, the final decision on the matter would be his, but he understood the gravity of the situation had reached a point that he could no longer exclude a functional part of the government. It was then he and his key staffed realized a critical reality, a reality he and others were not aware of.

The issue of the Article V Convention had been a topic of contention not just based on the information the Executive and Judicial Branches of government had informed them of. Many of the surviving legislatures had actually been in contact with their home states, and that was a factor the President and his staff had somehow overlooked or underestimated. The number was limited and seemed to be based upon their states reaching out to them. How these conversations had taken place was at first unknown, and the entire topic went unnoticed until the President requested a meeting with key members of both houses. It was then he realized, perceptions on the validity of an Article V Convention were already well entrenched in many members.

The issue may have been the validity of the State's assumed changes to the US Constitution, but it became clear the Legislative branch of government had their problem that would now rise to the surface as well. For two years, the federal government had struggled to stabilize the nation, and the struggle was continuing even as this constitutional crisis was taking place, but a percentage of the House and the Senate had grown more and more concerned over the enduring nature of the Emergency Warpower's Laws. The issue of the states bringing amendment articles to the US Constitution caught most of the Representatives by surprise, even those that had been in contact from time to time with their home states, but it seemed the time had come to address the very issue the states were concerned over. Both the Legislative Branch of the government and the States had a growing concern over centralized power. This viewpoint became very evident upon the President's first meeting with the leadership of the House and Senate. He had asked to meet with them on the issue of the Article V Convention to get their opinion. What they told him was an answer he was unprepared for. The surviving members of both chambers of the House were going to address the Article V Convention issue, but only after they discussed the Emergency Warpower's Laws. The time had come to define the limits to the very laws that had been holding the nation together for over two years. In the eyes of the President, the issue of his authority was now officially under review.

### Limited Change:

The discussion over the enduring powers of the special laws only lasted two days. It was clear to everyone the overwhelming opinion was those laws must have limits, and those limits would be set by the Legislative body of the nation. Although only 40 percent of the Senate and 30 percent of the House had survived the war, the authorities still constituted a legislative process. The Emergency Warpower's Laws were enacted at the moment in time when the survival of the nation was in doubt. That had changed, and everyone agreed. The nation may not survive as it once was, but it would survive. The requirement for Special Laws would continue, but they would be governed far more closely than in the past two years. The President or his legal replacement would be required to report to both chambers of the House twice a year. Changes to "Special Powers" as they would be called, would be reviewed and modified at that time. A simple majority of a collective vote in both chambers would be required to implement amendments to the Special Powers.

It was clear the nation was far from reconstructing the electoral process it had once operated under, but the states would be asked to recommend replacements for the representatives that had been with the federal government since the end of the war. It was decided that the process would begin one year from the signing of the new changes to the government. The states had to be given the right to help shape the future of the nation, or the nation would not survive as a Union.

When the issue of the Article V Convention was finally addressed, only one answer was agreed upon. Every state was going to be informed of the changes, and then they would be asked if they still wished to be signatories to the amended Constitutional Articles. The hope was, with the issue of the Emergency Warpower's Laws being addressed, a majority of the states would withdraw their support from the convention.

An All States Call was arranged, and the topic of the call was scripted in such a way as to entice all the states to attend." Changes to the Emergency Warpower's Laws and the reimplementation of the representative Process", that was the topic line. Initially, it worked except for Arizona, Missouri, Alabama, Wyoming, and Iowa. It was the Governor of Kansas who convinced the holdout states to at least listen to the discussion. It was also decided the visual impact of the call was critical to giving the right impression as to why the government wished to have the conversation. The Speaker of the House would be seated to the President's right and the surviving Senate Majority Leader would be seated to his left. The real purpose of the call was clear to everyone sitting with the President. The survival of the Union was still in question.

The President began the call by thanking all the states for attending and quickly acknowledged the desperate state of affairs the nation found itself in. In his opening statement, he never mentioned the Article V Convention or the documentation that had been sent by the states. His emphasis was squarely placed on the Special Warpower's Laws and the changes that would be becoming. He spoke of the efforts at the federal government's end to address these laws, and he asked the Speaker of the House, who was from Illinois, to give the details of those changes. When the speaker was finished, it was clear the volume and depth of the questions were going to require more time and interaction than could be accomplished on that one call. It seemed many of the states wanted a much greater explanation of the changes to the Emergency War-power's Laws, but one question set the tone for any follow-up conversations. The Governor of the State of Missouri ask when the changes would go into effect and did the changes allow the states to decide what assets would be moved from their states? Just when the President's Staff had begun to believe they may have resolved part of the crisis, the point of State's Rights came back to the forefront of the discussion. The an-swer was given by the President and again, the stance he took set the tone for the rest of the call. He was straight forward and blunt, and that became the point of failure. He informed the Governors the federal government would retain the right to take possession of any item vital to the future of the nation. His powers to do so would be reviewed by both chambers of the House, but until the vote to remove those precise powers, they would stand. As soon as he had made this statement, he added that in fact such a vote had already taken place and both Houses agreed the authority to commandeer items for the sake of the nation would remain for the foreseeable future. The conference call had only managed to resolve one issue. The states would not be given a voice if it was a matter of na-tional survival. The power of the federal government had not been checked, nor the authority of the President. What had changed was the process of reviewing those powers, and that was it.

The Governor of Kansas interrupted a statement being made by the Secretary of Commerce. He asked if the changes to the US Constitution brought about by the Article V Conven-tion had been reviewed and if so, by whom and what was the outcome? The call was over 30 minutes long when the point of the Article V Convention finally came up. Up until then, most of the Governors had been willing to hear the President address the issue of the Emergency Warpower's Laws, but now it was time for them to discuss the one question they had in-deed agreed to attend the conference call for.

The Governors were informed their Article V Amendments to the US Constitution were reviewed by the Department of Justice and were found to be invalid. When asked if both chambers of the House were allowed to review the amendments, the answer they were given most likely sealed the fate of the call. They were informed that given the procedural flaws in the State's "attempt" at an Article V Convention, the documentation was considered unreviewable by the Congress or the Senate. The Governors had no way of knowing if that was the truth, but one issue did stand clear. The federal government was not going to honor the results. When the explanation was given by the President, there was no response. The President was making a statement about the pending rotation of elected officials when the Governor of Arkansas interrupted him with a question. Was the US Supreme Court Chief Justice on the call? Was he in the room with the President's Staff? The Chief Justice spoke, and the Governors knew he was there. The Governor of Arkansas then made a request many in the room with the President had feared. The states as a collective asked the US Supreme Court to review the legality of the Article V Amendments.

Simply put, given the extenuating circumstances the nation had been in and would continue to be in, where the guidelines the state's followed adequate? The states were unanimous in their request for a Supreme Court review, and the federal government had no power to deny the request. The Chief Justice stated, given the gravity of the event, the court would review the case as soon as possible. No one else in the room said a word, and as soon as the commitment was made, the Governor of Arizona stated he was finished with the call. It was the Governor of Kansas that suggested the same body of experts that had delivered the Article V Amendments should be the ones to argue the case of the states. Everyone agreed, and a follow-on call would be held that week to set the final items needed for the hearing. The call ended, and as soon as it did, the message traffic between the states picked up dramatically.

**Other Events:**

The President's morning brief was set to be focused around the pending legal review, but events elsewhere in the world demanded the government's attention. For months the US had been tracking a radical movement in what had been Eastern Europe. A rogue Russian General had gained control of the territories of Estonia and Latvia. The city of Riga had become his base, and the Russian government had been unwilling and unable to expend the limited assets to deal with the movement. The nations of Lithuania, Belarus, and Poland had formed a provisional government within the past six months, and that group had been in constant contact with both the Russian government and the US over their concerns with this radical group. The morning brief indicated the Russian Warlord was forming a large raiding party set to move into Lithuania within the few days. The Russians and the US had agreed this group formed a real danger to the continued attempts to stabilize all of Eastern Europe. The US had consulted with the British and German governments, and it was clear they had no intention of expending assets to deal with a movement. France had not even responded to a request for input on the matter. This had not been the first time such an event had taken place in the post-war world, but it had been determined that if such actions could continue, they would significantly impact the ability to reach stability and without stability, there could be no real recovery. The Russians and British had already responded to two similar movements in the past year, and both nations felt it was time for the US to become involved in the whole process. Although the US had militarily evacuated Europe, they still could respond if tasked to do so. The SecDef informed the President what options they had, and the President instructed him they would talk about the matter after the morning brief. It was then the second issue was brought to the President's attention.

After the incursions into the Dallas Zone, the US had increased its intelligence-gathering operations to the South and West. The order had also been given to conduct an analysis of the overall status of Mexico and the other nations of Central and South America. This process was completed predominantly with signal intelligence and limited human intelligence operations. It was the human intelligence portion of the task that caught the US's attention. Events to the South of the nation had been monitored constantly, but not from an actual threat perspective. The task had been tracking what level of governance nations to the South had maintained, with a specific emphasis on Mexico. Once other assets were assigned to the task, it was clear a viable threat had been developing without the US's knowledge. Three groups had formed in separate areas, but with a unified command. These groups were made up of prior military members from a multitude of Central and South American countries, and they had dispersed to three locations, Reynosa Mexico, Carrizo Springs Texas and Goliad Texas. A member of the group near Carrizo Springs had been captured in a shootout with locals, and his story had been given to the intelligence team that was tasked to gather information in that area. The information was over a week old, and that was due to the tasking for the review of threats being given only in the past month. The member in custody had been a Captain in the El Salvadorian Army, and he stated his group numbered well over 300. None of them wore military uniforms, and they had traveled only at night in smaller groups. He informed the intelligence team the concept of forming large raiding parties had come about from a group located at a Shelter Camp just South of Mexico City. Rumors of the US establishing the Dallas Zone had been known for months, and it was those rumors that led to the formation of the raiding parties. At first, their goal was to raid locations around the zone and to do so disguised as South American Refuges that had traveled into the US for the sake of survival. The fact that hundreds of thousands of people had already been doing so, along with the collapsed borders, made their movements easier to execute. The three teams had also been allowed to travel with limited family members to further disguise their actions. When asked if these raiding groups were tasked to return, the answer pushed the topic to the level of immediately briefing the President. Their goal was to maintain their positions as long as possible and to move the seized items back to their main camp that was moving to Monterrey.

The individual had been in custody for over three days by the time the President was given the initial briefing. The groups that were found inside the Dallas Zone where thought to be splinter groups or scouting teams. After the briefing was completed, the President gave the SecDef one task, destroy the groups as quickly as possible to include the basecamp in Monterrey and Mexico City. The President understood it was useless to contact the government of Mexico on the matter, and the risk of exposure to the operation was too significant. What had started out as a well-organized raiding party had turned into, in the eyes of the US, an open incursion on US soil. The crisis in Europe would have to wait, or Europe, along with the Russians, would have to find a way to respond. Not only was the integrity of the US in question by the actions of the states, but an open incursion onto US land was now well underway.

The US Military had two missions at hand. One was to continue to plan for the occupation of the primary critical sites in the US, and the other was to neutralize an immediate threat on US soil. The priority was obvious, but the planning process had to take into account both missions as they would both consume assets that could not be replaced. To make matters far worse, the raiding groups were operating in an unconventional style. They traveled and dressed like anyone else in the area. Their weapons were concealed and determining who they were was going to prove to be a very intricate part of the mission. The fact their bed down locations were known would prove to be the one decisive advantage the US had.

The bulk of the forces tasked with the missions would not come from units inside the zone. Given the size of the raiding groups, it was deemed too important to maintain the maximum amount of security inside the zone. The problem became equipping and then moving the units that would be tasked. The military had been no different than the states. The best-equipped units in the nation had been moved into the zone. Although other organizations were capable of operations, most were not at acceptable combat readiness levels. "Re-leveling," as it was called, would take time and no one was sure what these raiding groups planned to do next. What did start immediately was the process of gathering as much information as possible on the actions of these groups. A detachment of Special Operations was tasked to find the camp outside Mexico City, and another was given the job of finding the camp in Monterrey. It was a collection mission, but it was authorized to turn into an assault operation based upon the decision of the on-scene commander. What the President and the rest of his staff understood was the reality that the US military was prepared to conduct combat operations on the sovereign land of Mexico.

*Contact:*

Two days from the briefing, the team tasked with the mission in Monterrey was in place. It was estimated the population within fifteen miles of the city was over 3 million. Finding a camp of military members was based upon analysis, the group in question would take and hold an old Mexican Garrison near the city. Those sites were known, and they were checked first. Drone overflights provided the locations within the first five hours. The mistake had been the members not believing they needed to continue their sanitized appearance. Weapons storage and electronic communications confirmed the right target. The one issue that was immediately sent to the rear for approval was the confirmation of a large contingent of Mexican military members within the group. Not only was the US preparing to conduct operations on Mexican soil, but they would be engaging Mexican Military members. It was determined these members were no longer reporting to the government and as such didn't represent Mexico.

The final confirmation the US team had located the right camp came from a snatch mission executed at the authority of the US Team Leader. Three individuals were taken traveling away from the camp, and they quickly confirmed everything the US had suspected, but their story was actually more alarming than anticipated. All three were US citizens and had military backgrounds. They were scouts for one of the smaller raiding parties and had been utilizing their Texas Driver's Licenses as positive identification if questioned by any locals. They had been raiding in the area of Laredo for over five months and stated there were at least 1500 members in their camp, not counting families. When asked about their knowledge of the two groups inside Texas, they said there were actually three, and they were nothing more than forward operating bases, FOBs. Their camps inside the state were replicas of the typical shelter camps that were located throughout the country. None of the three knew the exact location of the FOBs, but two of them had been to one near Brownsville within the last two weeks. All three were extracted back to the military facility at Ft. Worth.

It was clear the US force outside the camp in Monterrey was far too small to conduct combat operations. Moving additional forces into the area would prove to be challenging, given the rings of security that had been set up around the camp. It was also decided the location of the three FOBs inside Texas had to be positively identified and had teams in place prior to the main camp in Monterrey being assaulted. How much time that would take would become the issue.

Reports of violence and armed incidents had been so

prevalent since the end of the war; there was never any consideration to notify anyone at the federal level. By the end of the first year, the number of incidents had dropped dramatically, but they still took place at a level that most simply wrote them off. No one ever considered any such event was part of a larger, more organized operation and in fact, nearly all of them were not. It was not until the federal government asked the Texas state leadership what they understood of such events that they found an answer they were unprepared for. Law and order in most areas outside the controlled sections of Texas were based upon the authority of the County Judge. Responding to incidents had been and continued to be an issue for the locals. No actual tracking of such events had taken place, and the ability to do so was utterly dependent upon up-channel reporting. Areas that had once been known as the "Wild West" were precisely that once again. When asked if the state was aware of any more extensive than regular events near the areas of Brownsville or Carrizo Spring, the state had no answer. The state had not officially heard from anyone near the regions of Brownsville or Carrizo Springs since the end of the war. Travelers had spread stories, and these stories were quickly collected by the Intelligence Community, but no official reporting had been given at any point in time. When that explanation reached the President, his response set the tone for future actions.

" We seem not to own that part of our country anymore, but we'll change that."

The Collection Team was supported by several members of the Texas Rangers who had all worked the Brownsville area for years. They had been sent in a day after the snatch mission in Monterrey. Drones had been flying the area for the twelve hours before the team's arrival. Months earlier, the Rangers had heard rumors of a large group of what the locals were calling Bandits living on South Padre Island, and it was decided the team would work that area first. Within hours of their arrival, it became clear to them the so-called authorities in charge of the Island were not authorities at all. Padre Island had become a forward operating base for the organization out of Mexico, and it seemed everyone in the area had adjusted to their new environment. Another snatch mission was executed, and two members driving a Border Patrol Vehicle were collected. It was learned the group had taken quiet control of the Island nearly two months earlier and were using the location to run raids into Corpus Christi. Their primary targets were fuel and medical supplies, and the process of sending those items back to the camp in Monterrey was confirmed. The captured members estimated the team's strength to be over 200, but they were spread out over observation units, raid units, and rear security. The Brownsville Collection Team was ordered to remain in place with the task of collecting additional information.

The team assigned to Carrizo Springs was inserted at the same time as Brownsville, and they too had drone support before and during their initial operation. Like Padre Island, it took only a few hours to determent the raiding group was actually running the small town. Again, a snatch mission was conducted, and four members of the group were captured with one being a US citizen. It was determined the group had been operational in the area for over two months. When the US citizen was asked if he and those like him were leveraged when question by authorities, his answer didn't come as a complete surprise, they had not encountered local or state authority since they began their missions. They were tasked with raid missions on some of the larger ranches in the area and then worked their way to the assets that might be in Laredo. Their logistical movement process back to the main camp in Monterrey was identical to the process in Padre Island and Brownsville.

The Carrizo Springs Collection Team would change the dynamics of the US's approach. One of the Texas Rangers assigned to the team new several of the Ranchers in the area and the stored capabilities they had at their leading Ranch Houses. He recommended they attempt to make contact with two of them to ascertain what they knew of these raiding parties. The captured individuals were flown back to the Ft. Worth facility as soon as the team was given permission to contact the ranches. The movement was covert with the threat of the main ranch sites being in the control of the raiding parties. The first ranch was located just South of Asherton at Highway 83. The main Ranch House was empty, but there were signs of a recent gun battle that were far beyond what had been the norm after the war. It was clear to the team the Ranch had been attacked by a Platoon size force that was armed with light and heavy machineguns as well as 81mm Mortars. Five area ranch families had consolidated at that location just before the nuclear strikes. The team found confirmed kill sites based on blood evidence, but nobodies. They immediately decided to proceed to the next Ranch the Ranger knew had been heavily fortified. Upon arrival, they found the same results.

By that next morning, both Collection Teams had reported the same findings. Numerous locations were items that may have been stored or where people may have been fortifying themselves were found to be destroyed. The Carrizo Springs Team was ordered to make contact with the Texas Department of Public Safety garrison in Laredo, but the Texas Rangers advised they should not travel highway 83 given the large number of ambushes that had now been reported in the past week. The team approached and made contact when they were ten miles outside of the city. They were told to approach Las Tiendas Road and that a checkpoint was established at the intersection with 1472. Upon arrival, they made contact with a large force of over 65 armed men and women. Most were civilians, but several local and state law enforcement officers made up the command and control of the team. They escorted the Collection Team to the only part of Laredo they claimed to control, the Laredo International Airport. The Headquarters of the Laredo operation was located in an abandon Texas Army National Guard Armory.

A two-hour briefing was held between the Laredo Leadership and the Collection Team. The Laredo area had been uncontrolled since the end of the war. The events that happened around them were considered normal, and no one had any idea of any organized groups that seemed based on military tactics. One local law enforcement member did mention he had heard a rumor local drug gangs had been eliminated by some armed group and all of their supplies had been taken, but most just thought it was the actions of a rival gang from Mexico. Laredo was not a functioning city, but during the day, people in the protected zone around the airport had created a new normal, and that was a scenario found throughout the nation. To the locals, nothing had changed, but to the members of the Collection Team, the reality was new. The US had absolutely no control over its Southern Border.

A large part of the nation had been lost, and that was precisely how the government back in the Dallas Zone perceived what had taken place. The question became, what, if anything, could they do about this new reality? What level of resources would need to be expended? The President had a decision to make. Defend the historical borders of the nation or defend the zone the nation would rebuild from? It was not the first time the question had been reviewed, but it was the first time he was faced with the reality of foreign fighters on US land, killing US citizens.

The SecDef informed him the process of searching for and neutralizing an unknown number of groups would require assets that would need to be moved from the mission of securing critical sites. Simply put, covering both tasks was beyond the current capabilities of the nation, not to mention the increased requirements around the zone. The most capable military in the world was now stretched thin, just attempting to secure its own southern borders.

# CHAPTER THIRTEEN: BETRAYAL

The US Supreme Court was comprised of six surviving members. The ruling on the issue of the State's Article V Convention was 4-2 in favor of the states. The President was informed privately along with key members of his staff. The states would operate under the Emergency Warpower's Laws, but each state had the inalienable right to self-preservation, and as such, assets inside each state that would be considered by any ordinary person to be vital to the welfare of the members of that state could not be removed by a federal government without the state's consent. The Chief Justice's final statement was the one that every member of the federal government understood. The nation had survived for over 2 ½ years after the war and many things had changed, but the process of equal representation was a cornerstone of the country's Democracy and the time had come for that principle of government to return. The President asked if the representatives from the states had been informed of the court's ruling. The Chief Justice said they had not as he felt the gravity of the event required him to notify the President first. The President asked the Chief Justice to delay the court's findings for a few hours as the President and his Staff developed a format for an All States Call. The call was set. It took place seven hours after the court's ruling.

The ruling was not met with spontaneous joy from the states. All of them understood what was taking place, and everyone had been through the same nightmare together.

The reality was, the states had legally passed amendments to the US Constitution in a manner that was not historically accurate but did meet the intentions of the Founding Fathers. The President informed the Governors a detailed series of All States Calls would be held shortly with the intent of gaining each state's support or nonconcurrence on all matters covered by the Emergency Warpower's Laws. The first item reviewed would be the critical sites. Each state would be informed witch sites were in their territory and why the items were vital to the nation as a whole. Any state that had a nonconcur vote with the movement of critical assets would be asked to provide an answer for not only the federal government but for the rest of the states as well. Having the right to say no had become the rule of law, but giving an explanation was a logical request by anyone involved in the process.

The All States Call was relatively short and professional. The states had won, but what they had won was still not totally clear from the perspective of how it would impact each state. The federal government could no longer dictate to

the rest of the nation, but how this change to the 10th Amendment would affect the future of the Union was unknown. The first working group meeting was set for one week from the date of the Supreme Court's decision. By the time that next week was up, events had once again overtaken the nation.


### Lawful Orders:

The Supreme Court's findings had changed many things, but it did not change the needs of the nation. It did not diminish the priority of items needed to rebuild the country. Within a day of the court's decision, a meeting was held to determine the best path forward. The nation had been without a functioning economy since the war, and the concept of purchasing certain critical items from the states was quickly shot down. Prioritization was reviewed with the intent of approaching the most critical items as soon as possible. The logic was, the process of negotiating with the states would work itself out after the first few discussions.

High Voltage cable was chosen as the first item. It was critical to the goal of restoring power in areas of the Dallas Zone that had been damaged by both cyber and EMP events. The state with the largest production location as well as storage of the cable was Kentucky. The government was not only wanting to move what cable was still there in storage, but the goal was to move the manufacturing equipment as well.

The call with the State of Kentucky was held three days after the court's ruling, and the outcome was disastrous. The state was well aware of the cable issue, and it had plans already underway to utilize every foot of it they could salvage. It seems the federal support team that had been working with Kentucky had knowledge of this plan, but in the larger picture of events, it had never bothered to inform their higher headquarters. The short answer was no, and the reason behind the response was more than logical, at least to everyone in the stateside of the discussion. Kentucky then did something the federal government was not prepared for. They made a counteroffer. If the federal government assisted in restoring the wire manufacturing facility, the State of Kentucky would provide half of the wire produced to the government. It was also learned; the state had already conducted a detailed inventory of the wire stored in the state and had come to an agreement with Ohio and Tennessee to share what was recoverable. The state couldn't restore the manufacturing, and that was the reason they made the offer to the federal government. No one on the federal side was prepared to consider such an offer, and it was agreed they would conduct a follow-up call within two days to discuss the topic.

The Kentucky call had been a test. It was the government's first attempt to live under the pending changes to federal laws according to the amended US Constitution, and it was clear the process of negotiating with the states was going to be challenging. In standard times, this issue would have been worked out in a typical Supply and Demand market, but the US and the world no longer lived in normal times. One overwhelming fact became evident. What was critical to the federal government was most likely crucial to the states. To the senior members of the government, it was also evident, the states had begun their own concept of rebuilding, and the federal government seemed not to be part of their planning.

The President was briefed on the Kentucky call the morning after it took place. It happened to be the same briefing where he was informed the events in Europe were taking a dangerous turn for the worse. The Prime minister of England had called the President and notified him the Russians intended to neutralize the Rogue General and his forces. The Russian's surviving nuclear capability had been miscalculated, and it appeared a tactical event was going to take place within 24 hours. The appeal from England was for the US to intervene with its space-based abilities and perhaps avoid yet another nuclear event on European land. That discussion on intervention overshadowed the Kentucky call, at least at that moment. The US would not react to this event, but the debate consumed nearly the entire morning brief. It was not until hours later that the President asked about the call. He sat and listened to his staff interpret what had taken place before he finally turned to the Vice President and said, "I told you this wasn't going to work." The President called a meeting for 10 pm that same night, and that meeting set into motion events that would change the nation once again.

Options for the Kentucky issue were the topics of the meeting. Three were discussed. 1. Agree with the state's offer to assist in rebuilding the capabilities. 2. Inform the state the government would trade for the wire and manufacturing equipment. 3. Take the site and inform the state it was in the interest of the survival of the nation. The option of trading had the most support, but a fatal flaw was then realized. If the federal government began the process of bartering with each state, the items the states would wish to trade for would be exhausted beyond the point of supporting the Dallas Zone. Simply put, the government would be trading away a list as extensive as the critical assets list itself. It was also deemed impossible to rebuild the capability inside the state of Kentucky. Not only would that distract assets away from the Dallas Zone, but the assumption was it would set a precedent for other states the government could not keep.

The decision was made to seize the wire and the facility long enough to dismantle and transport key machinery items. Everyone in the meeting understood this act was illegal now, but only a handful disagreed with the necessity to violate the very changes to the constitution the nation had just passed. Two key members of the President's staff did disagree, the Secretary of Defense and the Speaker of the House. It was the Secretary of Defense that raised his concerns first. It was his opinion the states would see this act as a violation of law and word would spread quickly of what had taken place. The changes to the US Constitution had decreased the threat of rebellion, at least from the federal government's viewpoint, but an action such as the seizure of land and goods from a state would absolutely destroy any confidence gained from the legal changes. It was the President who asked the Secretary of Defense what alternative he supported. He stated he wasn't sure, but he highly recommended further discussions to take place with the State of Kentucky in an attempt to show them just how vital the issue was. After another hour or so of discussion, the decision was finalized by the President. The wire and the facilities would be seized. Later that same night, the Speaker of the House met with the Secretary of Defense. According to the Secretary of Defense, the Speaker voiced his concerns about the President's decision and then asked if the Secretary believed the order to prepare to seize the site was in his opinion, a lawful order. The Secretary is said to have not answered the Speaker but did state he was troubled by the task given him. The mission was to take place in two weeks. Everyone who had knowledge of the event knew there was one huge problem; keeping the states from learning of the event. In reality, there was a second problem. Would the Secretary of Defense execute the mission?

*Mistrust:*

The concept that would be employed to deal with the US's Southern Border was based not upon large scale unit movements, but the utilization of specialized teams that would gain the nickname of "Hunting Teams." Each team was the size of a reinforced Company and was made up of members from all the US services. Each team had drone support as well as an Air Assault package based on rotor wing operations. All combined, over a dozen teams, were dispatched to an area within 100 miles to the South and South West of the Dallas Zone. Each was given an area of operations, and all of them were able to call upon additional forces if required. Their mission was very simplistic. They were to seek out any armed group that was operating outside the knowledge or approval of any localized leadership. If these groups were found to be in defense of private land and made up of US citizens, then they would be identified and tasked with reporting their status once a week. Any hostile actions taken against the Hunting Teams would be met with deadly force. This process was developed and put into operation in a relatively short period, but word of the action was poorly communicated outside the zone. The Hunting Teams started their mission from the identified edge of the zone and worked their way outward. Within one week, seven of the teams had encountered armed resistance that had resulted in casualties. Only one of the hostile events involved US persons, and that event was contained within a matter of a few hours. The group that was encountered was conducting what had been anticipated in that they were protecting a shelter site of over 500 people. It was not determined if all 500 were legal citizens as that was not a task of the teams.

The process of securing the areas of greatest concern near the Dallas Zone resulted in an issue that although not unanticipated, was underestimated. Once again, rumors became a reality throughout the area. Reports indicated that most people just outside the zone were worried the purpose of the teams was to disarm anyone they came in contact with, to include US citizens. By the time this information made it to the President's morning briefings, the rumor was nearly a reality. Local leadership across the area continued to report the actions of the teams, and the stories seemed to grow more dramatic by the day. As the President was preparing to be briefed on the pending operation in Kentucky, a report came in that delayed everything.

The initial report came in from the team involved, but almost at the same time, several frantic radio calls came into the State of Texas' Department of Public Safety. A team had been conducting operations near the area of Buchanan Lake and had made contact with a large group near the town of Bluffton. The Team Leader reported they had come under heavy fire from a large force that had not identified itself. Drone intelligence identified several of the weapons as Galil rifles as well as the headgear of Salvadoran Special Forces. Air suppression had been called in, and the team estimated over a hundred hostiles had been killed. The number alone set off alarm bells in the Department of Defense, and a more significant Reaction Force was dispatched to the area. By the time the area had been cleared and made secured, it became evident several of the casualties were US citizens. US citizens being members of these groups was not new.

What was new was the percentage. Of the 68 confirmed killed, 38 of them were US. It was the news the Texas Department of Public Safety received that made this event a real crisis. This

Security Group had been known to those in the area. It had operated out of Fredericksburg Texas and was known to patrol along highway 16 up into the area West of the lake. How this information had not been communicated to the federal government was a question lost in the reality of a much greater issue. Since the end of the war, everyone understood locals had taken many requirements into their own hands, but the idea they would form a security unit with foreign nationals for the sake of securing their interest, that was unthinkable. Within a few hours, Texas DPS had the whole story. The reality was undeniable. Not everyone coming up from the South had the intention of harming others, but all of them did have every intention to protect themselves. The formation of this joint security force was a sign of just how much things had changed. People would continue to do whatever they needed to stay alive. From the federal government's perspective, foreign national military units had migrated into the US and had formed alliances with US citizens. In this case, it was not just US citizens, but local Law Enforcement. When the President asked how many other such units might be inside the US, the answer was one he already knew. No one had any idea.

The mission of the teams was changed. They were now ordered to positively identify all members of any security group they came across and remove any non-US citizens, by force if necessary. The US had pinned its hopes of rebuilding the nation on the Dallas Zone, and the zone had been chosen for several reasons, but one reality had now become clear. The Dallas Zone was located dangerously close to a part of the nation the government didn't control. The concept of the zone being under threat was the reason the teams had been dispatched, but the idea of US citizens forming alliances with foreign nationals had never been anticipated. Once again, the concept of the Dallas Zone would be questioned by those who argued against it in the first place. From the public's perspective, they understood only one thing. The federal government was out to control the states as they tried to survive. It was bad enough they would not help anyone outside the zone, but they were now preventing them from having the right to their own safety.

### Kentucky Incident:

The mission was briefed to the President and his key staff and approved, but not without several in the room questioning the possible repercussions. Again, it was the Speaker of the House who voiced the greatest concern. His words were strong as everyone in the room looked on. "There is no going back. There is no chance of trust surviving this event. Is this worth the possible destruction of the Union"? Not even the President responded to the question. It had become clear the states had not been striving for succession as the government had once feared, but it was possible, that concept could now be the outcome of the pending action. The issue of the states becoming aware of the mission before its launch quickly became the topic at hand. Everyone in the meeting was asked if any agency had information on the states finding out about the Kentucky Operation. It was mentioned the states had been holding an increased level of radio traffic for the past several days, but most of the intelligence-gathering networks were not privileged to the mission, and as such, their concerns of such increased activity were not immediately reported. It was not the first time they had observed a spike in state to state messages.

The consensus was, there was a valid risk of the states having knowledge of the pending event, but there was no evidence to support that theory. Once again, most of the people in the room were coming to conclusions, just as they had done on the states wishing for succession. Paranoia became a guiding force in yet another critical governmental decision. The President gave the order to speed up the timeline of execution of the mission as much as possible. He then asked the Secretary of defense what the earliest the task could be implemented was. Two days was the answer, and that answer was accepted. The Secretary of Defense then asked a question no one in the room had anticipated. What were the Rules of Engagement, ROE's, to be? At what point did members of the United States Military fire upon citizens of the US defending private property, legally protecting private property? The pause was broken by the Vice President. He recommended the military only fire if they are fired upon and that they must first correctly identify themselves. The President followed with his answer. They would be authorized to use deadly force to protect themselves. He then stressed to the room the critical nature of not just the Kentucky event, but any event in the future that would increase the chances of rebuilding the nation. The Secretary of Defense acknowledged the ROEs and then made a statement that may have changed more opinions in the room than anyone realized at that moment in time. The US Military had fired upon US citizens since the end of the war, but those were circumstances where law and order were being crushed beyond the ability of civilian authorities to cope with, and even then, the military was in Direct Support of Civilian Authorities. This was different, this was clearly a combat operation of seizing and hold, and this operation was against US citizens who were not breaking the nation's laws. It was then the Secretary of Defense made a request that would change the course of the whole event. He stated the civilian leadership of Kentucky and anyone at the site had to be informed the site was now under federal control prior to any military member engaging in any hostile action. By the tone in his voice, most in the room realized he was not recommending; he was placing a stipulation on the utilization of US forces on US soil, against US citizens. Nearly everyone in the room agreed with the recommendation, and the issue became timing and approach. How soon to the event, would the message be given? Who would it be given to and how. It would be the Governor that would be notified, but the issue of when became a complex discussion. The movement of the military units would be by air with advanced Scouts entering the area 24 hours before the main body arrival. This would allow the government to gain actionable intelligence as to the status of the site. Once that information was processed and the approach was finalized, the timing of the notification to the Governor would take place inside some predetermined window.

After the issue of notification was agreed upon and the process mapped out, the final, more significant issue was brought up by the US Attorney General. What was the course of action if the site was already held by the state? What were they willing to do if the state was already in possession of the site? The discussion was uncoordinated for several minutes and had become heated when the President spoke up. His words were final. He stated the website must be taken as the future of the nation must be preserved. It was then when the Speaker of the House stood up and said, "Ladies and Gentlemen, we may have survived the war, but it appears we will not survive our actions after the war." The Speaker then walked out of the President's meeting and resigned later that evening.

The units tasked were from the 5$^{th}$ Special Forces and 3$^{rd}$ Ranger Battalion. Only key members of both organizations were allowed access to the target package. To the rest of the teams, the mission was somewhere outside the US mainland. They had been assembled at a Main Operating Base, MOB, in Atlanta Georgia and the cover story was based upon the ongoing unrest South of the Dallas Zone. The Scout mission was tasked to members from 5$^{th}$ Group, and they departed 18 hrs. After the final word was given.

The states had been changing their coding processes every 24hrs since the day they realized the federal government was unable to break the encryptions. Message traffic about activities in Georgia were shared as soon as they were reported. Georgia had been observing essential federal facilities for well over a year, and the activity at the MOB near Atlanta was easily detected. The cover story of actions to the South of the Dallas Zone had been effective as this increased activity was written off as some potential response to that event.

The Scout Detachment had been on the ground for several hours when the first flash message was transmitted back to their command. The process was state of the art, laser burst transmission relayed by a series of satellites and went undetected by any civilian capability. What the initial message said was the issue. The site was occupied and not only occupied, but it appeared to be held by individuals in military uniforms wearing the patch of the Kentucky Army National Guard. Others were inside the sites as well, and several of them wore the uniforms of civilian police special operations units. The initial assessment was the target had a defensive force of over 100 well-armed and positioned members.

It took less than an hour for the Scout's report to reach the President. Somehow, Kentucky had found out about the mission, or at least that was the perception. The President called an emergency meeting, and all key players were assembled. Aerial reconnaissance had been completed hours before the Scouts arrived on scene and there had been no indication of activity at the site. That information led the President and his staff to believe Kentucky had become aware of the mission within the past day. How the information had leaked was not significant. What course of action could the government take now, that became the critical question? As options were being reviewed, someone made another vital comment. If Kentucky had discovered the mission, it should be assumed the other states had been notified. At that point, many in the room believed the event had grown to the point of being uncontrollable. The Secretary of State was the first to recommend calling off the mission, and he was quickly followed by the Attorney General and the Secretary of Defense. It was the

Vice President who made the comment they were past that point. If the states knew of the mission, then the damage was done.

The room was reviewing the pros and cons of calling off the mission when the next flash message came in. The Secretary of Defense read the message to the office. The Scouts had broken themselves up into three groups of six to gather more information on the forces at the site. Two of the groups had come under fire and had returned fire. Casualties were confirmed on both sides. The Scouts reported they were attempting to disengage and clear the target area. The Secretary of Defense informed his aid to order the Task Force Commander to extract the Scouts immediately, and he did so without looking at the President or anyone else in the room. In his mind, the event had gone exactly as he had feared.

The decision was made to contact the Governor of Kentucky and take every step needed to resolve the issue as quickly as possible. The Task Force back at the Atlanta MOB was placed on hold. The Scouts were extracted by air four hours after the incident. Their break contact distance from the target was over six miles, and it was unclear if any force was still in pursuit of them as they were extracted. The critical question was, did anyone observe the air package used to move the team out of the area? The call to the Governor's Office was placed by the President. It was nearly two hours after the extraction of the Scout Team, and everyone was still in the room with the President.

When the Governor was finally brought to the secured VTC, she seemed calm, but curious as to why the President had asked for an emergency call. It also struck her as odd the President had his critical staff in the room with him. To her, it was apparent something significant had taken place or was about to. She opened the meeting by apologizing for being late to the call, but she was being briefed on an event that had taken place at their powerline storage facility, and it was unclear what had happened or if it was actually over. The President stated he understood and asked her what she knew at that point. She informed him it appeared there had been another attempt on the facility, but given how often this had taken place, a defensive force that was stationed between that site and two others were moved into position before the event. She went on to say it appeared the group was only scouting the site for possible usable wire and that the President understood the value of such a site given the state's recent conversation with the federal government on the very topic. Her forces were able to detect the attempt and had engaged the criminals, but they had departed the area. Her forces were only allowed to pursue a distance of five miles, given the expenditure of resources needed to continue. The Governor ended her explanation of the event and then asked the President what the issue was he needed to talk to her about. The President answered by stating he was deeply concerned about such events given what they had now recently learned about the US's Southern Border. The President made a statement everyone in the room with him listened to in astonishment. He informed her they had come across information that several large groups of well-armed individuals, mostly non-US citizens had been rumored to be moving up into the central part of the country, and it was thought a few of these groups could be in the area of Kentucky. The Governor simply listened to the President and after a brief pause, stated that could very well be the pretext of what had taken place at the wire facility. The President went on to state these groups were far more capable than any others they had encountered in the past, and many of their members were US citizens. The Governor thanked the President for the information and requested her State Police Intelligence Division be kept in the loop of any additional information. As soon as she finished that statement, she informed the President she had an urgent meeting to attend and that she looked forward to speaking with him as quickly as possible and with that, she signed off.

The President had thought fast on his feet, but the question became, did anyone believe the Governor of Kentucky? If she genuinely did know of the pending mission on the wire, and most in the room thought she did, then why did she approach the conversation in that manner?

It was decided Kentucky knew of the mission and it was now an issue of had the other states been notified? Again, it was assumed they had been or soon would be. The only way to tell was to see what traffic had taken place between the states since the incident. There had been message traffic, but not at a level that struck the IC as unusual. If Kentucky hadn't relayed the event to others, then there was still time to stop the crisis from getting worse. The government couldn't break the encryption methods being used by the states, but it could deny the networks being utilized. The price they would pay for doing so was the states realizing who was capable of shutting down the communications network. What had been taking place was operating on UHV platforms. The ability to deny that level of communications across the nation existed, but other details had to be worked out before that event taking place. That required time and time was not what the federal government had.

The Governor of Kentucky had made a decision not to be the 2$^{\text{nd}}$ Civil War's, Fort Sumter. Her forces had identified the scout teams on their approach to the wire site. The exchange of fire had been the result of the Scouts splitting up with one team virtually walking right up to an Observation Post a half-mile from the site. By the time the word was given to disengage, multiple events had taken place. The State of Kentucky had followed protocols for such an event and had only sent one short message to the other states. In turn, the rest of the states didn't respond, and as a result, the level of traffic didn't indicate awareness.

The decision to interrupt the ability to communicate

between states was not supported by the majority of the President's Staff. The arguments were heated and ongoing as the Governor of Kentucky sent a message back to them. In light of the threats the President had informed the State of Kentucky, the state was increasing its defensive forces at the wiring facility until further notice. Kentucky also stated, it was confident no federal assistance would be required to defend the site, but the state would keep the government informed of any additional events.

Everyone knew what had taken place. The conversation over the wire production site had made the state of Kentucky fearful enough, and after the Supreme Court's ruling, it was clear the site would need increased attention. The scout teams were an indication the state was correct, and that action put several other states into motion. The list of critical sites the federal government had identified was not a secret, and as such, states now knew where they would need to concentrate their efforts, but that was if they deemed those locations critical to the state's needs.

The one way the government had to determine if the other states were aware of what had taken place was to observe other critical sites. Overflights were conducted within 24 hrs of the Kentucky event, and the information laid to rest any doubt the government had. Twenty-two identified locations showed signs of current activity with most showing various stages of response. Many of the sites had already been under the protection of a state force with the federal government limiting themselves to nuclear powerplant facilities. Most sites had been assigned to National Guard Units that had been nationalized during the war, and that explained why the Kentucky Army Guard unit had been identified. In all the discussions over the process of securing critical sites, the Secretary of Defense had been aware of the fact the National Guard had owned that mission. The difference was that the traditional list of locations had been based upon maintaining the nation during and after the war and not on issues that would be needed to rebuild the country. All of this was lost on a President who wanted to know once again, was the National Guard indeed under the Command and Control of the President or where they operating under the authority of the Governors?

The question of the National Guard became the issue, and the Secretary of Defense's explanation created a great deal of additional tension in the room. Command and Control of most National Guard Units had been left to the National Guard. Each state had always had organic Command and Control, some even up to Divisional level. Early in the conflict, as the National Guard was activated, they were given the order to mobilize in place and await further orders. With the speed and confusion of the war, those orders never came for most of the activated units. What the activation process had allowed was for the National Guard to gain access to equipment items they historically did not maintain, and this was especially true of ammunition. By the time the Secretary of Defense was finished with his explanation it was clear to everyone in the room over sixty percent of what was still functional in the US Military was made up of National Guard members and most were still inside their home states. Many that had been moved had been allowed to return to a Main Operating Base as close to their home state as possible. The question of the President of the United States genuinely controlling a large section of the military was a valid concern, with the Army being the primary issue.

The United States Navy, Air Force, and Marine Corp were deemed to be a non-issue, although the remaining strength of the Air Force was also nearly 60 percent Reserve Component. The conversation then addressed the issue of, had the Governors been able to communicate with their Guard Leaders without someone noticing? The bigger question became, had anyone really been paying attention? The repositioning of forces after the war was based upon support issues, and the composition of the forces themselves was never part of the equation. When asked what Main Operating Bases were commanded by National Guard Generals, the answer was three. The issue was, the majority of the Forward Operating Bases / FOBs / were manned by Guard leadership, and it was these FOBs that conducted nearly all of the daily missions that required interaction with state government. The Joint Assessment Teams' military attachments were predominantly National Guard members, and they worked with the states around the clock. The issue of desertions over the past two years was discussed in an attempted to understand if the effective force structure of the National Guard was equal to that of the active forces. The reality was, all estimates of force readiness had been consolidated from the beginning of the war. With that, it was assumed National Guard Units that may turn their loyalty to their Governors were combat effective.

Up until the time of the event with Arizona, few, if any inside the military had taken into consideration the issue of loyalty of the National Guard. That changed with the event in Kentucky, and it was now an issue that consumed the President's thoughts. States were taking control of assets that the federal government deemed vital to the nation's ability to rebuild, and the forces they seemed to be using to do so where federalized National Guard units. That perception proved to be inaccurate, and in a way, the President and his staff did not anticipate. Military members had been allowed to relocate as close to home as possible, and that process had been taking place for almost two years. Of those who walked out in the first year after the war, most did so for the simple reason of wanting to go home. When they arrived, they found their skills were in demand and even those that were not National Guard members often linked up with Guard Units. After the first year, the FOBs were vital support facilities with the MOBs being more of a contingent for overseas events or resupply for the FOBs. Although these two types of facilities stayed in contact, the priority and pace of the FOBs forced them to become much different than the MOBs made up of mostly regular federal forces. Again, until the Arizona event and then the Kentucky incident, this division of commonality had been either underestimated or simply overlooked. In the mind of the President and many of his key staff, the United States Military had become two distinct operations. One worked daily with the states and was made up almost exclusively of National Guard members, and one was a contingency force that controlled the nuclear forces as well as Naval and Air Operations. Although the Secretary of Defense didn't entirely agree with this analysis, he did understand the nation's continued course towards division had taken hold inside the military as well.

# CHAPTER FOURTEEN: THE DECISION TO FIGHT:

Again, each Regional Commander was tasked with assessing the status of his or her forces? Two questions were to be answered. "Were the members under your command likely to follow orders if tasked with moving against state held locations? What capabilities existed to resist potential military action in your Area of Responsibility"? The first question could not be accurately answered without an actual survey, but subordinate commands could provide a somewhat accurate assessment of the overall mindset of field units. A similar task had been given more than a year earlier, but it was assumed many units knew of the events with the states and the decision was made to retake the pulse of the force. The second question was almost rejected outright. Too many variables were not provided. Issues such as Mission Objectives and Rules of Engagement were not spelled out, and no Regional Commander wanted to go on record as to how he would attack or defeat US Citizens on US soil. In the end, the assessment of the Regional Commanders was inconclusive, and it was clear they were reluctant even to address the issue.

The analysis of loyalty showed the results most in senior positions. MOB's were expected to be more reliable than FOBs, but even then, the final analysis was alarming to governmental leaders. It was estimated that less than half of the remaining forces in the US Military would consider hostile actions with US Citizens as a legal order. The only caveat that showed why half of the force might agree was based upon hostilities initiated by a collective group inside the country. The events South of the Dallas Zone was the example given by most of the Field Commanders.

After analyzing this information, the question of communications was once again addressed. Did Regional Commanders have any additional knowledge of FOB's and unit's supported by FOBs communicating with the states on protective issues? It was a topic that had just been addressed, but it was clear senior leaders in the government were looking for just how much control they had left. Again, the events in and around the Dallas Zone had been made known to most of the force, and it was logical most of the states had asked their military support operations what the best course of action might be. In their minds, if organized groups were in Southern Texas, then they were in Southern New Mexico, Arizona and once they blended in with the local population, their ability to move North was a given. To the FOBs, the concept of the states asking them for support was why they were there. They may have heard about some of the tensions between the states and the federal government, but most were not aware of just how bad things had become.

It soon became apparent, the states had not convinced their National Guard Units to betray the country, but they had asked them to help defend sites the states deemed critical to their survival. Regional Commanders had not discussed the federal Critical Site List with any of the FOB's leadership, and in fact, only a handful of people outside the Secretary of Defense's key staff had any knowledge of the plan. This meant that when the states made their request to the leadership at the FOB level, it all seemed completely logical. It was soon learned, several of the FOBs even reported the request for support, and no one in the chain of command questioned a process that had taken place several times in the past two years.

In the end, poor communications between sites that had little day to day contact, the MOBs and the FOBs, along with little guidance on the Critical Site missions from the federal government in the Dallas Zone led to a scenario where US forces were doing their job, yet other forces were preparing to seize the very sites the FOB forces controlled. Once the Secretary of Defense was briefed on the current status, he developed a course of action for the President's review. MOB Commanders were still not informed of the situation between the states and the federal government, nor did they gain knowledge of the critical site plan. What they were instructed to do was to standby to recall their forces from the sites the states had asked them to defend. No explanation was given, and they were ordered not to inform any state official of the pending withdrawal.

If the federal government had been cautious not to let the local units know of the tension with the states, the states had been even more careful. The message they gave the FOBs was universal. There were threats, and they were beyond the abilities of civilian and local law enforcement defense groups to counter. The states believed that once the units were in place and were working with local leaders, they would be reluctant to turn on them if ordered. From the day the war ended, many of the military members had been with the locals every single day. Most were National Guard members, and most were from the states they were defending. Not only did the states believe this theory may work, the Secretary of Defense thought it as well.

The Secretary of Defense's brief to the President and his key staff was as simplistic as he could make it. He wanted nothing to be left to interpretation. Several states had asked the FOBs near them to help defend locations that were critical to the state's survival. The increased threat briefed by the

President to all the Governors was the primary reason. Most of the FOBs had become so interactive with the locals, the mission didn't seem out of the ordinary, and they had conducted such missions in the past. The Communications between the MOBs and the subordinate FOBs had become minimum over the past year, and most issues were based on routine logistical requirements. MOB Commanders had a minimal understanding of the tension between the states and the federal government. The bottom line was, the FOBs were supporting the states, and they believed they were doing exactly as they should be. FOB support missions were animated by green circles on a weekly status chart. No one had cross-referenced the weekly reports with the newly developed Critical Site List. The Secretary then put the issue in the most basic terms. The business of the FOBs had become routine, and this allowed their actions to go virtually unnoticed at the federal level.

The FOB weekly reports were compiled, and the map was shown to everyone in the room. Over 70 percent of the Critical Sites were designated with green circles. The states had a complete understanding of what the federal government had prioritized, and only the ones individual states had deemed unimportant to their survival were not in green. Some sites had limited support packages provided to the states, and according to the weekly reports, that was due to the states having their own robust defensive capabilities at those sites.

The Secretary of Defense was asked what options the government had, based on the information provided. He informed the President he had ordered all Regional Commanders to be prepared to withdrawal US Military Forces from the current deployment sites. He then recommended the President consider not withdrawing the forces but ordering the Regional Commanders to be prepared to take control of the sites. This action would simply require the MOB Commanders sending the message to the FOBs and their dispersed units. It was the Secretary of State who asked the question, "would they follow the order"? That option gained support in the room based upon the assumption most of the units at the sites were not aware of the status between the states and the government. The argument then became, just how much information should be provided and who should it be given to? Most agreed with the Secretary of Defense; the Regional Commanders had to know the complete story. They had to be brought up to speed on what had taken place, all of it. It was the Speaker of the House that then asked the question, "What if they don't see the order as lawful"? The changes to the US Constitution had been made, but the awareness level of those changes predominantly resided with state leadership.

The meeting had gone on for hours when someone suggested they tell the Regional Commanders there was a concern of infiltration of civilian defense units, much like what had taken place in Southern Texas. The Secretary of Defense replied that he would not lie to his force. He informed the President that if the force were lied to, any hope of maintaining their loyalty would be lost. Military members were used to not being given all the information of an event as that was the nature of many operations, but lying to them would prove to be disastrous. It was also decided, there could be no cover story. Units at each site would hear the state's version of what was taking place and would ask for confirmation. The President put an end to the discussion and instructed the Secretary of Defense that he and the President would brief the Regional Commanders and tell them what was at stake and they would do so immediately.

The President then asked if the plan to disrupt state to state communications was ready to execute. The answer was more complicated than he anticipated. The mission would require the movement of several low orbital assets, assets that now had limited fuel. It would not deplete their ability to maneuver after the mission, but every movement came at a price soon that refueling was no longer possible. Once the status of the mission was briefed, it was decided the plan would be used, but only after reports that critical sites were encountering hostile actions. It was the hope of the President and his key leaders; the local force commanders would be able to make the civilian leadership at the sites realize the price they would all have to pay for resistance.

### Commander's Call:

The call with all six regional commanders and their deputies took place four hours after the President's meeting was over. It was the President who spoke first. He told them this was going to be the most challenging discussion they had ever had in their lives, and the outcome could determine the survival of the unified nation. He asked who had knowledge of the recent Amendments to the US Constitution. All of them stated they were aware. It was then the President and the Secretary realized, nearly every FOB Commander had been part of some level of discussion with state and or local leadership on the topic. Not only did the Regional Commanders know of the changes, they all had an understanding of why. The Secretary of Defense stated he knew that two of the Commanders had been briefed, but the details as to what had driven the Article V Convention had been left at a very simplistic level. What had taken place was a series of in-depth discussions between the state government officials and FOB leadership, and this discussion had been ongoing since the day the states learned of the Supreme Court's ruling. What had not taken place was a similar level of dialogue between the Regional Commanders and their Superiors, to include the Secretary of Defense and their Commander in Chief. The President then asked, what they understood of the current status at the sites they were defending? All of them answer the same. Their task had not changed since the end of the war. They were to support the state and local leaders to the extent possible, and that included supporting them in their ability to safeguard assets they deemed critical to the state. It was then, one of the Commanders asked the question as to why they had been ordered to be prepared to take control of these critical sites?

Military members had been assigned to the JATs from the very beginning, and the stories of the issues that had arisen between the teams and several states were known, but problems had occurred in the past, and most FOB Commanders believed these were issues that would be worked out over time. It became apparent; the Regional Commanders had no idea just how bad things had grown between the government and the states. The President and the rest of the federal government had kept the military leadership in the dark, at least to the point the gravity of the situation was not understood. For too long, the fear of loyalty had driven the interactions with the military;Allowing members to relocate; overseas members back to the states, it had all been done for the sake of keeping the one organization that could hold the nation together content, or at least content enough they would follow their Senior Leaders. That changed with the Commander's Call.

Everything that had taken place between the states and the government was addressed by the President, and he left nothing out. He explained the Critical Asset List and why it was different from the list the nation had held for so long before the war. The Commanders were given a full briefing on the future of the Dallas Zone and why the critical sites were so vital to the zone's long-term concept. If the nation was going to rebuild, sacrifices had to be made, and the Commanders had heard that statement many times before. What was new to them was the level of resistance the states had placed in front of that plan. To the states, they were being asked to sacrifice too much. To the government, the sacrifices had to be made. When the President addressed the threats to the Dallas Zone, the issue of an unsecured Southern Border was not left out. Not only did the nation need critical sites, but the security of the zone itself had to be achieved. The President spoke to the issue of the rumors spreading to the South and West of the Zone. The Commander responsible for that mission as well as the Zone was the person the Secretary had communicated with the most. The President's point about rumors of what the military units were doing in the area was made very clear to the other Commanders, given everyone believed they would also come under the same public scrutiny if the critical sites had to be taken. Several of the Commanders commented there would be more than just rumors; there would be the extensive knowledge US forces had fired on not only civilians but other US forces. As bad as the situation was to the South of the Dallas Zone, it would be nothing compared to the conflicts at the critical sites.

When the President was finally finished addressing the Regional Commanders, one asked the question everyone on the President's staff knew was coming. Was the US Military's Commander in Chief ordering his forces to disregard the US Constitution? As soon as the question was asked, another Commander made a comment, "Is this a lawful order"? Immediately, the discussion became what alternatives did the President have? Had the government exhausted every other avenue and was there no other compromise that could be reached? To the Secretary of Defense, it was becoming apparent; the Commanders were reluctant to contemplate hostile actions to secure the sites. Past planning for Continuity of Government, COG, had always taken into account the possibility of using force on US citizens, but this was different. The country had survived the war. To the commanders, the nation was somewhat stable, and it seemed there was enough stability that compromise could be explored further. The Commanders did not feel the sense of urgency that typical COG planning had been based upon.

The President asked the commanders what options they might recommend? It was his way of allowing them some level of ownership in the crisis. It was then a statement was made the President and the Secretary of Defense had not considered. Let the FOB Commanders understand the issue and let them talk to the states. The concept of keeping the whole event as sequestered as possible had led the President and his staff to overlook the reality that local leadership was more in touch with the military than the government was. It also made the President realize the topic was most likely already underway between the states and the FOBs. Part of that theory had already been proven, but what the FOBs didn't know was the federal government's side of the issue. State and local officials had been complaining about support from the day the war was over and that was seen as the reason as to why the severity of the issue had not been unchanneled sooner. It had also become clear; the states had seemed reluctant to paint a picture of, "us against them," for the risk of losing what support they currently received. It was agreed. The regional commanders would brief the FOB commanders on the situation and then tasked them to contact senior state leadership. In almost every case, this would lead to the Governor's themselves being involved, especially once they were informed of the topic.

The Commander's Call was about to end with the guidance they would all meet again in four days when the commander responsible for the Dallas Zone and areas South asked if he could make a statement. He informed the President, his units assigned to seek out the armed groups near the zone were encountering increasing resistance from many of the civilians they were coming in contact with. The resistance was not in the form of hostile acts, but the overall relationship between the teams and the public was becoming a noticeable disadvantage. People were reluctant to provide information, and few asked for any form of assistance. The FOBs had been unable to shape the information messaging of the missions to a level the public acceptance. Although the teams had been ordered to modify their approach with the intent of not treating local defensive groups as potential foreign groups, that distinction was only possible after the groups had been detained and inspected. It was that inspection process that continued to create perception issues throughout the area. Everyone had known from the beginning how difficult it would be to seek out foreign groups given most were wearing civilian clothing. Types of weapons in the group's possession were usually the only indicators, but even then, all groups had to be handled the same, at least upon initial approach.

The topic had been brought up before, but in the past few days, FOBs that had these teams attached to them had suddenly seen a marked increase in flash reports. Three teams had entered an area near Canyon Lake, just West of the city of San Marcos and all three teams had come under fire as they approached the locations of several armed groups. In all three cases, none of the armed groups were based upon foreign ex-military members, but all three did have a large percentage of non-US citizens. It was the regional commander's belief the number of civilians moving into the Southern area of the Dallas Zone was growing and multiplying. The Secretary of Defense asked the commander for recommendations. The response was something the President did not want to hear. The suggestion was to stop the search missions and convert those forces into augmentation for the existing denial missions. The resources required were being expended while giving ineffective results and damaging the already weakened relationships with the civilian population. What the President heard was, the US no longer could keep massive movements of non-US citizens from entering the country. The commander stated he had a plan to augment the static defensive forces and it would be based upon roving patrols and increased checkpoints along hardtop roadways. It was something that was already taking place, but clearly, the scope of the threat had outgrown the ability to counter the event. The US could no longer defend its borders, and its only option was to increase the defense of the Dallas Zone. The Secretary of Defense recommended to the President that he inform the rest of his staff of this development as well as the Southern State's Governors and do so as soon as possible.

Two days later, the President addressed primary government officials as well as Governors. Almost all the Governors had decided to be on the conference call, even though the tensions over the sites were known by all. The topic was what compelled them to listen. The message had been sent out the President was going to speak to the issue of the Nation's Borders and the ability to secure them.

Once again, the President was straight to the point. It had become clear the volume of people from Central and South America who were moving into US land was beyond the control of the federal government. The resources needed to prevent the migration was beyond what the nation was willing to expend. The speculation was, this event would be temporary once many of the people discovered the rumors of normality in the US were false. This had been the case with El Paso directly after the war, and it was anticipated it would happen again. It was to be expected the Southern States would see a continued influx of non-US citizens for the foreseeable future. It had taken many of these people over two years to make the journey and intelligence indicated several million more were still moving North. The President then informed everyone on the call the priority would be to protect the Dallas Zone to the greatest extent possible and that would require the continued reallocation of military assets into the area around the zone. He went on to say that most of the people that continued to move towards the US were honest people who were just as desperate as any other person who'd survived the war. As he was addressing the issue of the morality of the situation, the Governor of Arizona interrupted him. Did the President intend to take military assets away from the state of Arizona?

Did he have a list of states that would see the reallocation of forces? The President's answer was predictable. He had not been briefed on the details, but he anticipated that briefing within a few days, and when he received it, he would be in contact with the impacted states. The Governor of Kansas was the next to make a statement. He asked the President if it was the federal government's intent to allow parts of the nation to become the property of foreign nationals. The Governor of Arkansas was the next to speak. He wanted to know how the federal government could be so sure these massive movements of foreigners would not merely continue moving North. What made the government so sure they would turn and walk back to Central and South America? As the Secretary of Defense was attempting to answer the question, an unknown Governor shouted out, "That's a great plan. So that's how you will pull our forces away from the places we are trying to defend". That comment put the conference call into a free for all that lasted almost a minute before everyone was muted. The President responded that only the forces required to secure the Dallas Zone to a much higher level would be moved. Every Governor in the call had been down that road in the recent past, but this time the issue was not machinery or raw materials; it was something the Governors had absolutely no say-so over. It was about federalized military forces. That call ended like the past several. Many of the Governors simply signed off, and the President decided to end the call.

### Call to Arms:

As had been the case since the first days of the war, paranoia controlled the thought processes of both the Governors and the federal government. The states were convinced the forces assigned to critical sites, made up mainly of their National Guard Units would be tasked to move into the area around the Dallas Zone, leaving the states unable to defend the sites from follow on federal forces. It was now clear, the only thing the government was concentrating on was the survival of the Dallas Zone. It was also evident; the identified sites would be taken regardless of what the amendments to the US Constitution had changed.

The Governors made a decision. They would sit down with their National Guard Leaders and explain everything they knew. Some had already done so, but at a very informal level and with a guarded approach to several of the more sensitive topics. That time was over. They would now be told what the Governors believed to be the truth, and they would be asked to consider any order to relocate as unlawful, given the federal government's intent to violate the US Constitution. Those conversations would take place over the next two days.

Communications between the states had increased dramatically directly after the President's call. Again, paranoia ruled any flow of logical thought. The states were going to resist the movement of their forces. It was time for the regional commanders to have their follow up call with the President and that set into motion a series of catastrophic events.

The Commanders were fully briefed on the issue of the additional forces for the Dallas Zone. The US was going to have to allow unhindered access into the country and the priority for the military was to protect two key elements of the nation's survival. One was the Dallas Zone, and the other was the critical sites. When the regional commanders asked why were the forces in place at the sites not just left there and other forces assigned to the buildup around the Dallas Zone, the answer shocked them. The President stated that most of the sites were protected by National Guard Units, and he had lost confidence in their loyalty. He explained once the states were informed of the need to allow the movement of millions of non-Us citizens into the US, many of the Governors stopped communication with the government. Three of the regional commanders had been on the call and had heard the

THE SECOND DARK AGES

remarks by the Governor of Arkansas. The President's point was clear. The Governors were going to attempt to regain control of their National Guard units, and that would place one of the two primary objectives of the US Military at extreme risk. The President's final words to the regional commanders were historic. "Ladies and Gentlemen, it is up to you to save the nation."

The question of lawful orders was lost in the crisis of the moment. Regional commanders needed to find out if their FOBs commanded by National Guard members were being approached by their perspective Governors. They informed the President they would make their inquiries and report back within 24 hours. For the President, that was too late. Although he did not tell the commanders, the President was going to authorize the neutralization of all state to state radio communications. The plan was not foolproof, but it would take out nearly 80 percent of the capability that was currently being utilized. Those were assets that could not be replaced, and it was an action that would leave the nation even more unstable. It was for that reason he decided not to inform the commanders.

When the briefing came to an end, the Secretary of Defense, privately informed the President, the denial of civilian UHF operations was an action the Secretary was convinced would do far more harm than good. Although the government could not break the encryption processes being used, the loss of equipment would be more devastating than the analysis had shown. He asked the President to delay ordering the operation until the Regional Commanders came up with a definitive opinion of what sites were now protected by National Guard units that would remain loyal to their states. It was only one day, and the Secretary was convinced the issue was not as dangerous as the President believed. The denial mission was pushed back until the Regional Commanders were heard from.

Seven states had made contact with their National Guard Leadership, and all seven had gained commitments not to take action against their own people. The issue of resisting federal forces moving on protected sites was a different and far more complex. Asking military members to resist fellow military members was a topic none of the seven National Guard Commanders could agree to. They would defend themselves if needed, but another reality was overlooked by the states. Although many of the FOBs had senior National Guard leadership, the forces themselves were mixed.

In most cases, the overwhelming percentage of military members were National Guard, but in almost every case, there still remained a mixture of Active and Reserve forces. The concept of the National Guard resisting orders was not as black and white as many of the Governors had anticipated. In reality, nearly every critical asset site had a percentage of Active and Reserve forces.

Eleven other states had been in contact with their National Guard Commanders, but agreements to remain loyal to the states were not achieved and, in several cases, it was not asked for. Most of the Governors had made contact with the National Guard Commanders to simply explain to them the status of the relationship between the states and the federal government. Article V changes were the CenterPoint of those conversations. It became clear to FOB Commanders the topic of "Lawful Orders" was not just an issue for the National Guard. What the MOB Commanders discovered; was the reality these conversations had been taking place since the changes to the US Constitution were announced. There had been discussions, but it had been considered low-level grumblings, and given the scope of everything else that had happened in the country, it just had not risen to the level of real concern. That changed when the states began to make contact and asked those contacts not to be revealed.

The Regional Commanders gave their findings to the

Secretary of Defense first. It was clear the information they provided him had commanders in a state of valid concern. If the FOBs were asked to take control of the critical sites away from the states and that action was met with resistance, a large percentage of the military members at those sites would not force the issue. The short answer was the FOB Commanders, and a large portion of their force would not see such an order as a lawful order. They then informed the Secretary this stance was going to hold true for a large percentage of the Active and Reserve forces as well. The FOBs had spent enough time with the state and locals; they simply could not take up arms against them for an act they felt was no longer illegal. The US Constitution had been changed, and the states were within their rights to keep the sites. The Secretary was then informed the forces that were going to be moved away from the sites and replaced had stated they considered that action as nothing more than an attempt to remove them from their state support role. If ordered to move, they would refuse the movement.

Of the top 50 sites the federal government had identified as critical to the nation's rebuilding, other than nuclear powerplants and support facilities, 38 of them were under the control of FOBs that had stated they would not remove state authority. The Secretary of Defense realized the news would need to be passed to the President in a closed conversation. His request to see the President and the Vice President only was granted. The meeting took place two hours after the Secretary had been briefed by the Regional Commanders.

The President listened to the Secretary of Defense until he was finished. He turned and looked at the Vice President and said, "we have lost the Union. At best, we will become a loose confederation of territories". It was the same reality most of the world had come to realize. The abilities to govern and control prewar national configurations were gone. The states had not worked towards independence, and they had not desired such a reality. What they wanted was the ability to provide for their own people, people who relied on state and local support to survive and not the federal government. The government had given a majority of its effort to the Dallas Zone, and from the first day the zone was announced, everyone outside that declared area believed they were on their own. The government had survived the war far better than any state, and the plans had always been written to ensure that the statement came true. The whole concept of Continuity of Government was based on the federal government. State and local entities were in the plans, but to most, they were an afterthought. The Vice President was talking to the Secretary of Defense when the President made the statement, "Do we have any options"? The Secretary explained the forces at the MOBs were Active Duty and Reserve, and the large majority of aviation units were located at the MOBs. He then told the President, even a percentage of those forces might not consider an order to take the critical sites as a lawful order.

Changes to the US Constitution had become known to most of the force, and although at the time, most of them had not realized what the event was all about, they did have an understanding now. Again, the question of options was asked. The Secretary's opinion was black and white. The President could let the states keep control of the sites, but that might lead to drastic changes to an already elaborate plan under development for the reconstruction of the nation. Concessions could be made to critical states with the hope of breaking the unity that had developed between them. Plans for the further development of the Dallas Zone would need to be changed as well. As the Secretary was speaking, the Vice President asked the most crucial question, "how do we regain the loyalty of the United States Military"?

The fear from day one had been the enduring allegiance of military members whose families and hometowns were impacted by the war while those same military members were not off fighting in some other corner of the world. The military had mobilized but had not deployed. The growing perception of the "haves and have nots" was just as prevalent in the military as it had been anywhere else. Those that served to support the locals had done so for nearly three years, and the bonds of commitment had been changing the whole time. The issue was, no one had indeed anticipated the level of change.

The President answered the Vice President's question. He informed the Secretary he was to have the FOB commander at the Kentucky Wire Site relieved of Duty are taken back to the MOB for review. The Secretary responded he was not sure the commander had committed any action worthy of his removal, given he had not been ordered to take the site. The order was to be given, and if the FOB commander refused, he would then be relieved.

A Heavy Quick Response Taskforce was ordered to deploy to the site and give the FOB Commander the ultimatum. It was the same force package that had been put together before. The MOB commander did not have command and control of the Taskforce as it reported directly to the regional commander. The event took place within the next 12 hrs in an attempt to limit any word of the mission. Word was passed to the Secretary of Defense the FOB commander would not be notified of the Taskforce arrival until 30 minutes before landing. The Taskforce would assume the primary mission of securing the site and the forces on hand would be lifted back to the MOB.

The mission took place six hours after the Secretary of Defense had briefed the President and Vice President. 30 minutes before landing the site was notified of the Taskforce's arrival. The regional commander was in constant contact with the force and in turn, he was reporting all events directly to the Secretary, who had the President and his key staff with him. The site had been under aerial surveillance for three hours before the mission, and the live feed was being observed by the President and those with him. The FOB commander met the Taskforce commander at the landing site, and no communications were heard from the team for over 30 minutes. The live feed showed the Taskforce had dismounted their aircraft and were in a holding area two hundred yards from the two commander's location. A large force had maneuvered into the area as the two were meeting and the President was informed it appeared the force was taking up a defensive position near the location of the Taskforce.

The first indication of conflict came from the aerial reconnaissance. Thermal signatures detected the small arms fire followed by several mortar rounds fired towards the Taskforce aviation assets on the ground. The timing between the small arms fire and the shoulder-fired weapons was reported four minutes apart. The first flash message from the Taskforce indicated they were taking fire from two directions and they had lost four rotor-wing aircraft. Without looking at the President, the Secretary ordered the regional commander to have the Taskforce disengage and leave the area immediately. As the President and the rest of the room watched, it was clear the exchange of fire was increasing on both sides. The live feed provided the Identification, Friend or Foe, IFF, on each member of the Taskforce, thus allowing the President and his key staff to witness in great detail what was taking place.

One hour into the conflict, it was clear the Taskforce had an objective in mind. It had broken into three groups with one providing cover for the other two maneuvering throughout the site. Aerial support had been observed targeting non-IFF marked vehicles moving in the general area. There had still been no contact with the commander of the task force, but communications between the taskforce elements and the aerial support package were monitored. Several massive explosions had been observed inside the main building complex, and three large fires were now visible in the feed. The inbound medical evacuation aircraft was heard in the communications, and one of the contacts on the ground estimated they had over forty members that would need immediate evacuation.

Three hours into the event, it was over. The Taskforce had secured the site, and the process of treating the wounded had begun. The Secretary of Defense asked the Regional Commander if he had gotten word to the Taskforce to disengage right as the fighting started. The commander replied he had not received a response from the Taskforce commander. He informed the Secretary he would have a preliminary assessment to him within the hour. The President and the Vice President were still watching the live feed as several other; ground feeds had now come up on the Command Network. The principal, wire production facility was burning out of control. Three storage yards were secured, but initial assessments showed, much of the wire had been moved. At that moment, the President's Chief of Staff informed him, the Governor of Kentucky was on the VTC wishing to speak with him.

Her words were emotional and straight to the point. "Mr. President. I didn't want to be the Fort Sumter of another Civil War. I hope you understand you still have time to stop this from getting out of hand". As soon as she was finished, she signed off. The President turned to his staff who had watched the short exchange and asked what the next step should be. The site was secured, but its value was gone. Word of what had taken place had already spread between the states, and many of the FOBs had been monitoring the communications as well. It was the US Attorney General who made the next comment. "There is no turning back now." As soon as he made a comment, the Secretary of Defense shouted, "there damn well better be."

The regional commander's report was provided just as he had stated. The Taskforce had 55 KIA and 120 WIA. The "Defenders" as they were referred to in the report were estimated to have 34 KIA and 150 WIA. The Taskforce had lost five rotor-wing assets with three more sustaining damage. The Defenders were being treated for their medical needs and would be flown back to the MOB within the next four hours. Eighteen of the Defenders killed were state and local law enforcement along with five civilians. Those taken into custody were going to be moved by ground back to the MOB as well. The names of all involved were being collected. The regional commander asked the Secretary of Defense what his follow-on orders were for the Taskforce, but the Secretary had no response for him. The site had been taken, and the cost of doing so was still being measured.

Within 12 hrs of the event, satellite and ground intelligence indicated, critical sites under FOB control in the states of Missouri, Illinois, Iowa, Arkansas, Mississippi, Tennessee, and Georgia had seen significant movements of inbound vehicles. As aerial platforms were moved, additional activities were reported in multiple states with critical sites. The President was also informed, almost all of the states had been in contact with each other since the event, but none of them, other than Kentucky, had made an attempt to contact the federal government.

The US military had been in combat against its own members as well as citizens of the US. Citizens and military members who were not stealing or harming others. Citizens and military members who were doing nothing more than the new changes to the US Constitution allowed them to do. They were within the law, and they had been attacked, or so the story was initially told. The commander of the Taskforce was killed in the confrontation, and what had been said in his meeting was never known. Who had fired first became an issue that both the states and the federal government would struggle to find out.

### The States Reactions:

Word of the event spread by two primary means. One was the states, and the other was the FOBs. Word spread to the MOBs as well, and rumors grew by the hour. From the beginning, it was clear the government was not going to control the perceptions forming all over the nation, and in the end, the world. FOB commanders learned of the stipulation that was given to the National Guard at the wire site, and every FOB throughout the country that had a majority of National Guard makeup quickly began to believe the government had lost confidence in them. Communication between the locals and the FOB leadership promptly became an open issue, and the discussions were frank. The states believed the federal government was breaking the law by taking critical sites without permission and orders to do so were unlawful.

Within three days of the wire site event, MOB commanders were reporting the situation at over 80 percent of the critical sites had become unstable. Several FOB commanders had been ordered back to the MOB Headquarters, but most had not shown up. Daily status reports had all but stopped and those that did come in painted a picture of a force that was extremely divided. It was the report from one of the FOBs in Missouri that forced the government into making a decision. The FOB commander had informed his units they would abide by the orders of the Governor of Missouri and not the regional commander or the federal government. Those members who were unwilling to agree to this decision were allowed to return to the support MOB. Of the 1400 members assigned, only 220 returned. News of the Missouri event quickly spread to other sites. By late that same night, less than half of the Forward Operating Bases were under federal control.

As the Secretary of Defense was briefing the President, one fact struck the most alarming note. All the FOBs that had decided to report to the Governors where they were assigned had a force that was 30 percent from the regular military. The message was clear, it was not just the National Guard that was questioning the federal government's stance, it was the regular force as well, and that perception was growing. Once again, the President asked for options, and this time the Secretary of Defense's answer shocked everyone in the room, everyone except for the Secretary of State and the Speaker of the House. The Secretary of Defense informed the President he believed the orders to remove FOB commanders and take control of the critical sites was in fact illegal. After the events at the wire site, the President came to the conclusion he could no longer carry out such orders. He then informed the President of his intent to step down as Secretary of Defense as soon as it was practical. Word of him doing so would have sent shockwaves through the force, and everyone in the room knew it. It was then the Speaker of the House made his statement. He was in agreement with the Secretary of Defense, and he was also aware that Congress was preparing an immediate inquiry into the wire site event. The room erupted into an uncontrollable discourse, and it was only after the Vice President shouted for everyone to stop that calm was restored. It became clear others in the room had not been supportive of the wire site event and in fact, most stated they had not been informed the event had been ordered. The discussion of a pending congressional Inquiry was taking place when word came into the room that changed everything.

The states had not just approached the FOB commanders; they had reached out to the MOB commanders as well. By the time the word of this change in events reached the Secretary of Defense, Three regional commanders had reported multiple MOB sites were requesting immediate legal clarification of the orders given for the wire site mission. MOBs in over eight states were in agreement; they had no authority to move on the critical sites unless they were under immediate threat from some hostile force. It was clear the states were getting their message across, and three of the regional commanders were now officially asking the Secretary for a legal opinion. This information was made known to everyone in the room, and it was the Vice President who stated the US military was now officially divided in its loyalty. The MOB commanders and the three regional commanders were not placing their support with the states that were speaking with them, but they were refusing to take any further action until a legal review was provided. The outcome was never in doubt. It was then the Secretary of State advised the President to order the US military to stand down from all orders concerning actions on US soil until further notice. Without military backing, the powers of the political leadership in the US was a moot point. The country came to a standstill.

# CHAPTER FIFTEEN:
# THE NATION DIVIDES.

Within two weeks of the orders from the President, the congressional investigation took place. The Secretary of Defense became the key to the hearing. Several others were brought forward and asked to give statements, and it was clear what had taken place. The President of the US had clearly attempted to circumvent the revised US Constitution. The defense of moving forces to deal with the growing threats to the Dallas Zone had little merit and did not factor in the findings of the investigation. Less than a month after the wire site event, Articles of Impeachment were being drawn up against the President. The man that had been responsible for the nation surviving World War III would be Impeached. The man who had saved millions of lives not only in the US but around the world would be removed from office.

The day the findings were made public, the Speaker of the House and the Senate Presiding Officer requested a meeting with the President and the Vice President. No one had forgotten what the two of them had done for the country, but under their watch, members of the US Military had fired upon their own Brothers and Sisters as well as Civilians. The military was deeply divided, along with the states, and the risk of another Civil War was a perception that had become a reality. It was also evident; the Impeachment process was going to be dramatic and would run the risk of further violence. The message both Chambers of the House brought to the President, and the Vice President was to step down. They were going to be given the option of walking away. After a lengthy discussion, both the President and the Vice President agreed. They would announce their departure within two days. And the process of replacing them began that day.

The Secretary of Defense had given the actual order to the regional commander that led to the wire site event. His status with the regional commanders was mixed. The three that had questioned the legality of the mission had lost confidence in the Secretary, and they made their position known to him. It was a short conversation that resulted in the Secretary informing the President he would resign the same day the President left the government. It was during that conversation between the Secretary and the President; an even more vexing issue came to the government's attention. As the regional commanders were speaking with the Secretary, the Secretary became concerned just how sympathetic the three regional commanders had become to the states in their area of support. He told the President he feared the loyalty of those commanders was an issue. They had spent over two years in their commands working the day to day struggles to keep the citizens of the US alive and safe. The US military had been and continued to be the backbone of survival, and that daily interaction had created strong bonds. All three had seen large parts of their assets moved to support the Dallas Zone and had done so with quiet reservation. These three commanders supported an area that covered twenty states, and they had been the states that led the drive to amend the US Constitution. His message to the President was clear. Stepping down from office was not a guarantee the US Military would stay united. Time, proximity, and hardship had changed the nation more than the federal government realized. The nation was different, and those who had run that nation had adapted to a new reality; a reality that was growing more and more independent of a federal governmental concept.

Like everything else after the war, the process of choos-

ing a new President and Vice President had to be modified. As
soon as the Congressional investigation had been agreed upon,
the idea the government may have to find a new President became an issue. The nation was still years away from a normal
election process, and the contingencies for such an event had
been written during a time with many different assumptions
than what currently existed then. The speaker of the House
would be sworn in as the interim. An attempt would be made
to hold a general election process with voting taking place at
Aid Centers for three days. That had been the plan, but the results were nothing the federal government could have anticipated and again, showed just how independent the states had
become.

Word of the President and Vice President stepping
down had not filtered out past some of the major support
areas. Life was hard, and the day to day struggle was far more
critical than to stay current on the actions of a federal government that was seen as doing nothing for the people outside
the Dallas Zone. Their connection with a federal government was predominantly based upon contact with US Military Support Teams. These teams had other agencies attached
to them, but their capabilities were minimal and dwindling
with each passing day. It was the US Military the people
looked to, and the idea that they needed to travel to vote for
a government that was doing nothing for them was not worth
the time and effort. As a result, large areas of the nation had
extremely low voter turnout. This meant the Dallas Zone and
US Military members made up a large percentage of the votes
that were cast. The only name they had heard on a continuing
basis was the person that was placed in the position after the
President's departure, and even to the ones that did have an
understanding of what was taking place, it still seemed like an
inconsequential issue. The entire concept of a federal government seemed to be fading away.

The Speaker of the House became the President of the

US, and to the nation, nothing had changed because none of it meant life would get any better. People were still dying and a rate that exceeded the birthrate by a factor of 10. The nation still did not have power, and the nation still was unable to move the caloric intake level above 800 calories a day. Life was hard and at times, almost unbearable, and a new President meant virtually nothing to the people who were still alive. In the end, avoiding a Civil War had been the goal, but the fear of such an event was still there.

The regional commander who had been in charge of the Dallas Zone was sworn in as the new Secretary of Defense. It was a move the new President had anticipated would bring some level of assurance to the other regional commanders. In fact, it had the opposite impact, and the President and his staff should have realized that fact from the beginning. The Dallas Zone Commander had been chosen based upon his understanding of the Nuclear Triad program. By the end of the war, the defense of the nation was based upon that program, and the President wanted that same person to be the Senior Military Officer inside the Zone. The logic had been flawed, given the commander had everything he needed to conduct his mission, plus he was the recipient of all the critical equipment items moved to support the zone. That had resulted in him being the most removed of the Six regional commanders. His needs and his issues had been different from his counterparts and as hard as life had become, which resulted in resentment, even when every effort was made to avoid that from happening. The Secretary of Defense had no idea what it was like to live outside the zone. For three years, he had little in common with the other five regional commanders, and nothing could change that.

What the Special Election for the Presidency had showed the government was just how disconnected the people were. The idea of holding elections to send replacement Senators and Congressmen to office suddenly seemed in question. The government feared the process was broken and they were right. During the discussions with the states, the ideas of holding elections to give the states a better voice had been reviewed, but it was clear that the concept would probably not solve anything. If the people were indifferent to a Presidential election, then why would they care about Congressional events? Those Representatives that had survived the war had done nothing for their constituents, or at least that was the opinion of most of them. They had become part of a separate nation that lived inside a zone that had a quality of life not available anywhere else in the country. They had become insignificant. The federal government was attempting to hold a nation together, but even as they tried, the reality was, the nation was changing, and they were truly powerless to stop the process.

The first VTC between the new Secretary of Defense and the regional commanders was a disaster. The topic had been, as the new Secretary worded it, "the stability of the force." What that genuinely translated into was the word, loyalty. Did the regional commanders have a better feeling for stability now that the crisis from the wire site had been addressed. The answer shocked him. No! Their response was, "no." The three regional commanders who had informed the previous Secretary they could not serve under him, where still of the opinion their forces were divided. Changing out the Secretary of Defense and even their Commander in Chief did not negate their commitment to the states and citizens they had gone through hell with. The call ended with a determination by the Secretary to visit each MOB as well as preselected FOBs in an attempt to explain what was essential to the nation.

When the Secretary briefed the new President, he made a dire prediction. Many of the military members would remain committed to the locals they had been with for several years now, and any attempt to change their environment could lead to yet another crisis. The option of rotating the commanders was reviewed, but in the end, that option seemed to have more negative consequences than it did positives. The President's closing comment was one the whole room had most likely been contemplating for some time. Was the government attempting to hold a nation together than had grown too far apart? No one in the room said a word, and the meeting ended.

### The Houston Incident:

During the war, the city of Houston had suffered two air burst nuclear strikes. One had been a two megaton device 15,000 ft over the Texas City area and the other a 3 megaton weapon at 10,000 ft over the area of Baytown. The targets were based upon oil refining capabilities as well as stored fuels in both regions. As such, the city of Houston had been designated off-limits with the Northern boundary being an area called the Woodlands, a Western boundary the area of Brookshire and the Eastern perimeter of Beaumont. Like every other major city in the US, this designation of off-limits was loosely enforced, given the expenditure of limited assets it would take to deny the areas physically. For the Dallas Zone, the levels of radiation exposer from the war were monitored by random sampling teams, and anyone that was found to be far beyond the known levels was considered to have come from one of the impact areas or had spent too much time inside them. Either way, they were removed from the zone and given a list of locations they could travel to for some level of support. It was a harsh reality that over the past three years, people had come to accept. Survival was no longer an issue for the minority, but a priority for the majority.

Movements in and out of the city of Houston were monitored, but only from fixed locations along major roadways. The ability to enter the city was as easy as staying off those significant roads. Houston did receive a higher level of attention given it was the closest city to the Dallas Zone that had suffered a nuclear attack. Overflights of the West side of the city had begun once the issue of armed foreign national groups being near the area had been discovered, but even these measures were limited and based on actionable intelligence. Random Scout Teams were sent into the area weekly with two missions. One was to assess the population that had remained behind. The second was assigned after the armed groups' events had taken place. Those Scout Teams had established a working relationship with several self-defense groups around the city and most worked well with the Scouts. Communications with many of these groups had been maintained for over two years, and they became the government's best eyes and ears for the foreign national groups. It was one of these self-defense groups that sounded the alarm on an event that further stressed the unity of the nation.

A report came into one of the Area Operations Centers / AOCs/ that a Self-Defense Group near the area of Sugar Land had been ambushed. They had put out an urgent call for support to two other groups they maintained radio contact with, and upon arrival, both of those groups had immediately called for support. All in all, over 150 armed members of three Self-Defense Groups had been overcome by an unknown force near highway 69 and the Brazos River, near Sugar Land. Two of the area sweep teams from the US Military were within 30 miles of the location, and they were tasked to make contact with the 3 Groups. One of the sweep team's commanders knew the first group that had called for help, and he knew their members were highly trained as most had left the service at the end of the war. He reported that if that group had been overrun and required assistance, then the force they were dealing with would have much higher than standard capabilities. Upon his request, additional air assets were tasked from San Antonia MOB to support the sweep team's response.

Five miles out from the known location of the incident, the sweep teams made radio contact with the groups. They had suffered heavy casualties and had lost contact with the force they encountered. They estimated the hostiles had continued to move parallel to highway 69 and that they were moving in a large convoy of civilian vehicles to include tractor-trailers. The locals had a checkpoint on Highway 69 and Alt 90, but that checkpoint had no radio communications. The air package had already moved ahead of the sweep teams, and as soon as they had the information, they began to look for signs of the force. The first sweep team was made up

of a Scout Company from 1$^{st}$ Cavalry, out of the Ft. Hood MOB. They made contact with the 3 groups, and their immediate assessment was the groups had suffered 60 percent casualties. The second team was a joint force with members from the Army and Marine Corps. They were more equipped to make contact than the Scout Company was, and so they were ordered to push towards the enemy. Air Ops spotted a large Convoy of vehicles with members dismounting near the Civilian checkpoint. As that report was being relayed back to the Operations Center inside the Dallas Zone, Air Ops stated the convoy had broken into four units with three pressing ahead towards the highway 6 intersection at a high rate of speed. Authority to engage had been pre-authorized in the area given the events that had been taking place, but this package was limited to two armed Apache Helicopters, and it was clear the enemy had deployed a rear defense to engage any force coming up the highway. The armed air package was tasked to support

the 2$^{nd}$ Sweep Team still moving towards the blocking force and the other air asset. A Blackhawk was tasked to keep in contact with the three breakaway units.

News of this event reached the Secretary of Defense, and he immediately made contact with the President. Everything about this event was different. The tactics and sheer size of the force was unlike anything they had seen. The Secretary of Defense had authorized the regional commander to use whatever force necessary to neutralize the threat, but at the time the President was being briefed, the sweep team had not made contact.

The team that had made contact with the three self-defense groups sent another flash report, and it was priority encryption. The Enemy KIA were European with a mixture of Russian and Ukrainian military uniforms. Weapons found on the scene were Russian made, and most of the self-defense group vehicles had been destroyed by Russian anti-tank weapons. It was the sweep team commander's assessment. They were dealing with a military unit, perhaps Battalion size in strength. As the senior commander in the event, he ordered the 2$^{nd}$ sweep team to make contact as soon as possible, but to hold a defensive position until reinforcements could arrive.

Upon receiving the flash message, the regional commander ordered an airstrike package to launch as soon as possible. The coordination for all actions would flow through the MOB at San Antonio. The Secretary of Defense was on a secured VTC with the regional commander within ten minutes, and the message was stunning to everyone back inside the Dallas Zone. A Russian force of over 800 men had penetrated the Southern United States and was pushing towards some unknown objective near the city of Houston.

As the President was being briefed, he asked only one question, how? How had a Russian combat force landed and worked its way into the US? The answer was as chilling as the government had realized with the other foreign national's events. The border was unsecured. Everyone in the room accepted that fact, but this force had to cross an ocean, and it had to do so undetected. The movement of ocean capable ships moving from Europe to Central or South America had been extremely limited. Records indicated only eleven ships had been logged making the journey in the past year. The war had reduced the US's ability to monitor the movements towards the Continental US, but it was believed the ability was still at a level that such a force should have been detected.

They were wrong and wrong to a degree much worse than they imagined.

With the reduction of a force presence in Europe, the US's efforts to monitor everything taking place there had become limited. The incident with the "Rogue" General should have been a warning as to just how blind the US had become. Large commercial ships had been tracked to the greatest extent possible, but the movement of other seagoing vessels was not a priority. The US had made a deliberate decision to leave Europe to its fate, at least for the foreseeable future, and that had resulted in losing situational awareness of matters other than affairs of state.

The event was ongoing, but the US government had to determine one key issue. Was the government of Russia, what was left of it, responsible for this force? The ability to communicate with the Russian government had been maintained. It had established itself in a small town called Tyumen on the Tura River. Contact was made, and the US President was strait to the point. He asked his Russian counterpart if they had any knowledge of the force that was inside the US? The Russian President was quick to answer, no. Again, the President was forthright in his next statement. He informed the Russian President the US would destroy this force, but they would take enough prisoners to find out the truth. If the US determined the force was working off the orders of the Russian government, the US would destroy what was left of the Russian nation. The Russian President became angry at hearing the words of the US President and responded by telling him that nearly 80 percent of the Russian military had already been destroyed or had walked away. Entire units had taken whatever they could gather and disappeared. If somehow one or more of those units had made its way to the US mainland on some revenge mission, the Russian government had no control over them and no knowledge of their intent. The US President answered him by repeating himself and the threat towards the Russian nation, and with that, he informed his counterpart they would be in touch as soon as the threat had been neutralized. The secure call ended.

The post-call conversations in the room were disorganized, and it was clear the ongoing event was keeping anyone from being proactive. One comment was made that did stick with the President and several others in the room. In the past, the Russians had utilized what was commonly called "Little Green Men" to conduct, unofficial operations. Little Green Men was a clever way of saying, Russian military members who were not officially recognized. It was the primary way they had taken the Crimea, and some in the room were convinced it was taking place again.

Although the US had maintained official contact with most of the nations in Europe, the reality was, only Germany, France and Switzerland had functioning national governments. In the three years after the war, Europe had become a conglomerate of small cities and towns that supported each other with no interest in international affairs or even supporting a national government. Keeping situational awareness of movements inside of Europe was indeed no one's priority. The event with the General was also seen as nothing more than a large band of Bandits out to capture wealth and power. What the US was facing on its soil was different. The enemy action was a well-laid plan to enter the US and disrupt the nation, but how and where was a matter of capturing individuals and finding out the truth. In the meantime, the President gave the order for the Secretary of Defense to be prepared to strike Russia or any other nation that might be responsible for what was taking place.

The 2$^{nd}$ sweep team had eyes on the blocking force as they had set up utilizing the massive flyovers at the intersection of Hwy 90 and Hwy 69. The Blackhawk had only been able to track one of the three breakaway units, and it was located moving on Hwy 8 near the intersection of 288 and Hwy 8. They had dismounted in the area of a location called the Clear Creek Golf Club. It was estimated this unit was near 150 in strength. The Blackhawk had been flying a patrol mission when the event started, and fuel forced it to break off the observation. The locations of the other two units were unknown at that time.

The Secretary of Defense knew they had a huge problem. The day to day air alert status was minimal given the threats were known to be small armed groups with limited little arms capability. The Navy maintained coastal alert missions and those assets were not in a position to support what was taking place, except for the alert squadron stationed at Corpus Christi MOB. Force generation for a real combat mission tasked out of Lackland MOB would take several hours, and it was decided the blocking force would be struck first by the package from Corpus. The short answer to the President was not a good one. The US was not prepared for such an event.

The enemy blocking force was struck one hour after the mission was tasked to Corpus MOB. A follow on Quick Reaction Force that had been in the area of Victoria was linking with the 1st sweep team as the airstrikes took place. 30 mins after the strike, the US forces had secured the area. The force that was destroyed was estimated at over 200 in strength, and the US had what it wanted. It had prisoners. They were taken to the Lackland MOB in San Antonio.

Notification was made to the President. The blocking force had been neutralized, and prisoners were removed for interrogation. What was not known was the intent of the mission and the location of two of the teams that had broken off. The President was informed the group held up near the golf complex would be struck as soon as the strike package from Lackland MOB was ready. Locals had been observing that same group, and they had also made contact with the other two. It was reported the other two groups had taken up defensive positions. One had been located near the Houston Zoo and the other near the University of Houston.

All three targets were struck within two hours of the blocking force being neutralized, but Battle Damage Assessment estimated that only 50 to 60 members of each force had been killed in the attacks. Local Defense Groups continued to locate smaller groups that had dispersed from the attacks, and those groups proved to be small enough the locals were able to neutralize them. Again, prisoners were taken and turned over to the responding military teams that moved into the area. The threat from this event was over, but the list of questions continued to grow.

The news of this event reached every state in the nation, and all regional commanders were ordered to increase their defensive posture until ordered to do otherwise. What the states understood was that a large, foreign military force had infiltrated the US from its Southern Border and had been engaged in the City of Houston. Why and how were questions the federal government could not answer, but the trust of the state in those answers was limited. Within a day of the event, rumors spread of the attack event being staged as an excuse to pull forces off of the critical sites, forces loyal to the states. No additional troops had been called for as the Dallas Zone had the bulk of the US's most capable units. That fact didn't stop the states from communicating their fears to each other. Trust had been lost, and the idea of a homeland invasion seemed nearly impossible. Even many of the FOBs found the story to be unrealistic. Almost everyone believed no Enemy of the US still maintained the ability to land a force on US soil.

The interrogation of several of the ranking prisoners revealed little information. What had been determined was that the force had come from a very contaminated region of Europe as the members' exposure levels were far above what the people in the US, Central or South America had endured.

Those in the US that had had levels that high had been on the East or West Coast and most had died in the past three years. The prisoners that did speak spoke a dialect of Russian attributed to Russia's South Western region. The Ukrainian uniforms all showed the members to be from three units assigned to the area just north of the Crimean. What was established was how they had made it to the US. It had been only has suspected. Several of the commercial ships that had been tracked had not been hauling aid to Mexico as their ship's ledgers stated. The process of observing these ships as they docked didn't exist, at least not at a level that would feed data into the US intelligence community. What was the size, capability, and intent of the force had not been obtained, and that was an answer the government back in the Dallas Zone would not accept.

The call that was placed to the Russian President was not set until another round of interrogation was completed. By that time, it was established most of the members were, in fact, Russian Military. When the call was made, the tension was beyond anything the US government had experienced since the end of the war. Not only did the Russian President deny any involvement in the action. He informed the US President the entire event might have been fabricated for a follow-on attack on Russian. The events that took place at the end of the war were still fresh in the minds of every Russian leader. The US and Russia had come to terms at the end of the war, and yet the US attacked again for the sake of parity. That explanation had been given in a harsh and short statement to the Russian Leadership, and soon after the strike with the reality being, the Russians had no way of responding. To the US, this attack on US soil was nothing more than a revenge event meant to disrupt the Dallas Zone, a concept that was well known throughout the world. Why the attack had taken place in Houston was still a mystery that interrogation had not exposed at the time of the call. The Russian President ended the call by making the statement the Russian Military still had options, and they were options the US had overlooked. After his comment, he disconnected his end of the VTC and the US President, and his key staff sat in silence. The war had been over for three years, but now, suddenly, it seemed a new war was about to start.

Forces were deployed in a full combat configuration in three major groups. Each Taskforce was Brigade in size with full aviation support. One was stage just Southeast of Laredo, and one was placed North of Victoria and the last was located North of Brownsville. The nuclear powerplant near Matagorda had its defensive force and was considered a hardened target. It was also determined if the attacking force had been tasked with the destruction of that site, they would not have driven passed it as they entered Houston.

The mission was to intercept any follow-on force that might approach the Dallas Zone, and every available imaging asset was tasked to that mission. It was the breakthrough from the interrogation process that set off the next set of alarms. A Senior Russian Officer was told not only he, but his surviving family would be moved into the zone if he would say to his captors what his units' mission was. It seems several of the senior officers had made the journey with their families, and once that was determined, the idea of offering the relocation became the primary tool for interrogation. The family members had been left behind with a small rear area detachment in Mexico, along with crucial resupply items. When the Russian Officer decided to speak, the details of what he said had to be verified if possible. It was far too alarming to give to the President without some level of vetting. The force had been moved over the past six months. Its size was over 4500 to include support elements. Its combat capability was based on an array of weapons, with a focus on shoulder-fired anti-air and anti-armor. Its goal was to disrupt the Dallas Zone to the greatest extent possible, and it would achieve that goal by attacking the first MOBs inside the zone. The Houston event was a distraction, designed to draw attention away from the main body force that had maneuvered in smaller elements, in civilian clothes and vehicles to a staging area near Weatherford Texas. When asked if he thought that the main body force was combat-ready, he stated it had been in place before the attack into Houston. The Russian Officer had no idea how soon after the Houston event took place; the primary mission would execute, but he did know the force was in position before his unit moving on Houston. This part of his story was discussed over and over again, but the story didn't change.

Two hours after the details had been learned, another Russian Officer was promised the same relocation deal, and he accepted. His knowledge of the Dallas Zone mission was far more detailed than the First Officer. The intent was a revenge mission for the US's attack at the end of the war. The units that made up the force now in the US had been in the Crimea at the end of the war, and their Generals had decided they would seek revenge at some point in time. It took them over two years to prepare the force, but the Russia Officer was convinced the spirit of the combat force, as well as their capability, would catch the US by total surprise. He stated the force would stage just West of Ft Worth Texas near a town called Weatherford and he was sure the force was in place. That was enough information to get the story moving forward, and it was a story that put the US government in a panic.

Why the main body had not attacked, yet knowing that prisoners would be taken was the question that came up first. The President asked the Secretary of Defense what actions were being taken. The Secretary had ordered the regional commander to search the area near Weatherford, and all assets were made available to him. There had been no radio communications that had been detected and only minor reports of small groups of armed men traveling in civilian vehicles. In an area that was well populated with people wanting to be near the zone, it was not unusual to see large numbers of armed civilians. What should have stood out was the fact they were seen in vehicles, given the short supply of fuel. The increased number of vehicles should have triggered some level of alarm. Why it didn't is still not known.

The entire discussion came back to the President's initial question. Was this an act supported by the Russian Government or not? It was the opinion of the Secretary of Defense that it was not. The President's question had been asked of both Russian Officers, and their answers were identical. When asked about their mission being sanctioned by the Russian government, they both replied, "What government"? Both had the same opinion. Russia had been without a functioning government at least one they were aware of, and that had held since the end of the war. They both stated the mission was based upon Russian Military member's desire for revenge and nothing else. Their leadership had developed the plan with only a handful of crucial members knowing what the actual objective was. The validity of their story was questioned by nearly everyone with the President, except for the Secretary of Defense. Rogue military groups had become the norm in the world, and to him, this event was no different. What the Secretary and his staff had underestimated was the scope and capability of this particular movement. In the eyes of the US military, this was just another version of a War Lord, one born from a collapsed state.

The Secretary of Defense made a comment that most in the briefing had not contemplated. With the Event in old Eastern Europe and now this attack on US soil, how many other groups like this one were out there? The US was no longer in a position to gather actionable intelligence on a global scale. Satellite assets provided some information, but the humanistic data was missing. It was the President who made a comment, "Is this going to become the new norm"? The world was a wholly destabilized place, and fortifying the US seemed the only option.

The call with the Russian President was not as tense as the previous conversation. The US let the Russians know they believed the attack was not sponsored nor supported by the Russian Government. The Russian response was tempered and given with little assurance. It was clear they continued to be in a precarious state. Three years had passed, and communications were taking place, but on a limited set of topics and considered very informal. The reality was, the Russian Military was in complete disarray, and the threats of unrest were far more prevalent than anyone had imagined. Russia was suffering from the same risk of breaking up, and the ability to control those events was even more limited in Russia than they were in the US.

The issue of responsibility had been cleared. The process of dealing with the pending assault on the zone was already underway as the President was speaking with the Russians. As the President was being briefed, areal assets, both air-breathing and space-based were concentrated on a 20 square mile area around the city of Weatherford Texas. A force of nearly 3,000 members should have been easily detected, once they assembled and it was estimated they had been doing just that for the past 24 hrs. The reality was, they never did gather. Four groups had used their location near Weatherford to reconfigure, but the entire fighting force had not assembled as a single unit. A separate Assault Team had assembled just outside the Ft. Worth MOB in an area called White Settlement. That team would be the first to strike, and the MOB was their primary objective. They had maintained their civilian clothing and moved into position with all their equipment utilizing FEMA vehicles they had seized in a raid just thirty minutes before their attack. There were no checkpoints between the area known as White Settlement and the MOB main gate, but the gate was not the point of attack.

Reports of the assault on the FEMA movement were coming

into the Sector Defense Operations Center, SDOC, when the attack began. Several anti-armor weapons were fired at five of the large airlift aircraft parked on the ramp at the MOB's airfield. All five aircraft were struck just as mortar rounds began to fall on the aviation fuel farm. Within minutes it was estimated that over 80 mortar rounds had been fired along with seven additional anti-armor weapons. Less than 20 minutes after the hijacking of the FEMA vehicles, the MOB aviation fuel farm was burning, and over two dozen aircraft had been damaged beyond repair. The MOB had been on heightened alert, and scout teams were in the area near the point of origin for the attack. It was suspected the enemy would maneuver away from the base as soon as the mortar rounds stopped, and aviation assets were dispatched in the direction of the attack. Four Blackhawks with a full Quick Reaction Force were dispatched. The first two Blackhawks were struck by unknown air to ground missiles, and the other two broke contact from the area.

The MOB in Ft. Worth was the primary military installation for the Dallas Zone, and as such, it was capable of full combat operations if needed. For weeks, the missions to the Southern area of the zone had been supported by the MOB at Lackland with additional support coming from the other major MOB at Ft. Hood. Although Ft. Worth MOB was the HQ of the US military, it was not configured or defended in a manner to repel such a massive assault, and it took hours to make that configuration happen

The Russian Assault Team intended to draw the attention of the US forces while the other groups maneuvered into the area. Their mission was to strike the airfield and then disperse into two smaller groups. These two smaller groups were to continue to assault the MOB but from different locations. The US had anticipated this tactic, but it didn't stop leadership from overcommitting forces that were needed to concentrate on the Weatherford operation. The MOB at Ft.

Hood was ordered to respond to the Weatherford area, and MOB San Antonio was tasked with providing maximum Combat Air Support.

MOB San Antonio had been alerted of the attack taking place inside the zone and was in the middle of generating a Combat Strike Package of over 30 fast movers and 20 drones when word came into it's Base Defense Operation's Center, BDOC , of mortar fire and anti-armor rounds being fired at the flight line. MOB San Antonio had been far more operational than the Ft. Worth, given it's tasking for support to the search missions. Even with that increased state of readiness, the MOB was still not configured for the type of assault that took place. Within 20 minutes of the attack on MOB San Antonio, it's aviation fuel farm was burning, and it had sustained over 30 damaged aircraft, most being fighters.

The Ft. Worth MOB had been struck, and the enemy was melting back into the thousands upon thousands of abandon homes and buildings in the surrounding area. Aerial platforms identified the team as it maneuvered away from the attack on MOB San Antonio. A Quick Response Force engaged the Russian team, and within 30 minutes, it had been neutralized. Seven wounded were interrogated, but their operational picture was limited to their teams' mission.

The response to the San Antonio MOB attack was being briefed when word came of another attack on the Ft. Worth site. Close Air Support was reassigned to Corpus Christi MOB, but that package had not arrived by the time the second attack began. The second attack on the Ft. Worth MOB was shorter in duration and consisted of only mortar rounds. Again, the flight line was the target and the First Responders who were reacting to the first event were forced to retreat. The attack lasted less than 5 minutes and again, the enemy forces retreated into an area of unoccupied buildings. When the news of the second attack was given, the President responded, "Do we not have a functioning military? What are we doing to stop this event"? Everyone in the briefing was confused and asking questions of people who couldn't give answers, and that made the situation even worse. The Secretary of Defense stated other air support was moving into the area from two FOBs near the Comanche Peak Nuclear Power Plant as they stood a higher level of alert than most. Comanche Peak was vital to the future of getting power back to critical parts of the Dallas Zone, and in fact, it had been operating at a minimal capacity for over six months.

To the US Military, it was clear this team near the Ft. Worth MOB was executing a diversionary mission. The Secretary of Defense advised the President the primary effort needed to be finding the main body that was said to have assembled to the West. By that time, the President and several others in the room no longer believed the two captured Russian Officer's story. Most were convinced the attacks they were witnessing in San Antonio and Ft. Worth was the work of the main body enemy forces, and as such, the priority would be to defend the zone itself and not press forces to the West.

Space assets could cover the entire area without burning critical fuel, and most had been put in place soon after the zone concept was started. IFF signals were attached to all US vehicles and aircraft, but over half of the ground forces no longer were equipped with the capability. This would lead to an imagery confirmation of vehicle movements. The US could see what vehicles were moving, and if an IFF signal was being sent. The movement of civilians had been limited to scheduled public transportation given the status of fuel on hand, and even then, that schedule was minimal. Most areas had a route that was run twice a day, and that was it. The assumption was, any movement of vehicles not on the known schedule would be considered hostile. That had been the day to day defensive plan inside the zone for well over a year. This event was no different. For a combat force of over 3 thousand to move, it would take vehicles, and that would make them known.

### *The Comanche Peak Incident:*

The enemy had taken longer to assemble than they had anticipated, and they understood the Dallas Zone would have air cover even with the operations at the Ft. Worth MOB. The strike on the San Antonio MOB was designed to not only confuse the US forces but to limit the strike packages that could be launched from that location. From the beginning, the decision to strike deep into the Dallas Zone or to strike areas vital to the zone would be made based upon the results of the two MOB attacks. The enemy decided to move on the most critical assets outside the zone. A force of nearly 1200 was tasked to assault the nuclear reactor site at Comanche Peak, and a force of over 300 was sent to destroy the transmission lines from West Texas Wind fields that were being routed into the Dallas Zone. Many of those lines had not been damaged during the war, and a large percentage of the Wind fields were still capable of producing power as soon as the disbursement grid was finalized. The US had been working on this project for over a year, and somehow, the Russian force knew it's every detail.

Comanche Peak had a defensive force of over 500. It was made up of a combination of units to include civilian agencies, but the bulk of the force came from the Texas Army National Guard. Its capability was limited to infiltration denial and limited anti-air. The threat assessment for the site in a post-war environment had never called for the ability to repel or destroy a real combat force.

The Russian Scouts had been in the area for weeks, and they had learned almost every detail of how the site was defended. A detachment from the main Russian body met up with two members of the scout team near the town of Granbury. The assault force was going to move as soon as the supply vehicles that staged in Granbury were taken. Once a week, a supply movement by FEMA moved through the city on its way to Stephenville where a sheltered community of over 150,000 lived. Stephenville had been designated as a staging area for those who were wishing to enter the Dallas Zone but had to be vetted before being assigned locations. After that process was completed, people were moved by civilian buses to predetermined locations inside the zone. The plan was to take this convoy and quickly move the short distance between Granbury and the plant.

The assault team took the 45-vehicle convoy in the city of Granbury, and by the time the word had been sent back, the team had arrived near the plant. The confusion of the assault on the convoy was so bad; the immediate reaction was it was the main combat force preparing to attack inside the zone. It had been two days since the strikes on both MOBs and reports of movements in and out of the zone had been overwhelming. The defensive force at the plant had been notified of the attack in Granbury and they had been fully briefed on the capabilities of the enemy force that was in the area. They took every precaution in their defensive plan, but the request for additional forces had not been answered by the time the Granbury attack took place.

Word of the attack on the plant came in a little over an hour after the vehicle event. Air assets had been up for two days since the MOB attacks, and the response to the plant was immediate. This time, the US aircraft were in full combat configuration and the ability to respond with air to ground was fully operational. A quick response force was tasked with a FOB in Stephenville. Word of the combat taking place around the facility at Comanche Peak showed the level of confusion. Live communications were being monitored by the Secretary of Defense, who was with the President and key staff. Some 30 minutes into the assault, it seemed the US forces were holding, and airstrikes were beginning to take their toll. The Secretary informed the President the enemy force was disengaging and moving to the Southwest. Air assets were still striking targets, but ground forces had been ordered to stay in place and defend the plant. Within another 30 min, all combat operations near the plan had stopped. Fuel and execution of resources drove everything the US government did, and this attack was no different. Two drones had been assigned to track the force that had broken contact at the plant, and two additional QRFs were tasked to neutralize the remaining enemy forces. Both of those QRFs were from Ft. Hood MOB, and their time to target was estimated at less than one hour. The Secretary informed the President the situation seemed to have stabilized, but the estimate was of a force of only 800, and that meant nearly 1500 were still unaccounted for. In reality, the government had no real idea of who was operating where.

Although the plant had not been lost, the damage was beyond expectation. The force assigned to the plant was not designed to prevent standoff weapons nor indirect fire. Initial reports, along with drone feeds, showed extreme damage to transmission lines and several support facilities in the compound. Reactor operations had been suspended as soon as the attack started, and the assessment was the facility was stable. It was the reports of the defenders and plant staff status that shocked the President. Within minutes of the search and clear operations taking place, it was evident the enemy forces had utilized chemical weapons. Those who came out of harden facilities were immediately impacted by an unknown agent. Chemical monitoring networks at the site had not been kept up to date since the end of the war, but several of the ones that did work indicated a weapon's grade nerve agent was in the area. As those reports came in, it was clear the enemy had dispersed several agents as they retreated. Within an hour, nearly 75 percent of those on the site were incapacitated. QRF forces that were still responding to the area were ordered to withdraw. A full strike package was ordered to neutralize the remaining enemy forces and the two QRFs from MOB Ft. Hood were called back. None of the responding QRF units were equipped to defend against the agents that had been used. The Russian forces had equipped themselves with weapons capabilities no one had anticipated, and their commitment to employing every weapon in their arsenal was absolute.

The US had lost it's only functioning nuclear power-plant and with it the ability to power critical areas inside the Dallas Zone. Emergency power became the only thing the government Headquarters had to operate from. The attack on the Ft. Worth MOB had forced the President and critical governmental members to an alternate site and the very fact that the process took place created rumors that no one would control. Word of the strikes on the power plant and two MOBs spread throughout the country and it became clear to the President he would need to speak with the Governors as soon as practical. As for the public that lived near the MOBs, they were fully aware that something very unusual had taken place, but the rumors of foreign national groups roaming the area of the zone were not new. It was not until the power plant attack and the news of chemical weapons being used that many began to realize something far more dangerous was taking place.

The emergency call with the Governors was scheduled for two hours after the news of the chemical weapons. Before the call, the debate was over just how much to say. The relationships were weak, and news of the federal government being attacked might have unpredictable results. The fact that such a comment would come up before the call spoke volumes as to the stability of the nation. The President decided the Governors needed to know everything the federal government knew, to include the unknown status of over 1800 known enemy combatants.

Every Governor was on the call. All had heard of the events in and around the Dallas Zone, but none of them, except for the Texas Governor, knew the status of the events. By the time the briefing was over, two issues were clear to everyone. The US had a highly capable foreign military force on its soil, and the location and actual size of that force were unknown. From the perspective of the Governor's, how this had happened was unimportant. The capability and the intent of the enemy were the primary concerns. Most considered themselves to be too far away from the threat to have any level of real panic, but just the idea that such an event could happen kept all of them more than concerned.

The Governor of Oklahoma asked the most obvious question. What measures were being taken to neutralize the threat? The Secretary of Defense went into great detail on what was being done, and he ensured all the Governors every regional commander was in constant communications with the Secretary's Staff. The topic then shifted to the use of chemical weapons and not only chemical capabilities, but biological and nuclear as well. It became easy for the President and his staff to see, the Governors were wanting to know if the situation was going to get worse. Confidence between the two groups had been lost, and the idea the Governors had to suddenly depend on any information given to them by the very government that had become hostile towards them was unrealistic. The President promised that everyone would be kept up to date on all actions and he ended by asking anyone who heard of unusual activity in their states to report it as soon as possible. It was that last statement that made many of the Governors have even more doubt. Why would the President worry about activities in other parts of the country? Was there more to the event than he was telling them? Again, the lack of trust ruled over every conversation between the states and the federal government. The call ended without a set follow on time for the next update. The President had communicated with the states, but the issue of trust remained the barrier the states could not overcome.

Three days had passed since the attack on the power plant, and the cleanup process had been underway for over a day when the next attack took place. It was clear the enemy forces that had struck the power plant had broken down into small groups, and even with the follow-on air operations, the ground assessment was only an additional 150 enemy forces had been killed. The constant utilization of air assets was limited to drones with several FOBs capable of supporting airframes remaining on alert. This time the attack was an ambush event. All movements outside the zone had been limited to military operations, but inside the zone, the task of keeping life as normal as possible had been the goal. A mobile clinic was attacked and destroyed near the town of Benbrook, and again, chemical mortar rounds had been used. Three of the convoy vehicles were taken and later found near Texas Christian University, just south of downtown Ft. Worth. The Campus had been converted into a special needs shelter, and the fact the vehicles were recovered in that area created a panic the government could not control. By the time word of the attack had been briefed, the decision had been made to limit all movement inside the zone with only military vehicles being the exception. The amount of vehicle traffic had been minimal in normal times, but the scheduled delivery of critical items such as food and medical supplies had made life bearable in the more remote parts of the zone. It became clear the ability to secure every roadway, and every movement inside the zone would logistically create a drain on limited resources that could not be maintained. Comanche Peak and the FOB at Ft. Worth were the beginning of a series of events that would change the future of the Dallas Zone concept.

*Assessments and changes:*

The US Military, along with the rest of the Intelligence Community, concluded the enemy's main fighting force had broken down into small cells that were highly trained and well equipped. That assessment was nearly correct. Special

Weapons Teams / SWTs / had detached from the enemy's main body. These teams were armed with chemical capabilities with several of the teams being armed with tactical nuclear weapons. It was a fear the US had contemplated but had no way of verifying. The ability of the force to arm themselves in Europe made the predictability of their capability impossible. The US had been conducting detection operations with every asset designed to do so, but they also knew the Russians had cloaking processes that could make detection extremely difficult. It was not until these detection assets began to alert on false positives that the US had to come to the realization such weapons were inside the zone. The Russians knew how to deploy false positives, and that process also sent the message they had the capability.

The decision had been made by the Russian forces; they would remain in civilian clothing, but when combat operations were to take place, they would change. It was their pride that made them demand this of their leadership. It was an easy sell given the leadership agreed. Their attacks were violent and based on speed. Over the next week, two dozen events would take place, predominantly on the Northern and Western sides of the zone. Each event was an ambush-style assault with the use of at least one chemical mortar round. The effect they were looking for was achieved. People who had gone over two years without feeling as if their lives were in daily jeopardy now seemed to sit in fear. Military and Civilian Patrols were increased in areas that continued to see the bulk of the attacks, but that did not give the public the level of confidence they wanted. Volunteer groups stopped after three days of attacks. When enemy forces were killed, it did virtually nothing to build trust. Anyone walking near anyone else was suspect. The fact the enemy was always found in uniform only confirmed to the public just how dangerous times had once again become. For the most part, people still did not live in single-family homes as it was too difficult to maintain.

Three years after the war, Shelter concepts were still the norm in somewhat modified configurations, but the fact was, large gatherings of people were the primary targets of the enemy, and the desire was to force them into leaving the area. Destroying confidence in the Dallas Zone was a primary goal, and that goal was achieved.

By the end of the second week, the Dallas Zone was paralyzed. Work on reconstruction projects had stopped. People began to push back into the areas where there were single-family structures even though they had no drinkable water and no reliable source of food. The Dallas Zone had come to a standstill, and the government seemed powerless to prevent it from happening. Large areas were swept by combat forces, and it was a tactic that was not new to many of the members of the military. They had conducted such operations in Iraq and Afghanistan, but this was different. This was their homeland.

Several teams were discovered and neutralized. Intelligence gained from these teams was telling. They had no radio communications and no written instructions. They had no idea where the other teams were located or what their missions were. What surprised the US Forces the most was a reluctance to be taken alive. Six, five-man teams had been taken out and of those only two members were taken alive. Several members showed self-inflicted wounds, but most died in head-on assaults on overwhelming US Forces. It was clear there was a hatred for the US, unlike anything the US Military had experienced.

The Russian force had changed its tactics. Except for the SWT operations, the force was broken down into groups ranging in size from 5 to 10 members. The concept of the main body force had changed again. Only one combat sized unit would remain intact. This 150 member unit would remain inactive until a later date and act as a maneuver force for a mission only it's two senior officers were aware of. The nuclear-capable SWTs remained attached to this element. In and around the zone were over 100 cells capable of creating tremendous damage in a concise period. For two weeks, the attacks had started and ended within 10 min. By the second week, the zone was averaging over 30 events per day, and the US was expending assets at an alarming rate. It was the death of a thousand cuts, and it was working.

The briefings with the President and his key staff were consuming most of their day. By the beginning of the second week, a more important meeting was held with the intent of changing the approach to the attacks. One issue immediately became apparent. The consumption of fuel for maneuver elements, both air, and ground, had gone up over 400 percent. Most of these responses were ineffective, given the short duration of the attacks and the ability of the enemy to move back into their surroundings. It was classic Guerrilla Warfare, and it was working. Single chemical mortar rounds fired into known high-density sites were the most common attack but clearing the footprint around every site that met that target description was impossible. The old concept of " See something, say something" was ineffective. Most civilians had no way of communicating what they may have seen, and the volume of reports was so high, the response process had spread the force in a completely disorganized fashion. What the President wanted was new ideas, new options. He wanted something that would show the public the zone was under control.

The decision was made; the military would greatly expand fixed observation positions throughout the areas the majority of the attacks were coming from. There was a great deal of resistance to the concept given the appearance of a militaristic state with everyone being questioned at all times. The purpose of the zone was to rebuild society, and that required people feeling as normal as they possibly could. The guidance was given. These observation points would not be checkpoints. People would not be stopped and questioned unless stringent requirements were met.

The concept of Observation Post, OPs, was not new in the post-war US, but the idea of them looking inward was. Not only was the idea unique, the sheer volume of these Ops was evident to the public. Within two days of the plan being approved, thousands of Ops became apparent throughout the Northern and Western areas of the zone. It was a process that would give the political leadership something to tell the public, but it was also a tactic the military knew the enemy would adapt to and it only took two days for that fear to become a reality.

A scheduled clinic was held in the city of Burleson, South of Ft. Worth. These events typically resulted in anywhere from 200 to 300 people showing up. The capabilities were limited, but the perceptions of some level of health care was critical to the zone's social fiber. After two weeks of constant attacks to the North and West, people were avoiding large gatherings in those areas, and that placed stress on events such as mobile clinical sites that were taking place in what was thought to be safer areas. The cell that struck the Burleson clinic had observed the change in defensive tactics. They were aware of the complete process that was now conducted one hour before the clinic assets arrived. They were aware of the drone coverage in the area of the clinics, and they also knew a QRF would be within five minutes of the site while the crowd was there. The event itself would have a security detail that was more than capable of repelling a small cell operation. But, the purpose of the Burleson attack was to show the US the cells had been successful in moving deeper into the zone. The defensive force was equipped with chemical gear as was the medical team, but many members of the medical staff had refused to have the chemical gear near them as they believed it would only create a perception of separation between the public and the staff. Three rounds fell on the structure where the clinic was being held, and all three contained nerve agents. The plan to disburse the crowd worked well and the casualties numbered less than twenty. Two additional rounds were fired with an adjusted impact area. It was apparent to the defenders, the enemy had continuous eyes on their target, even as they were moving the people away. Drone coverage of the clinic had been pulled for a priority mission away from the clinic site, and as had been the case, the attack was over in less than three minutes. The QRF that moved into the estimated area of operations for the enemy came under heavy fire that included three vehicles being struck by anti-armor weapons. That was new. The idea that a cell had made it into the Southern area of the zone was one thing, but the ambush of a responding QRF had not taken place since the strikes had started.

The Burleson attack was unlike the others, and that resulted in the President questioning the Secretary of Defense at a point in time when he had no answers. The frustration levels were higher than at any point since the end of the war, and everyone knew that is what the enemy force was trying to achieve. To the public, the fear that no location was safe was the perception, and it only took a day or two for that perception to become a reality. People continued to move away from areas that were dependent on large gatherings. Power that had been restored to distribution sites had been lost with the attack on the power plant. The government knew things were getting worse, not better.

The scheduled call with the states took place only a few hours after the attack in Burleson. The governors were told the truth. It was the opinion of the government the enemy had broken their force down into five to ten-member cells, and the purpose of these cells was to create as much panic inside the zone as possible. The government no longer believed the enemy intended to fight a force on force, conventional battle somewhere inside the zone. A long conversation took place over the tactics of the enemy and their continued capabilities. The Secretary of Defense told the group the enemy had utilized over 120 chemical rounds in the attacks, and it was nearly impossible to state how many they had left. The Governor of Iowa asked the question the government had simply not stopped to contemplate. Could the enemy only utilize the chemical weapons through Mortar rounds? The Secretary's answer indicated just how overwhelmed they had been. The concept of the enemy having means of disbursement had not been reviewed.

The events of the past two weeks had made the government completely reactionary. To the Governors, it was clear the federal government was nearly paralyzed. They had placed the nation's hopes on the Dallas Zone, and now an enemy was inside that zone destabilizing its day to day existence. The Governor of Missouri then asked a question most had not even considered. Was there a plan to move the federal government if needed and if so, what would become of the Dallas Zone? To the federal government, the zone was the building block of recovery. To the Governors, it was the seat of a federal government that had abandoned the states. The President answered the question in two parts. There was a plan to relocate the government if needed, but it would be temporary, and they would return to the zone as soon as practical. Then the President made a statement the governors were not prepared for. He informed them he knew they were and had been communicating for months and that the intent of these conversations was for the federal government not to understand what was being discussed. He stated he understood the division his predecessor had created between them, but the time for that division needed to come to an end. The US had been unable to anticipate the events that were taking place, and there was no guarantee that future events may not happen. In short, he was admitted to the states the ability to defend the nation from a world that had fallen apart was not there. Yes, the country could defeat anyone left on a typical battlefield, but the ability to control and overcome what was taking place in and around the Dallas Zone did not exist. The world had changed far beyond any of their imaginations could have predicted, and there was every reason to believe the US may not survive those changes. If two Divisional Commanders could put together such an elaborate plan to strike the US, then what else was possible? He painted a picture of a world controlled by War Lords, War Lords that now had access to weapons stockpiles left entirely unguarded.

The US was divided, and the world saw the nation as vulnerable, but still, the land where recovery had the highest odds of taking place. If the federal government could not protect the Dallas Zone, then how could it protect the nation? As Governor after Governor responded to the President's words, that theme held true. How could the federal government guarantee anything to anyone? Yes, nuclear weapons were still operational, at least for a few more years. Yes, the US had spaced based weapons, again for a short period, but those were deterrents to Nation States, not to roving bands of raiders. The conversation had drifted off the topic of what was taking place inside the zone, but the President and others in the room could sense the indifference many of the states seemed to show. The call ended with an agreement to hold the talk again in three days. The President had painted a picture for the states he hoped would begin to heal the rift between them and the federal government. By the time the call was over, it was clear, the division was far worse than anyone in the room had imagined. As bleak as the conversation had been, the issue of nuclear weapons being in the hands of the enemy was not revealed. The next call was set for three days, but before that call could take place, the future of the nation would change again.

# CHAPTER SIXTEEN: THE ZONE'S NUCLEAR NIGHTMARE

Within a day of the Burleson attack, events took place in Mansfield, Grand Prairie, Waxahachie and the city of Arlington. Each target had been some type of distribution operation up until the attack in Arlington. The distribution center attacks were the standard; chemical mortar rounds hit and run. The attack on Arlington was a well-defended communications field. It was the first tactical target since the strikes on the MOBs. The defense of the site was far above average. The indirect fire footprint was patrolled around the clock. This time, it was the civilian actions in the area that led to the event. For over a week, locals had begun to post their own checkpoints on most major roadways. The approach to the communications site had two. The military movements into the site had complied with the civilians given their understanding of the nervousness of anything or anyone in a military uniform. The rumor of enemy cells moving throughout the area wearing US uniforms was just one of many that now had the public on edge.

The convoy of six vehicles approached the second civilian checkpoint, and by the time the vehicle occupants realized what was taking place, they were killed. The cell had neutralized the civilian checkpoint and manned it just as it had operated for days. On the approach, nothing seemed unusual. The vehicles were taken without a single distress getting out. Their approach to the communications Entry Control Point was just as it should have been. The cell had observed every detail for over a day before the mission, and it went off without a hitch.

Word of the attack on the communications site was up channeled as soon as the assault began. It was immediately determined chemical weapons were being utilized. The enemy was in full chemical gear. The attack lasted a little over 20 minutes. By the time the defending force had completed putting their chemical suits on, the attacking force had made it to the main building. The defending force was made up of US Army MPs, and the drill of fighting while changing into chemical gear was well-rehearsed. The same was not true for the military and civilian communications members. In the 20 minutes, the attack had covered, over 100 communications support staff and 25 defenders were killed. An additional 30 members, both military and civilian, had been killed at the checkpoint.

As the President was being briefed, the value of the site became known. It was more than a simple communications operation location. It was a satellite link and the primary site for such operations after the strike on the Ft. Worth MOB. It was the most complex operation of its kind in the zone, and it had been rendered inoperative. The attacking force had departed the area leaving behind four dead and two wounded. The cell had been estimated to have had ten members. The location of the remaining members was not known at the time of the President being briefed, but like in all the other attacks, even if they were caught alive, they would have little intelligence value. The US had redundant satellite communication networks, but the attack was a significant loss to the overall program. Over 60 percent of this capability had been lost in the war, and it was estimated the attack constituted another decrease of over 5 percent. One impact that was immediate to the President and his staff was the temporary loss of secured VCT operations with the states. His next call would have to be conducted by a secured phone only and the explanation as to why would only make the issue of confidence worse.

The Arlington attack was being reviewed with the primary issue being convoy and route security when the next report came in. The detection operations for nuclear fingerprints had alerted on two locations near the Ft. Worth MOB. The area around the MOB had three previous alerts that proved to be false positives placed by the enemy, so when word came in of these two alerts, the reaction was guarded. After the attack, the defensive operations around the MOB had increased dramatically. A three-mile clear zone had been established, and no one was allowed inside the area. It was patrolled by drones 24/7, and the number of combat patrols required nearly 1400 members on 24 hr rotations.

At any given moment in time, well over 2,000 men and women of the US military were defending the MOB. It was home to not only the US Military Headquarters but the government as well. Both had stayed in place during the first attack, but after the discovery of potential nuclear weapons in the area, both had developed alternate sites. The ability to move the President and key staff by air or ground was on constant alert. The news of nuclear detection was not taken lightly by the President's detail. The areas that had shown to be hot by an airborne platform had two assault teams responding within minutes of the alert. Motion detection cameras in the area indicated nothing and two additional drones were flown in ahead of the teams. The location was at the base of the Highway 820 bridge on the South bank of Lake Worth. The second detection point was near an abandon shelter center that had been a mall, just South of the MOB's runway. Once it was obvious, the two detections had taken place within minutes of each other, and once it was clear for everyone to see the two sites were strategically placed at ether end of the MOB, the decision was made to move the President and his key staff. A fierce argument erupted between the Secret Service and the military personnel with the President over moving him. The military was convinced the best course of action was to stay in place. The President was in an underground facility that had been designed to survive nuclear attacks, given the MOB at one point in time had been a Strategic Air Command base. The Secret Service quickly relented, and the President ordered all essential government members to be brought inside the facility as soon as possible. He was unaware this drill had been rehearsed repeatedly, and the process would take less than 30 minutes to execute.

The locations of the two signatures were struck by air assets within 15 min of the initial notification, and the assault teams moved into the area within minutes of the strikes. The signatures had been lost just before the airstrikes and again made this event unusual. Decoys had been detected over the past week, but they never moved or went away. The strike on the highway 820 bridge completely destroyed both North and Southbound roadways. The attack on the second location was against a small warehouse complex. Searches of both were well underway when the first device detonated. It took place at the MOB front gate in a convoy of FEMA vehicles waiting to pass into the complex. Analysis later indicated its yield was between 1.5 and 2 kilotons. The process of moving critical and essential government members into secured locations was nearly complete when the first device went off. The President and his key staff were already in the day to day hardened facility they had worked from for the past two years. There was no doubt to anyone in that facility what had just taken place. Although the President's location was underground and located nearly a mile away, the impact was tremendous. Even though the order was quickly given for all responders to stay in a covered location, many did what was natural to them; they moved towards the impacted area. Thirty minutes after the first device detonated, the second one exploded inside an area known as The Point on Lake Worth, Just Northwest of the MOB. The distance away from the first device was far enough that instant damage was limited to the impact of the shockwave, and many of the responders were able to recover.

Unlike during the war, the US had no nation-state to strike back against. They didn't even have an idea of where the enemy was located other than they were dispersed throughout the zone. The question of retaliation was not the priority. The only problem that mattered at that time was how many devices did the Russians have? Mapping the impact of the two strikes was already underway with the intent of moving people away from the fallout areas when word of a third detonation came. The MOB at San Antonio had been struck from inside. The estimate was the device was the same size, but the enemy had managed to get the weapon inside the base. The MOB at Ft. Hood was made aware of the events, and they prepared for an imminent attack. The MOB at Corpus Christi was alerted as well, and they began to take every precaution possible. Ft. Hood's had one distinct advantage. It was a massive facility with assets that operated in a dispersed environment on a day to day basses. It was the alternate site for the US government, but the issue would now be getting there. Was the attack over? Was there time to move the key elements of government? These two questions could not be answered and once again, paralysis set in. A decision had to be made and, in the end, it was the Secretary of Defense that made that call. The MOB at Ft. Worth had been destroyed. Vital assets such as aircraft and other equipment items had been moved after the chemical attack, but that attack's impact area had been limited enough the decision had been made for the government to continue to operate from its primary location. With that option now gone, the movement of the government to

Ft. Hood was conducted on the ground to an extraction point, and then crucial members would be flown the rest of the way into MOB Ft. Hood. The greatest fear was based on the enemy anticipating the movement. It was decided the President and key staff would only be moved to a site just north of the MOB and flown by rotor-wing assets the rest of the way to the alternate site. The aviation mission took place from the old airfield that had been located at Meacham International Airport. Two FOBs were established at that site, and the security vs. distance to the location was deemed worthy of the movement.

The President and key staff landed at MOB Ft. Hood two hours after the attacks. The rest of the government was moved over the next six hours, and by the time all movement operations were completed, the impacts of the strikes began to take shape. People in and around the Dallas, Ft. Worth area of the zone witnessed the two detonations. For two weeks they had endured the hit and ran chemical attacks, but none of those events compared to what they witnessed. Everyone in the area knew the government worked from inside the MOB. They knew the primary headquarters for the US military operated from there as well. Although the detonations were small in comparison to the events of the war, they were still nuclear attacks and the fear of such events returned throughout the population. By the time the President was able to hold a proactive meeting with key staff, he only had one question. How could they stop the attacks?

### The Negotiations:

It had been determined that several vital Russian leaders had brought their families with them and that these family members had been left in Mexico with a security detail. The mission was tasked to Special Operations Command with everyone else in support. The site was to be located, and the

Russian family members were to be taken at all costs. The enemy could not be found as a collective fighting force, but what was dear to their leadership was hidden inside Mexico. They would become the bargaining chip. They would be the ones to pay the price if the attacks didn't stop. The mission launched the same day the attacks took place.

The Provisional Government of Mexico had been operating out of the city of Monterrey, but the communications with any government had been sporadic since the end of the war. The government had changed hands countless times based on who had the power to execute a coup against the current leadership. Given this reality, in the eyes of the US, Mexico was without a functioning government. Making them aware of what was taking place was out of the question, and several of the US President's advisors were convinced the Russian force might have even made deals with local Warlords. The US would operate on Mexican soil, and they would not inform any level of Mexican authority.

Of the eleven ships the US was aware of that had traveled from Europe to the Central American area, four had docked in Mexico at the Port of Veracruz. That is where the search started. Less than twelve hours after landing in the area, a flash report was received. One of the US teams had located the compound. The site was covered by high altitude drones, and it was the team leader's opinion they should move quickly to minimize their presence being noticed. The security detail was made up of an estimated force of over 100 heavily armed men, but no local militias seemed to be involved. A large assault force was requested, and that force launched from MOB Ft. Hood within two hours of notification.

The plan was to take the site and then hold it until the assault force was on the scene. The decision had been made not to wait given the risk of detection. The US team on the ground numbered thirty-five with armed drone and rotor-wing support. Within an hour of the President giving the order to take the site, the team sent a message they were inside the compound and holding their position. Electronic denial operations had prevented any signals from being transmitted within a thirty square mile area of the site, and confidence was high. The enemy force inside the US had no idea what had taken place.

The team stated they would need extraction for over 100 civilians. It was clear; the Russian force had brought more than just the families of a few senior leaders. Nine hours after the operation started, it was over. All the Russian civilians were being flown back to the MOB at Ft. Hood, along with five enemy casualties. The US lost seven members and one rotor-wing asset, but they had what they needed. They now had a bargaining point; the enemy force could not ignore.

The capture mission had taken less than two days to execute, and it had been successful beyond expectations. The same could not be said for the status of the Dallas Zone. The communications with leadership still inside the zone were constant, and the image they painted was disastrous. Within an hour of the attacks, people began to gather at many of the distribution sites. They were seeking guidance and information. The sites were communication hubs as well as points of distribution, and people wanted to know what had happened and what they should do. Reports began to come in within hours after the strikes of large movements heading East on Highway 20 and 30 as well as South on Highway 35. Almost everyone was on foot, but it was clear support vehicles were being taken and many of them by force. By the time of the enemy attacks, the zone's population had been nearly 20 million people. The areas just around the zone comprised another estimated 5 million. As people were suddenly fleeing the zone, they were moving into areas that were already occupied. Controlling the movements was impossible. The few checkpoints that were established in defense of the enemy forces were overrun by people wishing to leave the area. To the US government, one picture captured their reality. US citizens were once again fleeing areas they believed to be dangerous. The Dallas Zone had become a warzone, and everything the government had tried to accomplish was being lost in a sea of panic.

Initial reports of damage from the Ft. Worth MOB was catastrophic. Aviation assets had been moved, but many of the supply buildings that had been developed in the nearly two years the zone was under construction were gone. The MOB had been the focal point for storage and primary distribution. The threat of that site being destroyed had disappeared after the war, and the only fear had been theft and civil disobedience. Disbursement of assets had taken place, but the large percentage of bulk items had been warehoused on the MOB. It would take days to conduct the final damage analysis, but the snapshot assessment was over eighty percent of what was stored there was unusable. Casualties figures were estimated to be over 4,000 killed and 6,000 severely wounded. The fallout field was mapped within the first hour of the two detonations, and both devices were going to leave a highly contaminated area crossing right through the zone.

At the end of the initial briefing, it was the Secretary of State who made the first comment. "It appears the Dallas Zone project has been destroyed." Not everyone in the room agreed, but the options on how to continue with the program seemed difficult to imagine. One thing was agreed on. The states needed to know the scope of what had taken place, and nothing was going to be left out of the discussion.

Multiple states had attempted to contact the government, and most were given a generic description of what had taken place. All of them were informed the President would be conducting an All State's Call within the next day if not sooner. It was decided to hold that call until the capture mission had been completed. It was hoped the mission would show the states the federal government was working on a process to stop the attacks and perhaps provide some level of comfort. The All States Call was held twelve hours after the completion of the mission in Mexico. Every aspect of the three nuclear strikes were explained in detail. As questions were asked, they were answered to the best of the government's ability. When Ohio asked what the government intended to do about the attacks, the mission in Mexico was briefed in detail. The US intended to contact the enemy force, something that was already underway by the time the All State's Call was held. Several states then asked what the concept was behind the capture mission, and a few asked the location of the Russian family members. It was the Secretary of Defense who answered both questions. The US would demand the enemy force surrender immediately and turn in all their arms. If they agreed, they would be reunited with the families and transported to an undisclosed location in Europe. It was the last part of the plan many raised concerns with. Returning an enemy that had armed itself in a dysfunctional Europe could easily lead to a repeat of events. That was the general attitude of those who didn't support what they had been told. The President added the US would not allow any sea movements towards the Americas without prior knowledge and approval and that assets would be put in place to ensure that capability was maintained. None of the vessels that had left Europe for the Americas had been aggressively tracked, but that would not happen again. A Fortress America concept would be the plan, and that plan would be enforced at all costs. The discussion was ongoing when one of the states asked what would happen if the enemy refused the offer. Again, the President gave the answer. The US was prepared to intern the Russian Civilians at a location too far removed for the enemy to have any chance of reaching them. They would never see them again. It was understood the intent of the enemy moving their families with them had to have been based on staying somewhere in either the US or Central or South America. The Secretary of Defense was convinced they

were going to stay where they had been located and thus secure the port for additional movements from Europe. That
comment moved the entire discussion in a new direction. The
states wanted to know, was there a threat of a follow-on force
and how did the US know only one combat force had been
planned. The reality was, no one knew. Assets had been moved
to monitor ship traffic from Europe and Africa, and there had
been no detection of any movements since the attacks had
begun. Could there be a follow-on operation? The US needed
to know, and it needed to convince the states it was capable of
solving the crisis.

Discussions about the amount of damage to the Dallas Zone's capabilities were limited. The government wanted
to wait until a more detailed damage assessment was completed, and thus, a follow-on call would be held in two days.
At the end of the call, the Vice President made the comment
it seemed like the states were looking at this whole event as if
it were someone else's problem. Many in the room agreed, and
a few even questioned the value of the follow-on call. It was a
comment that was quickly dismissed.

The Russian cells had witnessed the two nuclear
strikes, and they knew what their orders were. Once they saw
the events, they were to attack the movements that would be
taking place as people were trying to leave the area. They were
to wait three to four days after the strikes and then choose
targets along any of the major roadways going out of the zone.
The tactics would not change. Ambushes would last less than
five minutes with a handful of chemical mortar rounds. The
intent was not to maximize casualties. The intention was to
continue the panic the nuclear strikes had created.

The government's decision was not to attempt to stop
the movements but to escort them as much as possible. The
theory was, the more the people saw someone was watching
over them, the more reluctant they would be to continue to
move away from the zone. A force deployment was generated

from all the FOBs in the area as well as additional units from three MOBs. All in all, over 4,000 US military members would be assigned to primary roadways with the instructions to escort the groups and provide support as needed. Air assets were a priority as they gave the public a visual sense of security.

Three days after the nuclear events, that small sense of security changed. A patrol near the intersection of Highway 30 and 80, just East of Dallas, reported an assault on a significant movement of civilians. They had been taking cover under an overpass at that location when they came under attack from the South. The patrol estimated the mortar fire came from a street called Samuell Blvd, just south of the overpass area. The patrol had heard the weapons fire, but by the time they maneuvered into the area, the attack was over. It was estimated over 100 civilians had been killed and another 200 were suffering from the exposure to the chemical rounds. Overpasses and chokepoints had been identified as primary target points by both the enemy and the US military, but the zone had thousands of such locations. As the decision was being made to move the civilians off the main roadways, reports of numerous other attacks began to come in. It had been three days since the nuclear strikes, and it was clear the enemy was starting a new phase of their plan. People were on the move in the Northern sector of the zone and distinguishing between enemy movements and civilians became impossible.

That same evening, the first of the leaflets were delivered. They showed the Russian family members being loaded onto support aircraft in Mexico as well as being interviewed in the US. The written message was simple. "We have all of your family members. If you want to see them again, you will stop all hostile actions and turn yourself into any government authority you come in contact with. You will have your leadership contact the US Military as soon as possible. Do this, and you will see your loved ones again. Don't, and they will be moved to an unknown location where you will never find them". The message was clear. Surrender and surrender immediately. The leaflets were dropped in every area; there had been enemy contact. The photos validated the story. Within a few hours of this event, Psychological Operations aircraft began flying. Frequencies were given out over the giant voice networks. It only took a few hours before the government started to get their answer.

The first cell to surrender was located near the Southside of the city of Arlington. Five members approached a military checkpoint. They were unarmed, and several spoke English. Within the next 24 hours, it was estimated that over 150 cell members had surrendered. Initial intelligence from debriefs indicated the cells had no electronic communications network. The timing of their events was preplanned, and cells that were to operate together knew so before the mission started.

The leadership of the operation was still in the Weatherford Texas area but would have relocated after the nuclear detonations had taken place. Most of the cell members who were surrendering were not connected to the families in custody. That fact surprised the interrogation teams. Of the members who had turned themselves in, almost all of them stated they had joined the mission to escape Europe and find a way to live somewhere in the Americas. The plan had been for the combat teams to destroy the US Dallas Zone along with the government and then retreat to Mexico, where they would set up their own community.

By the time the official briefing was prepared for the President and his staff, the number of surrenders had reached over 250. The story of why most had come and what their plans were shocked some in the room, but not the Secretary of Defense or the President. Europe was a wasteland with radiation levels five times what they were in the US. The idea of escaping to an area that was cleaner and more stable was appealing not just to those who brought their families. Some of the senior leadership had planned the mission as a revenge event, but they understood there had to be something at the end that made it all worthwhile. In the short time since the leaflets had been deployed, the attacks had fallen off dramatically. The Secretary of Defense informed the President of the effort to find the command cell was ongoing. The government knew not everyone would surrender, but the impact of the family mission had taken a considerable capability out of the force. Since the time of the attacks, it was estimated over half of the enemy force had been captured or killed. The danger was, not knowing the capabilities of those who were left. The leaflet program would be expanded as well as the Giant Voice operation. The President ended the meeting by giving one order. He wanted the people in the zone to know the enemy was surrendering. He wanted them to see the fight was not over, but the enemy seemed to be giving in. Again, as had been the case for over two years, it would be the Giant Voice aircraft and the leaflet process that would get the President's message out.

The senior Russian commanders had relocated to an area called Willow Park, and it was a local landowner who noticed them first. Their camp seemed too well organized, and its defensive perimeter was militaristic by design. He had watched the site for several days from a distance. Several of the men who lived in the same camp as the landowner decided they would make contact with one of the military patrols that had been working that area for months. Most of the patrols had designated locations where the locals could meet them if they had an issue. When they told the patrol about the site near the Southside of Lake Weatherford, air assets were called in immediately.

A flash report was given to the Secretary of Defense. The imagery of the site confirmed over 30 members in civilian clothing with fortified fighting positions. Several shipping containers for air to ground weapons were also identified. Two Special Operations units were immediately dispatched to the area with the task of validating who was in the compound. A little over six hours later, the target was confirmed. The language being spoken between the members was Russian, and several members were addressing two individuals as General.

The strike on the compound took place two hours after the confirmation. Both SF teams were tasked with clearing the site as soon as the strike was over. A total of 23 bodies were accounted for, and US forces would continue to search the immediate area for several days. It was determined the base-camp was not a Command and Control facility, but merely a "Hide" for the senior leadership. Several of the members who had surrendered stated the plan calls for the cells to reform near the Weatherford area two weeks after the nuclear strikes. From there, they would make their way back into Mexico.

Within a day of the strike on the enemy senior leader's location, a new set of leaflets were distributed. Again, they were based on photos taken at the scene of the strike, and the message was clear. The remaining cell members would hear the news over the Giant Voice network as well as from the leaflets. Their leadership was dead, and most of their unit members had surrendered for a chance at a normal life. Again, photos were crucial for the message as new leaflets showed the processing of those who had surrendered. The messaging to the enemy continued to have a duel impact. The public that was still moving away from the area began to slow their pace. Most knew they were out of the impact zone of the nuclear weapons, but the threat of continued ambushes kept some of them moving forward. A day after the strike on the senior leader's location, two additional traps took place. Word of these events didn't reach the general population, and the impact of the two events proved to be minimum. In the opinion of the Secretary of Defense, the enemy force had been broken. Residual pockets of resistance would be expected, but the ability to continuously disrupt the Dallas Zone was no longer there.

*Assessments:*

The assessment briefing took place three days after the enemy command element was destroyed. The dead from the three nuclear strikes was estimated at over 2,100 with over 3,500 severely wounded. Device analysis, as well as plume modeling, had been completed and the areas that would be impacted were already clearly marked. The losses of material goods at the Ft. Worth MOB was the primary topic. Equipment items that had not been distributed throughout the zone had been devastated. Several significant manufacturing capabilities that had been moved into the zone were stored at the MOB until proper installation could take place. More importantly, a relocation process from server farms across the nation had been underway for well over a year, and that storage area was destroyed in the second blast. This loss of data was considered the single most significant impact of the attacks. The discussion on how to repair the power plant ended with no real answer. The damage to transmission operations was extensive, but in the end, the reactor operations were still deemed safe and functional. The blast had also destroyed a crude water purification production process. The site on the MOB had been producing portable purification devices that were distributed throughout the zone. That production capability was lost.

As the meeting continued, it was becoming clear to everyone involved the impact on the day to day capabilities of the Dallas Zone had been severely degraded. The relocation of the US Military Headquarters to the MOB at Ft. Hood was already underway, and it was decided the government itself would remain at that location for the foreseeable future. The population movement inside the zone had slowed, but the percentage of people who had moved away from functioning distribution sites was estimated at over 1 million. The shift away from the Ft Worth MOB had also created another issue, and it was a topic leadership had nearly forgotten about. The Measles outbreak that had taken place prior to the attacks had been brought under control by separating those who were exposed from the rest of the general population. Two of the centers that were established to deal with the patients in the immediate area of the MOB had been abandon after the attack. Infected or highly contagious patients had been moved or were moving on their own, and the risk of an overall breakout was once again a primary concern. The list of issues continued to grow, even as the briefing took place. One thing was clear, the Dallas Zone concept had suffered a significant setback, and it would take additional resources to stabilize the plan.

When the President asked what measures could be taken to show the country was back to being proactive, security became the topic. In the All Sates Call, it was apparent the Governors wanted to know just how dangerous the attack had become. Most referred to what had taken place as an invasion, and it was a mental picture that stuck with many in the room. The task of tracking movements from Europe had been set as one goal, but the initial threat had started with other armed groups coming up from the South and the concept of how to counter that threat had not been finalized. The question became, was the Russian Warlord event going to happen again? It would be a topic the Governors would want an answer, and many inside the federal government wondered the same thing. The assessment briefing came to an end, but the next issue had to be addressed. The President needed to speak with the states, and they needed to know where the nation stood.

# CHAPTER SEVENTEEN: ARTICLES OF CONFEDERATION.

The crisis in the Dallas Zone had gone on for weeks, and in that time, the communications with the states had been minimum. The President had addressed the Governors on two occasions, but the day to day interaction had all but stopped. Each time, the states left the conversation with more questions than answers. Communications between the states had gone virtually unnoticed, and in fact, two large meetings were held in Oklahoma with no mention at the federal level. The day to day events had been tracked thanks to the interaction with the forces located at the FOBs and several of the MOBs. None of the forces outside the Dallas Zone or MOB Ft. Hood or Corpus Christi had been tasked with any possible support. Even when the three nuclear strikes took place, the MOBs outside the Dallas Zone area were only made aware of the event through message traffic. To everyone not involved with the zone project, what was taking place seemed as far away as any other event in the world.

When the President finally set a date and time for the next All States Call, most of the states where not even sure the attacks were over. They had heard about the surrender process, but they had no idea just how much damage had been done. When the call took place, it was clear the Dallas Zone concept was in serious jeopardy. It was also evident it was only a matter of time before the federal government would ask for more support from the states. The call ended with a pledge from the President to stay in better contact. It was a pledge the states were no longer genuinely concerned with.

Although the President had made a commitment to stay in better communications with the states, the next several weeks were far more challenging than he had anticipated. The issue of trust South of the zone had become an event that had to be addressed. Patrols were increased throughout the area, and after the enemy attacks, the attitudes towards any armed groups they came upon were much different. The government was far more paranoid than in the past, and the locals paid an ever-increasing price for that paranoia. Several clashes took place, and word of these events spread far faster than the government's ability to explain them. The government was struggling to stabilize the area, and communications with the states continued to be at a minimum.

Twice, the government had attempted to hold a working-level briefing with the states, much like the ones that had taken place for the past three years. The federal support team members had become the coordination points between the FOBs and MOBs to the Governors. Day to day interaction with their federal agencies back at the Ft. Hood MOB had become sporadic at best, and little guidance was given out. To the Governors, it was apparent; even the so-called national support teams were getting little to no support. They relied on the MOBs and FOBs for information, but those locations had little interaction with matters the support teams would be required to work on. In reality, the support teams had become state assets.

It had been three months since the last All States Call and the President started the conversation with an apology, an apology that wasn't needed. As he explained the current status of the events taking place, the Governor of Kansas interrupted him and asked if he would like to hear the status of the states. Since the attacks, the perception inside the federal government had been based upon assuring the states the government was functioning. In fact, that attitude had predicated most of the calls even before the attacks on the zone. Most of the President's staff was not surprised by the event. His predecessor had been met with an adversarial attitude for over a year and a half, and it was clear that approach had not changed. The response was professional, but everyone could tell the President was not pleased with the interruption. Again, the President apologized for being one-sided, and he made it clear he valued hearing from the states to the greatest extent possible. As soon as he was finished, the Governor of Georgia asked if the federal government had ascertained if any additional hostile forces were inside the nation. The Secretary of Defense was giving his answer when the Governor of Tennessee asked about the armed groups from Central and South America. Had they been located? Had the threat of them penetrating further into the country been neutralized and if so, how? The fact of the matter was, the issue of the armed groups had nearly fallen off the table as soon as the Russian Warlord event began to unfold. Within ten minutes, not a single Governor on the call had any confidence the federal government had an idea who was in the country and what their intent was. The Secretary of State attempted to paint of picture of these groups merging with US citizens for the simple goal of living somewhere more secure than where they had come from. That answer proved to be disastrous. The Governor of Oklahoma let the Secretary of State finish his explanation before he made a comment, "What if the people in Oklahoma don't want to join with these invaders"? From that moment on, the President and his staff changed their efforts to attempting to nullify the states' fears over continued movements into the nation. It was that very topic that pushed the conversation even deeper into the adversarial corner. The discussion was securing the countries' Sothern border and the actual effort it would take to accomplish the task. When the Secretary of Defense commented it would take more than the forces assigned to the Dallas Zone area, the issue once again became apparent. The federal government was going to relocate forces from the MOBs and FOBs outside the zone. It was the topic that had ended one conference call already, and it was the topic that concluded the current call. Force realignment would be reviewed with the states in less than two weeks, and there was no avoiding the issue this time around.

When the call was over, the President asked for opinions and feedback. Again, the feeling the states didn't really care about the status of the Dallas Zone seemed unanimous. It was also clear the issue of force reallocation was going to be a disputed topic. The concern over taking control of the critical assets sites was gone, at least then. The urgency was securing the country's southern border and the forces that the task would require. The President had informed the states the realignment discussion would take place in two weeks. He gave the Secretary of Defense one week to brief the plan to the President and his key staff.

The topic in the room then switched to the actions of the states. They had created a strong bond with most of the FOBs and many of the MOBs. They knew they had two weeks to come up with their own plan; a plan based on keeping the forces that were in their areas. The Secretary of Defense stated he would hold a conversation with the regional commanders within the next two days, to determine what options the states may consider. In the meantime, the issue of securing the area around the zone had once again become the primary task for the government. If that task was not challenging enough, the growing tensions between locals outside the zone and the patrolling forces had to be addressed. Given the events of the Russian Warlord attacks, what level of acceptance of foreign nationals on US soil was the government willing to accept?

It was a question the President tasked his key staff with, and they were to report back to him within the week.

The day before the President was due to receive the briefing on Foreign Nationals on US soil; US forces were engaged in a firefight near the town of Hebbronville. It was the largest hostile exchange outside the zone. The event lasted over two hours, and when it was over, nearly 80 people had been killed or wounded. The group was said to have been raiding supply movements between Hebbronville and Falfurrias that were organized by local settlements. Three days before the engagement, an ambush had taken place that resulted in over 20 members of the local communities' security detail being killed or wounded. The patrol found the hostile group and had determined the location of their basecamp. The attack on the camp took place with the support of armed drones and rotor-wing assets. News of the ambush and the follow-on assault on the camp spread outside the area around the zone. The locals who had been conducting their own relief missions had a functioning shortwave radio. They had been in contact with other independent camps for well over two years, with some of them being as far away as Kansas and Wyoming. Many of these camps had held their own exchange operations and had become very self-sufficient. This particular camp was well known outside the State of Texas. When word got out of the attack, several Governors were immediately informed. Although the hostile force had been found and neutralized, it was the makeup of the force that set other events into motion. Of the members killed in the basecamp, over 80 percent of them were not US citizens. To the civilian sites South of the Dallas Zone, this was not a new issue, and many had come to the realization, this was most likely the new normal. To those outside the State of Texas, this event was just another indication the federal government was unable to control the nation's security. It was not the first time this type of incident had taken place, but this event was the catalyst for a more significant issue that would drive the states further away from the federal government. The event would become known as, "The Falfurrias Incident," and it would become something the federal government could not control.

The Secretary's briefing was short and to the point. To truly control the Southern border of the US, 1 out of every 3 FOBs would need to be redeployed. The estimate had changed since the last time the question had been asked based upon a better understanding of the potential threat. No one could guarantee the Russian Warlord event would not be repeated, and the danger of such a capability coming from Central and South American Territories had already been proven. It was the Secretary's next statement that caught everyone in the room by surprise. Even with the increased capabilities, the timeframe this tactic would remain effective was estimated to be five years. The expenditure of assets to continue the required level of operations and the lack of manufacturing meant the US Military would be unable to use some of its most vital assets for the mission past the predicted timeframe.

Simply put, the US had five years to resume some level of production, or the concept of defending the nation was going to be lost. The President had heard this estimate before as the Speaker of the House, but the consumption rate was drastically different based upon the day to day requirements. Not only would the nuclear weapons program become questionable in a little over five years, but the complete capability of the US Military was now in doubt. In five years, the US would have a much more simplistic military with minimal ability. In short, the most technologically advanced military in the world was also the most fragile.

The President understood what his predecessor could not. The US was no longer capable of defending the nation as a whole. To reallocate the forces needed would leave the rest of the nation virtually defenseless, and even that concept was predicated on the states agreeing to the plan. Once again, the issue of what to defend became the primary topic. The Secretary of Defense's plan to protect just the Dallas Zone, only required certain assets being pulled away from the FOBs and MOBs, but even then, his conversation with the regional commanders left him believing that would be a difficult task. When the Secretary had completed the briefing, the Chief Justice of the Supreme Court made the comment everyone in the room remembered. "Mr. President. You have the choice to protect an old border of our nation and most likely fight a Civil War in the process, or you have the choice to accept what I see as reality. The US is no longer the nation that it was". Many in the room disagreed with the Chief Justice, but the President would not argue. Instead, he stated he would leave it up to the states to decide. The President would not send US forces to fight US forces. If the states could not agree to the reduction, then he would have his answer. They would hold the All States Call in one week and determine the fate of the union.

The government had no idea of the meetings in Oklahoma. Departmental rumors had circulated, but nothing was seen to be at a level worthy of informing the President. The idea that several states had met to finalize Articles of Confederation would have set off alarm bells everywhere, but the reality was, the federal government had been in a crisis footing with the attacks and awareness of state events had been nearly nonexistent.

For over two years, the consistent issue had been the federal government's inability and unwillingness to support the needs of the states truly. Once the Dallas Zone project was announced, the perception everyone outside the zone was being left behind could not be stopped. With the issues of force reallocation and critical asset ownership leading to an Article V Convention, it was clear to most states, the concept of the Union had weakened past a point of return. No state had openly spoken of secession, but that was the crime the previous President had all but convicted them of.

By the time the Dallas Zone attacks began to take place, many states had convinced themselves it was time to act. The meetings in Oklahoma were, in fact, signatory events. The first had ended with New Mexico, Colorado, Arizona, Kansas, Oklahoma, Missouri, Iowa and Arkansas agreeing to a form of Confederation that would bind each member to support the other to the greatest extent possible, while also declaring their exit from the Union. Several states were in favor of the process but had raised questions over the possession of federal assets already on their land, with the military being the primary issue. The initial group had all but been assured the military forces on their land would remain loyal to the states they were serving, with the stipulation that if an actual conflict were to arise with the federal government, they would not fire upon other military members. Another sticking point had been the reality many of the states still had representatives in the federal government. The fact that almost all these individuals had not been back to their perspective states since the end of the war made the issue of ignoring their legal status a plausible answer. In most state's opinion, they no longer represented anything other than federal viewpoints.

When the second meeting was held, the states of Mississippi, Louisiana, Georgia and Alabama agreed to sign on. The second meeting also continued the process of refining the relationships between the states. The terminology of, "Articles of Confederation," was chosen for a reason, for this was the model the states agreed upon. At what point in time and how this new confederation would be explained to the old federal government was the most exceptional point of contention. In the end, it was the President's request for another All States Call that gave the states the answer they were looking for.

The states had not been the only ones in communications over the issue of leaving the government. The conversations had been taking place within the MOBs and FOBs for months. Most had been informal, but regional commanders had warned the Secretary of Defense on several occasions that discussions were being held and the topic of loyalty had been the issue. Estimates had been made, and the Secretary had informed the President more than once of what they could be facing. Although regional commanders had told the Secretary of the discussions, they had not spoken a word of the two meetings in Oklahoma. The lack of trust of FOB leadership towards their MOB was more significant than the regional commanders had understood, but the sympathetic stance of many MOBs was an issue the regional commanders had wholly underestimated. The day before the President's All States Call, the Secretary of Defense decided it was time to inform him just where this issue stood. The conversation was brief and to the point. If given a choice, an overwhelming percentage of the US Military would side with those they had spent the post-war years with. Armed with this sobering reality, the President would still hold the call.

### The Call:

The states were prepared to announce their decision to leave the Union. Rumors of such an event had reached the government, but it had been decided if the topic was going to be approached, it would be up to the states to make the statement. The President would make his appeal first and then wait for the states to respond. He spoke for a little over twenty minutes and covered every vital issue over the requirements to protect the boundaries of the nation. It was clear to everyone on the call, without the forces moved from the FOBs and MOBs, the US would not be able to safeguard who was moving into the country or even where the movements were taking place. The President ended his briefing with this statement, "Ladies and Gentlemen, I need to know where you stand. I need to know if you are willing to save the Union"? The answer was given by the Governor that had been chosen to speak for the newly aligned states. The Governor of Missouri was that person. His words became historical. "Mr. President. We have witnessed the birth of a new world. We have survived the war that we have all feared for decades. Each of us understands the changes that have been forced upon us, and all of us have done our very best to keep some level of civil society, but a new reality is upon us. What was once true is no longer so. We cannot move into an unknown future based upon the dreams of the past. Grasping for realities that no longer exist is not what those who have worked so hard to survive deserve. The needs of a nation that cannot provide for its people must not take priority over the desires of those same citizens to survive. The dream of rebuilding the nation may be achievable someday, but we all know that day is very far away, and what must take place now is the simple act of survival. The Dallas Zone was a concept born from a government that was and remains unable to provide for all the citizens of the United States. Your dream, Mr. President, was never the dream of the states outside the zone. The sacrifices asked of us have been too much. The response to our needs has been all but ignored and all in the name of something that has no value to us. Mr. President. If you and your government wish to continue chasing your dream of rebuilding the nation, then that must include supporting everyone and not just the location where your government resides. Having said this, we all understand your inability to do exactly that. The nation is no longer capable of providing all things to all peoples, and that is why a group of us have decided to form a new Confederation, a new block of unity based upon realistic goals and the desire to help everyone and not just those chosen in some small slice of the country". With that, the Governor of Missouri was finished. It was the Vice President that spoke first, and his question was emotionally charged. Was the Governor of Missouri announcing the succession of states from the Union? The Governor of Arizona responded, "yes."

For the next hour, the conversation was focused on how such an act was illegal, given the standing federal laws.

The counterargument was simplistic. Historical standing laws were simply no longer applicable to the new environment they all lived in. During this discussion, the President had remained silent. Those that argued from either side knew he had not spoken since the Governor of Missouri had announced the split, but they knew he was listening and contemplating what this event truly meant. When the Governor finally spoke, his question was to the Secretary of Defense, and everyone knew the answer would determine the outcome of the discussion. He asked the Secretary if he had the forces needed to defend just the zone, not the borders and not the surrounding areas near the zone, but just the zone. The Secretary's answer was obvious. If only the zone were to be secured, then the government had sufficient forces and resources to accomplish that mission.

What that would mean to the rest of the nation was obvious. The states would be on their own. Incursions onto US soil would not stop as most of the world understood the US to be the land where survival and recovery would take place at a pace, unlike any other nation left after the war. Everyone knew the primary entrance into the US was from the South, but those wishing to enter from the East and the West or even the North could do so if they understood the cost. The East and Westcoast were highly contaminated, but not at levels any higher than most of Europe and far below levels in China. The point was easy for everyone to understand. If the states broke with the federal government, then their ability to defend themselves would be significantly reduced. For the states, it was an issue they had contemplated from day one. The call ended with a compromise to meet again in the morning. Everyone had problems to consider, but to the states of the new confederate, a prolonged discussion was nothing more than an act of appeasement on their part. Their minds were made up, and the chances of turning back were nonexistent.

When the call was over, the President looked at those in the room and stated, "we may now be the smallest, most powerful nation in the world." No one questioned how the states had come to such a complex agreement without someone becoming aware of the events that had to have taken place. In reality, most in the room understood precisely how it had happened. The states were interacted with when the government needed to, and that was about it. Their point was valid, and everyone knew it. The states that had not signed on to the new confederation were almost entirely dysfunctional, to begin with. Northern Tier states such as Minnesota, North Dakota, Montana, and Idaho had not even joined the call. Most of the population in those states was so fiercely independent, their reliance on even state government was nonexistent. To the President and his staff, the states that mattered to the dream of rebuilding the nation were the ones that pulled away. The idea of forcing them into staying in the Union was out of the question. The destruction that would have been required was unacceptable to everyone in the room, and the Secretary of Defense made it clear the US Military would not go to war with its own.

Compromise was the objective of the next call, and the President knew the only way to find such a goal was to ask the states what it would take to stay in the Union. The discussion on how to approach the next meeting lasted well into the night, and by the time it was decided, everyone needed to sleep before speaking with the states again. It was clear the nation was going to change, no matter what compromise was agreed upon. The last two people in the room were the President and the Vice President. The President had asked his Vice a question, when the Vice President stopped his answer and said, "We no longer have national Holidays. We no longer have Thanksgiving, Easter, Christmas, or the Fourth of July. Every day since the end of the war has been all about survival. Every day has been about living until the next sunrise. Perhaps we lost the nation three years ago, and we are just now realizing that truth? The Dallas Zone has not saved the nation; it has torn it apart". The President understood the new confederation of states was little more than a signed document. He knew almost everyone in those states had no idea such an event had taken place, and he knew they probably didn't care. The President's decision was one he could not escape. If he gave up the idea of the Dallas Zone and committed to supporting the states to the greatest extent possible, would the states remain? That was the thought process he was contemplating right up until the time of the follow-on call.

The call took place at noon the following day. Once again, the President started the conversation. His position was blunt. If the government gave up the Dallas Zone concept and focused those resources on the states to the greatest extent possible, would they remain in the Union? The Governor of South Carolina spoke first. Her state had not signed the Articles of Confederation, but they were leaning that way. Her question was as blunt as the President's. If South Carolina agreed, what precisely was the federal government capable of? What tangible assistance could South Carolina count on? It may have been one Governor asking the question, but it represented the thoughts of every state on the call.

The topic of support went on for over two hours, and one fact remained unchanged. The states had gone three years without any real federal support, other than the military, and that reality was not going to change for several years to come, if at all. Explanations were given about the revitalization of key industries such as medical and power, but the idea of those two items becoming available seemed impossible. Again, many on the federal side argued the concept of a build-out from the Dallas Zone would expedite support capabilities, but to the states, all they heard was the federal government's reluctance to give up on the zone. Just before it was agreed a break was needed, the Governor of South Carolina spoke again. Her words set the tone for the rest of the meeting. "We have been talking for a day and a half now. If I had to vote tomorrow on leaving the Union, I am afraid I would say yes". As soon as she made her statement, she walked away from the screen and did not return after the break.

When the call resumed, the Governor of Missouri spoke first. It was apparent to the President and his staff the states were about to approach a topic they had discussed in detail. The states had a concept for a new government that would include a federal government, but with a structure, they anticipated the federal government would not agree to. In short, the states proposed the government sign onto the Articles of Confederation. Instead of the states leaving the Union, the federal government would reshape the nation into its original form of governance. The core issue of this proposal was made very clear. The states had legally changed the US Constitution, and it was the federal government that violated that change. To the states, there was no going back to a system they no longer trusted, but there was an opportunity for the government to join what the states had created. To the President, the options were limited. The Union could dissolve into an immature Confederacy of States without a centralized government, or it could agree to join the states in a new Union. The discussion went on for over three hours before it was decided the federal government would need to review the concept put forth by the states in much greater detail. The states agreed to meet again in two weeks but made it clear their newly formed alliance would not wait. They would continue with the development of processes needed for the new agreement as they waited for the federal government's answer. The call ended with the President making the statement, "I truly believe, all of us have a common goal, and that is the preservation of the United States." He was wrong, and he knew he was wrong. The states had one goal, survival.

*The Decision on the "Zone":*

The hit and run attacks had not stopped, but the frequency had drastically diminished. As the government continued the process of finding the remaining cells in and around the zone, the real issue was the concept of forming a new government. What the relationships would be and how they would be managed would take a great deal of work, and most of that effort would only come after an initial agreement to approach the concept was agreed to. In the discussions that had taken place, it was clear the issue of the Dallas Zone was going to be a major sticking point for the states. What the President and others understood was the reality the states would not support the Dallas Zone concept to any level that required sacrifice on their part. It was the concept of the zone that brought the government into yet another crisis.

The Secretary of Defense, as well as the Vice President, argued the zone was the only option to rebuild the nation, but the Speaker of the House and the President argued there would be no union to restore if the states no longer recognized the federal government. All sides understood the impossibility of supporting individual states but letting the states who had signed onto the new form of government go would mean the end of the Union. It was also impossible to expand the zone without the assets held inside those same states. At the beginning of the second week of discussions, the government was deadlocked. The President had four days before he would keep his next conference call and his government was no closer to a decision than they had been the day the last call had ended. Two days before the next call, the issues at hand would change once again.

MOB San Antonio had received two reports from two FOBs, one near Alice Texas and the other assigned to the Laredo area. Within hours of each other, both reports indicated large movements of armed individuals moving by vehicle. One was heading for the Laredo Airport, the primary distribution center and one heading towards the MOB at Corpus Christi. Imagery indicated each group was dispersed over a five-mile area and numbered anywhere from 300 to 500 in strength. Further analysis showed both groups to be armed with small arms as well as an assortment of indirect fire weapons to include short-range rockets. Markings showed most of the equipment was from the Mexican Military. As the scenario was being briefed to the President, reports of similar size groups moving on the cities of Del Rio and McAllen came in, but it was the regional commander's report for the areas of New Mexico and Arizona that made the event different than anything the US had witnessed. A FOB stationed between Nogales Mexico and Tucson, Arizona had come under attack. Contact had been lost, but intelligence showed a large force heading towards the city of Tucson's MOB. Within the hour, the picture became clear; someone had organized an attack with a force of over 4,000. All indications were the strike forces were made up of Mexican and Central American Military members. These units were much more than raiding parties. They didn't have the capabilities of the Russian force that invaded, but they were far more dispersed and moving on much weaker locations than the Dallas Zone.

As the reaction forces were being alerted, a FOB just South of Albuquerque New Mexico reported making contact with a large hostile force that had been heading towards a distribution point in the city of Norman. That was the report that shocked everyone on the President's staff. That force had traveled several hundred miles inside US soil undetected. If the impression had been the US was unable to secure its Southern border, that impression had become a reality. That series of events brought about another undeniable truth. The MOBs and FOBs and even the regional commander had reported the hostile actions to the states at the same time they reported them to their typical chain of command. By the time the MOB at Tucson was given instructions on what assets would be provided to them, the MOB commander responded he believed he had adequate forces responding from two MOBs in Colorado. To the Secretary of Defense and the President, the message was clear. The new alliance between the states was reacting without the guidance or authority of the federal government. The attacks into the US were a dramatic indication of just how vulnerable the nation had become, but even more importantly, they were an indication of the concept of governance in the nation had changed. The states were working together without the federal government's knowledge or approval.

By the day of the President's call with the states, the enemy forces had been neutralized. Arizona had decided to occupy the city of Nogales, Mexico, and they had not asked for permission to do so. The forces used to conduct the operation had been tasked by the regional commander, and that commander had not informed the Secretary of Defense of the mission until it was underway. Everything about that event indicated how the call would go. The states had one stance. Was the federal government willing to agree to the Articles of Confederation or not? The government had its own question. In the eyes of the states, what was to be the role of a centralized government? As soon as the question was asked, the federal government had its answer. A centralized government would act as a coordination point, an agency responsible for capturing and articulating the issues between the states. It would have no authority over them. It would have no regulatory power. It would act as a facilitator and nothing more. The opinion of the states was unanimous and steadfast. Virtually thousands of issues would need to be worked out, but the overall concept was clear. The states intended for a centralized government to have no authority over them. The entire structure of the US government would be completely rewritten. Even the meaning of "The United States" would change. The states made one further point very clear.

The members of the House and Senate still residing with the

federal government would no longer represent the states they had come from. As far as they were concerned, those members were officially members of a government that was not recognized. Another reality came to the attention of the President. By the time the second call had taken place, the states that had not signed onto the Articles of Confederacy had done so. The Dallas Zone was on its own. The remaining territory of the State of Texas had been receiving support from the zone, but only based upon their proximity. In the eyes of the states, the federal government was made up of the State of Texas.

The call lasted over six hours before the Vice President asked the question many on the federal side wanted an answer to from the beginning. "What would happen if the President said no"? The Governor of Arizona answered his question. " If you do not agree, then we will remain as we have been for over three years. We will be part of the nation you have not supported. We will do what we have been doing since the end of the war. We will take care of ourselves. We will no longer recognize any authority you believe in having over us, and we will both go our separate paths". Everyone knew the government's ability to provide the states even limited support had been dramatically reduced and they knew it had become unrealistic to expect anything above what they already received. What had set this whole process in motion was the Dallas Zone, and everyone on both sides knew it. The zone was the federal government's answer to recovery. To everyone else, it was the lifeboat that left them in the water.

It was the President who asked the final question. "If we end the Dallas Zone project, will you stay in the Union"? The President had anticipated the answer to his question would be complicated and might take hours to validate. He was wrong. The answer came from the Governor of Oklahoma. "No. No, we will not go back on what we have moved forward with". The President asked for a one-hour break, and everyone agreed.

The President's words to his crucial staff were clear. He intended to inform the states he would agree to the Articles of Confederation, but the Dallas Zone would remain. The Speaker of the House objected, but the Vice President made his point even more precise than the President. The Speaker was powerless. Those he represented were not recognized by any of the states. He held a position that no longer existed. The decision was for the President and the President alone to make. How the Dallas Zone would be supported without the required assets residing in the states was a valid question and the answer was given. The states would be asked to help based upon the level of equal support provided to the same states. To the states, this meant the federal government was willing to trade. Most of the strategic reserves of fuel resided with the federal government.

The ability to eventually restart chosen nuclear reactors belong to the government as well. It was going to become an issue of bartering with the other states and the Republic of Texas, as the Dallas Zone would be referred to from that point on, would hold key parts of that process. That was the President's plan. He would declare the Dallas Zone to be the capital of the Republic of Texas. A Republic that would loosely join the Article of Confederacy. When he was finished explaining his concept, those in the room that doubted his vision chose not to challenge what they had heard. The President would give his proposal to the states, and then they would all work from there.

The announcement of the Republic of Texas shocked every state on the call. They questioned the amount of thought put into such a concept, and they asked if the leadership of Texas was in support of such an idea. From the beginning of the Dallas Zone project, Texas had been nothing more than a conglomeration of independent towns and small cities that had relied on nothing more than local support, much like the rest of the nation. When the federal government relocated to the facilities at MOB Ft. Worth, it quickly became clear the level of support many of those Texas population centers would receive was far above the rest of the nation. Even sites as far away as Abilene and Lubbock had benefited from the zone development. Three years into the post-war period, the dependency of Texas on the Dallas Zone project was undeniable. Shortly after the nuclear exchange phase of the war began, the Governor and many of his key staff had been killed in a fire that swept through their underground Emergency Operations Center. By the time many in Texas began to worry about a state government, it was apparent the federal government and the large MOBs inside the state were their best bet for survival. The short answer was, the federal government was the government of Texas, or as many Texans came to believe, Texas became the federal government.

The states would have their Articles of Confederation. The details would be worked out over the next several months, and the Republic of Texas would hold a special status in the new Confederacy. They would not be a voting member, but they would become what the states had offered. Texas would become the mediator of issues between the states. No one on the call believed it would work, but no one was willing to make that statement, at least not openly. When the meeting ended, the Governor of Georgia asked the President a sobering question. What would they call him? The United States of America had become just a title, a title that would be placed in future history books.

# CHAPTER EIGHTEEN: YEAR FOUR:

It took six months for the newly formed government to develop even the most basic operational laws. To most of the people, what had been called the United States, did not matter. To those who made up the new government, many believed that someday the old system would return. Their theory was, what had taken place didn't matter, or it was an event agreed to get the nation past the crisis years. A functioning centralized government was no longer essential or even expected by those who had survived the war.

By the fourth post-war year, an established program for bartering between the states had been developed. The Republic of Texas was still seen by many as the old federal government, but the items needed for survival were too important to let perceptions stand in the way. The new normal was acceptable to everyone in the territories. The world's recognition of the changes that had taken place still did not matter. Most of the world had no functioning governments passed the concept of local alliances. Borders had not been defended since the end of the war, and other versions of a "New Normal" had developed uncontested.

The death rate in North America had slowed, but it still outpaced the birthrate by nearly 200 percent. People were still dying from complications of radiation exposure and malnutrition. The caloric intake had remained below 500 per day, and the infant mortality rate was over 20 percent. In postwar terms, the situation was still in freefall. Groups migrating up from Central and South America had continued to move into the Southern Territories of the old US. Those that were guarded by armed groups were intercepted, but a process of integration had become acceptable if not to the government, then to the people in the region. Labor, healthy labor, and skillsets had become more important that antiquated concepts of national borders. The states of Arizona and New Mexico officially resisted the migration process, but reality overruled the desires of political leaders. The old US had no defined Southern Border, and there was nothing anyone could do to change that fact. The Northern Border with what had been Canada was even more irrelevant. Except for the missile sites, the government in Texas spent zero effort observing or controlling the North. The northern tier states had agreed to the Articles of Confederacy, but they proved to be the most independent locations in the newly formed government. Year four began with the same issues the country had been facing for the past three years. Individual survival daily was all anyone was trying to achieve. The concept of rebuilding a "Nation" or even a "state" was simply unachievable.

### Degrading Capabilities:

The concept of surviving a major conflict had been analyzed and updated for decades. The fact the war took place in a far different manner than anyone had imagined had resulted in many assets being unaffected by the impact of the war. As stated earlier, the military had a shallow execution rate during the war, but many of its assets were extremely technologically advanced, and by the beginning of the fourth post-war year, the price of failures increased dramatically. Nowhere was this more obvious than in the area of aviation. By the beginning of the fourth year, the military estimated that only 20 percent of its aviation ability remained. Aircraft didn't become inoperative due to significant mechanical issues. It was often the smallest of parts that grounded hundreds of fixed and rotor wing assets, pieces that had not been stockpiled and items that could not be replicated. The technology was no longer available to keep the military flying, and it would not return.

In year four, this same issue began to deplete the military's wheeled fleet as well drastically. All of this had been predicted, but the ability to solve the problem was merely overwhelming. As dramatic as these issues were, the notification of the status of the nuclear deterrent became the primary topic of concern. In just two months, over 70 percent of the systems required to conduct a coordinated nuclear strike was offline. The issue was once again technological upkeep. Parts were expended and could not be repaired or replaced. Satellite networks still functioned, but many of the components required to control and utilized those networks failed at an alarming rate. Some of the most advanced devices ever designed were orbiting the Earth, but the capability to control them was gone as well as the ability to execute the targeting process for the nuclear arsenal. With little chance of achieving these weapons effectively, the decision was made to deactivate them, and with that, the old US was no longer a nuclear power. The remaining tactical nuclear weapons would be held in reserve, but even those systems would run out of time. For the military, nothing could be replaced, and so the plan became to learn how to cope without them.

### Communication Failures:

The world had survived for almost four years off of two forms of primary communications, shortwave Radios and the Emergency Command and Control Networks operated by the US government. By the fourth year, many of the shortwave networks began to fail. Communications both at the official and private levels were decreasing, and it was noticeable to the new government in Texas. A process to assess inventories of functioning networks was developed, but many states withheld information fearing what little assets they had left would be required elsewhere. It was a fear that had not gone away. When two critical satellite networks became inoperative, the only communications the new government had with Europe was based on shortwave radio systems. The world was going quiet, and there was nothing anyone could do to stop it.

### Regional Review:

#### Europe:

The radiation levels in Europe had not changed. The prevailing theory continued. Many parts of Eastern Europe were so contaminated; it was accepted that no one was living there and if they were, any attempt to support them was impossible. From Central Germany down to Southern Italy and West to Portugal, the concept of governance was based on small territorial operations, much like the township concepts of old Europe. Everything East of Eastern Germany all the way to Kazakhstan was officially labeled as "unknown." It was accepted pockets of organized communities existed, but the ability to communicate or the desire to do so was simply not there.

#### Middle East:

Nothing had changed in the Middle East. Egypt, Turkey, and Israel were communicating with the outside world, but little else was taking place. Travel to the region was conducted by those in the area, but from the perspective of the Americas, the Middle East was a distant land with unknown issues and would remain so for decades. In the fourth year, communications with Turkey would end, and it was based upon the same problem the US had come to terms with. The lack of replacement parts ended Turkey's shortwave radio capabilities.

#### Africa:

South Africa was in communications with the US from the

day the war ended. Morocco and Algeria had gained some form of organized communications capability, but again, by the fourth year, much of that was lost. Although the US didn't understand the nature of the event, it was known some level of alliance had been agreed upon between Morocco and Egypt with Algeria being some version of a lesser partner. What this alliance was based upon was not known, but it was speculated it must have been over the issue of food supplies and protection for those were the only issues that truly mattered to any group of people trying to survive. The level of concern over some African agreement was marginal. All of Africa was not capable of impacting any other region of the world at so this alliance was not seen as a threat, at least not yet.

What Africa did have going for it was the fact the war had not been fought on its land. The loss of the World Wide Web collapsed every aspect of Africa's economy, but it had physically survived far better than Europe, Asia, The Middle East, or North America. Yet, for all of its positives, Africa suffered from one huge issue more than the rest of the world. Without medical support, disease would remain virtually unchecked. On a continent ideal for rapid growth of contagious illnesses, Africa would continue to be swept by sickness. In the second and third years after the war, nearly 40 percent of the population would die from the disease. The people there understood a simple life of hardship and that lifestyle did not change.

Year four portrayed an Africa that many in the US anticipated was in a far better position to rebuild than most of the world. It was for that reason; the government decided to provide both South Africa and Egypt with communications capabilities at all costs. Like South America, Africa was seen as a key element to the chances of rebuilding the US. The question became, was Africa willing to be such a vital partner?

*South America:*

461

Year four for South America was not much different from year three. People had still congregated into small towns and villages based upon agricultural support. Satellite imagery indicated fishing villages along the Amazon River had increased in both size and number. Brazil and Argentina had maintained communications with the rest of the world, and again, the new US government made an effort to keep the lines of communications open with both nations. The vast majority of people migrating into the Southern regions of the US were from the Central American Nations. It was later learned, Brazil had violently rejected several attempts by these same Central American citizens to relocate inside Brazilian land. It was speculated this reaction by Brazil contributed to the movements of Central Americans to the North, rather than South. Brazil was also observed reestablishing several of its railroad routes by the beginning of the fourth year. Its rail system was far less complicated than that of the US, and much of it was based on the mining industry. An attempt was being made to establish a railroad link between Brazil and Argentina and the US intelligence agencies anticipated that connection would be established in year four.

In the early months of the fourth year, the new US government noticed an evident distancing in communications with both Brazil and Argentina. Shortly after that, the US sailed a three-ship Taskforce to the port of Itaqui for a requested Port of Call. The ships were denied entry the day of their arrival and no reason was given. The stage was set. The government in Texas was convinced the relationship with the two powers of South America was in doubt. A second task force was dispatched to Caracas Venezuela, and upon arrival, it relayed they had observed Brazilian naval ships in the port. The concept of realigning with South America had been challenged by the nation the US had always anticipated would become a significant player in the world. Year four would see North America reevaluating its future with South America.

*Asia:*

The beginning of year four found the same decimated Asia as year three. Imagery showed a continued migration of Chinese away from the areas impacted by the war. Movement South was the constant theme, and by year four, tens of millions had pushed into Myanmar, Vietnam, Laos, Thailand, and Cambodia. Radiation levels on the Chinese East coast where as high as Eastern Europe and Russia. The Cities of Shanghai, Hangzhou, and the areas around them were so hot; not even scavengers ventured into the zone.

No official communications with any group claiming to be the government of China had had contact with the US or any other nation. Units of the Chinese military that were away from the warzone had limited communications, and it was determined most of these groups headed up the movements into the nations to China's South. Like Russia, China continued to be a concept on paper only. What had been the Chinese nation was no longer evident, and there was no sign of that changing anytime soon.

The status of Indonesia was unknown. Given the decreasing capabilities of orbital assets, that region was not covered for analysis. Like Eastern Europe, the area of Indonesia, to include the Philippines, was officially labeled, "A Dark Zone."

The beginning of year four for Japan showed a measurable improvement over the past three years. Radiation from mainland China continued to be the most significant issue, but the people of Japan were adapting faster than anyone had anticipated, and that fact was attributed to the reality they were the only nation that had already found a way to survive a nuclear attack. The fishing industry provided the Japanese people a higher caloric intake than most of the rest of the world, and with nearly four years of no commercial fishing, the areas that were fished were able to supply an abundance of food quickly. What Japan didn't have was the ability to move forward. With no global trade taking place, Japan was limited to the resources on its Islands. By year four, it was developing a crude sailing fleet, and this phenomenon was monitored as closely as possible with limited intelligence resources. Japan had one other advantage, like England, Japan was a remote nation. The mass migration from other nations was nearly impossible, and that allowed Japan to concentrate its limited assets on its own people. Some attempts were made to land on Japanese land, but they were met with stern resistance. Reports had been seen for two years of Japan sinking large ships sailing into Japanese waters. In normal times, this would have been an outrageous act, but nothing in the world was considered outrageous by year four. Japan was what the Chinese had feared for over a thousand years. It was the nation posed to be the regional power long before China would ever regain any form of government.

*Australia*

The most capable nation in the region going into year four was Australia. In years two and three, the planned movement of English citizens to Australia had accounted for over 2 million additional people being relocated. The impact of the war had resulted in the deaths of over 8 million Australian nationals, but the landmass of England was severely damaged from the war and the agreement to have voluntary evacuations to Australia benefited both nations. Papua New Guinea had entered into an alliance with Australia, and between the two, the ability to stabilize both countries was very successful. As was the case with everyone else, the primary issue was medical support and disease, but with a large landmass and a small population, the ability to distance the people from sickness decreased the impact of outbreaks dramatically.

Australia's relationship with the US was stronger after

the war than before. Both nations understood the fate of the world would depend on specific nations being able to stabilize as soon as possible. The Australian government realized their unique location guaranteed one of those stabilizing nations would be them. By year four, both the US and Australia were exchanging information daily. Both were extremely limited on what physical support they could provide each other, but the fact the US had a stable ally became a psychological victory. Australia was prime to become the center of rebuilding the Pacific region.

*India:*

By year four, India's status had also begun to stabilize. The communications with the US were inconsistent, and it was clear the issue of localized Warlords had become an overwhelming concern. India's nuclear arsenal had been in question since the end of the war, and by year four, based upon the US's declining abilities to respond, the decision was made to take action against what was left of India's nuclear weapons program. The US still maintained a global reach capability, and the locations of India's fixed weapons were known. The risk of the mission was based upon the reality many other weapons were highly mobile, and their exact location would not be based on reliable data. Satellite technology made searching for these mobile weapons possible, and the decision was made that would be enough to execute the mission. It was estimated the operation would account for over 70 percent of India's remaining weapons with those that may survive not having the ability to reach the US. The whole topic of India's nuclear weapons program brought into question any weapons that might still be functional somewhere in the world; weapons with the ability to strike the US mainland.

By the time the India mission was complete, locations in Pakistan were struck as well. England and France had taken actions to secure their weapons soon after the end of the war, and both were able to convince the US government all weapons were secure. In the end, not everyone in the US leadership was utterly convinced, but the risk did not outweigh the need for potential future relationships. India and Pakistan had been a very different story and posed a threat that could not be tolerated. The reality was, neither nation had a functioning government to oppose the actions taken.

India's population before the start of the war was estimated at nearly 1.3 Billion. By year four, no accurate global estimate had been completed, but based on radio communications from regions all over India, it was believed the population was perhaps less than 300 million. Like the rest of the world, most had died from disease and starvation. Those that claimed to represent some form of leadership made such claims for small sections of the nation, and the US had not "officially" heard from the Emergency Operations Center for the Government of India for over two years. India was what it had once been, a tribal collection based upon military units that had sided with local groups. Intelligence gathering on the status of India, like many other parts of the world, simply did not exist.

### Year Four's Conclusions:

The US's own status of government had changed. Although some believed the "old" concept of a Union of states based upon a centralized government would return, the reality was, most of the people didn't care, and some didn't even know there had been a change. The facts of the fourth year were the realities of the third year. Staying alive and staying safe would remain the daily goal of every individual in the nation.

One other issue did make year four unique, and it was something that had been anticipated. The depletion of supplies and networks that had been part of the survival process for the nation became a reality. Systems designed to get the nation past the initial few years of war were failing. As some had anticipated, the consumption of these programs had taken place at a pace well above average. Nowhere did this decreasing capability have a more significant impact than in the military. It was in year four the government realized the total combat capability of the US had been reduced to approximately 30 percent of its prewar status. This issue was compounded by the fact the military was no longer a "unified" body. In the new operation of government, states maintained control of assets in their territory except for nuclear programs. Although this had been agreed to at the beginning of the new government, the repercussions had not been fully anticipated. By the end of year four, many believed the ability of the nation to act in a unified manner to protect itself no longer existed. The will to survive at the individual level had manifested itself entirely to the very idea of governance. Those that had dreamed of the nation once again being unified would come to the reality that dream was lost.

Not only did the concept of a unified government seem a distant memory, but in year four, even the value of states came into question. The overarching goal of survival forced the issue of a state's importance. As areas continued to reorganize, many larger settlements began to develop their own rules as well as requirements. This was not new in year four, but by the time most states began to attempt the process once known as "mutual aid," it had become evident the same stance the states had taken against a federal government had become the foundation of many localized settlements.

State-level support and or state level requirements met a higher level of resistance. Like the old federal government, states often had little to provide, and this was especially true in the states that had initiated the pushback to the federal government. Year four would see the first of several violent events not against a federal government, but against state operations. The attempted reestablishment of a railroad line between Kansas City and Tulsa Oklahoma was one of the more prominent events. Three large settlements near the area of Wichita Kansas were not given priority to connect to the line the state was attempting to restart. That issue led to two violent clashes resulting in the destruction of miles of rail line near the town of Palo Kansas as well as the first reported incidents of US military forces firing on each other. To the government still operating in the Dallas Zone, the trend was growing by the day. The states would be challenged just as the government had been, and the ability to control this phenomenon was nonexistent. People were reorganizing based upon survival, not tradition or heritage. In the fourth year, state lines and state requirements would become as irrelevant as the old form of government.

In year four, what was true in the old US was true throughout the world, and in fact, in most cases, it had already taken place two to three years earlier. People saw little need for any form of governance above what it took to keep them safe at the very local level. Nationalistic pride was nearly a distant memory. Not only were people not interested in more significant issues outside their area of contact, but they were also agreeable to any form of leadership that provided what they were looking for, food, and safety. Those who provided some level of comfort were given nearly complete support. The minds of progressive thinkers were lost in the value of survival. By year four, the world had fallen too far for anyone to worry about the future past the next meal and staying alive until the next sunrise.

### The Dallas Zone in year four:

As the world struggled with the "New Normal," the only resemblance of the "old" US was trying to find its footing. As concerning as the continued incidents between the states were, the stability of the zone was even more challenging. Like the issue of the state's boundaries and requirements, the areas to the South became less sympathetic to the zone's concept. Infiltration all along the old Texas border slowly changed the demographics and with that change came a change in viewpoints. By the end of the fourth year, the area between old El Paso, McAllen and Corpus Christi Texas had little in common with the zone. The areas to the Northwest of the zone such as Lubbock and Amarillo relied more on day to day interaction with larger settlements in New Mexico and Oklahoma. The strikes by the Russians inside the zone had resulted in many of its essential citizens moving further East, and as such, they began to develop ties with groups in Louisiana where food was far more abundant. The dwindling capabilities of the military required the MOB in San Antonio to be moved back to Ft. Hood as well as moving the operations at Corpus Christi to Galveston Island.

The zone would shrink two times in the fourth year ending with its Southern boundary becoming located in the city of Hillsboro. The Ft. Hood MOB would be the largest operation outside the zone with its primary task of defending the Southern and Western approach. MOB Ft. Worth would be responsible for the area north of the zone, and MOB Galveston would be tasked with the East. In the end, the Dallas Zone would end the fourth year nearly half the size it had been.

Support operations to those near the zone stopped halfway through year four. Again, the nuclear strikes on MOB Ft. Worth had depleted over 60 percent of the long-term support items such as heavy equipment spare parts. Bartering with the states had become the only viable option for keeping the zone functioning, something the old federal government was committed to doing at all costs. As a result of the discontinued support, those in the area around the zone became more unreliable. Throughout the fourth year, alliances with those coming up from the South increased at an undetected rate. To those who had planned and built the Dallas Zone concept, it was becoming evident the zone was in real danger of falling apart. Talk of a government in exile spread throughout the states. To most, the government that was nearly in exile didn't exist anyway.

Year four ended with the world still living with darkness at night. Fires remained the primary source of heat and light. Food was still the most sought-after commodity, and people all over the world were still willing to kill for it or serve anyone to receive it. Nations and borders had become irrelevant on a global scale. The world was grinding to a halt. Success was achievable only at a local level, and the definition of success was nothing more than stability.

# CHAPTER NINETEEN: YEAR FIVE:

## *THE NEW NORMAL.*

*The Old Northwest:*

For the US, Year five saw the accelerated decay of the old concept of states. Several of the Northwestern states abandon the idea. Territorial leadership replaced what had been state and local government. As some of the larger settlements attempted to impose their requirements on a region, those nearby would often move away. As a result, large numbers of transient groups became more and more common. Also, moving away from Winter resulted in large numbers of groups migrating into areas that were more established. These movements were not always met with open arms. The old Northwestern states lost control of an even more valuable commodity than just state government. They lost control of the military organizations that had supported them. The concept of a unified federal military was gone, and by the fifth year, many of the units had broken into collectives based upon the settlement's the members attached themselves to. The entire Northwestern area of the old US had become a land of nomadic groups, moving based upon food, weather, and disease. As a matter of record, this area included the old states of, North Dakota, South Dakota, Montana, Wyoming, Idaho, Oregon, and Washington.

In the Midwest, agricultural production, for the most part, had stabilized the issue of migration. Those that had entered the old US from the South seemed to have no desire to migrate into areas that had a level of Winter the migrating people were not prepared for. The Midwest witnessed a caloric intake that climbed back over a thousand calories a day,

and by the 5<sup>th</sup> year, the number one trading commodity had become food. An established trade route based on old highway 70 and 35 allowed items to be moved with relative ease. The site of large modified wagon trains still made most people stop to realize just how far society had fallen. By the end of year five, many of the major highways in the states of Missouri, Kansas, Iowa, Illinois, Indiana, Kentucky, and Nebraska had been repaired to the point travel between the states as possible. It was the amount of time it took to travel these distances that people had to adjust to. If someone agreed to trade an item from St. Louis to someone in Nebraska, it would take over a week for that item to be delivered. Navigation on the main rivers was minimal given the lock networks had been non-operational for over five years.

Governance in the Midwest was still intact with each state still operating, but at a much-reduced level. In the Midwest, the primary purpose of government was to formalize and pass laws that had been agreed upon between adjoining states. No state could function as well on its own as it could as part of a greater collective and that had led to coordinated laws and agreements, but the issue of localized communal law was impossible to overcome.

The Midwest was the only area of the old US that had begun the process of production of simple goods. Although no form of currency was in operation, items that were produced were traded at both the individual, local, and even state level. Items such as agricultural equipment made up 90 percent of what was produced. In short, the Midwest was stabilizing at a level that was nearly identical to colonial times. The Midwest was not what it had been, but it was stable, and with stability came the hope of progress.

*The Old South:*

In the South, the states of Tennessee, Mississippi, Alabama, Georgia, Florida, and South Carolina had formed a working conglomerate similar to the Midwest and traded with the Midwest consistently. Like the Midwest, agricultural production had become the stabilizing element. The advantage this area had was its fishing capabilities. Fishing fleets were never a complicated process, and the skilled craft of making and maintaining large nets was never lost. The Southern states could provide a food staple different than the Midwest, and that became the bulk industry between the two. The challenge became the inability to transport the seafood product long distances without proper refrigeration. Salt manufacturing was not taking place, so even the process of packing the items in salt was not possible.

Both the South and the Midwest had a common mistrust in what was seen as the old federal government inside the Dallas Zone, and this continued to limit the level of interaction. The Southern states saw the government in the zone as a group who still longed for a past that would not come again for decades if ever. Although interaction took place, it continued to be informal and guarded at almost every level. The states of the South were working towards a new future, and that future didn't include what was still taking place in Texas. Louisiana was seen as a boundary, and as a result, the people of Louisiana became more dependent on the Dallas Zone than they wanted to be. The same held for the state of Arkansas, but the willingness to interact was not as restricted as was the case with Louisiana.

Given that fact, Arkansas had become a significant source of timber for the Dallas Zone, and as such, most in the Midwest and South were cautious in any dealings with them. The South, like the Midwest, was stabilizing. A new "normal" was slowly taking shape, but progress was still decades away.

*The Old Southwest:*

The Southwest had quickly become a completely different story. The loss of a unified effort between what had been the federal government and the states of Arizona, Utah, Nevada, and even Colorado had taken a dramatic tole by the fifth year. Waterways had been unregulated since the end of the war and water was the life's blood of these states. The ability to grow a sustainable crop was all but lost without controllable water. Given the nuclear impacts on California, the population of these states had risen dramatically just after the end of the war. The military had supported large shelter camps, but as the equipment needed to provide even the most basic amount of water began to fail, it was clear, the people had to move. By the end of the fifth year, the population of the Southwestern states had decreased over 80 percent, and with that, the ability to govern or even the logic behind governance was lost. Like the East coast, the Southwestern states became virtually uninhabited. The concept of nomadic groups was the norm, but the ability to support or even track them was impossible.

*The Northern States' New Alliance:*

The states of Wisconsin, Minnesota, and Michigan had been working in conjunction with the territory of Ontario for over two years. The migration of US citizens into that area of Canada was the driving force behind this event, but the severity of Winter had taken a large percentage of the lives that had sought to move into what they thought was a more stable environment. As the collapse of the US government took effect, these three states entered a regional compact with what was left of the government in Ontario and part of Manitoba. Although the Winters were far more challenging to cope with than in the past, the lakes provided a viable source of water and food.

By the end of the fifth year, trading with the Midwest

became a common practice. Navigation down the Mississippi River became the primary mode of this trading process and as such, many larger settlements had established themselves along the river. This concept was not just genuine along the Mississippi River, but every major river in the Midwest and Southern states. Cities that had once been major commerce centers on the rivers were once again establishing themselves. Items from Canada were being sold in New Orleans, and the rhythm of day to day life was stabilizing.

*The Dallas Zone:*

Year five saw an accelerated decline in the technological equipment still being utilized by the old federal government. Power production units numbered less than fifty, and the ability to repair them was no longer possible. Communications with other nations were still taking place, but the total number of contacts had been reduced to less than fifteen. The last satellite data collection on world population centers took place early in year five. The final estimate showed a world population of a little over 1.5 Billion people. What was understood by just about everyone still working to stabilize the Dallas Zone was how unrealistic it had become to think of the US as a unified nation. Those that had called themselves, "the government," came to accept the reality they were nothing more than one of the larger communities the US had evolved into. The continuity of the government could not be maintained, and the only hope became to preserve the process of the old government in the hopes that someday, it would become the cornerstone of whatever the old US would become. By the end of year five, the concept of the US government was gone. There was no singular announcement or decree. The government of the US disappeared into the day to day lives of those inside the Dallas Zone. The last page of US history had been written, and the ending had no defining moment.

*The US Military:*

By year five, most of the sophisticated electronic equipment, both weapon systems, and support networks, were inoperable. Ships that had been utilized for reconnaissance missions were pulled back into US harbors. Aircraft utilization was limited to moving nuclear warheads that were being disassembled. Coastal radar networks were able to cover less than 20 percent of the old US coastline, and that was concentrated along the Texas coast. Not only were replacement parts gone, along with the ability to manufacture new items, the individuals who manned very technical positions had left in such large numbers, the knowledge base to continue any level of operation was nonexistent. Units that had been assigned to territories and states continued to communicate less and less with military leadership inside the zone. By the end of year five, not only was the concept of a United States gone, but a military force designed and tasked to defend it was gone as well.

*The World:*

1.5 billion people created a baseline population that would allow humanity to continue, even with the loss of modern medicine and technology. The exploration units that had been sent out in years three and four had found a universal environment. Those that still lived were doing anything and everything they could to stay alive. The concept of traveling to some other location to find a safer life was limited by the ability to travel. Ocean-going vessels required items that were no longer available. Smaller ships were utilized, but the scope of their adventures was limited to coastal movements. Sailing from one continent to another was taking place, but the ability to sustain such support was not there. Those that did manage to travel were often welcomed by those they encountered if they brought with them a skill or youth.

It had been estimated the average age of the world population was somewhere around thirty to forty years old, and infant mortality was placed at over twenty-five percent. Even worse, the odds of a newborn making it to the age of fifteen was put at less than 40 percent. In one of the final conference calls between several nations, it was agreed that the population of the world would decline for at least another ten years before stabilizing somewhere around 400 million with the majority of that population centered on the African and South American continents.

One universal agreement had been reached by those nations that could communicate. The knowledge of what the human race had achieved had to be maintained. The technological achievements, as well as the advancements in science and medicine, had to be protected for future generations. No one knew how long it would take to regain the ability to utilize that data, but knowledge could not be lost. What made this commitment almost impossible to achieve was the reality that nearly all of this data was stored electronically. Large volumes of baseline data were in written form, but the truth was, most of what was needed to understand any hope of rebuilding society was kept in electrons. The world had gone digital and the ability to show that data fifty to a hundred years in the future was a huge challenge, a challenge that would need to be solved, if possible.

### The Author's Final Thoughts:

As I stated at the beginning of this report, I had no intention of developing a novel. I fully realize the limitations of what I have tried to accomplish with this document. My ability to validate statements and events is extremely limited, and as such, I did not attempt to do so. My word and my integrity are what I based this report on and in the end, that is all that I have. Over the past two years, as I've been piecing this report together, the attempt to capture the accomplishments of the human race has continued, and I consider myself lucky

I was asked to be part of that process. In my previous life, this document would have been reviewed a dozen times before it was finalized and moved through the halls of the United States Military Headquarters, the Pentagon. Perhaps someday that will be the normal process again, but for now, this is the story of what took place as I understand it. Humanity is on the path to a new future, but the past cannot become something that no longer matters. Over 6 billion people died, and somehow, that price must ensure the future is brighter than we all currently believe.

CPSIA information can be obtained
at www.ICGtesting.com
Printed in the USA
LVHW040203291019
635549LV00002B/224